THE MEXICO NOVICE

John Evans was educated in state schools and at Oxford University. After several years teaching English in Paris he became a mountain shepherd and sheep farmer in the French Pyrenees. He began writing in 1982. Now a full-time writer, he lives with his French wife and daughter near the Pyrenees.

JOHN EVANS

The Mexico Novice

FONTANA/Collins

First published in Great Britain by Fontana Paperbacks 1988
Copyright © John Evans 1988

Printed and bound in Great Britain by
William Collins Sons & Co. Ltd, Glasgow

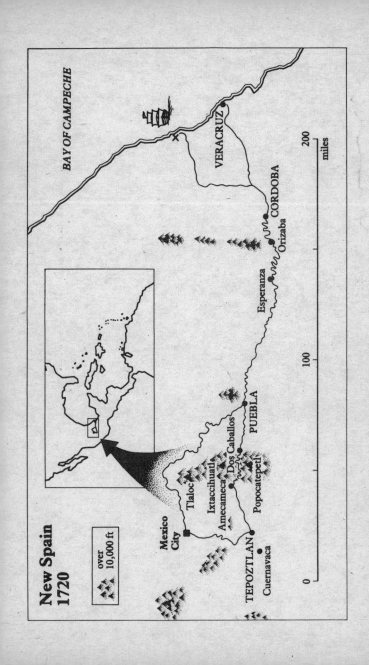

CHAPTER ONE

'Ruth?'

An animal scurried away through the undergrowth, but there was no reply. Habbakuk Parton waited a second more before moving on, stepping quietly. It had only been the creaking of a branch that he had heard. His sister was not yet there. In any event, he would have been surprised to have found her so far from the house. Her minutes of freedom were counted.

Some way further on, Parton stopped by a clump of bamboos and looked about him, breathing in slowly. The earth smelled good – damp and fresh from the evening's cloudburst – and the blossom in the orange grove which he knew was to the left behind the house was giving off a heady scent. He would always recognize, even in thick night, the woods around Salem – the particular sway of the high cabbage palms in the breeze, the sound of the place, its echo, the way the noises of birds and insects came to him; and, to the north, the familiar dark mass of the Blue Mountains outlined against the Jamaican night sky. He had spent thirteen years of childhood at Salem. It was time enough to know a place by heart.

The big white house was still there, he could see it now, pale between the trees a few hundred yards ahead. He slipped into the shelter of an untidy thicket. It wouldn't do to start the dogs off. If the alarm went up now, Ruth would in all likelihood be caught in the act of sneaking out to meet him. That must be avoided at all costs. Yates made her life a misery enough as it was.

He doubled back in the darkness and circled round towards what had once been the garden, a fenced-off place with flowers where they had played as children. They had built, he remembered with a grin, a model plantation with plots of grass for cane fields and little palm leaf shacks, and they had peopled it with lizards. The greens had been the masters and the browns had been the slaves. That had seemed natural enough to him as a child, he thought, but it did so no longer. He thought of Mardi, the runaway slave who had stayed on the island of Hispaniola to lead the fight against slavery, who had turned for an instant and waved as the sloop had taken him off the island at the end of his mission, ten months ago now. He had promised to return, but he could foresee no chance of doing so. Man proposed, and the Service disposed.

'Hab?'

'Ruth!'

His sister was running to him, into his arms. 'Oh, Hab!' Her eyes were shining in the darkness. 'It's good to see you!'

'It's good to see *you*,' said Parton, hugging her. 'How are the two of you?'

'We're fine.' There was a silence. 'Much the same, really.'

That was his sister, thought Parton. A few minutes whispering in the dark was all they would see of each other in months – even the exchange of letters was difficult – and she would pretend that everything was fine so as not to worry him. But he knew what 'much the same' meant for the girls. It meant living poor, close and cramped, cut off from the world – even church, he thought with a surge of anger, even *church* only at Easter and Christmas. Wearing twice-resewn clothes, waiting hand and foot on that old bastard Yates who kept them shut away and watched them like milk on the boil. Because they made cheaper drudges for him than black slaves? Because they mustn't find husbands and have children who might have legal claims to lay one day? Or simply because their very presence re-

8

minded people of the Parton family and of the injustice that had been done? Did the miserly old hypocrite know himself why he treated them like that?

'That doesn't reassure me,' he said.

'Nonsense.' Parton was sure Ruth was smiling. 'It's bearable.'

Ruth. The serious one, good-looking, thoughtful, careful not to hurt. Parton reached out and gave her shoulder a squeeze. Ruth was twenty-one, unmarried and still under the sway of her stepfather – *our* stepfather, Parton corrected himself. It had been so long since Yates had any power over him that he was forgetting.

'And you?' Ruth was asking. 'You must have some news. Out with it!'

Parton laughed. 'They're going to make my fortune. Not this week, next.' Ruth believed in him, and he wasn't going to tell her straight that good news was something he hardly dared hope for.

'So they'll be paying you prize money?'

'Apparently they will, but there's some sort of dispute on between the Crown and the Admiralty. Cameron explained it to me. The Admiralty, as a court, judges prizes at sea, but the Crown is claiming jurisdiction because the prize was taken on land.' Parton hurried on to hide his annoyance. 'But I'll get the money sooner or later. It's just a question of waiting.'

'Yes. I understand,' said Ruth stoically. She and Rachel never did anything other than wait, thought Parton. He cursed the Lords of the Admiralty. The same callously indifferent men who had sent him to Hispaniola to foment a tailormade slave revolt on behalf of London trade and financial interests, were now squabbling over the prize he had succeeded in stealing from the French while he had been there, the emeralds of the Portobello Virgin – one of them probably the biggest emerald in the world. Back in London, greedy eyes were fixed on that, and no one had a thought for the obscure Jamaican Lieutenant who had done the dirty work. Parton could see the pale oval of his sister's face turned up to him. She knew so little of his work. Would she have been as proud of him had she known? The waters of rivalry between Britain, France and Spain, of the struggle for America, were muddy, deep and treacherous. Parton swam in them efficiently – he had to. It was at times like this, here at Salem, his sister beside him, that it all came home hard to him. He looked over Ruth's shoulder and saw the house caught in the moonlight. If only the waters of his family life – if *that* could reasonably be called a family life – had been less deep and treacherous than the waters of international rivalry.

The house stood there, its two fine white storeys solid, its shutters blind, the twin columns of the portico its only concession to ornament. It had been built by his grandfather, one of the first Puritan settlers of Jamaica, back in Cromwell's time half a century before. Sixteen years had gone by since Parton had been inside that house. It was no longer his childhood home. It was property, real estate, an object to be bought or sold, married off, inherited – or stolen.

Yates, owner of a small estate nearby and himself a widower, had married the Parton children's widowed mother in time of trouble and had stolen Salem from the Partons. Stolen was the word, even if everything had been perfectly legally tied up when Parton's mother had died. Parton himself had been got rid of, dispatched by Yates to Barbados at the age of thirteen to work his indentures with a sugar planter – in other words, to be a slave. He had run away to sea and Yates had seized the opportunity to have his disappearance legally registered. The Parton son and heir, Yates had hoped, was well and truly out of the way.

He was wrong, thought Parton with a surge of battle-lust. The account will be settled, Yates. As soon as I weigh enough, in wealth and social position, to bend the law as you do, the reckoning will be squared.

'Hab.' Ruth's hand was on his forearm. 'I'll have to be going. I'm afraid to stay out too long.'

'Isn't the old man in bed?'

'Yes, but William's there with a bottle and one of the kitchen girls.'

Parton stiffened. William Yates was old Yates's son and Parton's hated childhood enemy. 'But I thought he was married and settled up towards Seaforth?' he objected.

'He is,' replied Ruth with a toss of the head. 'He married one of the Marchant girls with an eye on the estate. But he has to be on his best behaviour up there, church and fine sentiments and so on. When he feels like getting drunk and playing around with a slave girl, he rides down here on pretence of family business.'

'Often?'

There was a silence. 'More and more,' said Ruth in the end.

Parton frowned. 'Is William giving you any trouble?' He paused, trying to pierce his sister's expression in the darkness. 'Tell me, Ruth!'

Ruth faltered. 'It's not me . . . It's – oh, I wish I were wrong about this, but you should see Rachel now, Hab. She's beautiful. I may be biased, but it's true, she's a beautiful girl.'

Rachel had been a toddling three-year-old when he had been banished from Salem, thought Parton and now she was nineteen. The years went by, his sisters grew into young women, and he hardly ever saw them in broad daylight. Beautiful, for sure Rachel would be beautiful. 'And William?' he murmured.

'Doesn't take his eyes off her.'

'God Almighty!' Parton swung round in anger. 'If he as much as—'

'Sssh! Quiet!' Ruth was gripping his sleeve. 'Didn't you hear anything? Over there? There it is again!'

Parton heard it too. A footfall? He peered towards the house.

Ruth's grip on his arm tightened. 'Look!'

A pinpoint of light, perhaps a candle flame, swayed between the bushes thirty yards away and disappeared. There was a crash, a mumbled string of curses and the light appeared again. 'Who the devil's there?' The voice was thick and unsteady.

'It's him!' breathed Ruth. 'William! He mustn't catch me out of the house! They'll lock me in at nights and I won't be able to get out to meet you!'

Parton leaned forward. 'Stay here in the shadows and don't move!' he whispered. 'I'm going to draw him off. As soon as the coast's clear, hurry back. All right?' Ruth nodded. 'My love to Rachel. I'll get word to you again as soon as I can. And Ruth—'

'Yes?'

Parton kissed his sister's cheek. 'We'll beat them. All of them!' He turned and slid, bent double, into the blackness behind a mass of overhanging vines and crept rapidly towards the crumbling remains of the old fence, pushing through a large gap, tearing away a piece of rotten wood as he passed. He looked out between the leaves to the candle flame and lobbed the piece of wood well over to William's right, into the driveway. It hit the beaten earth with a dull thud.

'Hey!' The candle moved abruptly. 'Whoever you are, I've got a pistol here and the bugger's loaded and primed! Come any nearer, and I'll blow your brains out!'

Parton glanced back towards the garden. Ruth would still be waiting. He would have to lure William further. He crept on, scuttling from cover to cover, in a wide arc towards the driveway.

The candle was still. William was not moving. This time, Parton threw a clod of earth which shattered against a treetrunk and set the candle in motion. William was in the driveway now, walking up it towards the main gate. Parton

12

scrambled through the untidy scrub in the same direction. Ruth would be on her way back to the house. The dogs were keeping quiet, that was good. He reached the edge of the driveway near the gate ahead of William. He inched forward and looked back. The candle was swaying from side to side and William was muttering. It was too far for Parton to hear what he was saying.

Then the candle went out.

It took Parton several seconds to realize what was happening. William had turned round and his body was blacking out the flame. No doubt satisfied he had ventured far enough in defence of the house, he was walking back. Ruth, Parton was sure, had not had time to return safely. Even if William didn't actually catch her, he would be almost certain to see her. If, that was, he went on walking down the driveway. . . .

Parton shot out of the bushes and sprinted after him. He was perhaps forty yards away when William heard him and stopped. At thirty yards, William was turning with a curse. At twenty, William was facing him, the candle held high to see better. At ten yards, the pistol came to bear.

The range was deadly.

But William was drunk. Before he had gathered his wits enough to press the trigger, Parton's fist beat into the side of his jaw. The pistol jumped from his hand and rattled off into the darkness and the candle fell and went out. William's knees buckled and he slumped to the ground in an untidy heap, still mumbling.

Parton caught his breath and looked down at his old enemy. He and William had fought each other more often than he cared to remember, but it still felt good to hit that hated face . . . No, he told himself, it's time to go. Ruth will be back in her room by now.

Then he thought of Rachel and threw caution to the winds. He reached down, took William by the shirt-front and hauled him to his feet. Their two faces were inches apart. William had put on weight, realized Parton, looking at the pudgy features. Too much good living. He stank of rum.

William's eyes widened. 'You!' he gasped.

'Me.' Parton could feel his blood rising, the frustrations of his night visit coming to a violent head. The Yateses had done too much harm to him and his. He fixed his eyes on William's. 'Listen to me, William.' He spoke coldly, the words clearly detached. 'We're going to have a fight, as we used to when we were boys. Remember? You're older than me, you were bigger, remember? You used to like giving me a beating until I learned to fight back and thrash you in return.' He pulled William closer. 'That's what I'm going to do now. All right?'

William's head wagged from side to side, his mouth open. 'Wha – what for?' he asked stupidly.

Too stupidly to be true, thought Parton, feeling rather than seeing William's hand slip downwards. He caught it and held it still. 'Need a knife now, do you, William?' he asked, searching for it with his other hand, finding it at the other's belt, drawing it and throwing it aside. 'Just bare fists, like when we were boys.'

'Help!' called William, twisting away. 'Help! The house there! *Help!*' A racket of wild barking broke out at the house as he ran down the driveway. Parton was on him in two strides. He caught him by the shoulder, swung him round and hit him hard in the mouth with his left fist. With the dogs barking and the house waking, he only had time for one or two blows and they would have to count.

One was a fist which drove deep into William's fat midriff, expelling the air in his lungs with a whoop. That was for the thirty-odd miserable pounds a year which was all Parton had left after cashing in his pay warrant. The second was a knee that came up with force into the other's face as he jack-knifed forwards, straightening him up again. That was for the condescending smiles on the Kingston

14

magistrates' faces when Parton had tried to obtain justice. The third was another fist hard into the pot-belly and that was for the penniless vagabond the Yateses had made of him as a youngster, the good-for-nothing who had killed another man in a drunken brawl and had been forced to run to the Navy to hide from the law . . .

William was on the ground, gasping for breath, blood pouring from his nose. Parton bent, took him by the hair and yanked his head up. There were shouts back at the house and the dogs broke out into a new frenzy of barking. 'William!' Parton's voice was urgent. 'Can you hear me?' William nodded slowly. 'Then listen.' Parton bent closer. 'Rachel, my sister Rachel.' William's eyes widened. 'They're saying all over Morant that you've got your eye on her. Is that true?'

William stared at him, frightened, and tried to shake his head. The shouting at the house was clearer now. Parton only had seconds left. 'William, if you as much as lay a finger on Rachel, do you know what I'll do?' William was silent and Parton shook him. '*Do you know?*'

'No,' mumbled William through swollen lips.

'I'll tear you apart. I'll kill you. Touch Rachel and I'll kill you. Is that clear?'

'I'll have the law on you, Parton.'

'You'll need a witness,' said Parton dryly, letting go of William's hair. He turned and walked briskly up the driveway. There were lights coming from the house now. He would have to disappear quickly. The main gates were closed and padlocked, but Parton climbed the fence and dropped into the darkness on the other side. The woods would cover his escape. The fury was over now and he felt momentarily drained. He leaned back against the fence and closed his eyes. Had he achieved anything useful by what he had done? William would leave Rachel alone, but that didn't change the fact that the girls were still hostages. God damn it, that prize money would help. He shook his head and slid quietly towards the trees.

Somewhere in the darkness close by, a man cleared his throat.

No, thought Parton, stopping dead. Perhaps there *is* a witness.

'Lieutenant Parton?' A dark bulk moved forward.

'Yes?' Parton had heard that voice somewhere before.

'Seaman Paterson, sir, and compliments of Captain Cameron, sir. He said I'd like as not be finding you down this way.'

Parton breathed out as relief flowed through him. 'All right, Paterson. What's the Captain want?'

'There's a fuss on, sir. He said it was urgent. You're to make straight for Port Royal. He wishes to see you immediately, sir.'

CHAPTER TWO

'*Hijos de puta de una ostia de puta de madre*! Heave on that thing, damn your idle bones!' The Spanish bosun's spittle flew through the torrid air, punctuating his curses.

Parton shifted his hold on the capstan bar and his face creased with effort as he heaved. Lousy little half-rotten Spanish flea pit, he thought, and only a skeleton crew. Good thing the run's a short one.

'Heave!'

Parton heaved again. Swaying up the stu'n'sail booms was not the most demanding work on board ship, but a few more hands on the capstan would have been welcome. Still, he reminded himself, if they hadn't been short-handed he and Seward wouldn't have been taken on, and they would have had to wait at least a week for another passage.

'Heave!'

Parton glanced up as he pulled on the bar. The last boom was almost up to the topsail yardarm. A few more turns and the monkeys up there could get on with it.

It was some time later, all the same, when the bosun finally let the capstan crew rest. Parton wiped his face with his shirtsleeve and sat with his back to the starboard bulwarks. It was leaden hot, the sky was pale and coppery and the Bay of Campeche as flat and steamy as a plate of soup. He closed his eyes.

Henry Seward, dogging Parton's footsteps, collapsed on the deck beside him. Parton opened his eyes and looked down at the younger man. Seward was fighting for breath, his face bathed in sweat. No, decided Parton, it would take months at sea to make him look like a sailor. Try as he might to conceal it – and Parton suspected he didn't try all that hard – there was always something of the young gentle-man, stylish but often condescending, in his bearing and manners. In everyday life, Seward, son of a rich London merchant, was in charge of the family concern's business in the Caribbean and the Gulf. With his tall but stooping build, his pale complexion freckled and reddened by the sun, the short stubble of his light-brown hair which told of his habit of wearing a wig, Seward didn't look the part at all. Thank God no one on the *Santa Teresa*, short-handed as they were, seemed to give a damn who or what he was and that the passage would soon be over.

Seward sat up next to Parton, exhaled noisily and raised his brown eyes to the heavens. Parton, contrasting with Seward not only by his more powerful build, his deeply-tanned skin and dark, tousled hair, and his air of being quite at home on board ship, but also by the sometimes for-bidding coolness of his clear, grey eyes, looked across at the other with a smile.

'Is this due to go on much longer?' asked Seward.

The smile faded from Parton's face. 'I don't understand,' he said in Spanish. 'I don't know the language you're using.'

Seward shrugged and smiled nonchalantly. 'Oh,' he said with an ample gesture, 'there's nobody near to hear!'

'I don't care.' Parton was irritated. Seward didn't have to insist on being right when he had made a blunder. Parton could have done without that let's-not-get-vulgarly-upset condescension in the smile, too. 'Listen,' he went on, still in Spanish, 'on this trip, we only speak one language. You accepted that right from the start and that's the way it has to be.'

'*Muy bien*. As you wish,' replied Seward curtly in Spanish. 'Not another word in "that other language".' He opened his hands, palms up, and inspected them ruefully. The blisters of the first days had skinned, leaving bloody holes where a seaman's hands were calloused. 'What was the point of that backbreaking exercise we've just carried out?' he asked, looking up.

'The stu'n'sails? With this wind—' Parton held up a finger in the listless breeze, '—the master's crowding on all the canvas he's got so as to get this old tub into port before the weather turns.'

'A storm?'

Parton looked up at the brassy glare of the sky and sniffed loudly, enjoying the alarm which was creeping over Seward's urbane features. 'Smells heavy enough,' he said, straight-faced. He and Seward, posing as Spanish seamen, had signed on the *Santa Teresa* a week before in Havana. When they reached Veracruz, they would jump ship. Veracruz was a restricted port and the only way in was on a Spanish vessel. Even then, Spanish citizens themselves were carefully checked on arrival. Parton and Seward, as bottom-rung nonentities, were to slip through the net. It was the kind of thing Parton had done time and time again. 'Don't worry,' he said with a brief laugh. 'This old nutshell's been bobbing around the Spanish ports for years and she's not ready to go down yet. We'll get into Veracruz some time tomorrow.' He lowered his voice. He could reasonably tell his guide which way they were to go now that they were so close. 'And from there, we're going to Cordoba.'

Seward looked at him and nodded. 'All right. Cordoba's no problem. It's on the main road up to the capital. You've nothing to do in Veracruz?'

'Nothing beyond getting horses and provisions for the road.'

'Good. It's a filthy over-heated place in the marshes and it's riddled with yellow fever. We'll get out of it within the hour.'

'How soon can we make the journey to Cordoba?'

'Less than two days with good horses.'

Cordoba on the nineteenth of June, thought Parton. Things could have been worse. Only three weeks since the night Cameron had sent Paterson out to bring him urgently to the house in Port Royal.

Cameron had been in an unpleasant mood, remembered Parton. Sharp, unbending, tough. At times like that, his Scots brogue broadened, his eyes became pale, unflickering discs and his long pipe stem repeatedly stabbed the air to underline his assertions. The little room which served him as office and dining room had been thick with pipesmoke. Cameron had commanded at sea before taking on his present functions and he had kept the habit of living close in a confined space. He had also, thought Parton, kept the habit of exercising authority like a flail.

He had fumed about officers who couldn't be found when they were needed and wasted hours of precious time. Parton had let the storm go by. Cameron was fully aware of Parton's problems, but he never admitted to knowing, never showed sympathy, even in his very rare avuncular moments. That night in Port Royal, it had been the contrary. Cameron had reminded Parton, in veiled but forceful terms, of how much he owed the Service. Not simply the Navy, but *the* Service; the department he, Cameron, represented as commanding officer for the Caribbean and Central America and on whose secret lists figured the name of Habbakuk Parton with the rank of Lieutenant for which he could thank God . . . and so on.

This was softening-up, Parton had thought, before the announcement of some impossible mission. All the same, when Cameron had at last got to it, what he had said had been disconcerting. 'The first thing,' he had begun, 'is that the less you know about what you are to do, the better. I am going to give you precise orders and little more. A piece of the story here and there – I'll not fill in the blanks.' The waving pipe stem had forestalled objections. 'I have my reasons! It is vital that you succeed in this mission. Vital – but we have to envisage the contrary.' Cameron's voice had dropped. 'If you fail, Lieutenant, our losses must be cut.

We must not add to failure by providing the enemy with the means of striking an even greater blow. Do I make myself clear?'

'I think so. There are secrets in this affair that I must not be capable of revealing under torture.'

'Exactly.' Cameron had coughed and tried to look uncomfortable. 'I'm sure it won't come to that, however. I have every confidence in you, young man.'

It had been Parton's turn to clear his throat. Cameron had pretended not to notice and had pointed with the pipe stem. 'There are three years of careful, delicate work behind this operation. And tonight, Lieutenant, I have received dispatches which tell me that it is at last time to move.' He dropped his voice. 'The old enemy, Mr Parton.'

'Spain?' Parton had rather been expecting France.

'There's surprise in your voice, young man, and that is the result of habit.'

Parton had stared.

'A habit we've all been indulging in for too long now,' Cameron had explained. 'The habit of seeing Spain as an old colonial power with no future. Nothing could be further from the truth. I grant you that chronic inefficiency and near bankruptcy have long been typical of the Spanish–American empire, but this should not blind us to that empire's immense resources—' Parton had nodded, thinking of Spain's vast possessions in Southern and Central America, of the silver mines of Peru and New Spain, '—Nor to the fact that many things have changed in Spain. Philip V is not a mad old Spanish Hapsburg, but a French Bourbon and they have other ideas on how to rule a country, believe me. The last few years have seen increased efficiency, a new impetus to industry and trade, higher output of the silver mines and an important series of administrative reforms which are what interest us tonight.'

'Office work, sir?'

'In a sense, Lieutenant. But I doubt if your side of the operation will be as peaceful as that might suggest.'

'I can hardly say I'm surprised.' Parton had grinned.

'I didn't expect you would be. Now listen. Three years ago, the Spanish began reorganizing their colonial Civil Service, shaking everything up, changing the rulebook and moving all their people round.' The pipe had stabbed home the importance of the last remark. 'Of course, we've been watching all this carefully, both out here and back in Europe – partly because we have to know what's going on, but above all because in such circumstances men go up and men go down, and those who go down are rarely happy about it. I don't think I need tell you that such disgruntled men may become . . . disaffected?'

Parton had agreed. Men who had an axe to grind could be persuaded to betray their country. It was a spy's business to look for, find, and secure such men.

'Now,' had continued Cameron, 'we have, by long, delicate and utterly secret tractations – and you are not to be informed by which channels – reached an agreement with such an official. The difficulty of approach and the time taken are proportionate to the official's importance.' He had leaned forward. 'The information he can bring us is crucial, Lieutenant. It is vital to one of the essential tenets of our New World doctrine – control of the seas.'

Parton had studied his superior's lined face and had been reminded, beyond the stony and unbending disposition, of the man's power and importance, as spymaster and masterspy, meticulous observer of the international scene, leader of Britain's secret attack and defence in the Caribbean and Central America.

'The Spanish build their strength on silver, gold and stones. The French claim vast tracts of territory, from the snows of Quebec down to the Mississippi, which will take decades to settle. We occupy less ground – a few islands and the seaboard colonies – but we settle them, farm them, make them *live*. And we back them with seapower. I believe, Lieutenant, that our strategy is the best of the three.

If it is to succeed, we must maintain control of the seas – and this brings us back to our Spanish official. If we win him over, he will strengthen our naval power and weaken Spain's at the same time.'

'If? Didn't you say we'd reached an agreement with him?'

'His price is fixed, but one major condition—' Cameron had leaned forward again and steadied his eyes on Parton's, '—remains to be met. This man is not only unhappy about how he has been treated in office, but he has another grudge. He says the Franciscans have stolen his son.'

'The *Franciscans* . . .?'

'The Romish religious order, Lieutenant. He says they have stolen his son.'

Parton had shaken his head in disbelief.

'Let me explain as far as I can without telling you too much. Suffice it to say that the boy's mother is far away, that the father's work does not allow him to keep his son with him and that the boy's education was, as a result, entrusted to the Franciscans some years ago. Now the Franciscans claim that the boy is, to all intents and purposes, an orphan and they want to make a monk of him. They have removed him to a place unknown – no doubt a monastery or seminary or suchlike – where he is due to become a novice. And our man, quite simply, wants him back.'

'As part of his price?'

'It's a *sine qua non*. He won't come over to us without the boy.'

'Where is the boy?'

'Somewhere in New Spain.'

There was a silence and Parton had had the definite impression he was dreaming. New Spain was a vast Spanish viceroyalty stretching from the Panama isthmus in the south all the way up to the enormous northern missionary territories, California, Arizona, Sonora, Nuevo Mexico, Coahuila, Los Tejas. 'Somewhere in New Spain,' he had repeated leadenly. 'How many years are you giving me?'

'Nonsense!' Cameron had replied impatiently. 'They won't have taken him off into the wilds. He's probably in one of the larger monasteries where they have schools – in all likelihood, in one of the big towns.'

'And if he's not?'

Cameron had given a patient little sigh and shrugged. 'In that case, your mission will be a little more difficult.'

'What help can I get from the father?'

'None. You don't know the father. He doesn't know you. There'll be no contact between you.'

'So how am I to go about looking for the boy?'

'You will go to the town of Cordoba where the boy used to live. There, *in the utmost secrecy*, you will go to see an old woman whose whereabouts I am going to give you – and which you will keep strictly to yourself. The Spanish must not be able to work back from her to our man.'

'Who is she?'

'The boy's former nurse. She will inform you further – but be careful, she must not tell you too much!' Cameron's smile had suddenly become glassy. 'She mustn't tell you the boy's name, for example.'

Parton had attempted to conceal his consternation with sardonic laughter. 'I'm to go to New Spain, to look for a boy whose name I don't know and who's hidden away in a monastery God knows where . . . Perhaps now we'll get on to the really difficult part of the assignment?'

The glassy smile had remained. 'Shall we? Have you heard of the Holy Inquisition, Lieutenant?'

'Of course. Religious fanatics who ferret out heretics. What have they to do with it?'

'I'm not absolutely sure they have anything to do with it. Let's say there are strong reasons why you might fall foul of them.'

'In port?' Parton remembered that it was Inquisition officers who boarded ships arriving in Spanish American ports to check incoming passengers. If you were a heretic,

Protestant, Jew, or Moor, you were refused entry to the country.

'And elsewhere. They're not just a religious force, Lieutenant. They deal in politics too. And in espionage.'

Parton had not been aware of that. 'But all the same,' he had objected, 'they're only priests . . .'

'Our information is that there's little priestly about them. And listen, Lieutenant. In a country like New Spain, by far the largest single power is the Church. She owns at least half the land, half the towns, she's laden down with money to the point of being the country's major banker. There are vast numbers of clergy. They run all the schools, hospitals and poorhouses. There are convents and monasteries everywhere. They even deal in contraband trade, no matter the goods. The Church is far from being simply a religious institution.' The long pipe stem had pointed emphatically. 'And this immense power has a secret police force called the Holy Inquisition, whose task is to defend Church and State alike. The Inquisition is long-established and rich, provided with special premises staffed by highly unpleasant experts in interrogation and torture. And the Inquisition is feared. Every monk, friar, nun, or parish priest may be an agent of the Holy Office, in every town or village. People denounce their neighbours, children their parents. Believe me, in Spanish America the Inquisition is a terrifying and all-pervasive force.'

Parton had nodded. It was true, he knew from experience, that people from the Spanish colonies spoke of the Inquisition in hushed tones.

'Worse still,' Cameron had continued relentlessly, 'the New Spanish Inquisition is particularly efficient. It's led by a man who interests us a great deal.' His eyes had narrowed. 'His name is Ignacio Palafox. He's a member of the Dominican order, which is specially associated with the Inquisition. As Inquisitor-General, Palafox is one of the most powerful men in New Spain. Some would say, in view of his wide-ranging secret powers and his political influence, that even the Viceroy himself can't stand up to him. Again, don't confuse priests with priestliness, prayer and meditation. Palafox is simply an extremely ambitious man at the head of a powerful police force – a secret service, if you prefer. He also keeps several mistresses and has an unhealthy reputation – well, perhaps I don't need to go into details. Just remember he has hidey-holes people never come back from and don't say I didn't warn you.'

'It sounds as if I won't be saying anything if they catch me.'

Cameron's eyes had swung back to Parton's. 'I hope you won't,' he said quietly. 'That's why you must not know the name. To put it simply, the boy's identity is the father's identity. Once the Spanish have the one – and inevitably the boy's abduction will bring it forcibly to their notice – they will also have the other. If they react quickly – and everything will be a question of time – they will be able to arrest our man and make him talk. That will be a disaster for us. Not only will we lose our man and the secrets we want him to bring us, but also agents of ours and friends of ours who have come into contact with him during our long tractations. Do you see? The boy's name is dangerous. Not even you must know it until the very last minute. Up to then, there must be no risk of the Spanish learning the name.'

'Mm. Can't we get the man out beforehand?'

'No. It works both ways – if the traitor's name is known, the Spaniards will secure his son and the abduction will become impossible. Our man simply won't budge until the right moment. Clear?'

'Yes, sir. It's going to be a race.'

'Exactly. The old woman helps you locate the boy. You make careful plans. At the last possible minute, giving the Spanish no time to manoeuvre, you strike and go. You must bring the boy to the coast forty miles north of Veracruz on the night of the tenth of July. A ship will be waiting for you.'

'On that night alone?'

'I'm afraid so. The coast is well patrolled and a vessel of ours can't afford to wait for days. And above all, the operation is an exchange which . . . no, I can't explain the details to you, suffice it to say that everything must happen in one night.'

Parton had thought it through. 'I don't know inland New Spain,' he had said, looking up. 'As it stands, I've scarcely a dog's chance of finding the boy.'

'The difficulty's been taken care of,' Cameron had replied, putting down his pipe. 'I'm not sending you into New Spain alone. I've found you a guide, a fellow who has a thorough knowledge of the place. When I spoke of spying on the Spanish, did I mention the Seville and Cadiz trading houses?'

'No, but I know what you mean.' Spain's under-developed industries were chronically incapable of producing manufactured goods and supplying them to her colonies in sufficient quantity and hence at a reasonable price. Foreign traders – British, French, or Dutch – were unofficially welcome to trade with Spanish America as long as they used companies in Seville or Cadiz as figureheads to get round the colonial monopoly laws. The same footholds in Spain and her colonies could also be used for purposes of espionage . . .

'So, Henry Seward is the son of a merchant in London who's given us a helping hand once or twice in the past. They work through a house called *Rodriguez y Cuevas* in Cadiz. Henry was sent out here to learn trading the hard way and he spent four years in New Spain travelling as agent for *Rodriguez y Cuevas*. He speaks excellent Spanish, he knows the roads and towns, he'll take you where you want to go – and I suggest you go under the trade cover, since he's used to it. *But—*' The pipe had left the desk again and risen in warning, '—his task is strictly limited to that. He knows nothing of your true mission and must not learn anything, for the same reasons as those which oblige me to leave you in ignorance of a large part of the story. Seward, Lieutenant, is not an officer, he's a young man of good family. You must bring him back to me alive and kicking.'

On the *Santa Teresa* as she boomed sluggishly across the Bay of Campeche, Parton looked away from Seward. He must not allow apparently supercilious manners and Cameron's insinuation – that Parton could risk his life, while the young man of good family had to be protected at all costs – to annoy him. The two of them were going into dangerous territory and discord could be fatal. It was up to Parton to avoid it, to prove that he was capable of succeeding in a mission in collaboration with others and not alone as in the past. He looked across at Seward and grinned. 'If money can buy them in Veracruz,' he said, 'we'll get good horses.'

The old woman's sunken eyes lit up in understanding. 'Ah, you are the one they said I should expect,' she said almost eagerly. 'Please come this way, Señor.'

The house was modest, single storeyed and whitewashed and it was in one of the poorer quarters of the mountain town. It formed a U-shape round a sun-drenched and immaculate courtyard with a well in the middle. Taking care to follow Cameron's strictures on secrecy, Parton had slipped into the cover of the little courtyard before calling softly at a window, rather than knocking at the door in the narrow street outside. He had come to the house by a roundabout way from the tavern where he had left Seward and where they were due to meet again later. All had gone as planned. They had jumped ship and avoided Inquisition control at Veracruz before hiring horses and riding inland to Cordoba. It was the nineteenth of June.

'My name is Margarita,' said the woman, turning towards

Parton as she led the way. She had Indian blood, he thought as he looked at her. She had wide cheekbones, a flattish nose, olive skin. She was wearing simple black homespun mourning and round her neck hung a tiny silver cross. She seemed truly delighted to see him and Parton found her likeable. 'Of course,' she was saying, 'when they brought the message from Señor—'

'No!' Parton almost gagged her with his outstretched hand and the old woman stared at him in shock. 'Excuse me,' apologized Parton. 'But it is important not to say too much. Didn't the message explain?'

'Oh,' she faltered, 'of course. I was forgetting. How stupid of me! Forgive me, Señor, an old woman . . .'

'It's nothing.' Parton lowered his voice. 'Just tell me what the message told you to say. Do you understand?'

The old woman nodded. 'Please sit down, Señor.' Margarita gestured to the single chair in the sober little room. 'Perhaps I can offer you something to drink? I would be pleased to go out for some wine, or perhaps some *aguardiente*?'

'No thank you,' said Parton hurriedly. If he sat on the chair, he would break it, he thought. 'Please, Señora, be-have as if I were not your guest. If you go out for *aguardiente*, what will your neighbours think?'

The old woman's hand leaped to her mouth and she actually blushed. 'They mustn't think . . . A widow like me, Señor!'

Parton repressed a grin and decided he really did like the old woman. And if she had a personal reason for not wanting the neighbourhood to know of his visit, so much the better. 'Now, Señora, the boy,' he said softly.

'The Franciscans,' she whispered, fingering the little cross round her neck. 'Who would have thought it of them? Such a fine boy too, so quick, so lively, so good! Señor, I was his nurse – I looked after him, I brought him up. All these years I was like a mother to him.' There was bewilderment in her eyes. 'Why did they take him away? Such a little boy! They said I must see him no more and they shut him off from the world and his poor old foolish nurse!' She broke off, tears in her eyes.

'Why do you say "such a little boy"?' asked Parton gently.

The nurse looked at him in surprise. 'He was eight years old just after Easter, Señor.'

It was Parton's turn to stare. 'But I thought he was about to become a novice? I imagined he was older . . .' Cameron had not seen fit – or had not dared? to tell him that the boy was only eight. Damn Cameron. Parton had sincerely imagined a boy of at least twelve or thirteen, a boy who could fend for himself, walk all day, ride if he had to . . . 'I'm sorry, Señora,' he said. 'Please tell me what the Franciscans did.'

'They said he was an orphan and he belonged to God and to the order of St Francis. They took him to the seminary in Mexico City.'

'Is he there now?'

'I have had no news, Señor, but I believe so. It is there you must go if you are to look for him.'

Neither good news nor bad, thought Parton. The only road in New Spain which appeared to deserve the name went on from Cordoba up to the mountainous capital. He might have hoped to find the boy nearer to the coast, but at least he had not been taken to some far-flung province. 'How can I recognize him?' he asked. 'I've been told you can help me.'

'One moment.' The old woman went over to the prayerstool in the corner of the shady room and fumbled amongst a hanging loop of beads and slender chains which Parton had not noticed when he had come in. 'He will recognize this,' she said, coming back and holding out one of the thin chains. 'You are to take it with you.'

Parton took it. From the chain hung a bronze medallion

the size of a farthing. On one side was an embossed image of a saint. He turned the medallion over. On the other side was engraved the letter 'M'. He looked up.

'He wore it as a baby,' she explained. 'He is sure to recognize it, especially as the initial is mine. I gave him the medallion when he was tiny and he wore it until he was, oh, five or six.'

It might not be such a bad idea, thought Parton. 'If anyone else were to see this,' he asked, 'would they – could they – know whose it was?'

Margarita shook her head. 'A child's medallion? Myself . . . himself . . . his father no doubt . . . and now you, Señor. No one else.'

'Good.' If the medallion fell into the wrong hands, it would not automatically lead to the boy and hence to his father – although, from Parton's point of view, it was a very tenuous link indeed. Before it could be of any use to him, he would have had to narrow down the field . . . 'It would help if you could give me an idea of how he looks,' he said.

'Handsome,' said the old nurse, soft-eyed, 'Slim, dark. He has brown eyes. He'll have grown since I saw him. . . .'

A slim, dark boy of eight in a seminary in Mexico City who would recognize the medallion in Parton's hand. Better not to think too much about it. He nodded to the old woman. 'I must go,' he said, wondering where to hide the medallion. The chain looked just long enough. He managed to fasten it round his neck. In New Spain, almost everybody had something of the sort round their necks.

The old woman crossed herself. 'I am praying for him,' she explained. 'That you will bring him back and that I shall see him again.'

'I'm going to try,' said Parton, moving towards the door. 'Goodbye, Señora, and thank you.' He looked out cautiously into the empty courtyard and stepped over the threshold into the sun.

'I shall go on praying after you have gone.'

Parton looked back and smiled. 'Thank you. It may well prove necessary.' He turned and crossed the courtyard quickly, feeling a little cheap. If he found the boy and brought him back, it would not be to see the old nurse. He disappeared from her sight round one of the wings of the house.

He looked around carefully. The afternoon was quiet and empty. Below him the ground dropped away in a series of man-made terraces, drystone walls holding back the earth of the mountain slope, forming long strip-like gardens where Indian corn and vegetables grew. Parton went silently down a flight of rudimentary stone steps to the first terrace. He walked along it in the shelter of the wall, invisible from the houses above, the waist-high flags of maize partly hiding him from the gardens below. Five hundred yards further on, he climbed another flight of steps and looked out. An alley threaded upwards between two houses. No one was in sight. Parton walked through the alley, gratefully noticing that the stone walls on either side were blind. He came out into a street which was not the old woman's, turned immediately left and began climbing towards the town centre. He must not relax yet. He would take a roundabout route through the town before going back to the tavern where Seward was waiting.

Cordoba was a stone-built, prosperous town. It was on the main road from Veracruz to the capital and the air of the lower mountains made it a refuge for Veracruz traders who feared the fever-ridden marshes below. Parton left the poorer quarters and climbed into the oldest part of the town, seeing rich family houses where gloomy stone knights with long beards flanked windows and balconies topped by carved scrolls and escutcheons and stared fixedly across at their opposite neighbours. Parton climbed on slowly, looking around him, glancing back from time to time with care.

He left a narrow street and came out into a broader

thoroughfare. A little further and he would turn back towards the tavern. He was about to cross the thoroughfare when he saw a movement over his shoulder. It was little more than a blackish blur, but it intrigued him. He waited for a horse and its rider to go by, his sense of danger alert. He crossed the road and turned away from the tavern. He took a sidestreet and followed it for a way, turned through an alley into another narrow street, walked down it for a hundred yards, then stopped and looked around as if unsure of his way.

The dark blur had indeed been black. It was the black of a priest's cassock. When Parton's head had turned, the priest had jumped for cover into a porch. It had been an abrupt movement like that which had given him away in the first place.

However, the dark-skinned man in a filthy Indian blanket was less clumsy and Parton was not sure that his suspicions were justified. Then the man's brief, uncertain glance towards the porch where the priest was hidden confirmed them. If there were others, Parton did not know, but of one thing he was sure. The priest and the man in the Indian blanket were shadowing him.

CHAPTER THREE

Parton turned and walked slowly back down the street towards the two men. He needed a closer look. The simple black cassock of his first follower seemed to be that of an ordinary parish priest. 'Every parish priest,' Cameron had warned. And the second man? An Inquisition hireling? Of course, it might not be that at all – the cassock in itself meant nothing. It could be a disguise. In a country of brigands, the two men might simply be common thieves who had picked out an obvious stranger to the town and were making ready to waylay him. It would be easy to learn if this were so.

The priest was out of sight in the porch. The man in the blanket, caught out by Parton's return, had no choice but to keep walking. The street was narrow and Parton was bound to pass close to him. Parton looked beyond him to the end of the street as he approached, watching the passers-by on the wide thoroughfare he had left minutes before, then he lowered his eyes to the filth-strewn ground.

The man – he was certainly an Indian – went by on the other side, head bowed, his eyes turned away from Parton. Parton walked on slowly, alert for a sign of the hidden priest, ready for the scuffle of feet, the swish of movement, the attack from behind. It didn't come. He reached the end of the street. The men were not footpads. They were following him for other reasons.

When had they latched on to him? He had been careful. He was sure there had been no one when he had left the old woman's house. Had she betrayed him? No, he could swear to her loyalty. Had a neighbour of hers seen him and reported his presence? But why and to whom? Was the old woman's house being watched? That was possible. Cameron had insisted on the utmost care being taken in approaching her. If that was it, they had been damn well hidden. Parton could hardly believe it, especially when he thought of the priest's uncertain movements. All in all, there was no way of knowing how long they had been following him.

He turned into the light of the wide street and mingled with the passers-by. From the corner of his eye, he caught sight of the cassock again. The priest was still tailing him and the Indian would no doubt soon be back, too. It was time to get rid of the two of them, although the last thing to do was to let them know they had been seen, or give them the idea he was going to run. His gaze at the buildings and the passers-by was apparently casual, but he was looking for the way out.

The passers-by were too thin on the ground to allow him to lose his pursuers among them. There were the big houses – with their open gates through which he could see courtyards and gardens – but, if he tried one as an escape route, there was the danger of being trapped with no exit on the other side. Still, there was little else available. There would always be a window, or servants' quarters, or stables . . .

He was on the point of deciding which house when he saw the small square with the fountain. At the top of the sloping, paved square, water jetted into a semi-circular basin, the overflow running down the middle of the square in a stone gutter. Rising symetrically on either side of the fountain, meeting above it, were stone steps with black wrought iron railings. Then the steps went on, straight upward between grey house walls, towards the highest part of the town. It was like a funnel, thought Parton. His pursuers would hesitate to show themselves clearly on the steps and that should give him a few extra seconds at the top.

He turned and crossed the square, taking the right-hand side and climbing the steps until he was over the fountain.

He turned his head a fraction and looked back. The priest was at the bottom of the square, hesitating. The Indian was not to be seen, but he could not be far. Parton began to climb.

He climbed slowly. Undue haste would give the game away. His shadowers would be crossing the square, would be at the foot of the steps by now. He wished he could look back to be sure, but he must not show the slightest sign of suspicion. To keep his eyes from the fatal downward attraction, he looked up. Above the rooftops rose twin church towers, elegant and finely decorated. He climbed on. The last steps were ahead of him. At the top, he would turn right – slowly, deliberately. . . .

He reached the top and turned. He caught a glimpse of black way down the steps. He turned slowly, as planned. Then he was round the corner of the house at the top and could no longer be seen. He broke into a run.

He was in a street which seemed to skirt the hilltop. He decided he would go higher. He ran across the street and sprinted up a sidestreet, turned right, then left. He did not stop running. He turned right again. Without breaking his stride, he glanced back.

The Indian was twenty yards behind him, running silently.

It was impossible, thought Parton. He had changed direction several times. The Indian must have been really close, really close to him at the top of the steps to have followed. Of course. It was simple. He hadn't climbed the steps. He had come some other way. Parton had under-estimated his pursuers and now he was in deep trouble. He had given the game away, he had lost the advantage of surprise and he could no longer hope to shake off the Indian. He turned a corner and sprinted. There was only one way now. The Indian would have to stay there in the empty back streets. Alive or dead.

A doorway, thought Parton, or an alleyway, or just a

space between houses. There, ahead, what was that? A narrow passage, no daylight in it, dank walls, stinking of cats and rot. Parton ran in for several paces, stopped and came softly back, fighting to silence his breathing, shrinking against the wall. The Indian would look twice before running in, of that he could be sure. The man had already proved he was no fool. Parton would have to win on speed.

The Indian was there, he had checked his advance and was peering into the gloom of the passage as he came on. His eyes widened as he saw Parton at the last minute, much closer than he expected. He tried to stop, but his impetus brought him on, unbalancing him as he came within Parton's reach. Parton gripped the filthy blanket and heaved the Indian bodily into the passage, swinging him round in the same movement and slamming him into the wall. There was a hollow thud as the wind left the man's body. Parton pulled him forward and rammed him back again. The Indian's head whipped back and hit the wall. Parton let him go and he slid down to the muddy ground.

Parton looked out cautiously. The street was empty. He turned back and bent over the Indian. 'Who sent you?' he asked.

The man looked at him, glassy-eyed. 'The Holy Office,' he murmured.

'The Inquisition?' The Indian nodded, and Parton turned away. The search for the boy had scarcely begun and already the Inquisition was on to him. He turned back to the Indian, all the questions he needed answers to fighting for priority in his mind.

The man was struggling to his feet, a knife in his hand. Parton had no choice. His foot lashed out and his boot caught the Indian squarely under the chin. There was a dull crack and the man sagged back with a sigh. Parton would get no answers to his questions.

He went out into the empty street and walked briskly

away. He breathed in deeply. The knots in his stomach loosened a little. Now he had a fair chance of escaping. He walked on quickly. There was music in the air, he realized suddenly. He changed streets twice, climbing. The music became louder. He walked towards it. He could hear fifes and drums, but it didn't sound military. Music meant a fair or a market, a crowd in which to disappear. He had to become inconspicuous and he had to leave Cordoba. The music drew him on.

He came out into a bustling tree-lined avenue. Crowds were coming and going and at the end of the avenue he saw an open space packed with more people, behind them the church with the fine towers he had seen from lower down. He walked towards it. The hubbub grew.

The square in front of the church was filled with dust and noise and people. He plunged into the crowd, deafened by laughter, shouting, applause, singing, the beating of tambourines and guitars and the whistling of fifes. It was not a fair – there were no stalls, no tradesmen. He pushed his way further in, making for the middle of the square, wondering what to do about Seward who was waiting at the tavern. He would have to wait longer, that was all. There was nothing else to be done. Parton was going to mix with the crowd and let it hide him until he could find a safe way out of town.

It was some sort of feast day, he decided. People were well dressed, there were dancers, some wearing masks, and everyone seemed to be in the best of moods. Girls wore dresses with long, flounced skirts, red, blue, or white, which swirled as they moved. The double doors of the church were open and rows of white-robed choirboys carried embroidered banners and chanted, their singing drowned by the noise of the crowd. In front of them, surrounding a silvered shrine decked with flowers, priests in lace surplices swung censers, spreading clouds of perfumed smoke. Some kind of religious feast, decided

Parton as he moved forward. He looked twice at the priests, uneasy. His priest was not among them. He looked back. No sign of the black cassock in the crowd. Perhaps he had succeeded in throwing him off.

A shoulder banged into his back and he whipped round. '*Perdona*!' A dark-complexioned man was grinning at him. A group of dancers spun by, dust flying. Parton told himself he had to mix if he were to be inconspicuous. These people seemed friendly enough. He smiled and nodded at the man, then pushed into the group of dancers and began to dance. He frowned down at the weaving feet, concentrating. How the devil did they dance this thing? It was fast like a jig but the steps weren't the same . . .

'*Hombre*! Dance the *seguidilla*!'

Parton looked up. The entire group was laughing fit to burst. Parton laughed too, shrugging helplessly. 'I don't know the dance,' he said. There were howls of laughter. 'Perhaps he knows the *sevillana*!' called the man who had banged into Parton's back. 'Pilar, dance it with him!'

'Ah, no!' Pilar was a tall, heavy-boned woman in blue. Her dark hair was swept back from what had been a handsome face and her eyes were lined in black. 'The *sevillana* is no joke, my little husband! Except perhaps when you dance it!'

'I'll teach him, then!' offered the husband. 'Watch!' His left hand in the arched small of his back, his right arm raised, he lifted his head abruptly, tipped forward his flat, wide-brimmed hat and looked with burning eyes into Parton's. Parton grinned, knowing he was being made fun of, not caring as long as the dancers were hiding him. He looked out uneasily over the man's shoulder. *The black cassock*. The priest was there on the edge of the square, thin-faced, examining the crowd.

Parton bent forward, letting the man in front cover him. A tambourine crashed, the dancer spun round superbly, everyone was laughing. Parton half-turned, bending still further, pretending to choke with laughter. A quick glance told him that the priest was still there. He seemed to be alone. Parton began to choke in earnest.

'Hey, *hombre*!' His new friends surrounded him, slapping him on the back. The dancer was pushing a small wineskin into his hand. 'Lay the dust!' he invited. Parton took it and straightened up. He could no longer see the priest but that meant nothing. He drank a draught. The wine was strong, sweet and warm. It was hot in the middle of the crowd and the all-pervading scent of incense was sickening. Where had the priest gone? Had he found the Indian? Parton had no choice but to stay where he was and play the part.

'Where did you learn to dance like that?' someone asked.

'I was born in Cuba,' lied Parton. 'We don't know your dances there.'

'Of course!' said the dancer. 'You have the *criollo* accent of people born out here in the Indies. We should have guessed! As for us, we are from Andalusia.'

Parton's glance raked the side of the square where the priest had been. 'And you have come out here to settle?' he asked, looking back to the Andalusian and his friends, interested for the first time in who or what they were. They were several years older than he, and, in their short-jacketed suits of clean grey or brown worsted, they looked like tradesmen or craftsmen in their Sunday best.

'Not long ago,' replied the dancer. 'My name is Espinel. You will have guessed that Pilar is my wife.'

'Roca,' nodded Parton, introducing himself, and looking off to the other side of the square. If the priest came back with reinforcements, he would be trapped. But how could he leave the crowd and risk being seen?

'Are you expecting someone, Roca?' asked Espinel. 'Someone pretty, perhaps,' he added with a knowing look.

Parton turned, surprised. 'Oh, no. I'm just passing through, travelling with a friend.'

'And is your friend coming on the pilgrimage too?'

'This is a pilgrimage?' asked Parton, gesturing round at the dusty, shouting crowd. Good God, he thought, aren't pilgrimages supposed to be serious affairs?

'Señor Roca,' said Pilar archly as Espinal turned to find the wineskin, 'you don't know how to dance and you don't know this is a pilgrimage.' She was watching him. 'Must we think you have fallen from the moon?'

'Perhaps!' Parton forced himself to laugh, catching her eye. No, there was no suspicion in her look. There was more than a hint of invitation. Parton ignored it and turned to her husband. He needed the cover these people were providing and he wanted no complications.

'Which way are you travelling?' asked Espinel, passing the wine.

'Up,' said Parton guardedly. He had a story ready if need be, but he preferred not to have to answer questions.

'To Mexico City?' Squealing fifes and shrieks of laughter had drowned Espinel's words, but Parton had understood. He nodded. 'So are we!' yelled Espinel over the noise.

'I thought you were settlers,' shouted Parton, pointing to the ground to signify 'here'. As he did so, the priest came into view again, pushing into the crowd, peering to right and left. Parton couldn't swear to it, but it seemed to him the man had turned to signal to someone behind him. Parton moved closer into the group of friends, lifting the wineskin to hide his face.

'We are leatherworkers,' Espinel was saying. 'We have to go to the capital to register with our Guild before settling to trade.'

The priest was coming closer. Parton leaned forward and pointed to Espinel's belt. 'Is this an example of your work?' he asked.

'It is.' Espinel held open his jacket to show off the belt. Intricate, hand-sewn motifs drew arabesques on its supple, dark-tan leather.

'Marvellous. How is it done?' asked Parton, raising his

41

head a fraction and looking briefly over Espinel's shoulder. The priest was moving away, still prying from right to left. The crowd closed over him and Parton straightened up.

'A secret!' laughed Espinel. 'Our mystery!'

Pilar looked at her husband. 'If Señor Roca is coming on the pilgrimage,' she said, 'why not . . .'

'Of course!' beamed Espinel. 'We must adopt him!'

'Adopt?' asked Parton, horrified. He wished he knew what these people wanted from him.

'Yes! It's the tradition! A young man alone cannot come on the pilgrimage without being adopted. We have food, firelight, company – and our carts are ready and waiting for us down the road! Roca, let us adopt you!'

'But I'm not alone,' fenced Parton. 'And . . . where is the pilgrimage going?' He glimpsed the priest's back again between dancers.

Espinel clapped him on the shoulder. 'Don't worry! Tonight we shall be at the shrine of Our Lady of the Mountain not far from the road to Mexico City. Tomorrow, when the procession comes back to Cordoba, we, the Andalusians, we shall go on towards the capital. Why don't we all travel together?'

Parton watched the priest disappear on the edge of the square. He had called up reinforcements, or he was about to do so. The crowd could hide Parton and the pilgrimage was a way of leaving town unnoticed. The Andalusians' friendliness was cloying, but at least they could get him out of Cordoba. Better the Espinels than the Inquisition.

'I'll have to go and get Benidies at the tavern where we were staying,' he said. He and Seward had chosen their Spanish names beforehand.

'Not at all,' said Pilar. 'I'll send the boys.'

'We have three sons,' explained Espinel proudly, 'and two daughters.'

'Wonderful,' said Parton. 'But I can go myself.'

'No, no!' insisted Pilar. 'I'll send the boys. Did you say your friend's name was . . .?'

'Benidies. At the sign of the Three Reals near the livery stables. Please tell him he should pay our reckoning and bring our packs with him. And thank you!' he added in relief as Pilar began to thread her way through the crowd.

'It's our pleasure!' said Espinel. Parton looked at the Spaniard's broad smile and wondered where the pleasure lay. No, he reasoned, the Espinels couldn't know who he was. Pilar was coming back, pushing round a group of masked dancers. 'The boys are on their way,' she announced. 'They—'

'Look!' interrupted her husband. Parton turned sharply, afraid the priest was back. 'My dear,' called Espinel, 'come here, will you? Roca—' Espinel turned to Parton with an obsequious smile. '—our daughter Consuela!'

The girl smiled shyly and Parton nodded politely. Consuela was a lumpy girl of about twenty-five, showily dressed in red with a long, flounced skirt trimmed with white. So that was it, thought Parton, relieved to know what he was up against. The Espinels had a daughter to marry and the pilgrimage festivities offered a hunting-ground for eligible bachelors.

'Consuela!' came another voice. 'Oh, there you are!' A second girl pushed her way through the crowd. 'The last of our children,' said Espinel offhand. 'Consuela's little sister Gabriela.'

Parton saw the girl's head lift at the slight. Then her eyes left her father's and came to rest on the newcomer's. Parton swallowed as his glance took in long-lashed, dark, impetuous eyes, jet-black hair swept up into a chignon, superb matt skin, a blue hand-me-down dress clinging too tightly to high, firm breasts and down to hips where the long skirt flared. Parton nodded and looked away, seeking refuge. 'Little sister' indeed! The girl must be seventeen or eighteen, her body perfect and those black, passionate eyes. . . . No complications, he told himself. He needed the cover the Espinels could give. His eyes went back to

Gabriela for only a fleeting second before he turned to Espinel and said, 'Pleased to make your family's acquaintance.' It sounded lame and he laughed, clowning, pushing Espinel out of the way of a drunk-looking dancer. The Andalusian laughed too, passing the wineskin. When Parton looked back in Gabriela's direction, the girl had disappeared.

'Here's your friend!' called Pilar.

Seward was making his way through the crowd towards them, led by a dark young man and followed by two younger boys carrying packs. Parton realized there was movement in the crowd. The choirboys and priests were lining up to lead the procession from the square. Then Seward was there and Parton was introducing him to the Espinels and explaining that they were going with the pilgrimage.

Seward looked round with an uneasy grin. 'It's quite a holiday!' he said with apparent effort.

Parton glanced anxiously to the edges of the square as they began to move with the jostling mass of pilgrims. 'Let's enjoy it while we can,' he replied tautly, only slightly relieved to see no priest watching their departure.

The night was cloudy and black, but the embers of a hundred camp fires dotting the mountainside cast a reddish glow on rocks and blanketed sleepers. It was late and the pilgrimage was at last becoming silent. 'At last' was no exaggeration, thought Parton as he picked his way up the slope, searching for a spot which commanded a view of the road in case search and pursuit should come, even at this late hour, from Cordoba. The pilgrimage to the shrine in the mountains was the pretext for an immense drinking bout – even early in the evening's festivities, he had seen people blind drunk on the cactus beer they called *pulque* and if there had been laughter there had also been fights and a rumour that someone had been knifed to death over on the

44

other side of the slope. With the Andalusians, there had been drinking too and there had been music and dancing all evening – harsh, haunting melodies, tapping on the wood of guitars, cries that seemed part of the music, swirling dances in the firelight. Parton's eyes and ears were full. He chose a spot well clear of the nearest sleepers and lay down, wrapping himself in a blanket. He would not sleep, but it was restful to lie in the darkness, hearing the distant rush of a mountain stream, occasional muted voices and somewhere, behind a woman's laughter, the drifting notes of a last melancholy guitar.

The pilgrimage had provided good cover, or so it seemed. At least, they were out of Cordoba and they had mixed well with the Andalusians. As Roca and Benidies, the Spanish American and the Spaniard born and bred, their pre-arranged story since jumping ship was that they were agents of *Rodriguez y Cuevas* on their way to the viceregal capital to obtain a licence to extend their trade in cotton goods to Guadalajara and its province. On a somewhat similar quest, the leather craftsmen found the whole thing natural. What was more, Seward's professional experience had provided him with a thorough knowledge of New Spain's complicated laws and conventions and he was proving to be a mine of information for the would-be settlers. The result was that Parton and Seward's story was going over perfectly, even giving them a certain standing with their hosts. Perhaps they should accept the invitation to travel all the way to the capital, thought Parton. Hiring horses at the next town was the last way to be inconspicuous. The Andalusians' group was large, more than a score in all. It was a family group, neither too rich nor too poor. It would undoubtedly provide good cover on the road. The only argument against it was the time the journey would take – the Andalusians spoke of over a week. But after the events of Cordoba, Parton felt obliged to give more weight to safety than speed.

Stones rattled and he lifted his head, instantly alert. A skirt swished against a rock.

'Roca?'

The voice was muffled and he could not identify its owner. Pilar? Consuela? He feigned sleep.

A hand brushed his shoulder and he peered upwards. A woman's head was bending over his, in shadow. Then the head lifted and a red glimmer from a distant fire reflected in black depths he immediately recognized. Gabriela spread a blanket on the ground beside him.

'I have come to lie with you,' she said matter-of-factly. There was a rustle and her face was only inches from his. 'To lie beside you, if you prefer!' Her voice was playful. The smile on her face, now that he could make it out, was gently mocking him. He stayed stock still. Pilar he could have put off, Consuela he might have been able to discourage, but there was only one thing he wanted to do with Gabriela. The very lightness of the touch of her thigh against his was unbearable.

'I liked you as soon as I saw you,' she went on softly. Her breath smelled of lemon and some sweet spice, cinnamon perhaps. Her mouth would be delicious, thought Parton. He moved back slightly and she bubbled with laughter. 'So I followed you when you left the camp fire,' she said.

Parton summoned up his energy and propped himself up on an elbow. 'Gabriela, please. Your parents—' It was laughably weak and he broke off.

Gabriela lay beneath him, her smile still mocking, her eyes black on his.

'We're only talking,' she said maliciously. 'What else is there to do?'

It was a practical matter, Parton told himself. He had decided that the Espinel family was good cover for him and he must do nothing to rock the boat and lose it. He reminded himself of his shadowers in Cordoba and the sinister organization they represented. He and Seward needed to disappear, not to make themselves conspicuous. He looked away from Gabriela and sat up. She laughed and sat up beside him.

'Do my parents terrify you as much as that? I can't believe it. You don't look like someone who's easily frightened.'

'It's not that.'

'Do you know what my mother is doing right now?' Parton shook his head. 'She's with your friend Benidies. I don't think they're discussing the weather.'

Parton turned. It was true that Pilar and Seward had been the last at the fireside when he had left. 'Are you sure?' he asked.

'I saw them go off together. I was hiding in the shadows, watching which way you'd go.' She laughed briefly. 'With that genteel air and all he knows about the law and the Guilds and so on, he's very eligible indeed. My mother desperately wants an eligible bachelor for Consuela, but she's not above trying him out first. I thought she was going to make a play for you, but his standing went up during the walk here this afternoon, while yours went down. Except with me.'

Parton smiled. 'Thank you.' He felt annoyed with Seward for having so quickly forgotten their need for a safe cover, but in fact, he realized, he felt relieved at the same time that Pilar had chosen the younger man. Still, this was likely to cause trouble . . . 'How does your father take this kind of thing?' he asked.

Gabriela snorted. 'He pretends not to see. All that matters to him is marrying off Consuela, then me, and bringing two good sons-in-law into the family business with my brothers. That's all he lives for. To become a respectable master craftsman at the head of a prosperous family concern.'

'Is that such a bad thing?' asked Parton neutrally, secretly relieved by Gabriela's affirmations.

'You should see the price he's willing to pay for it,' she replied warmly. 'Years back in Spain of bowing and scraping and bribing guildsmen, to no avail. Now he's brought us all out to America and he'll go to Mexico City and grease more guildsmen's palms and lick their boots in hopes they'll grant him the rights he needs! He has no pride! And he'd happily marry off poor Consuela to her mother's lover and pretend he didn't know what he was doing. That's Espinel!'

'Espinel?' It seemed a strange way for a girl to speak of her father.

Gabriela looked at him for a second before replying. 'He's not my father. My mother won't admit it to me, but I know he's not. What did you think of the music and dancing tonight?' she asked abruptly.

Parton frowned at the change. 'I liked it,' he said guardedly, not wanting to show himself too ignorant of Spanish customs.

'What you saw was nothing,' said Gabriela, leaning forward. 'Tonight there were no *gitanos*, no gypsies, because they are forbidden to emigrate to America. The gypsies know another music, another dance,' she whispered. 'It is called *flamenco*. It is more noble, more perfect than the other dances you saw tonight. It seems to be magic. It is – I wish I could explain it to you! It is cruel and gentle at the same time. It can make your heart leap and your blood run cold at the very same moment. Can you understand that?'

'Perhaps,' said Parton, looking into Gabriela's shining eyes.

'No, Espinel is not my father. Whatever lies my mother tells, I know the truth. The whole town back at home knew it. My father is a gypsy, a dancer renowned from Seville to Granada.' Her hand was on Parton's. 'I know I am his daughter and I shall be a dancer. Oh, the New World is perhaps a marvellous place, but Espinel brought me out here against my will and I'm going to go back to Spain as

48

soon as I can find a way. I will find my father and even if it is secret and forbidden, however difficult it may be, I will live with the gypsies and I will learn to dance.'

Parton looked at her for a long moment. 'You know what you want,' he said softly at last.

'Don't you?'

He bent forward and kissed her. Her hands came up to his face, his neck, slipped inside his shirt, caressing. The little girl of the family, thought Parton, pulling her down beside him. His hand cupped her hip, holding her to him and her nails scratched his shoulder, her teeth caught his tongue. Her dress was a tight sheath above, a flowing mass of skirts and underskirts and petticoats below. He began to lift them and Gabriela rolled over on to her stomach. 'There are buttons all down the back,' she said. 'It's the only way.'

Parton leaned over her, unbuttoning, sliding the dress over her shoulders. There was soft down at the nape of her neck and in the hollow of her back. The last button was low, over her buttocks. He slipped his hand inside, untying a knotted tape and pushed her drawers down. The skin between her thighs was like velvet. She groaned, broke away, tugged at her dress, pulling it off, tearing away skirts and underskirts, while Parton too tore off his clothes. He pulled a blanket over them as she lay facing him, raising her thigh, hooking her knee over his hip, and he held her by the waist and pushed up slowly until he was inside her.

'Two hours until dawn, Roca,' she said, her black eyes on his. 'Let them be mine.'

CHAPTER FOUR

'The biggest city in all the Americas!' announced Seward from the top of the rise, pointing.

Parton came up to join him where the road skirted northwards round a shoulder of the volcano Tlaloc and looked down into the fifty-mile-wide Mexico valley. Snow-capped mountains hedged it round on all sides. Below, hazy in the middle of the valley, he saw a vast expanse of water, and beyond it, around it, the great dark mass of Mexico City, capital of New Spain.

The journey had been long. It had taken eleven dust-ridden days to climb through the rising valleys and along the endless loops the road traced on steep mountain flanks and in the approaches to higher and higher passes. There had been no travelling faster. The Andalusians' mule carts, in a long day's climbing which exhausted the mules, covered a bare twenty miles. Parton had several times considered leaving the group and hiring horses to move ahead faster, but the thought of the Cordoba Inquisition had decided the issue each time. He could not be sure, in spite of appearances, that the Inquisition had given up pursuit. Word might well have been sent to other towns. The Andalusians' cover was good and he had stayed with it.

The country was strange to him, his familiar Caribbean world far behind. Day after day they had climbed into the thinner air of the mountains on the rising, rutted road – mud after an evening storm, dust the next morning after an hour of sun – seeing the scores of Indian carriers, the *tamemes*, bent under crippling loads, leaning forward and trotting so that the weight on their backs would not pull them back, while their ragged families ran beside them.

Even the children carried what they could. The rich rode by in sedan chairs carried by other Indian bearers and fine horsemen in leather and silver cleared the way ahead of them with a disdainful shout. Hovering above the landscape in the shimmering haze, long trails of cloud floating after their summits, the white, snow-capped cones of the high volcanoes, near and far at once, unreal, snow and ice up there and down below nothing but heat and dust and more road to tramp before nightfall. The towns had been stranger and stranger to Parton's eyes as they had come closer to the hollow heart of New Spain: the lavish expense, the lace and pearls and silk of the Spanish gentry in filthy streets where beggars lay dying, the white and gold of elaborate spires and towers, the fanatical splendour of Puebla de los Angeles, city of a thousand churches with its tiled façades of blue and green and red and black, its enormous population of priests and monks and nuns, like guardians of a holy city . . . Parton had been invaded by the dizzying impression of entering a secret empire, like Marco Polo journeying to Cathay, or like Cortes. Had not Cortes made exactly the same journey as Parton, to look down into the same valley at the same city, capital of the Aztec empire he had been about to conquer?

But Parton had resisted the invasion with force. He had clung to practical detail, transposing Cameron's instructions on to the reality of the country around him, pumping Seward daily for information, memorizing every stretch of the road as they climbed, fixing in his mind the obstacles, the dangers, the difficulties, the towns and even the smallest villages, the relays where horses could be changed – because the way back down the road had to be covered much faster than it had been climbed.

For, as the Andalusians and their fellow travellers left the Aztec ruins by the marshy confines of the lake and came in among the rows of crumbling adobe huts of the poorest and furthest-flung of the Indian quarters of Mexico City, it was the evening of the first of July. Parton had nine days in which to find an inconspicuous boy in the great city, kidnap him, and get him safely down to the coast.

The second of July had scarcely begun when Parton left the lodgings he and Seward had taken in the *barrio* Santa Maria a few doors from the Espinels and made his way to the city centre. Seward had not been exaggerating. Mexico City was vast, several miles across. Parton had never seen a city as big. He left behind the dirty little streets of private houses and came out into wider avenues, already swarming with people, the gateways of magnificent public buildings a to and fro of clerks, officials, servants and citizens on business. Parton stopped by a beautifully laid out park with fountains and flowerbeds and looked around. The first thing was to learn what establishments the Franciscan order had in the capital, and if he could do so without Seward's help, so much the better. The best way was probably simply to ask a Franciscan friar. If he played the part right, he would be running little or no risk. Even after what had happened in Cordoba, every monk or priest in New Spain couldn't be on the lookout for him. Asking for directions was perfectly innocent. The problem was, he could see no friars in the growing crowds around him.

Perhaps it was too early and they were all at prayer or at mass. He looked up. He saw several church towers above the rooftops and made for the biggest.

They were the towers of the cathedral. Parton walked down the side of the enormous, richly decorated structure and stopped at the edge of the vast square in front of it. The square was filled with market stalls and people, thousands of people. If you wanted to find a crowd in a New Spanish town, he thought, you had to look for a church. He avoided a group of beggars who came running towards him and walked into the square. In an hour the market would be over. The sun was already beginning to hit hard through the clear mountain air.

He pushed his way in among the stalls and shouting vendors. The alleys stretched for hundreds of yards across the square and the crowd was thick. After arrays of saddles and harness, he saw bales of cotton and lace, stalls of oil and wax sellers and candle makers, pitches of household utensils, brightly painted ceramics, jars and bowls and jugs in blues and yellows and reds, then, on mats on the ground, Indians and *mestizos* were selling fruit and vegetables, drinks, cooked food. There were dark-green watermelons and sweet peppers, chillies, squashes, baskets of lemons, limes and oranges, maize, tomatoes. Parton bought a couple of *tortillas* from an Indian woman who was cooking them over a charcoal fire and ate them ravenously. The crowd jostled and he stepped aside. A man in threadbare grey homespun pushed past him. The cowl was down and the tonsure, like the chin, badly shaven, the eyebrows dark and prominent, the eyes sternly fixed ahead. The friar was by and already going out of sight in the crowded alley.

'Señor!' Parton ran after him. Damn it, how were you supposed to address a friar? Play the boy from out of town, thought Parton, the country cousin. 'Señor Friar!' He caught up with the friar and touched his arm. The man turned, menacing, ready to beat away a beggar.

'Señor, please! Help for a stranger who needs directions in this enormous town! Just *directions*, Señor Friar!'

The man looked irritably at Parton and pulled him aside into the relative calm of a passage between two stalls. 'Quickly! I have no time to waste!' he groused.

'Thank you, my Father!' said Parton. 'I hope you're a Franciscan, after all.'

'I am. Now tell me what you want. I have no time for tomfoolery.'

'Good!' smiled Parton. 'You see, I'm from Remedios and my name's Lopez! I expect you recognize it!'

The friar looked at him blankly. 'Lopez?'

'From Remedios! Now you remember, don't you?'

The man sniffed, deep creases forming from the sides of his nose to the corners of his mouth. 'You don't smell of *pulque*,' he said. 'I suppose you're mad. May God have mercy on your soul.' He turned to go.

'But my cousin!' insisted Parton, holding him back. 'Lopez from Remedios! He's here with you, with the Franciscans in Mexico City! My cousin Jaime! He's at school here in a Franciscan college and I've been searching for it since yesterday so I can visit him and give him the money the family sent for him!'

The Franciscan wiped his brow wearily. 'There are thousands of us in the capital, young man, and I know none of the schoolboys. What's the name of his school?'

'The fact is, Father,' said Parton, scratching his head, 'that I don't remember the exact name. Not exactly. It starts with Saint. Saint something's, that's for sure. He's there to become a friar like you, father.'

The friar sighed. 'You mean your cousin is a novice?'

'Not quite. He's about to become one.'

'The boys who are preparing their novitiate are at the Seminary of St Francis,' said the friar testily. 'Is that it?'

'Perhaps,' Parton looked doubtful. 'He couldn't be anywhere else, could he?'

'Not if he's due to become a novice.'

'Then that's it! I knew it began with Saint! I told you so, didn't I?' said Parton joyfully.

The Franciscan looked at Parton and shook his head. 'Suffer the little children,' he muttered. 'Down the avenue over there,' he said, pointing. 'Go down it until a wide street with trees crosses it. Turn right into that street and walk about half a mile. The Seminary of St Francis is in a small street on the left. There's a statue of our Blessed Founder on the corner of the building. You can't miss it.' He looked at Parton severely. 'But they won't let you see your cousin. I don't know what gave you the idea you could. The seminarists are in strict retreat except on certain feast days when families may visit. The next one will be Assumption.'

Parton's mouth dropped open. He had a vague idea Assumption was in August. 'What about the money I'm supposed to give him from the family?'

The friar glanced down to Parton's hands and shrugged. 'Whatever you have to give, you will hand in at the gate. We share all earthly goods, my son.'

Parton caught the look in the harsh eyes and fumbled in his pocket, handing the friar a small coin. 'For good works,' he said piously.

'It shall be counted thee,' said the Franciscan as his hand closed on the coin. Parton watched him disappear in the crowd. Then he turned and threaded his way in the opposite direction for a while before skirting round the edge of the plaza and leaving it by the avenue the friar had indicated. He reached the wide street with trees and turned right, walking quickly. There were fewer passers-by here, although the roadway was busy with carriers and carts. Several buildings had carved stone façades and statues and he studied them as he walked. Parton's strictly Protestant upbringing had left him rather short on the lives of the saints, but he was fairly sure that the founder of the Franciscan order was St Francis of Assissi. On the corner of a grim-looking, blank-walled building a little way ahead was a statue of a man with a beatific smile and a doe nuzzling his hand. That was it. Parton crossed and walked beneath the statue round the corner into the sidestreet. The wall was as bare and windowless as out in the main street and the statue was the only decoration. There was a closed door with a grille. He walked past it, looking up. There were not even attic windows, not even bull's-eyes. There had to be gardens and cloisters on the inside, he thought, to let the light in. The blank wall ended and a private house followed. Parton looked in casually through the gate as he passed. A musically dripping fountain in a courtyard, flowers, a tree, a high, blind, white wall, the seminary wall no doubt. No way in through there.

He turned left. Along this side of the seminary were more private houses. A narrow alley led back to the main street, the high seminary wall running its entire length. He came out on to the main street and checked again that there were no doors or windows. There were not. The Seminary of St Francis was surrounded by windowless walls or by houses which did not communicate with it. There was only one entrance, the small door with the grille.

He turned beneath the statue again, crossed the narrow street, and stopped, looking at the door. How could he get in? A shutter was closed on the inside of the iron grille. 'Strict retreat', the friar had said. What would happen if he went up and knocked? Would the shutter open? What kind of story could he tell? Cousin Jaime from Remedios wouldn't do this time. Could he offer a contribution? The friar had said gifts could be left at the gate. If he offered enough, might he get invited in? But then, how would he give the friars in there the slip and find out for sure if the boy he was to kidnap was there? And how would he get the boy out? Ideally, he needed to find a way of breaking in without, all the same, risking too much at one throw of the dice. The contribution idea was possible, but he would be seen close up and it might yield no returns at all.

Two men brushed past him, one limping heavily and leaning on the other's arm. Parton saw the leg uncovered to the thigh, the mass of purulent sores and he turned away involuntarily. The beggars on the cathedral plaza had been clean and healthy compared to these.

'For the love of God!' The stronger of the two was hammering on the seminary door while the limping beggar sat with his back to the wall. Parton shrank back and watched. At least he would see what happened when someone knocked on the door. 'Brother Friar! Open up, for the love of God!' The hammering was louder.

Parton saw the shutter open and a face appear behind the grille.

The beggar clawed at the door. 'Alms and assistance, Brother Friar, for the Blessed Virgin's sake! We are dying!'

There was a chink of metal on the stone threshold. 'Go with God,' called the friar from within and closed the shutter. The beggar on the ground was on the coin in a flash. 'The filthy bastard,' he muttered, staring at it. 'The filthy bastard! Look!' He held up his hand. His companion's eyes widened and he turned back to the door, kicking and hammering like a madman. 'It's a *tlaco*! Worthless! *Bastard*!'

There was no hesitation. The door opened sharply and a young, strong-looking friar appeared in the doorway, a heavy stick in his hand. He pushed the beggar away with the stick, then, as the man came staggering back towards him, hit him a crack over the shoulder. The beggar squealed and stepped back into the street.

'Move on!' shouted the friar. He poked the beggar on the ground. 'Get on with you!'

'And what do we do with your lousy alms?' whined the beggar. 'This token ain't enough to buy a handful of flour, you cheating boy-fancier!'

The friar rounded on him and the beggar scrambled to his feet and limped away.

'On your way!' shouted the friar, stick flailing. 'Take your poxy sin-ridden sores elsewhere!' He was beating the two men off down the street. 'Dying men should find comfort in Mother Church! Find a priest, confess and die!'

Parton walked quietly down the street until he was opposite the open door. It gave on to a dim corridor, light at the far end of it. There was no one in sight. The doorkeeper was on his way back and Parton walked busily on down the far side of the street. With a final imprecation towards the beggars, the friar shut the door and a bolt slammed into place.

A slow smile came to Parton's face as he walked on.

'Stop!'

Seward's razor wavered and stopped an inch from his cheek. He turned, wide-eyed, as Parton came into the room. 'Afraid I'll cut myself?' he asked.

'No,' said Parton, pulling at the curtain that separated their two ill-furnished and expensive rooms. 'I need your help, preferably unshaven.'

Seward sighed and pointed with his razor. 'Just when I'd got some hot water.' Steam rose from a brightly painted bowl on the window ledge. Hanging from a nail above it was a polished brass disc in which Seward's features were reflected. 'It hurts to throw it away.'

'I'll use it if you'll lend me your razor,' said Parton. 'Is hot water as hard as that to come by?'

'She made me pay for it,' said Seward with a nod in the direction of their landlady's apartments. He handed the razor to Parton. 'What are we going to do?'

'Tell you when I've finished,' said Parton, soaping his face. 'Did you buy the fruit from her too?' There was a pile of fruit on the table in the corner.

'No, that was Pilar. A present for us.'

'Motherly of her.' So Pilar had already paid a neighbourly visit. Seward's bed did look ruffled. Parton began to shave.

'She'd already been out to visit the big market on the *Zocalo*, the cathedral plaza. It's an impressive sight.' Seward paused. 'But since you've been out this morning, I suppose you might have seen it yourself.'

Damn, thought Parton, applying himself to shaving carefully around the scar which ran under his jaw. Pilar had been at the market earlier. Had she seen him with the friar? Apparently not – unless Seward was being tactful and pretending he didn't know. Damn it, it was annoying. 'I'm afraid I've no time for sight-seeing,' he said sharply.

Seward marked a pause. 'I wasn't trying to probe,' he said at length.

'I'm sure you weren't,' said Parton conciliatorily, finishing and rinsing the remains of soap from his face. He needed Seward's help, he reminded himself. 'What annoyed me was the idea that Pilar might have seen me somewhere in town. I wouldn't like the Espinels to know too much about what we're going to do now, for example.' He peered into the brass disc. He looked smarter. He turned and grinned. 'Are you up to facing a friar with a big stick?' he asked. 'If you're quick, he won't hit you.'

When the shutter opened, Seward clasped the grille with his filthy hands, pressed his face to the bars and shouted, 'I am Alpha and Omega. Give me sustenance, give me bread!'

The shutter slammed to on to his fingers and he let out a howl of pain. 'Iniquitous one!' he yelled, kicking out at the age-darkened wood of the door. 'Give me bread!' His blows doubled.

Parton watched from the corner of the street, admirative. Seward was playing the part of the mad beggar to perfection. Parton looked out towards the main street, fearful that Seward's performance might attract unwelcome attention out there. Fortunately, the streets were empty at the hour of the *siesta*.

The door opened and the athletic young doorkeeper was there with his stick. Seward clawed at him.

'Impious son of iniquitous parents!' he shouted. 'When will the Lord's servant have bread?'

The stick swung and cracked into Seward's ribs. Seward stepped back and Parton, watching, winced. 'Bread,' whined Seward, 'bread for the servant of the Lord . . .'

The friar advanced on him, stick raised. 'Blaspheming, idle beggar! Servant of the Lord, indeed! Move on or I'll shake your idle bones!'

Parton slid from the corner towards the door. Seward only had to take the man a little further . . .

It was as if Seward had read his thoughts. He dodged the stick, grappling with the friar, shouting. The Franciscan pushed him away and plied the stick, forcing him off down the street. Parton walked quickly to the door and looked in. No one was in sight. He stepped into the corridor. It was dim and flagstoned, with an alcove for the doorkeeper. Shouting was still coming from the street. Seward should break off now before he got himself into real trouble.

Parton was through the corridor and into a cloister and no one had challenged him. He slipped into the shelter of a dark corner. The cloister was empty, the sun beating down on to the bare patch of earth in the middle. Back in the corridor, the door slammed and the bolt banged home. Parton had about half an hour in which to search the seminary. When Mexico City's bells rang four o'clock, Seward would attack the door again to cover Parton's escape.

The friar was muttering. Parton stayed where he was, waiting to be sure the man was not going to come through into the cloister and see him nosing around. Silence came down again like a leaden cover. Would the friars be sleeping as most people did in the afternoon? And the boys? Would they have the right to sleep too, or would they have to read or meditate or pray? 'A strict retreat', the friar on the market place had said. The very thought of young boys being shut off here between the stone walls made Parton shudder. He had a sudden vision of lines of kneeling boys surrounded by fanatical friars with sticks and whips, screaming about sin and blasphemy. He shook his head. That was New Spain again. The country was unbalanced, ringing with religion, cavernous with priests and cloisters. It made Parton uneasy and yet it was there, into the musty odour of prayerbooks, the shuffling of bare feet and the chanting of Latin, the fanatical eyes and the grey, unhealthy skin, that he had to go to find a boy of eight and get him away to his family.

Parton stirred and moved silently forward over the flagstones. Thoughts like that made him really want to succeed. There were windows along the inner wall of the cloister. He went cautiously to the first and peered in. There were tables and benches in the large, otherwise empty room beyond. A refectory, thought Parton .

Further down the cloister, at the end of the refectory, was a doorway which gave on to a dark vestibule with a staircase rising to the right. Parton climbed the stairs quietly. There were two doors in the landing at the top. He bent to the latch and looked through the wide hole it had, like all latches, worn in the door. The room beyond contained shelves of manuscripts and books and a large desk. Through the latch-hole of the second door, he saw a gaunt, white-haired friar sitting dozing at a table in a simply furnished room with a bookcase. Parton wondered if he weren't looking at the superior of the seminary. He made his way softly downstairs again. Across the cloister, directly opposite, there was a similar door. He decided to leave it for the return trip. To the left, after two more windows of what seemed to be another part of the refectory, was an opening which he reasoned should lead to a second cloister. He slipped through it, looking back anxiously to be sure he wasn't in the doorkeeper's field of vision. He could see a pair of sandalled feet on the flagstones of the corridor, but nothing more. The friar must be sitting back in the alcove. Between the two cloisters was a narrow, roofed-over space where blocks of stone lay with mason's tools. There would always be something to repair in a place like this, Parton supposed, noting that there were no doors leading elsewhere.

He looked out into the second cloister. It was larger than the first and just as empty and bare. Opposite was a big building with double doors which would no doubt be the chapel. On the left were two doors and Parton started there. The first gave on to a short corridor with a staircase. At the end of the corridor was a closed door. Parton looked through the latch and saw a roomy kitchen with clean pots and pans hanging against a wall. There was a passage on the far side which would lead through to the refectory. There was a marmalade cat lying curled up on a chair, but there was no one in sight.

He climbed the stairs. A long landing ran the length of the side of the cloister, doors leading off it at regular intervals. Parton counted a dozen of them. They had grilles in them like the outer door and the place had a prison-like air. He crept to the first and risked a look in. A friar was lying asleep on a bed. There was no one in the second. In the third, a friar was kneeling by the bedstead. Parton had seen enough to know that these were the friars' individual cells. He went back down and out into the empty cloister. The next door was shut and locked. He found a crack in the wood and peered in. He could see little, but after a time he made out barrels and sacks. The place looked like a storeroom and probably went with the nearby kitchen.

He turned to the chapel. One of the doors was ajar and he slipped inside. There were windows above him, along the cloister wall at second-floor level and rays of light obliqued down on to the wooden pews. There was a high leaded window above the altar too. It must give on to the gardens or courtyards of the private houses on the east side of the block. It was the first time he had seen anything that looked remotely like a way in or out apart from the street door. He studied it, reckoning rough distances. It might be useful when the time came.

Apart from that, the chapel held nothing of any interest. He began to feel vaguely anxious. He had seen only a few friars and no seminarists as yet. Afternoon heat or not, the place was strangely quiet for a place where young boys lived. Disused was the word which almost came to mind. Still, the other half remained to be searched and conditions in such a place would no doubt be strict. He left the chapel quietly but hurriedly. Time was going by.

The windows on the third side of the cloister gave on to a large room with high desks of the kind you had to stand up at, and a rostrum for the schoolmaster. It was the first clear evidence he had seen that the place was indeed a school. But there were no pupils, no master. He climbed the staircase which followed. There was an open door at the top and he glanced inside. He made out a row of beds and shrank back against the wall by the door. Here he had to be careful. If the boys were sleeping, there might well be monkish watchdogs. He inched forward, listening for the slightest sound. He looked round the door jamb and swept his gaze rapidly across the dormitory. It was empty, the beds bare, blankets neatly folded at the foot of each.

Parton cursed and hurried back down the stairs. He now had the definite impression that something was wrong. The seminary seemed so empty – and it was as if it had been so for some time. He slipped through into the first cloister. There were windows and a door, following the now-familiar pattern. The classroom behind the windows was as empty as the first. The staircase beyond led to a second dormitory, empty too. Parton went in and looked round. A fly buzzed listlessly. That was it, he thought. The impression of disuse came from a combination of tidiness and neglect. Everything had been neatly arranged and then left. He ran a finger over the edge of a bedstead, leaving a clear trace in the dust.

There were no boys. The place was practically empty. However, the classrooms and dormitories showed that there had been pupils in the seminary. How long ago had they left? Why? Where had they gone? The friar that morning had been quite affirmative when he had said that a boy preparing for his novitiate would be here, but he had been wrong. Was it a case of the left hand not knowing what the right was doing? Parton touched the bronze medallion at his throat. Almost a day had gone by in the capital and he still had no more than this scrap of metal to find the boy with. He had to start all over again.

A bell chimed, muted, distant, then another, closer to. Parton turned and left the dormitory. As he hurried down the stairs, he heard banging and shouting from below. Seward was at his post and exactly on time. The irascible doorkeeper would probably react quickly. Parton took the steps two at a time. Noise didn't matter now. What did was to get to the door before it was too late.

He turned left out of the doorway and immediately saw patched grey homespun about a foot from his face and approaching fast. Something thudded into his back and his nose flattened into the homespun. He gulped for breath, blood running from his nose and slid back on to the man behind him. Shaking his head to clear it, he launched himself under the arm of the man in front, wrenched free and ran for the door.

'Bar the door!' came a shout. 'Get him!'

Parton slipped on the smooth stone as he rounded the corner of the cloister, righted himself and had time to see four more Franciscans ahead of him, while the young friar with the stick blocked the exit. His first two attackers had been joined by two more, and they were right behind him. He might have accepted odds like those on open ground – but here, resistance was useless. That meant talking his way out of it.

'Leave me alone!' he squealed as two friars seized his arms and pulled them back harshly. 'What've I done wrong? Let me go!'

'What are you doing here in the seminary, my son?' The voice was calmly authoritative. Parton looked up to see the white-haired man who had been sleeping at his desk.

There was nothing sleepy about him now as he came forward. Banging and shouting came muffled from the door and Parton wished Seward away and out of this.

'I asked why you were here,' the white-haired man repeated. His eyes were grey and alert.

'I'm doing nothing wrong,' said Parton in a scared voice. 'Tell them to let me go.'

'Tell me first why you are here.'

'I didn't know it was wrong, Father,' whined Parton. 'I didn't even know what this place was, a church or a monastery or what. The door was open and I came in to look around, that's all.'

The Father Superior's eyes widened. 'To look round?'

'Yes. I'm new in the capital, I was visiting all the fine buildings and this door was open and I didn't know it was wrong to come in, I swear I didn't and I haven't stolen anything, Father, you can search me!'

The Superior looked sharply towards the doorkeeper. The friar shook his head. 'Impossible, Father!'

'Impossible?' protested Parton. 'The door was wide open and there was no one there! How else did I get in, then?'

'Well, Brother Diego?' The Superior looked at the doorkeeper again.

'That's to say . . . Perhaps there was a moment when I was chasing that mad beggar off down the street. Listen to him, Father!'

Parton willed Seward away as the Franciscans listened to the hammering on the door.

'Are you going to let me go now, Father?' he asked piteously to try to put an end to it. The tonsured head turned towards him. Parton hoped that fear and near-tears and the blood caking from his nose would be mask enough, but the eyes were not the eyes of a fool. There was a short hesitation, then the Superior's head shook slightly.

'No,' he said. 'You will take him to the Calle Alvarado,' he ordered. 'All of you will escort him. He must not escape on the way.' He moved away.

'What?' pleaded Parton. 'Please, can't you let me go?'

The Franciscan turned back. 'I have no choice in the matter,' he said quietly. 'You are in a place where you should not be.' The eyes rested on Parton a moment longer and Parton wasn't sure if he didn't see pity in them. Then the old man was gone.

The friars hustled Parton into the corridor. He marshalled his forces. Wherever the Calle Alvarado was, he didn't intend going there. Brother Diego and another friar were ahead of him in the passage, two men were holding his arms and the rest were following. Seward was beating a tattoo on the door. He would be in their way when they opened it . . .

The bolt slid back and the door opened. For a moment, Seward stood staring in astonishment while Parton made enormous eyes at him and no one moved. Then Parton ducked and pulled forward, shouting. Seward jumped at the friar in the doorway, kicking out. Diego lifted his stick. One of Parton's arms came free. He turned to wrench free the other. The friars behind pushed forward in confusion, the whole group tumbling forward and somewhere back there someone was holding on to Parton's arm for dear life and he couldn't get free.

He heard a sharp tap and Seward shouted in pain. Parton heaved his way over the threshold, pulling his captors with him and grabbed Diego round the waist with his free arm, hauling him round so he couldn't strike again. The strong young friar brought his elbow back into Parton's face, once, twice. Parton felt his nose bleeding again. Someone was on his back now and blows were raining on him. His arm was still caught back there and the weight of the man on his back was almost disjointing it. Then the tide rose and pitched him forward as the friars pushed out into the street, kicking as they passed, going on to deal with Seward whom Parton could no longer see. Seward must not be captured too. Parton turned his head as the friars forced him to his feet and saw Seward taking kicks and blows as he was hustled away down the street. Parton was trailed in the opposite direction, towards the statue of St Francis on the corner. It was a relief to know that Seward would go free, even if he had brought the younger man into momentary danger. Parton was lifted bodily now, held by arms and legs and carried off. He saw no more of Seward.

Breathless and cursing, the friars carried Parton across the main street – he saw trees above – through several sidestreets and across an avenue. Parton tried to keep track but the movement was rapid and he could see little but the tops of buildings and blue sky. They turned a corner and went down a street for several hundred yards and stopped. Parton was set on his feet again, surrounded, solidly held. He looked ahead.

Facing him, on a corner, was a grim, stone building. Its only windows were high, narrow slits, its only door, between massive stone columns on the corner itself, of black oak studded with great iron rivets. It looked like a prison or a madhouse – except, he noticed, that there was a stone cross above the door. In the street – the Calle Alvarado, he remembered – a crowd was gathering to watch. People were pointing, some were laughing. He caught the glance of an old woman who threw her eyes up to heaven and crossed herself.

Then the door opened and Parton was dragged brutally forward. Into the door, beneath the cross – and, last fleeting detail as his eyes were raised in the second he was pushed inside, a carved escutcheon with gilded lettering at the foot of the cross.

Something in Latin, the words abbreviated. The door closed heavily behind him and it came to him suddenly that he had no need to be a scholar to understand what he had read.

Offic. Sanct. Inquisit.

The Most Holy Office of the Inquisition.

CHAPTER FIVE

The room was bare. There was not a stick of furniture. Were such places always like that? wondered Parton. There were black patches of saltpetre on the walls and the same charcoal-like substance flowered in the cracks between the damp stone blocks of the floor. It was somehow penetratingly cold in spite of the afternoon heat outside, although it was true there was no window, just a barred opening above the door through which filtered weak light. Parton pulled his jacket to and shivered.

A key clattered and turned in the lock and a man stood profiled for a moment in the doorway. Parton could see little of him except that he was of medium height and that he wore black. As he shut the door, the light passed over his features for a second. The face was inconspicuous right down to the greying goatee beard. He came forward, walking with a slight stoop. Parton couldn't help feeling something, not weak, but inoffensive about the man. He looked more like a clerk or a shopkeeper than one of the terrible agents of the Inquisition Parton had been dreading.

He stopped several paces from Parton, facing him. 'You are not praying, my son?' There was mild surprise in his voice.

Parton stared at him without replying.

'Most men in your place kneel and beseech God's mercy!' This time there was an imperative sibilance in the voice that warned Parton not to presume. He knelt on the damp stones and bowed his head.

'My son, I can hear you,' said the priest.

What does he want? thought Parton. Should I talk, explain? Or should I be praying and crossing myself? How are you supposed to behave in front of the Holy Inquisition? He looked up at the priest.

'I didn't do anything wrong, Father!' he protested. 'Or if I did, I didn't mean to!'

'Tch!' The priest held up a calming hand. 'You misunderstand me, my son.' In the dim light, Parton could not be certain, but it seemed to him he saw benevolence in the priest's eyes. 'I am not here to interrogate you. I am here to confess you and bring you spiritual comfort before you are put to the question.'

Parton's knees began to hurt as the cold rose from the damp flagstones. He gaped, playing for time.

'Come, my son, we all have sins to confess. It will lighten your soul.'

You must take me for a fool, thought Parton. 'I have nothing to confess, Father,' he said, lowering his eyes.

'Nothing? Then why are you here?'

'I – I meant no harm! I didn't know it was wrong to go in that door, Father, I swear I didn't! I was visiting, looking round, that's all!'

The priest almost laughed. 'What do you mean, visiting?'

'The city, Father!' Parton widened his eyes as the priest searched in them. 'Such a great city, so many buildings, palaces, churches, the cathedral! In two days, Father, I have done nothing but walk round the city, admiring the fine buildings, but I have done no harm!'

'Why two days?'

Parton looked astonished. 'But . . . because I came to Mexico City two days ago!' he said as if it were a fact no one could be ignorant of. Where should he say he had come from? Remedios wouldn't do. This time it had to be a real place, a place he had seen and could describe, could answer questions about.

'Where are you from?'

'Esperanza, Father,' replied Parton, remembering the village thirty or forty miles from Orizaba on the road up.

'Which Esperanza? District of Orizaba?'

The question could be a trap thought Parton. Still, the Esperanza he was thinking of was probably within the limits of the district of Orizaba. He nodded.

'Why have you come to the capital?'

'To look for work.'

'Is there no work in Esperanza?'

'Not for the fifth son of a smallholder.'

The priest was silent. Parton watched him anxiously. Then the priest said sharply: 'You were seen entering a staircase in the seminary and it was some time before you came out again. Why?'

'For nothing, Father, I swear it!' The priest was cross-cutting his questions, benevolent one minute, harsh the next. Cameron had warned him that the Inquisitors were experts in interrogation. 'If they say I stole anything, they're lying! You can search me! I didn't go there to steal, I was just looking!'

'Then why did you fight the good friars? Why did you try to escape?'

Parton gulped back indignation. 'They hit me first!' He brought his hand up to his nose. 'They nearly broke it! Then they said they were going to take me somewhere and I didn't understand where and I was scared. That's why I tried to get away in the street. Father,' he pleaded, clutching at the hem of the black habit, twisting the rough cloth between his fingers. 'I've done nothing wrong, please . . !'

The priest bent and removed Parton's hands patiently. The long black cape opened, revealing a white habit beneath. 'What are the duties of a Christian to Holy Mother Church?' he asked.

Parton stared up the narrow line of white framed in black leading to the scrawny neck. That was the worst kind of question possible. If they were to get on to religion, he had had it. The priest looked down at him, his mouth a tight thin line.

'To go to mass,' adventured Parton, 'and to confess your

sins.' What the devil else, he wondered. 'To obey the priests,' he went on, searching his infidel memory, 'and do penance, and . . .'

The door clicked open and Parton, almost dropping with relief, heard soft footsteps coming into the room. The priest turned to the newcomer whom Parton could not yet see.

'Well, Brother Lazaro, does our young man know his catechism?' The voice was smoothly polite, almost caressing, but Parton could not repress a shiver. It was not his imagination, it was not the cold in the room. The ice was in the man's voice.

The first priest sighed. 'No more than a donkey, Excellency.'

Excellency? thought Parton, alarmed. Still hidden by the priest, the newcomer murmured, 'Will you be so good as to fetch me a chair, Brother Lazaro?' It was a question only in form. The priest left, shutting the door behind him.

The newcomer did not move from the shadows by the door. The light from over the door, such as it was, fell on Parton and he was sure that the man was watching him observing him. He could make out the dark outline of a tall figure and a pale blur above which was the face. A man accustomed to command, a man addressed as 'Excellency', in the Mexico City headquarters of the Inquisition. The man that Parton was trying to see clearly was, in all likelihood, the man Cameron had warned him about – Palafox, the Inquisitor-General of New Spain and head of the Spanish Secret Service in Central America. The cold from the floor was slowly invading every part of Parton's body.

Brother Lazaro came back with a chair and the newcomer had it set facing Parton. For a brief instant as he moved towards it, the light touched him and Parton saw a tall, well-built man in the black cowled cape and white habit of the Dominicans – although the cloth did not look like homespun and the large cross which hung at his chest was of rich silver and mother-of-pearl. A black skullcap crowned tonsured ash-grey hair. Beneath it, the high forehead and long, supple features denoted intelligence and force. The eyes were particularly striking, pale and expressionless like polished stones. They caught and held Parton's for a second, then flickered down as the man sat. Brother Lazaro was behind him, plunging him anew into shadow. How many times, wondered Parton, had the two of them played out the same little scene?

'Now.' There was a rustle of robes. Parton had been right in judging that this man was not dressed in homespun, but in silk. 'Perhaps, Lazaro, we should begin by asking our young friend his name?'

'Valdes,' said Parton quickly, changing names again. 'Luis Valdes.' Show deference, he thought, and added. 'Excellency.'

'Spell your name,' said Lazaro.

There was a dry chuckle from the newcomer before Parton could reply. 'Really, Brother Lazaro!' The tone was icily mocking. 'Our friend Luis doesn't know how to spell – do you, Luis?'

Parton shook his head. 'I have no education.'

'You see, Brother Lazaro?' There was a movement and Parton guessed that the man was turning back towards him, looking at him. 'However, I'm sure he has something in his pockets which can prove his assertion. A work permit, perhaps. Or just a simple letter?'

Parton frowned, feigning incomprehension. Thank God, he thought, that he was carrying nothing compromising. He had hidden most of his money back at his lodgings. 'No, Excellency,' he said, 'I have no papers.' Why should he have? People of the poorer classes didn't carry papers round with them, unless they were emigrants like the Andalusians.

The Inquisitor-General did not hesitate. 'You leave Esperanza to look for work in the capital and your family – please excuse me – is too stupid to ask for a letter of recommendation from the *alcalde mayor*?' The tone was brittle, peremptory.

Parton looked forward unblinkingly and forced himself not to show his alarm. This man had been listening to all that had gone before – from some secret hiding-place, no doubt – and now he was out to trap him. Why had he no letter from the mayor of his village? All Parton could do now was bluff. 'Don José is no friend of my family,' he said bitterly. 'If he were, no doubt there would be work in Esperanza for me and my brothers and I would not have had to come to Mexico City.' He leaned hopefully towards the shadowy figure in the chair. 'But perhaps you can help, Excellency . . . Don José is abusive and unfair! Everything in Esperanza is for his family and friends! Perhaps you can help my family to obtain justice! Valdes, Excellency, the name is Valdes!'

There was an icy silence. Parton decided he had gone far enough. But what else could he do now but push his bluff through and hope that the priests knew nothing of Esperanza and would not check? There was a rustle and the chair scraped. ·

'You say, Luis, that you enjoy visiting the buildings of the capital? Believe me, this building too is a fascinating place to visit. I would be delighted to show you some of our . . . facilities.' The voice was colder than ever and Parton could read neither release nor condemnation in it. 'Perhaps you will lead the way, Lazaro?' The man went back into the shadow of the wall.

'On your feet, Valdes!'

Lazaro could change his manner as others changed shirts, thought Parton as he stood up stiffly. His knees were painful. He followed Lazaro out of the door, the skull-capped Inquisitor coming next. The three of them walked down the corridor, closed doors on either side, in single file. Was it the moment to try something? Parton hesitated. The man behind him was clever. Parton considered it now certain that this man was the Palafox Cameron had warned him about. How many desperate prisoners had he seen, here in this dank stone fortress? He was probably armed. Even if he weren't, even if Parton succeeded in mastering the two priests, what were his chances of escaping from the headquarters of the New Spanish Inquisition? The walls were of stone, light came from skylights, the doors were heavy, locked and undoubtedly guarded . . . And perhaps, thought Parton suddenly, he's deliberately giving you this chance to admit your guilt by trying to escape. The thought was decisive. Parton followed docilely.

Lazaro took out a key and opened a door. Steps led down. Parton followed through the door. It slammed shut and a key turned twice. Light filtered down from above. The staircase was spiral in a square shaft of stone. The three men went down. Parton counted thirty steps. The light lessened. Forty, fifty. It was almost dark. They could only be beneath ground level, thought Parton, although the building was so strangely constructed that he was not sure from which floor they had begun the descent.

'Wait,' said Lazaro and unlocked a door. He beckoned and Parton followed him out into the daylight. He looked up. Above them was a high, vast stone ceiling pierced with gridded apertures through which came the light of day.

The quiet, cold voice of the Inquisitor-General came over Parton's shoulder. 'If a man were clever enough, my young friend Luis, to find a way of climbing up to one of those openings and strong and patient enough to free the iron bars, all this without being seen and recaptured, he would climb out – and believe me, no one who has passed through this place has not dreamed of doing this – only to find himself in a blank-walled courtyard from which there is no possible way out.' Parton heard the key turn in the lock behind him. 'So you will understand, Luis, that once you are in these chambers, you leave them only with my permission.'

Parton was cold, bruised and weary. There was an acrid taste at the back of his mouth. He brought up a hand and wiped blood from his face. The certainty settled into him. He was in the torture chambers of the Inquisition.

And strangely, there was nothing to be seen. The great chamber at the edge of which they stood was empty. The floor was wide and paved with flagstones, the stone walls were freshly whitewashed to half-height, the doors in the opposite wall painted the same colour. The air was cool and the place gave an impression of health and cleanliness. It was empty and swept clean, like a well-washed hospital.

It was on second glance that the details showed.

There was the floor. When Parton looked carefully, he saw that it sloped gently from either side to a central gutter which ran down to an iron drain. And there were holes in the floor, square holes, round holes, cut into the stone. The longer he looked at them, the more Parton saw patterns in their layout, rectangles, crosses, triangles – and when his eye followed through the lines they formed, it came to a solidly set ring or hook, embedded into the wall and hidden at first by the uniform whiteness. From the rigging and quickwork of a sailing vessel, Parton knew the mechanics of pulleys and blocks and tackles. As his eye scanned the tell-tale sockets and anchorpoints of the empty chamber, his mind set up the infernal mechanisms which would fit the pattern, calculating the terrible forces they would be able to unleash at a sign from the man beside him. From the corner of his eye he could see the black silk skullcap above the grey fringe and the long, pale face. The man was turning to him now, a sardonic lift at one corner of the precisely drawn mouth. The impression of power which emanated from him was not only intellectual. Palafox was well-made, younger than the grey hair suggested and undoubtedly strong. His blue eyes still betrayed no emotion.

'A pity for your visit, my young friend, that there is no work in hand for you to see. I should have liked to have been able to let you judge our efficiency by seeing a living example. But come.' He led the way to the middle of the chamber and pointed down to six square sockets in the floor. 'Here we place the uprights of one of our machines. Do you see? And there—' he pointed to the walls at either end, '—we run ropes to those rings from the uprights and we tauten them with blocks so that the machine is firmly fixed and cannot move. Then my little Luis, you are attached to the machine with your hands above your head . . . here and your feet down here. Our helpers have two winches to turn, one at each end. Can you imagine what happens?'

Parton gaped. He could full well imagine what would happen. He would be slowly racked until the joints gave way and only skin and muscle were holding him together. He flung himself at the Inquisitor-General's feet. 'Why are you showing me all this, Father?' he blubbered. 'I have done no wrong. *Please!*'

'Do not touch me!' The kick was rapid and precise and it pushed Parton back on to the floor. 'Come now, Luis, so frightened for so little? Let me show you something worth whimpering over. Cheng!'

From one of the side doors appeared a squat, ugly man in a blue tunic. His black hair was pulled back into a pigtail and his skin was yellowish brown like that of New Spanish Indians. He shuffled forward to Palafox's side and looked down expressionlessly at Parton.

'Cheng is the most gifted of my assistants, Luis. I had him brought here from China on the Manila Galleon and he cost me a deal of money. He is considered a great specialist in his country. Show him, Cheng.'

Still as expressionless, the Chinaman took a bundle of cloth from under his tunic and unrolled it. Parton saw the gleam of metal. Arranged on the cloth in a neat line, held by leather straps, were shining blades. Slowly and deliberately, the Chinaman took one out and showed it to Parton.

It was old. The haft was of intricately carved ivory, browned by age, and the blade – the blade looked perfect and razor-sharp, but it was no ordinary knife blade. The end was rounded, the cutting edge no more than an inch long. Cheng held up another, the ivory haft similar, the edge even shorter, hollow ground, wicked. Scalpels, thought Parton, surgeon's knives.

'Now imagine again, Luis.' Palafox was leaning forward and his mocking smile had totally disappeared. 'You are stretched on the rack, the pain is great, but still, foolishly, you are resisting the Most Holy Office, you are refusing to confess. Cheng begins his work. Do you know, Luis, how they execute criminals in China?' Parton's eyes rolled desperately and he shook his head. 'They peel them alive, Luis. Men like Cheng are experts. The layers of the skin, the muscles, the nerves, the blood vessels, little by little . . . It takes days to die – if I wish you to die. If not, Cheng will keep you alive for as long as I order him to.'

There was a silence. Parton began to blubber again.

'No, Luis!' The Inquisitor-General reached down and shook him by the shoulder. 'I want you to imagine it. It is long and most terribly painful. Imagine and look up. Look up!'

Parton looked up and saw daylight streaming through the grids above. A man would go mad, he thought. The agony of joints racked to breaking point, the slicing blades – and up there, constantly present, light, sky, freedom . . .

'Can you see the blue of God's heaven?' whispered the priest.

Parton dropped his gaze to Palafox's, wondering what kind of man he could be. The blue eyes were practically lifeless – you could see nothing in them, thought Parton, but perhaps a kind of cold menace. There was no light in them, not the slightest glimmer. They were the eyes of some underground animal, accustomed to living in the dark. What had Palafox to do with the blue of God's heaven?

'A nasty scar you have there, Luis.' A long finger traced the thin white scar under Parton's jaw. 'Did you do that with a ploughshare on the family smallholding?'

Does he know who I am, is he playing cat and mouse with me? wondered Parton. Or is he simply enjoying scaring the wits out of a country oaf? 'It happened in a fight, Excellency,' he quavered, knowing that the knife wound was too obvious to be denied, 'over a girl. But it was a long time ago. Please, I've done no harm, *please* . . .'

'Put him away,' said Palafox curtly, gesturing towards the doors in the side wall.

'Come on, Valdes,' ordered Lazaro, pushing Parton to his feet and towards a door. He opened it, pushed Parton inside and shut and locked the door, leaving him alone in the empty room beyond.

Alone. The relief, for all the control he had been exerting on his feelings, was tremendous and Parton only just checked himself in time. It was a trap, it could be nothing else. He was not alone, no one ever could be in that place. Everything in the Inquisition building was false-bottomed, false-sided, specially built. They were spying on him from somewhere, studying his reactions. What would Luis do? There was a table in the middle of the room with two chairs. Parton sat at the table and buried his head in his folded arms, pretending to sob. At least he could hide his face and think. It was hard to avoid fear, hard to concentrate, when he thought of what awaited him if Palafox decided to put him to the question. He had so much to hide, so much was at stake.

But that was beside the point. What mattered was why the Inquisitor-General had brought him down to the dungeons to give him this glimpse of hell. Did he – could he – really know who Parton was and why he was in New Spain? No, thought Parton. If the answer had been yes, he would have been on the rack at that very moment with the Chinaman unrolling his bundle of knives. Then was Palafox amusing himself with an innocent fool? It was possible. The man seemed to enjoy distilling fear. On the other hand, he was quite evidently highly intelligent and in deadly earnest. He was surely not frivolous enough to spend his time playing with an unimportant country boy. There had to be a more serious motive for what the Inquisitor-General was doing. He hasn't made up his mind, thought Parton. He still doesn't know who I am and what I was doing in that seminary. However, I *was* in the seminary and he wants to find out who I am.

The seminary was the focal point. Why was it empty, while a Franciscan friar sincerely thought it was in normal use? Why had the Superior said 'You are where you *should not be*'? Parton knew why, from his point of view, the seminary was so important. From now on, he had to assume that the Inquisitor-General had his reasons for considering that it was important too. Could their respective reasons be similar? It was not to be ruled out.

Parton checked his thoughts, surprised. There was a scent in the room, a quite distinctive scent. In fact, he realized, it had been there for some time – but not when he had been pushed into the room, of that he was sure. The room was empty, but the scent was there, slight but insistent, a woman's perfume, musk, nutmeg . . . a rich woman's perfume.

There was a woman and she was watching him. It was incomprehensible, but he was sure of it. What was a woman doing in Inquisition headquarters? Could she be one of the mistresses Cameron had said Palafox was notorious for keeping? Where could she be? He warned himself to be careful, not to show too much. He propped his head on his hands and, between bouts of apparent despair, inspected the walls of the small room, stone block by block.

The slit was high up on the wall to his right and it was about six inches long by an inch deep. He could have sworn, in the instant he looked into it, that he had seen a pair of eyes watching him and then withdrawing. Perhaps it was the lingering scent that persuaded him that he had heard a rustle of silk?

The door opened and Parton looked up. Brother Lazaro came into the room followed by Palafox. Lazaro, to Parton's surprise, sat at the table opposite Parton, while the Inquisitor-General stood slightly to the side, arms folded within the ample sleeves of the white habit, his pale eyes intent on the prisoner.

'Why did you enter the Seminary of St Francis?' began Lazaro formally.

'I told you, Father,' said Parton, wringing his hands. 'The door was open and I went in to look around. I didn't know I was doing wrong.' He had to push the bluff right through to the bitter end. His only hope was to persuade Palafox that he was indeed Luis Valdes from Esperanza.

'Are you a true son of Holy Mother Church?'

'Of course I am, Father!' Parton faked astonishment. Questions like that made him feel sick. If they ask me something simple, he thought, something to prove I'm a true Catholic like reciting the Lord's Prayer or the Creed in Latin, I'm finished.

'Have you anything to confess, my son?'

What would Luis Valdes do now? He would probably confess his sins down to the last and even invent a few for good measure. Parton stared down at the table trembling. 'I . . ,' he began.

'Quickly, boy!'

'Then yes Father yes I have!' Parton blurted out. 'The sin of the flesh, Father, with the neighbour's daughter and I committed it once – no, Father, forgive me, I must not lie, *three* times and yes, it was the complete sin, all of it and I didn't confess it, Father, it was on my mind but I didn't confess it!'

'Why not, my son?'

Parton was leaning across the table now, imploring,

acting for his life. 'I didn't want our priest to know, he's related to her on the mother's side and I was afraid to tell him, Father and please, please, please don't put me on the rack for it, please don't hurt me, Excellency, please!' He looked up.

Palafox was no longer looking at him. The eyes were distant, the features rigid and feverish patches burned in his cheeks. It's all up, thought Parton. I've pushed the bluff over the edge and it's all over.

'Despicable fool!' The Inquisitor-General's voice was thick, the silk and ice gone. He turned and walked rapidly to the door. His hand on the lock, he looked back briefly. 'Get rid of him, Lazaro,' he rasped. 'In the usual way.'

The bluff had worked, Parton repeated to himself. The bluff had worked. All the same, it was hard to believe that the late afternoon sun which was warming his back as he walked down the street was real, hard to believe that they had sent him packing with a penance and a strict warning never to go wandering round buildings like the seminary again. But it was true, he was free and he was walking down the Calle Alvarado.

Be careful now, he warned himself. It doesn't mean a thing. They may have released you to see where you go, what you do, whom you see. The bluff may not have worked at all or only partly. The first thing to do was to lose any possible shadowers. He looked around uncertainly, not quite sure where he was. He asked a passer-by for directions to the *Zocalo*, glancing behind him as the man explained the way. Either he was not being followed, he decided, or his shadowers were very, very good and he couldn't see them.

By the time he reached the plaza, empty now of its market stalls but thronged with a strolling crowd, the sun was reddening. He pushed through, crossed the square, walked up to the steps in front of the enormous edifice, climbed them and went in. Inside, he hurried through the faithful across six of the wide cathedral's naves, brilliant with candles and white lacquer and gilt-wreathed angels climbing to the dizzy vaults, and lost himself among scaffolding and masonry where work was under way on the seventh nave. He found a small side door and slipped out. He changed streets, changed streets again, doubled back, changed streets yet again, then chose a look-out point in a dark doorway, hid and waited.

An hour later, covered by night, almost sure he was not being shadowed, he took a long, roundabout way back to his lodgings in the *barrio* Santa Maria. He was troubled to see there was no sign of Seward but pulled off most of his clothes, lacked the will to finish, tumbled on to his bed and went immediately to sleep.

CHAPTER SIX

He had to preach a sermon in the cathedral and thousands of people were watching him. Obviously, when he wanted to speak he couldn't and everybody began to laugh. He raised his arm for silence. It had no skin on it. Cheng had done an expert job. All Parton could see was a pattern of veins branching over slippery muscles. He groaned and turned over in his sleep.

'What on earth's happened to you?'

He opened his eyes. Gabriela was at his bedside, carrying a candle and looking down at him in dismay. 'You're all bloody,' she said.

Parton looked down quickly at his arm. Ridiculous. Of course there was nothing wrong with it. They had let him go. It had been a nightmare. 'It's nothing,' he told Gabriela. 'Just an accident.'

Gabriela put the candle on the table, crossed the room and came back with a pitcher of water. She lifted Parton up, pulled his shirt over his head, laid him back again and washed his face with the cold water, patting it dry with the shirt. 'That's better,' she said with an almost motherly air which made Parton want to laugh. 'But you're covered in bruises. How did it happen?'

'Gabriela,' said Parton with a sly grin, 'I'm naked and you're fully dressed. How long is that going to last?'

Gabriela laughed, her black eyes on his, her hands behind her neck already unbuttoning the simple grey dress which was her every-day wear. Her clothes fell to the ground and she lay beside Parton. She touched his chest. 'Look at that bruise!' she said.

Parton's hand slid to the small of her back and he pulled

her to him. It had not been easy, on the road, to be alone with her. 'There's only one way to make me feel better,' he said, nuzzling her hair.

Gabriela pulled away. 'But tell me how it happened,' she insisted.

'I was robbed,' lied Parton. 'Waylaid by a gang of footpads in a dark corner. There was nothing I could do. Good thing I had little money on me. Now come here.'

Gabriela came.

What time it was when Seward got back, Parton did not know, but it was still dark. He disentangled himself from Gabriela's arms, rummaged for his breeches, pulled them on and went through the curtained-off doorway to Seward's room.

'Are you all right?' he whispered, finding a stub of candle and lighting it.

Seward nodded, trying a laugh. He had a swollen lip and a big bruise over an eye. Parton saw that he was trembling. He looked exhausted, as he sat heavily on the bed. 'I couldn't pick up your trace,' he said. 'By the time they'd finished with me and I managed to get back round to see where you were, you'd disappeared. I asked passers-by, but they took me for a beggar and avoided me. In the end, I thought they might bring you back to the same place, so I set myself to watch. At midnight there was still no sign of you, so I came back here.'

'You were careful not to be followed?'

'Yes. I'm sure I wasn't. I took a long way round and you know I know the town well. What did they do to you?'

Parton hesitated. Then he said: 'They took me to the Calle Alvarado.'

Seward looked up. 'Oh, no,' he said.

'Is it as well known as that?'

'Well known and feared. What did they do to you?'

'Put the fear of God into me then let me go. I was careful

not to be followed back too. I hope we've finished with them.'

'Mad friars and now the Inquisition.' Seward leaned back against the wall and closed his eyes. 'It's enough to make your flesh crawl.'

'Yes,' said Parton. If only you knew, he thought. It's not over yet. He looked at Seward. He had brought him into the game and put him in danger – against Cameron's orders not to reveal anything about the true nature of the assignment. But that was the way it was. The young gentleman couldn't be kept constantly out of danger, nor totally in ignorance of what they were there to do. Parton couldn't succeed alone without the slightest aid. Cameron must have been crazy to think that Seward could serve as guide on this mission without running risks. Anyway, Seward himself seemed to accept them without murmuring and that was a point in his favour.

'What now?' asked Seward, opening his eyes.

'Sleep,' said Parton, turning to the door. 'Tomorrow, we'll have to lie low. We can use the time to get some rest.' He slipped past the curtain and went back to Gabriela. Her eyes were on his. Rest was unlikely.

The third of July dawned and outlines of objects in the room paled. Parton had reckoned that the journey down to the coast, hiring the best horses and riding fast, would take four days. If he was right on that score, he had four days left in which to find the boy. Today could hardly count. Neither he nor Seward could go anywhere near the seminary. The best thing they could do would be to change lodgings in case they were tracked down to these. It would be better to give the Espinels the slip. And Gabriela? Perhaps Gabriela too. How could he take her with him? He looked down at her with a surge of regret.

She was looking up at him and he realized that she had been doing so for some time. He smiled at her. 'Awake?'

Gabriela did not reply immediately. She looked at him seriously, intently. 'Do you know,' she said at last, 'I think you're planning to do something dangerous. Something desperate. I could see it in your face while you were thinking.'

Parton laughed uncomfortably. 'And what else did you manage to read in my face?'

'Nothing. But while you were asleep five minutes ago and your friend Benidies slipped through to get some water from the pitcher, I saw his.' She paused, smiling up at him. 'You didn't tell me you'd *both* been assaulted and robbed by footpads.'

Parton did his best to look unconcerned. 'Didn't I tell you we were both together when it happened? It was in some dark little streets not far from the cathedral. There was a whole gang of them, too many for us. As I said, it was a good thing we weren't carrying much.' He stirred, making ready to get up. Gabriela, don't pry, he thought. It'll be the end between us. 'I could do with some water too,' he said, looking for the pitcher.

Gabriela lay still, watching him as he sat up on the edge of the bed. 'I can't see you being surprised and bettered by robbers,' she said, still smiling softly. 'And with Benidies there to help, it's downright unlikely. Anyway, I never did really believe your story.'

Parton turned on her sharply. 'What do you mean, story?'

'*Rodriguez y Cuevas*. I'm from Andalusia, remember and Seville and Cadiz are Andalusian ports. It's fairly common knowledge there that "Spanish traders" just give their name and signature to cover foreigners.' Her hand reached out to touch his arm. 'Don't be angry, but I don't think you were born in Cuba. I don't think you're even here to trade. I've somehow always felt that you were tense, ready for something much more dangerous and now I'm sure of it.'

'Perhaps you're partly right,' hedged Parton. 'I'm not

Cuban. *Rodriguez y Cuevas* is, as you say, a front for . . . foreign traders. It's difficult and dangerous playing this kind of part. Perhaps that's what makes me tense.' How was he to get out of this, he wondered desperately. If Gabriela had put two and two together, others among the Andalusians might have done so. Now it was sure that he and Seward would have to change lodgings and give them all the slip. And, damn it to hell, it meant sneaking away from Gabriela too. She was forcing him into it.

Gabriela sat up and leaned forward, her black hair, loose, tumbling over her shoulders. 'Who are you really?' she asked gently.

'I can't tell you.'

'Why not?'

Parton felt wretchedly torn between the imperatives of his mission and his desire to tell Gabriela everything, to keep her with him. She had already guessed so much. Did it matter if he told her the rest? If you're going to leave her, he told himself, it most certainly matters. Secrecy is vital. 'I'm sorry, I can't explain,' he said.

'You see? You *are* up to something more dangerous than trade and licences and cotton goods!' Gabriela laughed. 'Otherwise you'd tell me!'

Parton was silent. This was getting worse and worse. Whatever he did, whether he told her the truth or left her, Gabriela was, from now on, a potential danger to him and as such, perhaps she would be better with him, on his side, than abandoned, resentful . . . and seeking revenge. Or was that simply wishful thinking?

'Listen.' She shifted forward and sat beside him, her dark eyes on his. 'I don't mean to worry you with my questions. You don't have to reply. But I know you're someone strong, I know you're going somewhere, I know you're *moving* and that, I need. I'm sure you'll not be staying long in New Spain, you'll be leaving and I know you're capable of it. I told you I wanted to leave New Spain and go back to find my father, to find – oh, I don't know – my true life, perhaps! With you, I'm sure I can do it.'

Parton took her hand from his arm and stood up. He went to the table, poured water from the pitcher into a cup and drank. How could he possibly take her with him? He thought of the dungeon at the Calle Alvarado. Gabriela couldn't risk that, it was unthinkable. And what would be her attitude if she discovered that he was working against the interests of her country? The chances were that she might not be troubled, but then again, she might.

'You're thinking I'll be a hindrance to you. I won't. I'm determined to get away from here and whatever I have to do, I'll do, whatever you ask me to. I can help you. Let me try.'

Help? Against the Inquisition? If only she knew, thought Parton. But . . . she was quick, capable, disarming, determined. Use her, he could surely use her, especially today. He had so little time and so much still to find out. There was an errand she could run . . . Then what? Cheat her and leave her? Couldn't he decide later, after the errand? He turned to her. 'If I ask you to help me, will you promise me one thing?'

'What?'

'Whatever you do, you must keep away from priests.'

Gabriela burst out laughing. 'Priests? That won't be hard! Half of them think I'm bound for hellfire and the other half would like to help me on my way! I never go near them!'

Parton grinned. 'All right. Then listen . . .'

When Gabriela came back late that morning, Seward was still sleeping and Parton had prepared their packs for the move. Apart from clothes and blankets, each pack contained a pistol and a stock of powder and shot, a couple of candles and an extra tinderbox, knives, a coil of light rope and a ball of twine, a water canteen and a packet of dried meat – provisions which had been bought in Veracruz and which had not yet come into use. Parton looked up as he finished buckling the second pack. 'Already?' he asked, surprised.

Gabriela was radiant. 'I told you I could help you! And it wasn't really difficult!'

'No trouble with friars or priests?'

Gabriela shook her head. 'I didn't see any. I went to see the local tradespeople, that's all. If you want to know what's going on in a place, go to see the tradespeople, they always know. I found a butcher who knew, then a draper's wife – which means I'm sure the butcher wasn't talking nonsense. I told them I had a little brother at the seminary, but that it was all closed up and the Franciscans wouldn't answer the door.' A shadow crossed her face.

'Is anything wrong?'

'Well, I did have a little brother. He died last year.'

'I'm sorry.' Parton's hand found hers. 'Is that what made you choose the story?'

'Perhaps. Anyway, the boys from the seminary left a month or so ago and they haven't been replaced by new boys yet. They were taken to a town called Tepoztlán, not far south of here. It's a small town with a monastery, it seems.'

Parton was overjoyed. 'Good girl!' he whispered, taking her in his arms and kissing her.

'It was so easy! What—' Gabriela turned to follow Parton's gaze and her hands clutched involuntarily at his shirt-sleeves. Framed in the doorway, hands on hips, her black eyes flashing and her mouth tight with anger, stood her mother.

'All night and all morning and you haven't had enough, you little whore!' Pilar's voice cracked. She raised a theatrical hand and pointed outwards. '*Home!*'

Gabriela turned completely to face her. 'You're not going to call me a whore,' she said quietly. 'Not unless you admit to being no better yourself.'

Pilar stepped forward, speechless, and slapped Gabriela

rapidly twice in the face. Her daughter stood her ground, her eyes level. In a glance, Parton took in Gabriela's proud bearing, her way of holding herself like something precious, something that was not to be spilled, trampled on, contaminated, and he was suddenly sure that, whatever blows she might receive, Gabriela was mistress of her destiny, would win through in spite of what a shameless mother and a lying father could do. And he knew that his last hesitations were over and that he wanted to help her win through.

'Get out of here,' he told Pilar, stepping past her daughter and turning the woman round, bundling her towards the door as she stared at him poisonously, struggling.

'No!' Seward had come through the curtained doorway. 'Leave it to me,' he said as Parton turned. He took Pilar by the arm and led her out of the house.

Gabriela buried her face in Parton's shoulder and he held her close in silence. When she looked up, her eyes were wet with tears. 'Now I'm bringing trouble on you,' she said falteringly. 'She'll be back with half the neighbourhood before the day's out.'

'She won't,' contradicted Seward as he came back through the door. 'I've managed to calm her down.' He glanced towards Gabriela. 'If you go back now, the incident will be forgotten.'

Gabriela's mouth dropped open as she turned questioningly to Parton.

Parton looked at Seward and shook his head. 'We're leaving here now,' he said evenly, 'and Gabriela's coming with us. We'll cross to the poorer quarters on the south side of the town and find somewhere to lie low until it's dark. Then we'll take the road.' The frown on Seward's face was of surprise rather than annoyance, he decided. 'We'll need your guidance. Do you know a town called Tepoztlán?'

'Maria-Dolores, my dear girl,' said Palafox, raising his mistress's head, 'at any other time I would be delighted to succumb to your well-intentioned advances.' He pushed her gently but firmly away. 'Not now. I have far too much on my mind.'

Maria-Dolores, kneeling in front of the Inquisitor-General, sat back on her heels and looked at him through heavy-lidded, golden eyes. She was dressed like a princess. Her gown was of dapple-grey Chinese silk with a jabot of Flemish lace stabbed by a blood-red ruby. Her dark, luxuriant hair was powdered and piled high, held by pins of intricately chased silver set with pearls. Her face, powdered and rouged, was proud and finely built, the nose straight and delicate, the jawline a perfect oval – but the makeup gave it a mask-like appearance, the eyelids and lashes were too heavily darkened under the thin black lines of the brows and there was falseness in the heart-shaped taffeta beauty spot close by the pouting lower lip. Only the eyes told another story, soft brownish golden, strangely absent, the pupils wide. It was – perhaps – the mask of a rich and haughty woman on the face of a dreamy and sensual girl.

'Leave me,' ordered Palafox curtly. 'Tell Lazaro I'm waiting for his report.'

Maria-Dolores stood up obediently, crossed the richly carpeted room and went through the door without a word. A scent of musk and nutmeg lingered behind her. Palafox remained seated, staring thoughtfully into the fire – the depths of the Inquisition building were by no means warm, even in July – until the door clicked open and shut again and the bearded Lazaro announced himself by a discreet cough.

Palafox looked up. 'Well?' The enquiry was sharp.

'No use, Excellency. We've been totally unable to pick up his trace past the cathedral. He's thrown us off.'

With a gesture of annoyance Palafox stood up, a full head taller than his greying assistant. 'Who was shadowing him yesterday when we released him?'

'Porfirio, Excellency. I can't believe it was negligence on his part.'

'No. Porfirio is one of the best.' The Inquisitor-General's

pale brow creased as he stared back into the fire, his mouth a resolute line. 'This man's important, Lazaro,' he said without turning. 'We can be sure he's got something to hide, since he threw off Porfirio, and he did that so successfully that we can be sure he's no beginner. We already know he's a first-rate play-actor. He practically convinced me yesterday, he made me doubt.' He left the fire and looked at Lazaro, his lifeless eyes hard as stone. 'I should have racked the truth from him while I had him here. Now it will cost time and effort to get him back.'

'The seminary may be important,' proffered Lazaro with a self-deprecating cough.

Palafox shook his head. 'He's too intelligent to be seen there again. He'll keep well away.'

'I meant, Excellency, that we received a denunciation this morning which mentions it. Not so much a denunciation, a message. I thought I might permit myself to bring it to your attention.'

'Well, man, what is it?' Lazaro had sounded too pleased with himself beneath the practised humility of his manner for Palafox to show patience.

'A woman by the name of Espinel gave it in at the door. She said that she had been sent to inform that the young man from *Rodriguez y Cuevas* was the associate of the man from the *Seminario San Françisco*.'

'*Rodriguez y Cuevas*?' Palafox gripped Lazaro's sleeve. 'You're sure? Did she say more?'

'She left hurriedly saying she was in danger. They didn't take the incident seriously at the door, but when I received the morning report the reference to the seminary intrigued me, and I thought . . .'

'You were right, you were right,' interrupted Palafox, turning away. For a long moment, he seemed to be absorbed in studying the flickering of the fire. Then he said abruptly: 'What do you think our young friend Luis will do now, Lazaro?'

'I think . . .' Lazaro hesitated – better turn your tongue seven times in your mouth than speak foolishly to the implacable Inquisitor-General – then launched out uncomfortably. 'Since he was searching the seminary, I think he's after the boys.'

'So?'

'So he should end up in Tepoztlán.'

'Good reasoning!' Palafox's congratulatory smile looked more like a sneer. 'Luis wants to find the boys. Whichever thread he picks up, it will lead him to the centre of the web. The web was spun with that in mind, Lazaro, the whole plan was conceived to that end!' He crossed briskly to a desk and began sorting papers. 'Order the carriage and prepare the usual escort. Salvador will take charge here while we're away. We'll ride to Tepoztlán this evening after the heat of the day. On your way. Oh and Lazaro—'

'Excellency?' The stooping priest turned back in the open doorway.

'Aren't you curious about the message you were so right to bring to my attention?' The smile and the tone were dangerously silky.

'Naturally, Excellency, but. . . .'

Palafox stepped forward with the same smile. 'Close the door,' he said softly. The Inquisitor-General was actually pleased, thought Lazaro with surprise as he obeyed. 'Listen, Lazaro, it's like peeling a fruit. The first layer is a trading house in Cadiz called *Rodriguez y Cuevas*. No difficulty for us to peel away this layer and find a foreign trader – in this case, yet another family of Protestant merchants from London.' Palafox could not restrain a brief laugh. 'Peel away *that* layer, Lazaro and what do we find?' His voice dropped to a whisper. 'Jacobites, Lazaro, Jacobites. Good Catholics in hiding, fervent but secret supporters of James Stuart and above all, friends of Spain because Spain has always been the staunchest ally of the Stuarts. I made the acquaintance of the young man from

Rodriguez y Cuevas some two years ago when he was here to trade. His father and uncle had been, in their time, of some small use to me. Now it will be his turn. Because, Lazaro—' Palafox's smile became deadly. 'Not only is our friend Luis going to walk into a trap in Tepoztlán, but known to us while unbeknown to him, his faithful companion is a traitor . . .'

The sun's rays slanted from the west over the tops of the trees by the roadside where Parton, Gabriela and Seward stood. Below them the stony road looped down lazily to a roughly triangular cluster of clay-red roofs and greyish stone walls, more of a big village than a small town, lying shimmering in the heat among haphazard rocky hills and sparse, dusty vegetation.

'Tepoztlán,' announced Seward simply.

It was nothing remarkable, thought Parton. Just one burst of green and colour, of fields and gardens, hard by the little town in a hollow where there must be water. The rest was dust, stones, leathery-looking trees, apparent uselessness. There was no bridge, no ford, no reason for the town to be there. It was not on the main road to Cuernavaca, which they had left some miles back after having walked down from Mexico City all day and part of the night before. No, thought Parton, there was no apparent reason why Tepoztlán should be there at all.

Except the monastery.

The monastery was about a quarter of a mile out of town on the far side. To say that it was big, impressive, was to fall well short of reality. The entire population of the town could find refuge in the massive, block-like building, he thought. In fact, it would make a perfect refuge. Solid, plain stone walls rose to well over thirty feet, reinforced, no doubt against earthquakes, by enormous buttresses and cornered by great square towers. There were apparently no windows. The outer precinct and gardens were enclosed by another thick stone wall, of a height Parton found it difficult to judge from afar – six, eight, ten feet? There was only one gateway leading in through this precinct wall and as far as Parton could see from this angle, only one large door leading into the building itself. High above this arching doorway, two domed belltowers surmounted by gilded crosses were the monastery's only outer concession to religion.

'All that's missing is a moat and drawbridge,' he muttered.

'I might have guessed,' said Seward drily. 'You have to get in there.'

'It's surely possible,' said Gabriela. 'Where there's a will, there's a way.'

Parton looked down at her with a laugh. Her enthusiasm was contagious. He was committed to her now, he thought, committed to getting her out of New Spain. And she was, in turn, committed to him and to his mission, eager – too eager, Gabriela, he thought – to help. She knew his name. She knew that he was looking for a small boy in a seminary. In fact, in many ways, she knew more than Seward.

'Well, don't ask me to go up and knock on the door like a mad beggar,' said Seward. 'I bruise too easily.'

Parton looked across at him. Seward didn't often joke. Behind the younger man, the eastern horizon was closed off by the sawtooth line of the high volcanoes, the snow of their summits gleaming in the afternoon sun. Parton gestured towards them. 'What are they called?' he asked.

Seward turned and pointed. 'The biggest one there is Popocatepetl, and the second biggest, that one, Ixtaccihuatl. The other one up to the north over Mexico City is Tlaloc.'

Parton's gaze ran from one peak to the other, then swept down to the wide plain below. 'Indian ruins,' he said, pointing to a pyramid-like structure rising from the trees several miles on the far side of Tepoztlán.

'That'll be the old Indian town of Tepoztlán,' said Seward, 'all boarded up now and forbidden so that the Indians won't go back to their false gods.' He laughed briefly. 'At least, that's the Spaniards' story. They looted them first, of course.' He pointed upwards. 'Imagine old Cortes coming through the pass up there and seeing all those rich cities spread across the valley. It must have been quite a sight.'

Parton looked up. 'Which pass?'

'That one, between Popocatepetl and Ixtaccihuatl,' replied Seward, indicating a deep indentation between the two peaks. 'The old Indian road went through there.'

Parton looked at the pass, then back down at the ruins and fixed the site in his mind. For tonight, they were too far away, but they might come in useful as a hiding place later. Closer to, on a hillside well out of Tepoztlán, was a group of low buildings, some of them roofless, others intact. 'We could try those barns for a place to spend the night,' he suggested.

Seward nodded. 'Then let's be going. It'll soon be night-fall.'

The stars were paling one by one before the new light creeping from the east over the volcanoes as Parton and Seward came out of the broken-down door of the ruined barn where they had spent the night, and where Gabriela, with strict instructions to remain in hiding with their precious packs, was to wait for their return. Dawn on the fifth of July and two days in which to find the boy before running for it down the Veracruz road, thought Parton. Before the morning was out, they had to have reconnoitred the monastery and found out for sure that the boys, *the* boy among them, were there. Parton let the fresh dawn air give him hope. The monastery looked like a fortress, but it wasn't one. It was a school. It could be got into. Gabriela was right. Where there was a will, there was a way.

They slipped down the hillside, a wary eye open for early-morning farmers or herdsmen, towards a stony gulch which led down to Tepoztlán. A mile from the town, they left the gulch and skirted round through maize fields and trees until they were overlooking the monastery from a slight rise on the side they had been unable to see the evening before. Parton settled into the shelter of the trees and looked down at the massive pile. It looked grim in the early light. This side too was bleak, windowless stone. Perhaps, he thought, the place really had been built as a fortress back at the beginning of the Spanish colony almost two centuries before, when the Spanish still feared Indian attacks. His eye caught on a detail and he frowned. He moved round among the trees until he had a clearer view of the back of the monastery. Yes, there was a door, a small door, in the back wall. Above it and to its right, in the middle of the wall, was a big double door, no doubt a granary door. It was the first encouraging sign he had seen. He turned his attention to the precinct wall. The day before, it had looked the same height all round, but now Parton saw that it was not. If some parts were in good condition and at least ten feet high, others were less so, the mortar ageing and crumbling between the rough, unhewn stones and gaps forming where the wall was little more than a man's height and could easily be scaled.

Seward stepped back, watching Parton as he studied the scene, and wondering how much longer this nerve-racking game was to go on. It's because *you* know that you're trying to learn the secret of his mission and bring about its failure that you can't avoid the feeling that he knows it too, he told himself for the hundredth time. Parton doesn't know. He'd have killed you if he did. But why was he so cagey, so obviously uneasy in Seward's company, irritable at times, at others putting on a show of good humour and unconvincing friendliness? Didn't he have his suspicions?

Cordoba had probably been a mistake, thought Seward. He had set the Inquisition to shadowing Parton to find out what he was up to, but they had been inefficient, had failed and since then Parton had been wary, so very wary. Seward had scarcely had a moment of freedom in which to attempt anything. There had been the afternoon in which Parton had been prisoner – but Seward had been sincerely in ignorance of where Parton had been taken and he had found it impossible, in his bruised and filthy beggar's disguise, to persuade the Franciscans to take him seriously. They had chased him away again and in the end he had given up. Pilar, the next morning, had been a godsend. She had surely delivered the brief message which he had hurriedly given her while calming her anger against Gabriela. Pilar had sworn she would do as he had asked. He had been right to seduce the woman, she had finally proved useful.

But did that mean that his message had been understood, that it had got through to the right channels? Was Palafox, the man he had met two years before, still Inquisitor-General? Would the message – which he would be sure to understand even if no one else did – be brought to his attention?

Seward could be sure of nothing except that the waiting game he had been playing since Cordoba had to go on. He had no alternative but to cooperate with Parton, allaying suspicion by his readiness to help, hoping little by little to discover the true nature of Parton's mission, while waiting for the opportunity to denounce the man and put an end to his activities.

And to his life? Seward was not a hardened fighter and the question troubled him. Not for the first time, he brushed it aside. Parton was an officer in the secret service of the Protestant usurper from Hanover, George the First and Seward prayed the last, while the true King, the Stuart, waited in exile for the moment – which would surely come soon – to return to his rightful place on the throne of England and Scotland. Providence had placed in Seward's way a chance to strike a blow, however modest – and until he knew the secret of the assignment Seward could not judge how modest – for the cause. He tried to recall his feelings when Cameron had contacted him and he had realized that he was being asked, for his country's sake, to help in some kind of treacherous attack on Spain, the ardent defender of the true faith and the oldest friend of the Stuarts. For his country's sake, thought Seward angrily, he had better assist the Spanish than fight against them. It was in his country's interests that Spain be strong, that James Stuart be restored and that the Catholic religion be re-established. Seward thought of his family in London, of the years of hiding and false-seeming and fear, of his father and mother's lifetime of paying lip service to Anglican heresies and to false monarchs, bowing the head before the in-iquitous laws which discriminated against those of their religion. They had suffered too much, they had been too passive. It was up to younger men now, men like himself, to stand and fight for justice. No, he thought, there will be no pity. I shall do what I have to do and whether Parton deserves torture and death or not doesn't come into the reckoning.

He jumped as Parton touched his arm, pulling him back into cover. 'The back door,' whispered Parton.

The monastery door opened and the two men watched as a line of cowled figures filed out. They were carrying what seemed to be garden tools. The door closed behind them and they spread out in the grounds and set to work. The *chack-chack* of the hoes in the stony soil carried on the clear morning air, but there was no other sound.

Parton studied the scene. The gardens were laid out in vegetable plots interspersed by fruit trees and patches of dusty shrubbery, except at the back end, which looked fairly over-run. Some of the gardeners had gone off to the far side and could no longer be seen. On Parton and Seward's side, there were six men working in pairs. Two were down towards the front of the building and partly hidden by fruit trees. That left four within striking dis-tance, working two by two in different plots.

Parton watched as the friars worked on in silence. They gave no sign of splitting up as he wanted them to – on the contrary, each couple stayed closely together. He cursed under his breath. It occurred to him that the work in pairs prevented laziness because the men could watch each other carefully and no one could sneak off into a corner and rest. Perhaps this hard work carried out in silence was some kind of penance. Whatever it was, it was both a hindrance and an opportunity. A hindrance because he could not hope to approach the monastery with friars working all around it; and an opportunity because he might be able to replace one of them and get inside the building. The sun was well up now and the morning was moving on. He looked towards Seward. He was going to have to bring his guide into action once again and to hell with Cameron. There was no time to wait; no time to hatch another plan. What had to be done, had to be done that morning. He beckoned to Seward and whispered rapidly as the other bent forward.

'Am I going to get beaten up again?' asked Seward, dead-pan.

Parton grinned. 'This time, we hit them.'

'That'll be a pleasant change.' Seward grinned back before looking away.

Using the cover of the bushes and trees on the dry slope, they made their way down to the precinct wall and towards a gap Parton had pointed out in advance. Standing on a fallen block, Parton looked through the gap into the grounds. The two nearest friars were only fifteen yards away, their backs turned. The others were out of sight. Parton bent back down to Seward, whispered a few last instructions, helped him up into the gap and saw him over and down into the shrubbery below before he hauled himself up and dropped over quietly in his turn. The biting of the hoes into the soil covered the sound of their movements and there was no shout of alarm. Parton gestured forward. The two men snaked through the bushes until only a small plot of vegetables separated them from their two targets. They lay flat and peered out through the

101

fringe of the long grass and leaves which hid them from the friars' view.

The nearest of them had reached the end of a row and was leaning on his hoe, cowled head down, trying to look inconspicuous. Parton watched carefully. If some superior were surveying the scene from somewhere, he would surely react and call the idler to account. Apparently there was none. The second friar, reaching the end of his own row, tapped his fellow roughly on the arm and pushed him towards the next plot. The two of them crossed a narrow walk, turned round, and began hoeing, moving backwards, between the rows of plants towards Parton and Seward. Parton kept his hand on Seward's arm. The men had to be almost on top of them – but they must not have time to turn and see their assailants.

The first was at the end and about to turn. Parton gestured upwards with his head, leaped forward and tackled the further of the two, gagging him with his circling arm and pulling him back quickly into the bushes. He turned the man face down and pushed him to the ground in the same movement, hitting him behind the head with a short, stabbing blow. The man went limp and Parton looked immediately across at Seward. The second friar was lying on his back, blood dripping from a cut above his temple. Seward shrugged and showed a fist-sized stone in his hand.

Parton listened to the man's breathing. He would live. He began to strip his friar, indicating to Seward to do the same. The men were naked under their habits. Parton tied his man up using his waistcord and gagged him with a rolled-up ball of grass. The man's face was black-bearded and harsh. There was nothing soft or turn-the-other-cheek about these men, Parton reminded himself, checking the two friars' bonds. Then he and Seward hurriedly pulled the homespun habits over their heads and down over their clothes, stood up, picked up the hoes where they had fallen and began to work.

Parton breathed out. The alarm had not been raised. He glanced toward Seward and gave a reassuring grin, then raised his cowl to hide his face, watching Seward do the same.

They worked on. The soil was stony and dry between the rows of chickpeas. It was hot. The sun was high now and they were thickly, doubly dressed. It would soon be midday, thought Parton with a glance upwards. How long was the chore due to last? He started on yet another row, Seward beside him.

A handbell clanged somewhere and Parton looked up, his face hidden deep in the cowl. Ideally, he would have liked to have got into the monastery while leaving Seward on the outside, but it was already obvious that there was no way of doing this. Two friars were walking towards them, two more coming into view and it was not the time for confused, uncertain acting. The others were shouldering their hoes and making towards the back of the monastery. Parton grimaced regret to Seward and led the way forward.

The Englishmen fell into line between the two pairs of friars in the shadow of the great side wall of the monastery and shuffled on in silence. No one else was speaking, which was a relief. Parton looked down at his feet. His boots were practically completely covered by the grey habit. The lack of a waistcord was another problem. He shuffled in closer behind the man ahead, seeking cover from prying eyes, gesturing Seward forward in the same way behind him. They rounded the corner and Parton shrunk inside the cowl. The back door was open and already friars from the other side of the grounds were filing in. A man in black was watching them, counting heads. Parton squeezed as close as he dared to the man in front and kept his eyes down as he went past the supervisor, hoping Seward was doing likewise.

Then he was past the man and at the door and going through. The door looked heavy, with iron bands, double bolts and a solid lock. Inside, doors led off to the left, but they were closed. Perhaps there would be larders and storerooms, thought Parton. On the right, a flight of wooden steps rose to a trapdoor. The granary, he thought, glancing up as he went past. The trapdoor didn't seem to be bolted on this side and Parton could see no point in its being bolted on the other. Ahead, the friars filed on in silence in the cool, dark corridor. Parton began looking for a way to leave the line unnoticed along with Seward. These men were on their way, in all likelihood, to share a meal, or perhaps to prayers, or to some other activity in which Parton and Seward's imposture would be quickly noticed. The line crossed a small, cobbled courtyard, each man leaving his hoe or spade leaning against the wall as he passed, then went in through a narrow door. At the door, Parton glanced back. Seward was right behind him, head down, his cowl well over his features. The man in black was following the line, watching.

Parton cursed as he went in through the door and cursed again immediately as he saw another gaunt-faced man in black pointing the column round to the right and into a wide corridor. There was a growing smell of cooking. Parton looked round desperately, the realization dawning that it might well prove impossible to slip out of the line without being seen. On either side of the corridor, the doors were closed.

Behind Parton, Seward shuffled forward, his face still well covered in order to hide, if Parton looked back again, his growing jubilation at the idea that the men in black were Inquisition. He had to be sure, however, before making the slightest move which might give him away to Parton. The game was not yet fully played out and he had to keep his privileged place close to the British agent. But if a trap were being sprung, he thought with relief, Parton would soon be caught in it and he himself would be free of the anxiety which had been his constant companion over the last weeks.

And Gabriela? The thought was sudden and unwanted. Gabriela was a beautiful but stupid girl. She was Parton's.

Did that mean he should betray her too? Damn the girl, he thought. The force of his resentment surprised him. Why should the little slut matter to him?

She didn't, he told himself firmly. All the same, there was no reason to betray her to the Inquisition. Parton was an officer – an enemy officer, he reminded himself with a kind of thrill – and he could take what was coming to him. Gabriela was a girl and, Seward decided – the decision appeased him – he would mention neither her name nor her presence when the time came to tell what he knew. Parton would go to the block alone.

In front of him, Parton was fuming. The friars at the head of the line were beginning to turn into an open doorway and he could see yet another man in black beyond it, sealing off the corridor. Not a word had been spoken, but the column was under strict watch. He himself was at the door now, going in. In the large room beyond, lit on one side by high windows, the friars were taking bread, plates and steaming dishes from a long kitchen table in scrubbed white wood and shuffling on with them towards another doorway. Parton was now sure that these men were carrying out some kind of punishment, working for the community all day in silence, gardening and serving at table and perhaps doing other chores. There was food for a large number. Parton's hopes began to rise. It was his turn to take something from the table. He picked up two blue-and-white pitchers of water and walked on. Then he was through the door and into the refectory beyond and his heart leaped.

The boys.

There was row upon row of them, dressed in austere slate grey, sitting on benches at long tables, their heads bowed in silence. Parton ran a quick circular glance round the refectory. Two men in black were watching from a wide doorway at the side, the doors closed behind them. There were no other watchers or monitors. Friars were setting down plates and dishes. Parton walked forward, copying the movements of the men in front of him. There were about forty boys in all, he reckoned. They seemed to be grouped in rising order of age, the older boys at the back. The youngest boys at the first table might be six or seven, he thought, while the eldest were perhaps twelve or so. His eight-year-old would be among the middling ones, at the second or third table. The boys' heads were down and they were eating with intense application. Conversation was obviously forbidden during the meal and there was little or no movement. Almost all of them were dark-haired. That wasn't going to help. He stopped at the second table with his blue-and-white pitchers. Only the medallion could come to his aid. Could he show it to the boys as he poured water, without being noticed? If he had it round his wrist, for example . . .

He only needed one hand to undo the clasp. He passed a pitcher from his right hand to his left. The pottery was heavy and thickly made and he had a job holding the two pitchers with one hand. He gripped harder and raised his right hand to his neck.

The second pitcher slipped from his grasp and crashed to the floor.

The silence was suddenly total. The boys were staring, the friars were turning, all eyes were on Parton. He shrunk into his cowl and bent to pick up the shards, hoping the table in front of him would hide his face sufficiently.

'How very clumsy of you, my son,' came a voice from behind him.

Silk and ice. Parton froze. It was the silk and ice of a voice he knew. For a long moment, he stared at the blue-and-white shards on the floor, then he turned, slowly, unwillingly.

The side door to the refectory was open. Surrounded by Dominicans in black and white stood the Inquisitor-General, the corner of his mouth lifting in a brief, sardonic smile as his expressionless eyes met Parton's. At a gesture of his hand half a dozen men stepped forward.

Parton leaped to his feet, flinging his remaining pitcher at the faces of the advancing friars and ran for the kitchen door, grabbing a gaping Seward by the arm as he went.

Of course, it was too late. Every exit was guarded. There were friars and priests ready and waiting in the doorway, more behind them in the kichen. Parton charged at them with the energy of despair. It was as if he had charged into a wall. There was nothing other-worldly about these priests. They were made of very solid flesh and bone and the flesh was more muscle than fat. These are Palafox's henchmen, and he doesn't choose choirboys, thought Parton as a hard head banged down into his and a fist caught him in the ribs. An arm seized him by the neck and pulled him forward. He raised a knee sharply and the arm let go. He struck out towards a face and felt something give under his fist. Then they were on him from all sides and he went down under the weight of numbers, catching a glimpse of Seward, white-faced, arms pinned, then seeing the stone flags coming up towards him much too fast. His head hit stone with a hollow sound and a red shower flashed behind his eyes and all the fight went out of him.

He hardly registered the vaulted roof and the twists and turns as they carried him quickly away to another part of the monastery. A door clanged shut. He was laid out on a table and strapped down to it. He was searched. The priests took away the contents of his pockets. Then the medallion.

His mind was still so spongy that he tried to grab it back from the man who had taken it from round his neck, but he couldn't move. That was just as well, he reminded himself. They didn't know, they mustn't know, the medallion's importance, or they would track down the boy, his father, the British agents involved. God, his head ached. He blinked at the tough-looking faces above him. I fell into a trap like an idiot, he thought mechanically. His head really hurt and he closed his eyes.

He must have passed out and gone into a dream he thought, because he had the definite impression he could smell the scent, the rich woman's perfume from the Calle Alvarado, musk and nutmeg. But that was not entirely impossible, he told himself, coming to and looking up.

She was staring down at him through heavy-lidded, golden eyes. She was dressed in silk and lace. Parton wondered if what he was seeing was real. What was a sumptuous young woman like that doing here in this castle-keep monastery and before that in the Calle Alvarado? Could she be Palafox's mistress, or one of them? Could even as powerful a prelate as the Inquisitor-General show himself so openly with a woman like that?

'Maria-Dolores seems to interest you to a high degree, my little Luis . . . and I do believe you interest her too.' The door closed behind Palafox. 'She is a very striking young woman, is she not?' The priest's hand came into Parton's field of vision and the tip of his long, slender forefinger brushed the girl's lips slowly. 'She is my mistress, Luis. My favourite mistress, I should say – the most obedient, the most beautiful and the most depraved.'

The girl's eyes were on the priest's now. Her lips parted in a gentle snarl and her pearly teeth bit at the finger. An acute pain flashed through Parton's arm. He raised his head and looked down. The girl's long, manicured nails had drawn blood on his forearm by the strap which held it to the table. Her eyes were on his again, her nails poised anew.

Parton laid his head back and closed his eyes. God, into what sombre pit had he thrown himself? How had he let himself be taken in? Wherever Palafox was to be found, appearances were false. The seminary had been empty, the outwardly plain building in the Calle Alvarado concealed false levels, secret spyholes, its system of infernal mechanics, the Chinaman with his ivory-hafted knives – and now this grim, square monastery, supposedly a school, had served as cover for a well-sprung trap and, here in its dungeons, was the Inquisitor-General again and this masked whore with her perverted tastes and her hollow golden gaze.

And this time he was shot. This time there was no way out.

'Enough, girl.' The voice was soft, but the tone of authority would not be brooked. The girl's hand left Parton's arm and the voice went on. 'We must speak seriously, my little Luis. It is time.' Parton looked up to see the long face bent towards him without the slightest trace of the mocking smile he had expected to see. How had all this come about? How had the Inquisitor-General been able to prepare this trap? Had he had Parton followed? Had someone betrayed? The Espinels, thought Parton with sudden misgiving. He had made an enemy of Pilar Espinel, he had taken away her daughter, a minor. Pilar could have made trouble for him – she would surely have done so. Could that have come to Palafox's ears? But how could he have known about Tepoztlán? Had Pilar been close enough to overhear the name of the town the other morning when Gabriela had brought the information? And Gabriela, what would happen to Gabriela now?

'How fast you are thinking!' said the priest close to Parton's ear. 'You are wondering how I managed to trap you again, are you not?' He laughed softly. 'It is all ridiculously simple! I could not do other than trap you!' His voice dropped to a sibilant whisper. 'Everything in New Spain is under my control. You are deep in my domains, young man, and nothing here can happen without my knowing it and deciding what is to be done about it. You are no more than a very small fly caught in a web you could not avoid. I grant you, you played your part well the other day and you very professionally used the cathedral to shake off pursuit. But all that was useless.' He paused and bent forward, looking down into Parton's face. 'You were bound to come here because you were looking for the boys – and the boys are here.'

Parton looked towards the wall. He had nothing to say and he was not going to look the Inquisitor-General in the eyes.

'You see,' the soft voice went on not far from Parton's ear, 'this is not a Franciscan monastery at all. This place is one of many useful annexes to Inquisition headquarters in the Calle Alvarado. What are schoolboys doing in an Inquisition annexe? *All* the boys in this rather special school are the sons of important officials. That is why they are here and not in the loving care of their families.'

It was bad enough to have failed. It was perhaps even worse to be Palafox's captive. But to know that the Inquisition ensured the discretion of high-ranking officials by holding their children hostage, that everything had been fixed from the start. . . . Parton felt his fighting spirit drain away.

The Inquisitor-General's voice lost its customary silk and became harsh and pressing. 'Do you think Spain does not *know* that foreign powers have money to spend corrupting dissatisfied Spanish officials? Do you think there are no counter-measures, that we do not keep a close watch on those who might trade important secrets? And what better hold on a man than his children?' The priest moved round to the head of the table and gave a brief laugh. 'A blunter man than I would call these boys hostages. That really is too crude. I prefer to call them simply . . . guarantees. Now!' He leaned forward and looked down into Parton's eyes. 'The questions which face us are: which country are you working for and which official is preparing to sell secrets to that country? In other words, for *which* boy have you come here to throw yourself into the spider's web?'

Parton felt some of the fight coming back. There was a battleground, the other was defining its limits. '*The boy's identity is the father's identity*', Cameron had insisted on that. If Parton could shroud the question in mist, he might yet save something from the ruins of his mission.

There was a cry of pain from nearby.

Palafox smiled. 'My aides are in a hurry. Perhaps your friend will be the first to tell us what we want to know?'

Parton thought of Seward with a mixture of annoyance and shame. It would be so much easier to face torture alone, without the idea that he had dragged Seward into this and that they could cross-examine him for hours without learning anything important. Parton looked up at Palafox. 'He won't,' he said, shaking his head. 'He knows nothing of any importance to you.'

'Noble, but useless,' said Palafox, turning in response to a knock on the door. 'You will both be put to the question and there will be no mercy.' He disappeared and Parton turned his head to see the back of the black silk cape at the door. There was a muttered conversation. Parton brought his eyes back to the girl. She was watching him with a dreamy smile on her face. Her eyes were strange, there was something wrong with the smile. He looked away.

'So!' Palafox was back by Parton's side. 'Your friend has told us you are both English. Perfect! Enemies of Spain – and enemies of Holy Mother Church. You are heretics. *Protestants.*' He stared thoughtfully at Parton, his eyes narrowing. 'Protestants?' he murmured, leaving Parton's side and going over to the table by the wall. He came back, the bronze medallion in his hand.

'Is this yours, Protestant?'

'Yes.'

'The initial?'

Parton shrugged. 'I bought it at the *monte de piedad*. I don't know who put it in hock.'

'Which saint is carved here?'

'I don't know.'

'Of what possible use was this medallion to you?'

'Everyone wears something like that here.'

'You mean you wanted to look like a good Catholic?'

Parton nodded and the Inquisitor-General stared at him

again for a long moment, weighing the medallion in his hand. 'Perhaps,' he said at length. 'But I'm tempted to wonder if one of our boarders won't recognize this little bauble. . . .'

Parton tried to look indifferent. The last links were falling into Palafox's hands. Whatever happened he must not betray the importance of the medallion. There was just a slim chance that the priest would accept his version and forget the thing.

'I think we'll go and show it to them,' said Palafox and left the room, the girl following. There was a discussion out in the corridor of which Parton could catch nothing. Then the two cowled gaolers came in, unstrapped Parton from the table, tied his hands behind him and hobbled his ankles with a short rope. Two more friars opened the door and he was hustled away from the cell and down the dimly lit corridor.

They were not making for the refectory, thought Parton, scurrying because of the hobble and the speed at which his guards, no amateurs, kept him moving and constantly about to fall. He gave up trying to work out where they were. The draughty, echoing corridors looked alike and formed a genuine maze.

A door opened ahead of them and the guards dragged Parton through. He looked about him quickly. The last act was about to be played, he thought, here in this classroom. High-ceilinged and wide, the room was cold. There were books and sheaves of paper on shelves along the walls. The boys were sitting very straight and staid, eyes lowered no doubt on order, with slates on their knees. As in the refectory not long before, the youngest were in front and the older boys at the back. Two friars with canes were watching them from either side, and a third, hook-nosed, was conferring with Palafox in front of the boys. The girl sat on a high stool behind Palafox, the wide skirts of her magnificent gown shimmering grey and Parton glimpsed shoes of supple oxblood leather filigreed in fine silver thread beneath. She was watching him again. He looked away.

Palafox and the monk ended their discussion and the monk turned to face the boys. He cleared his throat and all heads rose in unison. The man was hatchet-faced with thick, prominent eyebrows. He crooked a grimy finger at the first boy on the right. The boy came forward hesitatingly and, at a signal from the tutor, knelt. He could not have been more than six years old and he was trying bravely to hide his fear. The place was loathsome, thought Parton. These boys virtual prisoners, hostages of Palafox's system, forced to live in the crypt-like shadows of this fortress, hectored by unwashed and brutal 'tutors', spent their days between prayers and Latin and the whip and enforced silence. Now Palafox was craning forward, studying the child's face as the tutor held out the medallion. He glanced up at Parton, back to the boy and shook his head. The tutor pointed the boy back to his place in silence and beckoned to the next.

Parton looked down at the floor. He must not look towards the boys. He knew and Palafox did not, that the boys from the front row who were now being called out to look at the medallion, were too young. Somewhere in the second or third row, and there were perhaps a dozen candidates as far as Parton had been able to see, was a dark-haired boy of eight who had worn that medallion for years and on whose face would dawn recognition at its sight. Palafox, scrutinizing each face, would not miss it. Then he would have the name and many men would be tortured and would die as a result. As for Parton, nothing he could now do could possibly worsen his fate. He might as well be hung for a sheep as a lamb. He tore away from his guardians and yelled: 'If you recognize the medallion, don't say so! If you show them you recognize it, *they'll kill your father*! Don't let them know, don't even blink when you see it!' A heavy blow sent him reeling. 'They want to kill your father—' Palafox was up and in front of him, screaming rage and the friars were on him and he fell, still shouting.

'Take him away!' screamed Palafox. 'Take him back and make him ready!'

Parton was kicked and beaten out of the classroom and run hobbling back through the corridors to his cell. This time, before being strapped down, he was stripped naked and his clothes placed with his other possessions on the second table. One of his guardians looked at him with a leer. 'You're in for something special,' he smirked. 'I've never heard him scream like that before.'

The door opened and Palafox strode into the room, his mouth a tight line. 'Very well!' He addressed Parton, visibly fighting for composure. 'You succeeded in throwing confusion among the boys. But you also admitted that the medallion could be recognized by one of them.' He leaned forward, his eyes stony. 'Now the games are over, Englishman. I want to know *which boy*.'

Parton looked him in the eyes and laughed. He had succeeded in placing the combat on the only ground where he had any strength. 'I've no idea which boy,' he said.

Palafox was silent, calming down, studying him. At length he said softly: 'Then I'm afraid you are going to suffer truly most horribly.'

'What do you have in mind for him?' It was the girl. Her hand was on the priest's arm and she was smiling her unsettling smile.

'Take him back to the Calle Alvarado and give Cheng his greatest challenge yet. I want him to suffer as man has never suffered before in the great chamber.' His eyes were on Parton's. 'But I want him to live, I want Cheng to keep him alive, I want his suffering to go on for a hideous length of time.'

'When shall we be leaving?'

'This evening when the heat has gone down.'

'Then we have time to begin?' She looked pleadingly at the Inquisitor-General, snaking her body in closer to his.

'No, my dear.' Palafox smiled at his mistress fondly. 'Our means here are too crude, we are ill-equipped and the men are little better than apes. Only Cheng can treat this man as I want him to be treated.'

Maria-Dolores smiled softly and produced a slim leather case from behind her back. She clicked it open. Parton could see red velvet lining and shining blades. His stomach tightened.

Palafox looked from the blades to his mistress's face and laughed briefly. 'So you have been taking secret lessons from Cheng! Confess, my child!'

'Is it a sin, my father?' The girl's voice was mock innocent, her body pressed close to the priest's.

'Maria-Dolores,' he said thickly. 'I shall be pleased to see what you have learned.' His eyes on the girl's, he stepped back to watch.

The girl's eyes gleamed dully as she chose a tiny blade and held it up to the light, watching it glint and feeling the edge with her thumb. Parton lay bound and naked. He was beginning to feel sick.

From Seward's cell nearby came screams.

CHAPTER SEVEN

The pain was rather like when you fell and barked your knees or your elbows when you were a child, thought Parton, or only slightly worse. It was bearable. He had not uttered a word during the half hour the girl had worked on him before Palafox had taken her abruptly away. It had been almost a game for the two of them, thought Parton. The serious things would begin back at the Calle Alvarado.

A nerve twitched from his neck down to his chest where the scalpels had left several square inches of lacerated skin. They had left him lying there, strapped to the table. Night had fallen and his two black-robed guardians, sitting by the door, had lit a candle to watch him by. The door was, as usual, locked from the outside and Parton knew that there were two more guards out there in the corridor. Mercifully, it was quiet out there. The screaming from Seward's cell, as long as it had gone on, had been harder to bear than the knives. It was Parton's fault if Seward was there and could give no satisfactory replies to the questions Palafox and his inquisitors were asking. Seward should have stayed with Gabriela.

She too was in terrible danger. Perhaps she would stay in the ruined barn for the night, but what would she do in the morning? Would she in her turn be arrested? Run, Gabriela, run, he willed.

He shook his head and tried to remain calm. If he were to stand a chance of holding out, he must keep his thoughts together, he must reason. The problem was, that the more he reasoned, the worse things looked.

Palafox, by now, must have realized that he had laid hands on an agent who could teach him a great deal. Not only did the Inquisitor-General want to know the identity of the boy and hence of the boy's father and the British agents who had worked on the case, but he would also want to learn whatever else Parton could give away. Parton knew that if he were to tell all he could about the organization of the Service, about Cameron, about other agents in the Americas, a masterspy of Palafox's power and intelligence could quite simply cripple the Service for years to come. Parton thought of the whitewashed dungeon with its swabbed stone floor and the gratings in its high ceiling and felt heavy with secrets, with future betrayal. The boy, the father, Seward, Gabriela and how many others, depended on him now? And he would crack, he would talk, no one could do otherwise faced with the long and excruciating process Palafox was about to put him through. He had no choice but to escape or die. Escape? He was strapped down naked and guarded in a locked cell deep inside a fortress. Die? How? Could he find a way of killing himself? Could he cheat his guards into helping him? A wave of darkness rolled over him as he thought of Jamaica, of his sisters who would be left at Yates's mercy, of Yates and William with whom he would not be able to settle the account. And of Gabriela too. Still the words came through, pitiless, logical: you must not reach the Calle Alvarado, you must die rather than talk.

A key clattered in the lock and he turned his head. The guards were getting to their feet. Then the door opened and the girl stood framed in the doorway. The nerve in Parton's chest twitched violently. The little game with the gleaming knives was about to start again.

'Out!' Maria-Dolores pointed to the door and the guards left without a word. The door slammed and the key turned. She was locked in with Parton. She came forward. The candle was behind her and he could not distinguish her expression. Could she become the instrument of his death? Could he get her to make a mistake with one of her knives?

She was beside him now. She had changed clothes – she was wearing a loose gown overlaid with white lace – and her hair was down in long, brown waves. She stretched out her hand and Parton seized up, holding his breath. She ran a tentative, long-nailed finger down the bloody pattern she had traced on his chest. Parton closed his eyes as pain lanced through him. It was worse than the knives themselves. The finger traced downwards, lower and stopped.

Parton opened his eyes wide. She was playing with him, inviting him. He could hear her breathing, rapid and shallow. Her eyes were dull, veiled, golden. . . . She threw herself on him with a strangled cry. The lace of the sumptuous gown ran rough and dry over the lacerations on his chest, showering fresh pain through him. She was sobbing convulsively, her lips working frantically over his shoulders and his neck. The skirts of her gown opened and she was naked underneath. Her thighs were parted and she was rubbing herself against him, he could feel hair and heat and moisture. He went cold.

'Please!' Her voice was raucous in his ear. 'Do it to me, *please*. I wanted you as soon as I saw you and now the knives and the blood and I can't hold back, oh please!'

Damn you to hell, thought Parton angrily as she knelt over him.

'Please! He lights the fire but he never does enough to put it out, he lets me burn, it pleases him, it's his way of torturing me! Oh, please, please!'

Priest's whore, madwoman, get off me! Parton wanted to shout, get away from me with your silk from China and your lace from Flanders and your silver and pearls and your rich slut's perfume and Spanish leather and your depraved tastes . . . Then the anger left him. Think, he told himself.

He stole a glance towards the door. There didn't seem to be a spyhole in it. Palafox had said they were ill-equipped in Tepoztlán and, if anyone were watching from some secret lookout, why had two guards been placed inside the cell to watch him? It was fair to assume that no one could see what was happening inside the cell. 'I can't move,' he said, looking up at Maria-Dolores. 'What can I do strapped down like this?'

The girl was off him in a second, fumbling with the straps at his wrists. The heavy strap over his waist was harder and she tore at it, hastily, clumsily. Then she unstrapped his ankles, straightened up, unfastened her gown and threw it towards the table by the door.

Parton lowered his legs from the table and stood up gingerly, his muscles aching. Maria-Dolores faced him, her hair flowing over her shoulders, her magnificent body naked and reached towards him. Go easy, he told himself. He had to humour her. At the slightest alarm it would be all over and the chance wouldn't come twice. She was against him, kissing him wildly, her heavy breasts pressed against his chest. It hurt less than the lace. He kissed her experimentally. He was going to have to summon up desire for this madwoman who had taken pleasure in carving his skin. Look at her body, touch her and let her touch you, forget who she is, he told himself. It was much less difficult than he had imagined. When she lay back on the table and drew up her legs, he penetrated her quickly, deeply and she growled like a cat. She closed her eyes and rolled her head from side to side, groaning. Parton risked a look round. On the table by the door were his clothes and money, her gown flung by them. There was a dark, flat object. He looked back quickly at the girl. Her eyes were still closed. He squinted at the dark object and recognized it. It was the slim leather case in which she kept her surgeon's knives.

The discovery must have surprised Parton into some subtle change of pace, because the girl's eyes flickered open again for an instant. 'Oh yes, do it like that,' she breathed, and her head resumed its rocking from side to side. Parton looked at the case. How could he get over there without alerting her? They would have to go over together, he decided.

He bent forward, slid his arms under her, and lifted her from the table. She'll open her eyes, he thought as he let her weight come slowly on to him. She did. 'Oh God that's good,' she moaned, looking at him with her golden eyes and crossing her ankles behind his back. 'Like that, yes, yes.' She closed her eyes again and Parton moved to the side. Little by little, he thought. The nerve in his chest twitched and he froze, letting it calm down. You can't stop now, he told himself. The nerve stopped twitching and he moved forward.

Maria-Dolores's breathing was ragged now, her head whipping from side to side, her eyes shut tight. Parton seized the opportunity and moved forward faster. They were by the table. The case was within reach. He would have to hold her with one arm while opening it to take out a knife. He shifted her weight.

'*Oh yes oh yes oh yes oh yes!*' Maria-Dolores arched towards him, eyes on his, her thighs gripping his waist, her heels digging into his buttocks, forcing him to her. '*Oh yes oh yes* OH YES!'

There was a knock at the door and a call from out in the corridor. The girl shuddered and the cries died away slowly in her throat.

'Damn them,' she said huskily, her eyes glistening. 'Let me down.' Parton lifted her away from him and put her down. She turned towards the door.

'What is it?' she called. 'I ordered you to leave me in peace!' Parton moved in close to her back, his left arm circling her, his hand on her breast. 'You will stay out there on guard until I call you!' There was an answering murmur of apology and assent from the other side of the door. Parton buried his head in the flowing brown hair and kissed the girl's neck. The case was by his right hand but everything had to be started over again. Maria-Dolores's breathing deepened and she pushed back against him, arching her back. Parton bit her shoulder and glanced at her face. Her eyes were closed.

'Take me,' she breathed, wriggling back in search. Parton's eyes slanted down desperately to the case. There was a little silver catch on it. He slipped it and opened the case.

'Quickly,' moaned Maria-Dolores, raising herself on tiptoe. Parton took a slim knife. The blade was only two inches long, but the point was wicked. He held it just behind her right ear and spoke softly into her left.

'In my hand is one of your knives. If I push it into the hollow behind your ear, it will go straight into your brain and you will die immediately.'

The girl froze and the silence was total.

'Listen to me,' whispered Parton. 'You know what's waiting for me at the Calle Alvarado. You know I have nothing to lose. Killing you with this blade will be easy and it will make no difference to my fate. So you are going to do exactly as I say. Do you understand?'

'Yes.'

'Good. We're going to move back a few steps. Slowly. *Slowly*. Now keep absolutely still.' Parton took his shirt with his free hand and pulled it quickly over his head. Dressing one-handed was not easy and he had to switch the knife from one hand to the other several times, but the girl seemed paralysed and did not make a sound.

'Now you,' he said, pushing the gown over her shoulders. She fastened it in front and slid her feet into silk slippers she had kicked off when she had thrown aside the gown.

'Over to the far side,' he ordered, leading her across the cell to a spot where they would not immediately be seen when the door was opened. He turned Maria-Dolores to face the door and slipped behind her with the knife.

'Now you're going to call them in. All of them, quickly, and don't try anything clever.'

The girl did as she was told. The door opened and one of the guards looked in. If he took fright now and locked the door again, thought Parton, there would be little chance of escaping from the cell. 'Tell them to *hurry*,' he whispered, pricking her skin with the sharp point.

'I said, come in all of you, quickly!' she called, her voice breaking on the last word.

The four cowled guards came in, frowning. One of them looked at the empty table in the middle of the cell and turned questioningly towards Maria-Dolores. Parton pushed her forwards towards the door to cut off the men's retreat, letting them see the knife in his hand. He spoke quickly.

'Do as I say or I will kill Palafox's mistress and he'll string you up for weeks at the Calle Alvarado to make you pay for such a blunder! Move on into the cell and don't make a sound. Go over to that wall and lie face down on the floor.' He was almost at the door but the men were hesitating, still under the surprise. 'Order them,' he breathed in the girl's ear.

'Do as he says.' Her voice quavered. 'Palafox will be furious if you cause my death.'

This time, the argument seemed to go home. The men shuffled over to the spot Parton had indicated and lay down without protest. Parton backed out of the door and glanced up and down the dark, empty corridor. The key was in the lock.

'Not a whisper when we are gone,' he warned the guards, pulled the girl out into the corridor and locked the door behind him, throwing away the key. 'Take me to my friend's cell first,' he said, pushing her forward.

'He's not there,' said Maria-Dolores in a small voice. 'He broke down and agreed to tell everything he knew. He's with Palafox now in the private apartments.'

If Seward told all he knew, it would not get Palafox far. Parton hoped his guide had had the good sense to make his offer before the ill treatment had gone on too long. Now he had to be rescued.

'This was his cell,' said the girl as they came to an open door. 'You can see it's empty.'

It was dark inside the cell, but Parton believed her. 'Lead the way to Palafox's apartments,' he said.

Maria-Dolores turned her head until the point stopped her. 'You must be out of your mind,' she said, genuine shock in her voice. 'There are armed guards all over the place up there. You won't even get through, never mind save your friend.'

'You'll get me through.' Parton pushed her forward.

'It won't work,' said the girl trembling as they walked down the corridor. 'You don't understand. What we told those idiots back there is nonsense. I'm just his whore, his plaything. He'd see me dead a hundred times rather than let you escape. He can easily change mistresses, but you're important to him.'

'This knife can kill both of us,' replied Parton. 'You first and me afterwards. Argue less and do as I tell you.' All the same, he could sense the girl's fear of Palafox and was sure she had not invented what she had just said. She seemed more frightened of the Inquisitor-General at a distance than she was of Parton close up and ready to kill her at a moment's notice.

She took a right turn and led the way to a stone staircase. At the top, the corridor they took came out on to the upper level of some kind of quadrangle or cloister. Parton felt the warm evening air and caught a glimpse of stars above. Gabriela was out there somewhere. Please God he could get out of this place and get to her before it was too late.

'After these steps,' said Maria-Dolores, 'we may come across armed guards at any point.'

'Go on. Tread softly.'

They went down a short flight of steps and into a long corridor. Barely perceptible light came trickling from somewhere far ahead. They were moving towards the front of the monastery, Parton thought. There was a soft enquiring call from further down the corridor and a cowled shape loomed out of the darkness.

'Tell him to stand aside,' said Parton, steadying the knife in his hand. The girl did as she was told. The guard disappeared and a door clicked softly.

'Where's he gone?' whispered Parton, pushing her on.

'Taken another corridor. He's gone to warn the others. I told you the truth. We don't stand a chance.'

'Keep going,' Parton told her. They walked on. The silence ahead was unsettling. If what the girl had said were true, an ambush might be set, well-armed men waiting for them in the dark. Parton peered over Maria-Dolores's shoulder into the dim light.

What happened was far from what he had expected.

It began with a low rumble like distant thunder somewhere in the depths of the walls, then a sudden metallic rattling like that of a chain being run out. There was a harsh grating swish and a loud clang ahead of Parton and the girl. She stopped dead. Parton could feel her heart beating fast. 'What is it?' he asked.

'An iron grid like a portcullis,' she said. 'The corridor's closed off.'

'We'll go another way.' Parton dragged her backwards. 'You said there were other corridors.'

'They'll have locked the doors. We've only got this corridor now. Oh, quickly!' She turned and pulled forward. There was a fresh rumbling, this time back towards the flight of steps at the beginning of the corridor. Parton checked her, fearing a ruse. 'No, quickly!' she pleaded, 'If they drop that grid we'll be caught like rats in a trap!'

They ran. The chain was rattling now. There was a loud explosion behind them and a pistol ball whanged off the stone wall. The rattling was all around them now. They sprinted to the bottom of the steps. There were more shots from behind and a ball whistled by very close. The girl ran madly up the steps, Parton following. He looked up. There was a grey blur up there just over the girl's head, and he heard the screech of metal on stone. He dived forward over the top of the steps and plunged her on beyond, rolling onwards himself, whipping his legs after him, every pore tingling in expectancy of the crushing, severing iron grid above.

The portcullis clanged to the stone floor inches behind his feet.

He breathed out and reached for Maria-Dolores, lying just in front of him. There were shouts and the sound of running feet back down the corridor. Another pistol barked. She had been right, he thought furiously, he was not going to be able to get through. He dragged her to her feet, threatening her with the knife again. 'We have to get out of here!' he said, pushing her into cover round a corner.

'Where to?' she gasped between breaths.

'The back door.'

'It's locked and there are no guards to open it.'

'The front?'

'It's guarded. They have the key.'

'Lead the way.'

They stumbled out into the cloister again. 'Right,' whispered the girl, 'and down those narrow stairs.'

Parton hurried her down, hearing the scraping above as the guards raised the portcullis. That would give them a few seconds. Maria-Dolores led the way through more dark corridors. The shouting was fainter now, although Palafox, alerted, would waste no time. 'Faster!' ordered Parton.

They crossed a courtyard and plunged through an open doorway. There was a patch of lantern light ahead. Parton pushed the girl on and into the light. There were two cowled guards. They stared in astonishment.

'Open the door or I'll kill her,' said Parton.

There was a moment of hesitation, then one of the guards pulled a pistol from his wide sleeve. 'No,' he said.

Parton inserted the point of the blade into the scented hollow behind Maria-Dolores's ear, punctured the skin and began to push.

'Do as he says!' she screamed at the men. '*Open!*'

'And give me that pistol,' said Parton, pushing her forwards and not letting up with the blade.

The man wavered only a second longer before shrugging his shoulders and handing Parton the pistol. His fellow unlocked and opened a small door inset into the great iron-banded oak ones of the main entrance. Parton stuck the pistol into Maria-Dolores's back and pushed her out into the night. There was shouting back in the depths of the monastery. He slammed the door behind him.

'The gate in the front wall,' he ordered.

There was only one sleepy guard at the outer gate and Parton clubbed him with the pistol butt before he had time to get up from his stool. He unbolted and opened the gate. Now what? He no longer needed the girl as a passport. But there was still so much to be done and she could be useful. She was a valuable card in the game and he held so few. 'That way,' he told her, pointing. 'And don't forget the pistol! Run!' Shouting broke out back at the monastery door and a shot rang out.

Parton and Maria-Dolores ran off into the night.

'Gabriela! It's me!' This had to be the barn, Parton was sure of it. He pushed Maria-Dolores in through the brokendown doorway and followed, calling Gabriela's name again.

'Mmm?' There was a scuffling noise from above.

'Gabriela, we have to go,' said Parton urgently, his feeling of relief short-lived. Palafox would not give them an instant of respite. 'Pass the packs down. Hurry!'

Gabriela was wide awake now. 'What happened?' she asked, passing down the first pack.

'Things went wrong.' Parton slung the pack over his shoulder and cursed as his chest hurt. 'We have to run for it.' He pushed Maria-Dolores out again as Gabriela climbed down from the ruined hayloft and picked up the second pack. Parton looked back towards the monastery. There were points of flame milling about back there. Palafox was sending his men out to search.

'Who's *she*?'

Parton turned to see the two girls eyeing each other in the vague starlight. However poor the light, the white lace of Maria-Dolores's gown was unmistakable. 'She's our prisoner,' explained Parton. 'A hostage. Look, they're out after us. We've got to go.'

'Where?' Gabriela's question was brittle, as if Parton's sudden reappearance in the middle of the night with a lady in lace had disconcerted her. Parton reached out and gave her arm a reassuring squeeze, looking out at the same time beyond her into the dark countryside, trying to remember. Then it came back to him. 'That way,' he said, pointing.

Maria-Dolores stumbled and fell for the third time on the rocky, difficult ground and Parton hauled her up, glancing back at the torches spreading out across the countryside behind them in the night. She wasn't acting the part, he thought – she was breathless and he saw tears glistening on her cheek. He remembered her silk slippers and didn't wonder. However, a little suffering would do her no harm.

'*Damn*.' That was Gabriela, off to the side.

'What's wrong?' called Parton.

'A rock! Or . . .' Her voice faded away then came back. 'There's no way through on that side. It's a jumble of stone blocks.'

'Thank God,' said Parton. He had been afraid they would go by in the dark. He peered ahead. He had expected to be able to make out at least a silhouette of the big pyramid, but there was higher ground beyond and it was acting as a dark backcloth. They would have to proceed by trial and error. 'This way,' he said.

It was not easy making a way through the rubble of stone blocks and the thick clumps of rampant vegetation which grew here and there among the ruins. It would be much easier for their pursuers with their torches. It was vital to leave no trace of their passage. The ground was dry and stony, but they would have to be careful not to break branches. Parton came out abruptly into a clear space. He began to make out massive looming shapes on either side. He stepped out into the space, dragging Maria-Dolores, Gabriela following.

It was a wide, stone-paved avenue. The buildings on either side sketched black, rectangular blocks against grey. He still could not see the pyramid, but any building would do as long as they could get into it without leaving traces for the searchers. He walked over to one of them and climbed three or four wide steps. At the top, there was no door. A creeper luxuriated over heavy wooden boards. If the Spaniards had boarded up the forbidden Indian towns, so much the better, he thought, but if they were to break in on that side, open as it was to inspection from the avenue, they would be quickly discovered. He went back down the steps and felt his way along the front of the building, still leading Maria-Dolores. Stumps of stone jutted out at shoulder height. Parton bent to one and found himself peering at a square-headed monster with baleful black discs for eyes. He turned away and felt along to the corner, plunging into the utter darkness between the building and its neighbour. He made his way patiently to the back, searching for an opening they could use.

The back of the huge building was completely overgrown with bushes and creepers. Parton pushed in carefully among them for some way and hit his shin on a low stone parapet.

Steps led downwards among the bushes. He found the top and went down, parting the branches gingerly. There was a boarded-up doorway at the bottom. He caught the end of a wide plank at the bottom of the doorway and pulled. Half of it came away in his hand with a dull crack. He tore away the rest and felt around. A thin draught came through the hole. There were no obstacles ahead and it was big enough to crawl through. Parton turned to Maria-Dolores. 'In you go,' he said.

Meagre first light filtered through from God knew where among the halls and passageways of the massive Aztec palace. Parton stared at the wall in the small room where they had hidden all through the night and realized that it was light enough for him to make out the joints between the stones. He sat up on the stone couch and swung his legs to the floor. A scorpion scuttled away, tail high, but Parton could see no snakes. The growing light was coming from a doorway to the left and he went towards it.

He had to take a look outside and make plans. Searchers might have been through the Indian ruins during the night without him hearing them through the thick walls of the palace, but it was now, with daylight, that the real danger of search became apparent. He found himself in a passageway, light flowing from the far end. Dust and rubble littered the floor and reptiles scurried as he passed.

The room at the end was many times larger than the one where they had spent the night and its ceiling was at least twelve feet high. A carved stone frieze of triangular patterns ran round the chamber at head height. The stone blocks of the walls were precisely hewn and there was no mortar between them. Light in the chamber came from above. An open-sided staircase rose steeply against the far wall to a long gallery which Parton thought must rise above the roof. He climbed the stairs and looked up. There was a flat roof supported by stone pillars. The gaps between the pillars had been boarded up, but the boards had rotted in a dozen places and light filtered through. Parton hauled himself up and looked out. Beneath him was the wide avenue, opposite a flat-topped building that he supposed was similar to the one they were hiding in, its façade studded with gargoyle-like monsters, disconcerting in the grey light.

He scanned the avenue, the buildings and the all-invading brush. He saw no one. He looked out over the bushes to the low, stony hills of the surrounding countryside. There had to be searchers somewhere out there. Palafox would not give up as easily as that. Parton thought he saw a movement on a hillside a mile away. He narrowed his eyes. No, it was impossible to say, the light was still too uncertain. He shifted his position and crossed to a crack in the boards on the far side and looked out, away from Tepoztlán.

He shrank back into the shelter of the pillar by his shoulder. The high pyramid he had seen on arriving at Tepoztlán was about four hundred yards away. Silhouetted against the dawn sky at its very summit was the figure of a skirted sentinel, arms folded across his chest. It was not a statue. The skirt of the monkish habit was moving in the breeze and now the man was slowly turning and staring out in a new direction. Palafox had placed a watcher high on the pyramid, from which the entire surrounding countryside could be surveyed.

Parton watched anxiously until he was sure that the sentinel was unaware of his presence in the gallery of the ruined palace. Then, from each side of the gallery, he made a thorough reinspection of the tops of the buildings all around. He saw no sign of other watchers. After all, one at the top of the pyramid was enough. The next thing was to look for a way out. The back of the palace, by which they had crawled in during the night, gave on to bushes and trees. With the sentinel looking in the opposite direction, it should be reasonably easy to sneak away on that side. If that proved to be true, the Indian ruins could go on being a useful hideout because it would be possible to come and go without being seen.

He looked back towards Tepoztlán. Yes, there were movements on a hillside far away – not close enough to worry about. Lower, those few red roofs were all that could be seen of Tepoztlán and the dark block half hidden between two rolling hills, like an upturned boat in the waves, was the monastery. Parton wondered what Palafox would be doing. Organizing the search, certainly, calling up reinforcements, using the power of his formidable secret networks, sending out word of the fugitives and of the importance of their capture. And apart from that? How angry would he be at Parton's escape and his mistress's capture? Would his anger blind him? Parton could perhaps imagine him angry, but coldly, lucidly so. Palafox would be waiting, knowing that, on home ground, all the chances were in his favour.

Parton left the gallery and went down the stairs. With the sentinel nearby, he couldn't leave Maria-Dolores free of her movements. In the small room, the two girls were still sleeping on the stone couch, Gabriela in her grey travelling dress, her hair tied back, leather walking shoes on her feet and Maria-Dolores in silk and lace, the gown filthy and torn, the tatters of those ridiculous slippers beneath. Oddly, they had both taken the same attitude in sleeping, heads on hands, knees drawn up, like children. Yet how different they were, thought Parton: the black-eyed, passionate girl of the people and the rich man's golden-eyed toy. He leaned and shook them by the shoulder, then turned and took dried meat and a water canteen from one of the packs. 'Here.' He handed the food and water over. 'It's all there is.'

Gabriela sat up, drank from the canteen and passed it without turning her head to Maria-Dolores. Maria-Dolores, staring about her, apparently terrified, ignored the gesture.

131

Parton studied her pale, tear-streaked face. Was there something more human in it? He remembered the knives. No pity, he told himself. 'Drink,' he ordered. 'Then you can start being useful. What will Palafox do next?'

Maria-Dolores sat back more calmly, drank and looked at him tiredly.

'I don't know his secrets,' she said at length. She shrugged. 'I imagine he'll send riders to all the nearby towns with your description – our description – and orders to the Inquisition in those towns to be on the lookout for us. Other riders will go farther afield, to the capital and beyond, because you'll doubtless have to try to get out of the country.'

'Hmm.' Seward was a problem. He knew nothing about the boy, but he held secrets all the same. 'What has Palafox learned from my friend?'

Maria-Dolores shrugged again. 'There I can't help you. I don't know!' she protested in response to an impatient gesture from Parton. 'I told you that he doesn't keep me – or indeed anyone – in his secrets! When your friend was brought to Palafox's apartments because he was ready to talk, I was sent away. I've no idea of what was said.'

'You could be lying.'

The golden eyes opened a little wider and held Parton's gaze. 'I can't see what I stand to gain by it.'

'Excuse me if I break in.' Gabriela shook her head slowly, looking from Maria-Dolores to Parton. 'But perhaps you could tell me now who she *is*? And who's this Palafox?'

'*She* is Palafox's mistress,' replied Parton, 'and Palafox is the Inquisitor-General of New Spain.'

'Is that all? We're up against the entire Inquisition?' asked Gabriela flatly, her eyes on his. 'I told you you were up to something dangerous, didn't I?'

Parton repressed a grin and concentrated on Maria-Dolores. 'What do you think will happen to Seward now?'

'If Palafox is satisfied there's no more to be obtained from him, I imagine he'll lock him up again for the time being.'

'Before?'

'An official or unofficial execution. He's a spy, isn't he?'

'Not really.' Parton's mouth tightened. It had been a victory to have escaped with the girl as hostage, but all the rest was defeat. All? 'And the boys?' he asked. 'What will he do about them?'

Maria-Dolores looked up in unfeigned surprise. 'He'll find out who the medallion belongs to, of course.'

'The boy won't say.'

There was a pause. 'Do you take Palafox for a gentleman?' asked Maria-Dolores, world-weariness in her voice.

Parton began to pace up and down in the small chamber. Defeat was all along the line indeed. Palafox was undoubtedly capable, if all else failed, of hurting and scaring the boys until one of them admitted to recognizing the medallion, even if the boy knew his father's life depended on his silence. Worse still, the boy could try to hold out in order to save his father and the process would go on . . . The boy's suffering would be, in a sense, Parton's fault. In either case, there would be pain, fear and death, including Seward's. If anything were to be done to stop it, it had to be done quickly, not only because of the coastal rendezvous on the night of the tenth. 'Before dawn tomorrow,' he said, 'I've got to get Seward and the boy out of there.'

'You're out of your mind,' said Maria-Dolores. 'You don't know him. Even if you try to cut your losses and escape from New Spain, you don't stand a chance.'

Parton turned sharply. 'I can trade you off. And if he doesn't give me what I want, you'll die.'

The girl sighed. 'Then make ready to murder me. I told you last night that he'd sooner accept my death than your victory. Worse still, now he'll be furious about your escape – and probably even more furious about my part in it.'

'What was her part in it?'

Maria-Dolores turned to Gabriela with a brief smile. 'Your friend took advantage of the fact that we were both naked and in an advanced state of erotic frenzy, to hold a knife to the back of my head.'

'*She* was in a state of frenzy,' said Parton quietly in reply to Gabriela's questioning frown. '*I* was strapped down and waiting to be transported to Mexico City to die. It was my last chance.'

Gabriela looked at him, a slow smile forming on her lips. 'A charming last chance,' she said softly.

Parton shrugged and looked down at Maria-Dolores, feeling the smart of the cuts her knives had made and wondering if Gabriela would find the other girl as charming if she knew . . . Maria-Dolores's gaze faltered and she looked away.

'What are we going to do?' Gabriela stood up decisively.

'Find a way of getting into the monastery, lay hold of Seward and the boy and get them out of there. Simple,' said Parton.

'Let me go out and try to get near the monastery or do something useful.' Gabriela touched Parton's shoulder. 'They don't even know I exist.'

Parton looked down at her passionate young features with a surge of tenderness, abruptly chased from his mind by the memory of Palafox's lightless eyes in the dungeon at the Calle Alvarado. 'No,' he said. 'It's too dangerous. Anyway, Seward might have told them about you.'

'Why? They've never heard of me – why should they ask questions about me? Why should Seward volunteer information they're not even looking for?'

Parton looked questioningly at Maria-Dolores. 'I told you I didn't hear your friend's confession,' she replied, 'but, as far as I know, Palafox has never heard of this girl.'

'You see?'

Parton shook his head. 'There's still a risk.'

'Can *you* go up and look around in broad daylight?'

'No. That doesn't mean . . .'

'And hasn't she just said that it's no use trying to exchange her?'

'She may be exaggerating.'

'It didn't sound like it to me. Look, let me just go into town and see if I can't learn something useful. You know what I told you about the tradespeople. It worked in Mexico City, didn't it?'

Parton hesitated. He could wait for night and try a last-ditch heroic attempt with Maria-Dolores as hostage – but the chances were that she was right and that they would both be cut down, shot, or captured before they even got inside the monastery. It would be a noble gesture, but it would do nothing to save the boy and Seward. Only ruse could get through the Inquisition's defences and it couldn't come from him as long as daylight lasted. Any man of Parton's build within miles of the monastery was going to have a hard time of it today, explaining who he was and what he was doing. There could be no more play-acting for Parton .

But an idea had been sketching itself, almost unconsciously, in his mind and Gabriela's mention of Tepoztlán tradespeople was giving it flesh. It was true that the chances the Inquisition was looking out for her were very slight and she might slip through, young and angelic, where no one else could. He looked back down at her.

'Perhaps there is something you could try,' he said.

Tepoztlán was the kind of town that was always hot and dusty, even in the morning, thought Gabriela as she crossed the one and only square in the middle by the small church. It seemed to be permanently asleep. A town which paid sincere homage to the *siesta*, slept comfortably at night and scarcely batted an eyelid in the morning. Marvellous. It was the kind of place she hated.

She looked round and reminded herself to be careful. The Inquisition was not to be trifled with, at home in Spain or out here in the colonies and Parton had warned her about the friars who, in his opinion, were largely hired mercenaries and not clerics at all. It had been frightening enough at first, sneaking out under the bushes and through the trees while Parton had watched the sentinel, then almost running into two friars hurrying along the path she had chosen further on and hiding herself quickly among some rocks as they had gone by. But she had walked the last half-mile into Tepoztlán openly and no one she had met on the road, not even the two black-and-white-robed Dominicans – Inquisition men those two – had given her a second glance. The Inquisitor-General's men were out and about, but they were not looking for her.

The girls she had spoken to by the bridge over the desultory stream had been a harder test. They had watched her keenly, critically, eager to judge the girl of their age who had arrived alone, dusty, travelling the road freely and saying she would take on work if any were to be had in the town. Gabriela had understood that pride could be fatal to her at such a moment and she had been humble and friendly and charming. By the time she had left the girls, she had learned what she wanted to know.

Tepoztlán was not a trading town and its few craftsmen and tradespeople were not getting fat on the monastery's business. The friars kept well away from the town in general and most goods they used came down the main road from Mexico City. However, the monastery did some occasional business in Tepoztlán – the blacksmith, for example, worked for them occasionally and there was a cooper, a carpenter, a builder, even a cobbler. They were of no use to Gabriela. She couldn't look for work with craftsmen like that and anyway, it might be months before one or another of them had a job to do at the monastery.

The baker was different. The girls had told her quite a lot

136

about the baker. He was bone idle, they had said and it was his wife and daughters who worked hard to provide the town with daily bread and *tortillas*. Such a fresh product couldn't be brought down from the capital and the baker's biggest customer was the monastery.

Gabriela left the square, following the girls' directions and hurried down an evil-smelling alley. He might take *you* on, had said one of the girls, eyeing Gabriela's charms. It seemed that if you worked for the *mestizo* baker, the best thing was to work with one hand and keep your skirt on with the other. Gabriela quickened her pace. Today was Thursday and Thursday was delivery day at the monastery – of course, thought Gabriela, food would not be delivered to a monastery on a Friday.

The smell of hot bread filled the air and drowned the natural odour of the alley. There was an open door a few yards on and a cat sat rubbing itself contentedly against the post. Gabriela looked in. On a table were baskets of bread and trays piled with *tortillas*. A puffy-faced girl a couple of years younger than Gabriela was heaping them on to another tray. She looked up as Gabriela's shadow fell on her work.

'Hello!' Gabriela composed a smile.

The girl didn't return it. 'What d'you want?' she asked, returning to her work.

Gabriela eased herself inside. 'You've got a lot of work to do, dear,' she observed.

'For the monastery and twice as much as usual,' said the girl. 'What d'you want?'

'Can I help?' smiled Gabriela, moving forward.

'P'pa!' called the girl sullenly.

A small, brown-skinned man with a pot belly appeared at the back of the shop, wiping his hands on a dirty apron and grumbling. The girl nodded at Gabriela without a word. 'What do you want?' asked the baker.

Smile, Gabriela told herself. 'Work,' she said sweetly.

137

The *mestizo* raised his eyes to the ceiling, lowered them to the floor and spat. 'You think I hire workers?' he said, turning to go.

'Please Señor!' The urgency came naturally to Gabriela's voice and the baker looked back over his shoulder. 'No money, Señor. Just food. That will be enough.' He had to accept, thought Gabriela. Those baskets and trays were going to the monastery and she was going with them. She remembered what the girls had said and eyed him. 'I ask for little, Señor . . .'

'What's this?' A harsh-faced woman appeared by the baker, peering over his shoulder at Gabriela.

'This vagabond wants to work for a few *tortillas*,' said the baker.

The woman stared Gabriela down. 'We don't need the likes of *her*.'

The baker looked speculatively at Gabriela. He seemed to be changing his mind about what might be done with the likes of a girl like that. 'You can carry a tray of *tortillas*, can't you?' he asked.

'Of course,' said Gabriela, picking up a tray. It was heavy.

'Throw her out!' shouted the woman.

'Hold your tongue, woman,' said the baker. 'You were complaining about all there was to carry to the monastery today. She can help you.'

'While you sleep!'

'I told you to hold your tongue,' said the baker.

'Oh, thank you, Señor!' said Gabriela. A glance from the baker showed that thanks would be for later. Gabriela would look after that when the time came.

'Hey, papa!' Two small boys ran excitedly through the door. 'Papa, the soldiers are here!'

'What soldiers, idiot?' asked the baker's wife, grabbing the elder of the two by the ear.

The boy turned a dark eye on her and wriggled away.

'The Regiment of the Holy Cross,' he said solemnly, rubbing his ear. 'Lancers. And musketeers too, from another regiment. They've cordoned off the town and you can't go in or out. And now they're searching all the houses.'

CHAPTER EIGHT

'They're not going to stop *me*,' muttered the baker's wife as she strode up the alley with a basket of bread under her arm, followed by her daughter and Gabriela with their trays. 'Soldiers are idle and dishonest,' she went on, leading the way across the square and glaring at a group of them who were waiting for a door to open opposite. Gabriela looked away and wished the woman would shut up. She heaved a sigh of relief as they left the square without incident.

The road which led out of Tepoztlán towards the monastery was straight, flat and dusty. The baker's wife and the two girls were still in the town when they saw the half-dozen musketeers in red and green standing in the shade of a clump of trees just after the last houses. 'There they are!' the woman grumbled. 'I suppose they're the ones who're going to try and stop us leaving town!'

Gabriela looked towards the soldiers. Beyond them, the monastery was in view down the road. Her heart began to beat faster and she reminded herself that they were not looking for her. At least, she hoped not.

'Halt there!' A musketeer stepped out into the middle of the road, his face in the shadow of his wide-brimmed hat. 'Nobody tell you ladies the town's sealed off?'

'Is that so?' retorted the baker's wife. 'Then who's going to deliver all this to the monastery? You, perhaps?'

Don't give them ideas, you old shrew, thought Gabriela frantically. They might agree, and I'll never get to the monastery.

'Father?' the soldier called towards the trees.

A black-and-white-robed Dominican limped slowly out of the shade. 'Yes?'

'These women claim to be delivering bread to the monastery.'

The old man peered across and Gabriela, the sudden taste of fear in her mouth, avoided his gaze and tried to look unconcerned. Now she would learn if the Inquisition had her description.

'Yes,' said the Dominican. 'That's the baker's wife. They're expected. You can let them through.'

Gabriela withheld an immense sigh of relief as the women moved forward. 'I should think so too,' said the baker's wife loudly. 'Annoying honest folk with no reason.'

'Hey!' called the musketeer.

They stopped and Gabriela cursed the woman's loud mouth. They had been on their way through and now they were in trouble. The musketeer walked up slowly and faced the baker's wife. 'For your information, lady, we're searching for a very dangerous outlaw. I wouldn't like to think what he'd do to you and these poor young girls here if he got hold of you. Good thing we're here to protect you, isn't it?' There was no reply. 'On with you,' the soldier said with a sneer. 'You go to the monastery, you deliver your bread and you come straight back. We'll count you in, all three of you.'

The road to the monastery was short and Gabriela could have wished it longer. The arrival of the soldiers had set her nerves on edge and she needed to calm down. But already they were at the outer gate and a friar in grey was opening it. He looked strong and cruel and so did a second one who was watching them in through the gate. Perhaps these were the mercenaries Parton had talked about. The gate slammed shut and there was no going back.

Gabriela gritted her teeth and fought against the fear which was seeping into her. She hadn't been recognized, they weren't even looking for her, she told herself. She looked at the great dark building towards which they were walking. It looked bleak and terrifying. Was the Inquisitor-

General in there? How many men, either fanatical Dominicans or mercenaries like those at the gate, did he have under his orders? What was she doing, trying to fight the Inquisition?

Gabriela was not worried by the idea that she was fighting against her country. This was not her country and she had nothing to do with these terrible men, nor they with her. She remembered the boy who was held prisoner there and had to be got away to his father. Would he be like her little brother? Wasn't that enough to want to do something for him? And she herself, didn't she want to escape from New Spain and to her father? Weren't these reasons enough? Still the gloomy building unsettled her, yet she knew she would need absolutely solid nerves to do what she had to do. Suddenly she imagined Parton, determined to save the little boy and his friend Seward, pitted against that building in the night. The main doors were guarded and there were no accessible windows. The monastery alone was a terrible enemy. Parton was strong, but he was only a man – and he was alone.

She was there to try to open the way for him and now she knew that she was going to do it. The three women were walking down the side of the grim edifice and Gabriela smiled briefly to herself. She felt capable again.

They turned the corner and came to the back door. The baker's wife knocked loudly. 'Very well, very well!' A voice came weak and muffled from within. A bolt grated and slammed back, then another. A key clattered and the door opened. The friar in the doorway was greying and no doubt a regular on the job, because he waved the women in without hesitation. 'You're late!' he protested as he bolted the door behind them.

Gabriela looked quickly about her. It was as Parton had said – the corridor, the doors, the wooden staircase climbing to the trapdoor. The baker's wife, contradicting the friar, was leading the way through an open doorway on the left.

Gabriela followed and found herself in a wide, airy room, cool and shady. She placed her tray of *tortillas* on a long table by the wall as she had been told to do. There was an open door on the far side of the room, but she could see nothing beyond it but barrels. Stores and larders, as Parton had said. Gabriela knew she had little time now. The friar was beginning to count the loaves. She backed slowly off towards the corridor.

'Thirty-four!' announced the friar.

'Nonsense, three dozen!' retorted the baker's wife.

'It's always the same,' sighed the baker's daughter listlessly. 'They have to argue the toss. We can go out and wait in the garden.'

'You'll wait in the passage,' said the friar sharply, looking up. 'We have orders to keep the door shut and bolted today.'

The two girls went out into the corridor while the dispute picked up again. Gabriela drifted towards the staircase and glanced up. The trapdoor had no bolts, Parton had been right. It shouldn't be difficult to lift.

A pale, young friar stuck his head out of a door further along the corridor and looked at her. 'Oh no, not *him*,' said the baker's daughter. Gabriela cursed. She had no time for interruptions. The friar was coming towards them.

'Well, well,' he leered, 'a new girl! How nice!' One hand reached out to pat Gabriela's cheek, while the other went down to pat something else.

Gabriela enjoyed the smack in the pimply face she gave him. 'Leave me alone, leave me alone!' she squealed. She ran up the stairs to the top and perched just under the trapdoor. She could feel it lift a little when she pushed up with her back.

The young friar stared furiously at her, his cheek reddening, while the bread dispute stopped and there was an instant of silence.

'Leave the girls alone, Brother Donatio!' came the angry

voice of the older man from the stores. 'And get back to your work!' The young friar made an obscene gesture towards the doorway, gave Gabriela a parting glare and left, while the argument picked up again in the stores.

Gabriela lifted the trapdoor, winked at the baker's daughter who was staring at her, horrified and climbed up into the granary. It was dark, but there was just enough light for her to see that the granary was practically empty. The light was coming through a crack in the door. Gabriela ran to it, light-footed. The door was wide and heavy and it was secured by a huge iron bolt. She slipped the bolt little by little until a fraction of the very tip still held in the socket of the doorframe. A determined push from the outside would open the door easily enough. She ran back to the trapdoor and stepped down on to the stairs. She had just lowered the trapdoor shut above her when the baker's wife came out into the corridor, the friar following. He looked up immediately and frowned. 'What are you doing up there, girl?' he asked severely.

'Hiding,' pouted Gabriela. She pointed down the passage to where the young friar had disappeared. 'I'm afraid he'll come back and *do* things to me.'

'Get down from there at once!' shouted the baker's wife. 'And take this tray!'

'And all three of you, on your way!' said the monk, unbolting the back door.

Outside, Gabriela listened to the two bolts slamming home and the key turning twice in the lock. Everything had happened so quickly she had had no time to feel fear. She glanced up. The granary door looked exactly as it had when she had arrived, solidly shut, oaken, a big iron hook set into the wall above it for hauling up sacks of grain. Only she knew that the door would be easy to open for someone who had used that hook and rope to climb up. She followed the two others round the corner of the monastery, trembling now the job was done.

The friars at the gate let them out. Down the road, Gabriela saw the clump of trees and the soldiers. The three women would already have been seen and the musketeer had said they would be counted back in. Gabriela was tempted to run for it into the brush and make her way back to the Indian ruins, but that would make her immediately suspect and what she had just done at the monastery would be found out. She had no choice but to go back with the other two and find a way out of town later.

She hefted her empty tray and trudged off unwillingly towards Tepoztlán.

Parton looked out into the deepening twilight in the avenue. Cicadas buzzed and the gruesome stone heads opposite cast longer and longer shadows, like sundials. The sentinel from the pyramid had gone by on his way back a few minutes before, no doubt obeying orders to come in at nightfall. That was one relief. The searchers who had combed the Indian town during the day had not found the broken boards under the bushes at the back of the palace and that was another. But Gabriela was not back yet and Parton was seriously doubting now that she would be.

During the afternoon, he had not worried. The fact that she was away for some hours did not necessarily mean trouble, far from it. It undoubtedly meant that she had been able to get near to the monastery – it had been agreed between them that, if she had not been able to approach it, she would come back immediately to the Indian ruins so that a different plan of attack could be tried. But now the delay was long and Parton was beginning to fear the worst. What did it change? Whatever happened, there was a last-ditch effort to be made that night. Everything was ready, the operation was planned in detail. Either it would come off, or it would not. If it did, he would free Gabriela at the same time as Seward and the boy. There was no point in blackening the picture. All the same . . .

It was now completely dark outside. There was no use in watching. He decided he would wait a few more minutes before leaving. He climbed down from the pillars and sat with his back to the wall in the gallery.

There was a rustle as Maria-Dolores, sitting off to the side, shifted. 'Is she really important to you?' she asked, her voice seemingly neutral. Parton did not reply. 'Because if she is and you sent her into Palafox's clutches—'

'Be quiet!' said Parton, leaning forward. Of course that was where the problem lay; that was the thought he was constantly trying to banish.

'She's young and pretty enough to give even him some real pleasure—'

'I said shut up!' Parton grabbed her wrist and twisted it and she cried out. 'She'll be back or I'll get her out! We'll wait, and we won't talk about that damn priest! All right?'

Maria-Dolores was silent for a moment. Then she said, 'I'm sorry. I don't know what made me say that.'

Once again, Parton was surprised. Maria-Dolores, during the day, had alternated – for no apparent reason – between aggressiveness and concession. There had been times when she had pushed him almost to violence and yet, when the searchers had been in the town (and she had heard their voices clearly and knew they were there), she had made no effort to elude his watchfulness and make her presence known. She had even been cooperative over his demands to know certain details of the layout of the inside of the monastery – although Parton was well aware that she could be lying to him and he was prepared for that.

'Not a sound!' he breathed suddenly, clamping a hand over the girl's mouth. The noise he had heard had not been caused by a lizard or a scorpion and it had come from within. He stared into the impenetrable blackness and held Maria-Dolores still.

'Parton?' It was Gabriela's voice and it was coming from the back of the palace. Parton stiffened, tightened his grip

146

on Maria-Dolores and did not reply. Outside, an owl hooted some way off and another replied. It would take a clever man to say if the owls were feathered or not. He could hear footsteps, shuffling in the debris, somewhere back there, near the room with the couch.

'Parton!' The voice was closer now, in the passage leading to the big chamber, Parton decided as he listened. The light footsteps were Gabriela's. He could hear no others. Outside, an owl hooted again. The sound came from high on a building, not from the ground.

'*Parton*!'

'Pssst!'

'My God, are you *there*?'

'Wait down there,' whispered Parton. He listened for a last time to the night outside, then took his hand from Maria-Dolores's mouth, pulled her up and led her down the narrow steps in the dark.

'You *bastard*! You scared me!' Gabriela ran, stumbled, fell into his arms. 'I was beginning to think all kinds of things. . . .'

'So was I.' He squeezed her affectionately. 'I had to be sure you weren't accompanied before I made a sound. Sorry.'

Gabriela raised her head to his and whispered, 'I did it!'

'Good, good!' Parton listened delighted to her story. 'Why did it take you so long to get back?' he asked.

'The soldiers. Tepoztlán was crawling with soldiers and priests all day long, the place was cordoned off and no one could leave. At nightfall they reduced the pickets, called most of the soldiers back to camp and I managed to sneak out into the countryside.'

'What kind of soldiers?'

'Lancers and musketeers.'

'Damn.' Mounted troops were bad news. The hours of darkness ahead, when cavalry could not risk itself on rough terrain, became even more precious. 'Where's their camp?'

'Near the stream among the plantations. I think most of them are back there for the night. I didn't see any at the monastery either.'

'Are you hungry?' asked Parton. He had eaten some dried meat an hour before.

'No. But I've brought some food!' Gabriela handed over a packet of *tortillas*. 'The baker kept trying – I don't need to explain – and his wife got so angry she threw this pile of *tortillas* at me and told me to go. No one was more pleased than I was!'

'Good,' said Parton, 'we may need these later.' He pushed Maria-Dolores ahead of them to the room with the couch and sat her down on it. Then he took the two candles he had prepared from the top of a pack, slipped one into his jacket pocket, struck a light with a tinderbox and lit the other, putting the tinderbox into his pocket with the first candle. Yellow light filled the small room. It would not be seen from outside, the room was too deep inside the thick-walled palace. On top of the packs, the ropes and pistols were ready. There was just Maria-Dolores to deal with now.

'Make yourself comfortable,' he told her. 'I'm going to have to tie you up.' He watched her face by the light of the candle.

She looked genuinely astonished. 'But – aren't you taking me with you as a hostage?'

Parton bent and began to lash her ankles together with the twine he had prepared earlier. 'You're a better hostage here. You said yourself they wouldn't hesitate to fire on you. And I'm not going to sneak you into the monastery just for you to call out and give the game away at the first opportunity.'

There was a sullen silence. Parton took her hands and tied her wrists together. 'You're going to leave me here,' she said accusingly. 'You don't trust me and you think I'm of no use as a hostage so you're going to get rid of me.'

'Not quite.' Parton tore a strip of lace from the hem of her gown. 'You're right I don't trust you.' He watched her closely. 'But, if I succeed tonight, I'll be back. You'll come with us, because I just might be able to trade you off in a tight corner.' He tore the strip of lace into two. 'But let's be clear. If I don't get back here to free you, it'll be because I've failed. If I fail, I'll die. I won't allow myself to be captured alive a third time to end up at the Calle Alvarado. If that happens, you'll stay here and you'll die slowly of hunger and thirst, unable to move, and—' he showed her a rolled-up ball of dirty lace, '— gagged.'

'No! Don't do that to me, please!'

'I can't risk you shouting for help, can I?'

She stared at him, mutely pleading. Not so proud now, he thought. There was something about her eyes that had changed, he wasn't sure what. 'So,' he continued deliberately, 'you can see that your best bet is to help me succeed so that I can get back here and free you. If you lied to me today when you answered my questions about the layout of the monastery, for example, now's the time to set that right and tell me the truth.'

She shook her head briefly, emphatically. 'I told you the absolute truth, down to the slightest detail.'

Parton watched her for a second longer, then nodded, satisfied. He passed her a canteen, holding it to her mouth. 'Drink before I tie the gag in,' he said. She drank and said nothing. He could trust what she had said, he thought. If she had lied, she was genuinely signing her death warrant. He placed the ball of lace in her mouth and tied it firmly in place with the other half of the strip. Then he took the two coils of light rope and slipped them over his shoulders, crossing them over his chest and hung the two pistols from his belt.

'And what am I to do?' asked Gabriela.

Parton pulled his jacket to and buttoned it to hide the white of his shirt. 'Come with me. I'm going to need a lookout on the outside.'

'Good. My eyesight's perfect.'

'There's just one thing I want your agreement on,' said Parton, bending closer to her. 'If I'm not out of the monastery within an hour, you must not come back here. You must run from here as far and as quickly as you can and forget you ever even heard of me.'

Gabriela swallowed and shook her head. 'I doubt if I'll be able to do that.'

Parton blew out the candle and led the way to the door. 'If I don't get out of there,' he said drily, 'you'd better try.'

Anselmo, the hatchet-faced tutor, was already waiting under the lantern by the carved and gilded door as Lazaro came into view and walked diffidently along the last few yards of the corridor. The two men looked at each other uncertainly. It was perhaps a little early. The slightest mistake today could have disastrous consequences. It was not the moment to annoy the Inquisitor-General. 'Perhaps we should,' sighed Lazaro after a long silence and knocked, opening the door as the voice from within invited him to. The two men walked side by side through a richly draped antechamber and into Palafox's study.

The room was brilliantly lit and, in contrast with, or perhaps in spite of, the bleakness of most of the monastery, lavishly furnished with fine ebony and rosewood, Chinese ivories and silk hangings and Oriental rugs. Palafox, sitting at a leather-topped desk in the middle of the room, turned towards them as they came forward. Both men watched for signs of danger. Apparently, there were none. The expression on the long face was neutral, the mouth tightly sealed, a slight furrow over the brows indicating displeasure, but no more. If the Inquisitor-General felt furious and humiliated by the Englishman's escape and the manner of it, if he was angry at the immense blunder his unfaithful mistress had made the evening before, or indeed, if he felt mortified or even jealous at the desire that had motivated Maria-Dolores's act, nothing showed on the surface. Lazaro, who knew Palafox of old, did not doubt that the feelings were nonetheless there – deeply hidden, but all the more dangerous for being deep.

'Lazaro.' Palafox picked up a thin sheaf of papers from the desk. 'Further messages for Mexico City. Are your riders back yet?'

'Yes, Excellency.'

'Send them straight back with these. Whom has Salvador chosen to take word on to Puebla?'

'Cristobal and Benito,' replied Lazaro, relieved he had seen to every last detail and could reply.

'Fine. No result from the search?'

'No, Excellency. But I'm sure that—'

'I scarcely expected one,' interrupted the Inquisitor-General, standing and smoothing the white silk of his habit. 'The Englishman's no fool. Is he, Anselmo?' The stony eyes left Lazaro and bolted on to the tutor.

'Ah – no, indeed not, Excellency. But of course . . .'

Palafox held up a peremptory hand. 'It's no great matter,' he said. 'If he doesn't come tonight that will mean he's decided to abandon the boy and try to escape. Either way we'll catch him. What have you done with the boys, Anselmo?'

'As you ordered, Excellency. In the dormitory as usual, no special precautions taken.'

'Good.'

The tutor coughed uncomfortably. 'And . . . what is to happen to the boys if he doesn't come tonight, Excellency?'

'Either he comes tonight or not at all,' replied Palafox curtly. 'So you will have them ready for interrogation tomorrow at dawn.' He turned back to Brother Lazaro. 'Have my instructions concerning the sentries been carefully carried out?'

'Completely, Excellency.'

'You're quite sure, Lazaro? The outer ring is sparse? The lancers are out of the way?'

'Absolutely.'

'Clear orders have been given to the inner ring?'

'Exactly as you explained to me, Excellency.'

'Good. Then I think that's all for the moment.' Palafox walked slowly across the study and turned to face his two subordinates. 'You seem a little puzzled, Anselmo?'

'No, no, Excellency.' The tutor wavered, then took the plunge. 'But – aren't we making it all too easy for him?'

The smile on the pale face was fleeting. 'Our Lord, Brother Anselmo, used parables to explain to the simple-minded and perhaps I should do the same. Tell me, Anselmo, when a fisherman throws his net, does he cast it open or closed?'

'Open, Excellency, and thank you, Excellency, I think I understand now,' murmured Anselmo unhappily.

'And once the fish is caught in the mesh, can it swim out again?' insisted Palafox.

'No, Excellency, it can't.'

The Inquisitor-General's gaze was withering. 'That will be all, my brothers,' he said and turned back to his desk.

Parton stopped under a sheltering branch in the last clump of trees and his grip tightened on Gabriela's arm, holding her back under cover. He could see no light – there was scarcely a star to be seen between the clouds over the looming bulk of the monastery – and no movement. A dog was barking over towards Tepoztlán and Parton thought he heard a horse whicker down where Gabriela had told him the lancers were camping. But here at the back end of the monastery, the night was windless, dark and still. Ahead of them was a strip of dusty open ground, a path and the precinct wall. Parton strained his eyes, looking for sentries.

There had to be sentries. Up to now, it had not been too hard. Sentries were spread out here and there in the countryside around the town and monastery, but for him and Gabriela, their clothes grey and their faces darkened with earth, it had been relatively easy to sneak through under cover of the trees and bushes. Now it would be harder. The corners of the outer wall were the most likely positions. To the right, the hillside rose black and Parton could not even see the wall, let alone make out the corner and a possible sentry. To the left, he could see the corner, but no sentry. The man could be in the covering shadow of the wall. It was annoying. Parton had chosen to approach the monastery by this end, not only because the granary door was at the back, but because the grounds were overgrown from the outer wall to the building. No other side would do. Should he try to get the man to show himself? Should he jump him? No. He had to get into the monastery silently, without trace. He and Gabriela would have to sneak between the two supposed sentries and reach the wall unseen and unheard.

He slipped back to Gabriela's side. 'We're going to crawl across,' he breathed. 'Keep your head down.' He dropped quietly to the ground and snaked out of the covering trees and in among the tufts of dry, spiky grass which dotted the open ground. The grass was over two feet high here and there and it gave a little cover. There was neither sound nor movement from the corners of the wall. After all, the night was dark and if Parton couldn't see the sentries, the chances were they couldn't see him. He looked back to see Gabriela right behind him, following the same course between the clumps of grass. He hoped to God there were no snakes in the immediate vicinity. He reached the path – no more cover – and crawled the last few feet quickly, getting to his feet as Gabriela joined him. They crouched for a moment in the shadow at the foot of the wall, leaning back against the stones and breathing again. No feet shuffled in the dust of the path, no challenge rang out. Perhaps Palafox had

153

chosen to concentrate his men inside the monastery, thought Parton. The thought was sobering.

He tweaked Gabriela's sleeve and led the way, crouching, towards a large breach he had picked out the morning before. The ruined masonry formed a mound of stones and mortar rising almost to the gap above. Parton crept up and looked into the grounds. They were dark and silent. He waited. He heard no voices, no clearing of throats, no stamping of cramped feet, no rustle of movement among the bushes. He waited still longer, watching the black shape of the great building for the least sign of light or movement. He saw and heard nothing. He straddled the wall. The stones were still warm from the heat of the day. He swung his leg over and dropped softly inside. Gabriela was sitting on the wall now and he reached up, took her by the waist and helped her down, fearing the sound of even a small stone falling. None did. Dry grass crackled lightly beneath her feet as he set her down. There was no reaction from the darkness ahead. He led the way forward, bent double, among the stunted bushes.

The back wall of the monastery with its two doors looked out on to a semicircular patch of paved ground surrounded by low, thick shrubbery. Parton left the higher bushes, dropped to his stomach, and crawled into it, Gabriela beside him. As they brushed against the plants the mingled scents of kitchen herbs, basil, thyme, sage, tarragon, rose in the air. Parton chose a spot from which Gabriela would have a sweeping view across the back and down one side of the monastery without having to raise her head above the plants which gave her cover. 'Stay here,' he breathed into her ear. 'Don't forget the signal.' Gabriela shook her head. Parton pulled his boots off and left them beside her. He gave her arm a parting squeeze and crawled out of the herb plot.

He crossed the paved space, crouching, in a few rapid barefoot strides. He shrunk into the shelter of the wall and crept along it, looking round both corners for signs of sentries, listening long and hard at the door for sounds of guards inside. All seemed clear. He waited in the shadows, listening. It was barely possible that no sentries had been set. Or, the thought came back to chill him, they were all on the inside. He would soon see. There was no going back now. He padded softly past the door and unslung the ropes from his shoulders. He looked up. This was going to be tricky.

The big iron hook above the granary door was about fifteen feet up. His two ropes lashed together were twenty feet long, which meant that, with the rope running in the hook, the two ends together would hang about five feet from the ground. The difficulty of the climb was that it had to be carried out in total silence – including that first jump for the ends of the rope. If ever his long years of dog-hard work as a sailor were to be useful, it was now. The first problem was getting the rope up there and into the hook. He took from his jacket pocket a bundle of twine and a piece of cloth, then a round pebble he had picked up on the way there. He wrapped the cloth several times round the pebble and tied the end of the twine firmly round all of it. Then he unravelled the bundle of twine carefully, spreading it in wide loops at the foot of the wall and attached the other end to the end of the rope. With another piece of twine specially prepared beforehand, he lashed the two lengths of rope together. He was ready. He listened carefully. Not a sound. He hefted the cloth-covered stone in his hand and looked up, fixing his gaze on the hook's black silhouette against the dark sky, lowered his arm, bit his lip and lobbed the pebble upwards.

At the first attempt, the stone fell short of the hook and dropped back to the ground with a dull thud.

Parton froze and listened for a long, long moment before relooping the twine on the ground and trying again, this time holding the end of the rope high in his left hand so that its weight would not drag on the twine.

The stone shot clear over the hook and down the far side, scraping the wall almost soundlessly as it fell, then, the slack having run out, it swung back and hit Parton on the shoulder. He caught it quickly and hauled on it slowly, feeding the rope upwards by degrees with his left hand. The twine must not break under the strain. The rope reached the hook and Parton hauled gently. It followed the twine through with scarcely a hitch. Now the rope was running freely through the hook and Parton could draw the twine in quickly. When the lashing between the two lengths of rope snagged on the hook, he stopped and cut away the twine with his pocket-knife. The two ends of the rope dangled in front of him at shoulder height.

He listened again before moving. Then he crouched and leaped for the double rope, catching it cleanly, swinging his legs up in the same movement and pushing off and up against the wall with his bare feet. His hands rose quickly one above the other, pinching the two ropes firmly together and, knees bent, he pushed off the wall for the second time, then hooked a foot over the threshold of the granary door. He hung for a moment almost horizontally, then he took a deep breath and speedily hand-over-handed his way up the rope and stood up in the doorway.

He looked out into the grounds and listened. He knew he had hardly made a sound in climbing, but one sharp-eared sentry would be enough. All was quiet. He turned and pushed the door steadily. Of course it might have been checked and rebolted since that morning – but no, the bolt slipped easily and he pushed the door ajar. He lifted the rope from the hook, coiling it over his arm, looked in farewell towards the herb garden where Gabriela was hiding, stepped inside and closed the door behind him, half-bolting it to keep it shut.

He leaned back against the wall by the door and breathed out. Now he was inside, he realized that the cuts in his chest had been giving him pain for some time without his paying any attention to the fact. He looked around in the darkness. Gabriela had told him that the granary was almost empty and that there were no obstacles between the door and the trapdoor. He put the coiled rope down by the wall where it would be easy to find again and stepped tentatively forwards and to the left, towards the trapdoor. His outstretched hand touched the wall and he followed it, feeling for the trapdoor with his feet. He found it, knelt quietly and listened. There was no noise below. He lifted the trapdoor a few inches and peered down into the corridor. He could see and hear nothing. He raised it completely and slipped down on to the stairs, closing it over him as he padded down.

The back door was not guarded and was of no use to him and he wasted no time in the dark corridor. He knew where he was going and only his fear of running into a guard or of making some sudden noise and revealing his presence, slowed him to a stealthy walk. The corridors were silent and in all of them played the same thin, cool draught. Before the small courtyard where the friars had left their gardening tools, he turned aside and made for the little-used wing of the monastery where the cells were situated. They could not be much farther now.

He stopped abruptly, hugging the wall. Ahead and to the left came a trickle of light. He crept towards it, back to the wall. It was coming from a passage which he was sure he recognized. At the corner, he risked a wary glance. It was the corridor which led to the cells and the light was coming from under a door down there. He stayed in silence, listening, back to the wall. There was a sigh and the sound of a chairleg scraping on the stone floor, then there was silence again. Parton looked out circumspectly. The door was the door to Seward's cell. On the far side of it was a dark mass, hunched against the wall. There was another sigh. Parton began to make out the figure of a guard, sitting on a stool and leaning against the wall and either catching an uncomfortable nap or cleverly simulating it. There was no sign of a second guard further down the corridor. Parton slipped soundlessly out of hiding and crept down the passage, sure now that the guard was asleep and alone. The man's cowled head was lolling on his shoulder. He swallowed, shifted in his sleep and opened his eyes. He did not see Parton immediately. Parton's left hand gripped the cowl at the neck as his right hand clamped over the man's mouth and he jerked the head forwards then smashed it back into the wall. The guard slumped. Parton let him slowly to the ground and turned to the door. The key was in the lock. He wished there was a spyhole to enable him to see if there was another guard within. He turned the key slowly, as silently as possible, inched the door open and peered in.

The light came from a guttering candle on the table. There were no guards. On a mattress on the floor, fully-clothed, lay Seward. Parton closed the door and hurried over to him. He was asleep, breathing normally, apparently not unconscious. His face was bruised and puffy and there were bloodstains on his shirt. Parton shook his shoulder lightly.

Seward's eyes opened and focused slowly on Parton's face.

'Wha-what are you doing here?' he asked, shocked. 'How did you get out of your cell?' He struggled to a sitting position.

Parton put a finger to his lips. 'I escaped last night,' he whispered. 'I couldn't get to you. So I came back.'

Seward pointed shakily towards Parton's cell. 'I thought you were still there!'

'They weren't likely to buoy up your hopes by telling you I'd got away,' said Parton quietly. 'Can you walk?'

'Yes. I'll be all right. Bit bruised, that's all.' Seward was silent. Then he looked at Parton and burst out: 'I suppose they scared me more than anything. But I've got to tell you something. I broke down and told them everything, who we were, our real names, everything I could!'

'You were right to talk!' whispered Parton. 'What you told them doesn't matter now. You don't know anything really important about my mission, so there was no point in resisting for hours.'

'But don't you see, if I'd known more, I'd have told them!' insisted Seward feverishly. 'I'd have given everything away like a damn coward!' He broke off, shame-faced.

'There are no brave men or cowards where the Inquisition's concerned,' said Parton. 'Don't blame yourself. You were right to talk. Now that's enough. We have to get out of here.' He helped Seward to his feet. 'You'll have to carry your boots. We mustn't make a sound.' He led the way to the door and looked out. The guard was lying by his stool and Parton judged he would not wake up for some time. All the same, he took the man by the armpits and dragged him into the cell. Seward was out in the corridor now and Parton locked the door on the unconscious guard. Down the corridor, all was dark and silent. Parton hoped it would go on like that. He felt Seward's nerves shaky and wondered how well the younger man would be able to fend for himself in case of trouble. Parton shelved the question for the moment and brought to mind Maria-Dolores's description of the layout of the monastery. A lot depended now on the truthfulness of Palafox's mistress. Parton was aware of the contradiction – but he had done all he could to ensure she had not been lying. Up to now, her information had been good. Please God it would go on that way. She had said that the boys' dormitory was not far from the refectory. Parton turned at the top of the passage and led in that direction.

For several minutes, the two Englishmen padded silently through the maze of corridors, Parton absorbed in remembering directions. It was vital to make no mistake, to waste no time. Above all, they must not go on beyond the refectory into the front of the monastery, closer to Palafox's apartments, where guards were always thick on the ground.

Parton recognized the kitchen doors and walked past them. To the right, a corridor led to the double doors at the side of the refectory through which Palafox had come when he had trapped them the day before. After the doors, the corridor narrowed as Maria-Dolores had said it would. Further on, deep in shadow, was the flight of stone steps she had told him to expect and which led upwards to the dormitory.

Parton and Seward were at the foot of the steps, peering ahead, when a sudden murmur of voices broke out behind them and a bolt was drawn noisily. Parton grabbed Seward by the arm and dragged him up the steps into the darkness. The refectory door was opening and light was spilling out into the corridor behind them. Parton pulled Seward on a few more steps and held him still.

'Nothing!' came a soft voice from below. The light flickered, almost touching the two Englishmen's feet and Parton could smell the resinous smoke of a torch. The guards had perhaps heard a noise and were checking. He eased upwards a step, helping Seward to do the same. Seward wanted desperately to call out, to bring the guards on to them, to put an end to the masquerade. Parton would be taken prisoner, it would be all over . . . But Palafox had been brutally clear. 'He will come to the monastery and I hope he will succeed in making his way in. Our intention is to capture him once he has identified the boy. But our friend Parton is a dangerous and resilient man. He may escape us yet again. If he does so, I want you to be with him. He does not and must not suspect you. You can slow him by playing on the torture you're supposed to have undergone, but you must do nothing to shake his trust in you.' Do nothing, thought Seward. Do nothing and hope.

'Take a look down there, but don't waste time!' came a whispered command from below. The sound of the refectory door closing echoed through the long corridors and Parton took advantage of it to cover the last remaining steps in one movement, lifting Seward with him. Then there were footsteps and the light brightened below. Parton shrank back round the corner, his back to a door and flattened Seward against the wall next to him. Light filled the steps, the torch no doubt held high down there. Opposite Parton, the light fell on to the bottom half of a large, iron-riveted door. Parton's pulse quickened. The dormitory, exactly as Maria-Dolores had described it. He waited in silence, making ready to deal with the guard should he climb the steps to carry out a more thorough investigation. But the man seemed satisfied, because the light lessened abruptly and the footsteps retreated. They went on to the far end of the corridor and the top of the steps was in shadow again. But the guard would be back and Parton had only seconds in which to act. He crossed to the door and tried the enormous wrought-iron latch. It was well-oiled and lifted easily. The door swung open. Parton held it just ajar and listened to the sounds coming from within. Someone was snoring gently. It was dark in there. Below, the guard's footsteps seemed to be coming closer again. Parton reached for Seward, pulling him close and breathed in his ear, 'When we're in, stay by the door and don't for God's sake make a sound.' Seward nodded. Of course I won't, he thought bitterly.

Parton slipped inside, bringing Seward with him and shut the door again softly, painstakingly dropping the latch. The air was thick and the place smelled over-crowded. A child turned in his sleep with a rustle and a sigh. Parton tapped Seward's arm to let him know he was going to move forward. There had to be friars somewhere to guard the boys and they were the first target.

Then, thought Parton, would come a far from easy part. Which boy?

*

Gabriela lay flat on her stomach in the scented herb garden and looked out from under a bush. To her left, she could see the end wall with its doors and, straight ahead of her, the heavily buttressed side wall of the monastery. Her eyes were by now adjusted to what was a very dark night and she had seen and heard sentries going their rounds on two occasions. They had come down the side of the building, had stopped at the end to inspect the two doors, had noticed nothing amiss and had continued their round down the far side which she couldn't see. As far as she could reckon, there had been a fair quarter of an hour between their visits. That was enough to give Parton time to get down and away when he got back; and if by mischance he came back to the door just when a sentry was passing, she would do her job. She would not give the all-clear signal and he would wait up there with the door closed until she did. Things might go wrong, but it was the best they could do in the circumstances.

Gabriela wriggled and wished she could get up and stretch her cramped legs. She had been lying without moving for almost half an hour now. Parton had given himself an hour in which to succeed. She thought of his hard, muscular body and pressed herself to the warm ground. Of course he would come back, she told herself. It was just a matter of waiting . . .

She jumped and narrowed her eyes. Was that a movement down the side of the monastery? It was. Someone was coming. It wasn't a sentry unless they came at quite irregular times. That was possible and it would be a problem. But the sentries had made enough noise for her to hear them before they came into view. This man was making no sound at all. He seemed to glide silently along the path, a tall figure in black, the face pale . . .

Gabriela felt suddenly, terribly, afraid. She shrank deep

into the cover of the bushes, closed her eyes for a second, then looked out again.

The man was reaching the corner of the building now and she could see him better. His walk was steady and controlled, his long features white, his hair grey. The black cape swished silkily against his shoes as he moved softly forward.

Without ever having seen this man before, with only a few scant words of description from Parton to go on, she was nonetheless sure beyond doubt that she knew who this man was. She was looking at Palafox, the Inquisitor-General of New Spain.

Then her heart leaped into her mouth.

He was walking straight towards her.

Palafox walked on past the herb garden and into the overgrown shrubbery behind Gabriela. She pinched her forearm hard as if to stop dreaming and turned on her side to see which way he had gone. She could no longer see him, but she could hear him as he made his way through the untidy bushes towards the wall.

There was a long silence. Gabriela raised her head as high as she dared and listened. Low voices came from the precinct wall. Palafox was talking to someone out there. The voices stopped and picked up further on. Gabriela presumed that Palafox and another man were walking along the wall together. There was a new silence, then a fresh murmur of voices further round.

Then Gabriela realized. Palafox was not walking with another man. There were sentries along the wall at regular intervals and Palafox was going the rounds, stopping and talking to each man in turn.

Had the sentries been posted in silence since she and Parton had come over the wall? Or had they been there all along, hiding in the shadows? What were the chances that she and Parton had really got in unseen? Gabriela began to feel like a rabbit in a snare.

*

Parton moved forward between the two long rows of beds. Halfway down the dormitory, he could make out a kind of big, whitish rectangle. As he moved towards it, it became clearer. It was a cubicle. A bedroom for a friar on dormitory duty?

He stopped in front of it and looked at it carefully. It appeared to be composed of curtains hanging from rails above. There were beds on either side and the wall behind, so there had to be an opening on the side he was looking at. He found the edge of the curtain and drew it stealthily aside. He could see nothing in there, but he could hear steady breathing. He inched forward and his knee touched something soft, the bed no doubt.

The man on the bed stirred in his sleep and turned over. In spite of the darkness, the movement was visible. Parton saw the man's head just beneath him. He slowly unhooked a pistol from his belt, settled it in the palm of his hand, the butt protruding and decided which way the man was facing. Then he pinned the jaw and neck with his knee while he struck down hard at the back of the head. The body jerked and went limp. Parton bent and listened to the man's breathing. The blow had been heavy and the man would not move for some time. Parton hooked the pistol back on to his belt and felt around in the darkness. The cubicle was narrow. There was a bedside table, nothing of any interest.

The curtain behind him rustled and a voice murmured, 'Anything wrong?'

Only Parton's eyes moved. He saw the dark outline of the head framed in the triangular opening of the curtain.

'Aureliano? Anything wrong?' The friar stepped into the cubicle and reached down to touch his colleague's shoulder.

Parton's arm shot out and he pulled the newcomer forward and into his rising fist. The blow connected with the chin, but it was too short and the man staggered over

164

Parton, kicking out wildly. Parton straightened up, pushed the man on to the bed on top of his fellow and struck down. He was not sure which of the men he hit. The newcomer was rolling away from him, arms flailing, grasping at the curtain. He was going to pull the whole cubicle down and raise the alarm if Parton didn't stop him rapidly. There was no room for a clean, decisive blow. Parton flung himself forward, hands to the man's throat and locked his thumbs over the windpipe. The friar thrashed wildly, raining blows on Parton's back and ribs. Parton squeezed. The blows became feebler. Parton held on. The blows stopped. Parton did not let go. When he was sure the friar was unconscious, he counted to ten before taking his hands away. He was already listening carefully. The fight had made a fair amount of noise and if there were other friars guarding the boys in the dormitory, they would be making ready for combat by now. But no, he thought, they would first have called out and raised the alarm. There were probably only two guards. There was whispering going on out there. He slid from the bed and opened the curtain. The whispering stopped as if by magic. Parton grinned and took the candle and tinderbox from his pocket. He struck a light and lit the candle, shading it in case there were windows from which it could be seen and left the cubicle.

He looked immediately at the four windows on the opposite wall. They were shuttered and there was no sign of alarm anywhere out in the building, but he decided to go on shading the candle all the same. He ran his eyes along the two rows of beds. A few frightened faces stared wide-eyed over the sheets in the half-circle of yellow light cast by the candle. One or two of the older boys were whispering excitedly, but a good many others were hiding under the bedclothes. Parton blessed Cameron from the bottom of his heart. He knew he had to reassure the boys, to win them over to his side. He beckoned Seward over from the door and set him to watch the two friars stretched out in the cubicle, then he looked round as the whispers got louder, not sure how to begin.

'You're the prisoner,' said one of the older boys.

'You're the one who said they'd kill our fathers,' said another.

'Sssh!' said Parton. There had been no condemnation in their voices, but it was sure that he must have frightened the boys in the classroom the day before. He grinned reassuringly. 'We must be quiet!' he whispered. 'There's a guard prowling about down by the refectory!'

Silence fell stonelike. Of course, realized Parton, there was no love lost between the boys and the friars.

'Why has he got a dirty face?' whispered someone.

'To hide from the friars,' said Parton. 'They can't see me in the dark.'

'Didn't you hear him fighting them?' rejoined one of the first boys scornfully. 'What did you do to them?' he asked, turning to Parton and sitting up. He had red hair and he was wearing a night shirt like the other boys.

'Sssh!' reminded Parton, glad to find an ally. 'I knocked them out.'

'Don't believe you!'

'Go and look! No, not all of you, just him!' Parton pointed to the red-haired boy. 'Show him,' he whispered to Seward. Seward held the curtain shakily open while Parton lit the cubicle with the candle. The boy looked in then turned back to Parton, his eyes shining. 'Completely knocked out cold,' he announced. 'How did you do it?'

'Hit him with this,' whispered Parton conspiratorially, showing one of the pistols at his waist.

'A pistol!' said the boy, awed. 'Bet it doesn't work.'

'Oh yes it does,' Parton assured him.

'Could you knock any other fried beans out?' came a new voice.

'All of them,' replied Parton firmly, supposing that fried beans meant friars. A buzz of excitement ran through the dormitory. '*Sssh*! We have to keep it a secret!' whispered Parton, pointing to the door.

'Who's he?' asked the redhead, looking at Seward.

'He was a prisoner too. We're escaping. We need help.' There was a fresh buzz of excited chatter and Parton waited for silence before adding casually, 'If you like, you can help us.'

'Oh, yes!' Heads nodded vigorously. 'What do you want us to do? Can I shoot a fried bean with your pistol?' asked the red-haired boy.

Parton shook his head, smiling. He had got them, he thought triumphantly. 'That would raise the alarm,' he told them, 'and we must be absolutely – *absolutely* – silent.' Forty boys caught breath as one. 'What would help us would be to have you hiding all over the place,' he went on. 'Something like hide and seek. The friars will be busy looking for you and in the confusion we'll be able to get away. What do you think?'

'Not bad,' said the redhead.

'I know a good hiding-place!' came a voice.

'Who doesn't?'

'I bet mine's better!'

'Quiet!' Parton stopped it. 'The first thing is to get dressed *without a sound*. No noise at all. All right?'

There were cho17ed whispers of assent. The boys dressed hurriedly, at great pains not to make too much noise, although there was some. Parton went over to a window, masking the candle, and listened. Out there was a cloister which gave on to the refectory and part of the kitchens. There were certainly guards down there. For the moment, all was quiet. He went to the door. No light came under it and he supposed that the guard had gone back through the refectory door after his inspection of the corridor. All the same, there was no going back down there with forty boys. Maria-Dolores had told him of a second door at the end of the dormitory and they would have to use that. The whispering was rising again and he turned to the boys and quietened one or two who were beginning to get excited.

'Now. I want you to split into two groups,' he whispered. 'Here,' he pointed to a space on his right, 'all the boys from ten upwards. And here,' he pointed to his left, 'all the boys who are less than ten. Got it?' The boys shuffled into place and there was a little pushing and shoving. 'Absolute silence!' warned Parton. 'Don't forget your shoes scrape on the floor.' The groups finished forming up and silence fell.

Parton beckoned to the red-haired boy. 'You're the leader of this group,' he told him, pointing to the younger boys. In the older group, he picked out one of the boys who had spoken first along with the redhead. 'And you're the leader here,' he said. 'Both leaders must check their men. Make sure no one's missing and no one's in the wrong group.'

The redhead turned back to him. 'All here,' he reported.

'Not one missing? It's important.'

'No, not one.'

'Nor here,' the second leader whispered.

'No one's in the wrong group? For example,' Parton whispered to the redhead, 'all the boys aged eight are in your group?'

'They're all here. No one's missing.'

'Good. Now we have to get out of here without the friars noticing. Isn't there another door down there?' He pointed to the shadowy end wall.

'Yes!' said several voices at once. 'Behind the curtain.' Parton walked towards a heavy baize curtain covering half the wall. He pulled it aside. There was indeed a door behind it. Maria-Dolores had said it gave on to a corridor

from which he could find his way back towards the granary.
He tried the door and felt his heart sink.

It was locked.

CHAPTER NINE

'The key's on the other side,' whispered the leader of the older boys. 'You can get it with a sheet –'

'Let me!' The redhead pushed forward with a sheet pulled from a bed in passing. He spread one end on the floor and slid it under the door for a foot or so. Then he took the other end, twisted the corner tightly into a point and poked it into the keyhole. There was a rattle as the key fell. The boy pulled the sheet back carefully and retrieved the key. 'Of course, I've had practice,' he whispered modestly, handing it to Parton.

'Good work,' grinned Parton. He went back to the cubicle. The two friars were still unconscious and looked as if they would be for some time. 'Ready to go?' he asked Seward.

'I'll be all right.'

'Come on.' Parton led the way back to the door. The boys were becoming impatient and Parton sensed that it was time to move before a rumpus broke out. 'All right, we're going,' he announced. 'But first a reminder. We must not be heard. No talking, no laughing, no scuffing shoes. Is that clear?' The boys nodded solemnly. Parton hoped that their fear of the friars would be powerful enough to keep them quiet. He unlocked the door, blew out the candle and looked out into the corridor. It was draughty and empty. To the left, it led to the cloister and there was a little vague light from the kitchen or the refectory at that end. To the right, the darkness thickened.

Parton turned back and whispered, 'The older group first. Turn right outside the door.' He stepped out, letting the boys through, hissing softly at them as they passed to quieten them. If they were to get out of hand now, all would be lost. The redhead led the younger ones out, then Seward followed, shutting the door. The two men followed the boys down the corridor.

They were making a tremendous effort, Parton recognized, but even so some noise, shuffling, light footfalls, an occasional cough, was inevitable. He wished there had been some other way of doing things, but he couldn't think of one. If he were to have taken the boy alone and left the others in the dormitory, the Spanish would have had no difficulty in learning the name. The longer Palafox was kept in ignorance of the boy's identity, the greater Parton's slim chances of success would be.

The older boys ahead were stopping at a crossing where corridors branched in several directions and a flight of stairs led down. Parton moved up and whispered to the leader. The older boys filed off down a side corridor on their way to hiding-places they had assured Parton were good. They would need them, thought Parton, wishing them luck. He drew the leader of the younger group aside. 'Do you have an idea for a really good hiding-place?' he whispered.

'I know one, but I don't know if you'll be strong enough,' said the boy dubiously.

'I expect I can manage. What would I have to do?'

'There's a crypt under the oratory down there.' He pointed. 'I saw it wide open one day when we were at prayers. But usually there's a great big stone slab over the top of the steps.'

'What's in it?'

'Statues. Nothing much, really.'

'Won't there be any friars in the chapel?'

The redhead looked at him askance. 'At night? Not likely.'

Parton thought quickly. The oratory was not far. He doubted if the stone slab would be too much for him. And the hiding-place sounded good . . . 'All right. Lead the way,' he said.

He rejoined Seward and they followed the boys down the

stairs. There was less noise now that there were fewer boys. Parton watched them go down and thought: I've narrowed it down. *The* boy was one of the eight-year-olds ahead of him. If all went well, he would single him out in the next couple of minutes. The boys were down and going through a corridor now. There was some clatter at the oratory door as they went in before Parton could hold them back, but, as the group leader had forecast, the place was empty. The red lamp over the altar cast a dim light. Painted plaster cherubim smiled down as Parton, Seward and the boys followed the redhead to the side of the chapel. 'Here!' he whispered, pointing down.

Parton bent to the carved slab. He felt round its edges until he found a spot where he could grip it. He heaved. The slab was heavy, but he lifted it slowly and leaned it against the wall. A draught came up from the hole at his feet, proof that there was at least some fresh air down there.

Now was the time. . . . 'Before you go down,' he whispered, 'listen to me. That medallion yesterday. Did they show it to you again?'

'Yes. But after what you shouted, nobody owned up to knowing it.'

'But one of you recognized it,' said Parton softly.

The silence was suddenly tense.

'Don't worry, I'm not with the friars. I'm against them. You know that,' Parton reasured them. 'One of you, a boy of eight, recognized that medallion because it was his. I want that boy to understand that I don't want to do him any harm. His father sent me here to look for him. That's why I had the medallion. But the friars took it from me and tried to use it to find out which of you it belonged to. I shouted to stop them from doing it.' He paused.

'Are you going to take me away from here?' came a small voice.

Heads turned. 'Fernando!' whispered someone.

'Yes,' replied Parton, trying, like Seward, to see which boy had spoken.

'To my father?'

'Yes.' I hope to Christ he's going to *want* to come, thought Parton.

'Why didn't he come for me himself?'

'He couldn't. He sent me in his place.'

'All right.' The boy came forward. In the reddish light cast by the altar lamp, Parton saw a slim boy of medium height for his age, with dark hair and eyes. One more test, he thought. He bent to the boy's ear. 'Whisper to me who gave you the medallion,' he breathed.

'Margarita,' whispered the boy without hesitating. 'My nurse in Cordoba.'

'Right,' said Parton. 'Down you go,' he said to the red-haired boy. As the boys trooped down the steps into the crypt, Parton found himself wishing he could take them all away from the dismal place. He hated the idea of shutting them up down there. But they would be retrieved before too long – dreary hours for them, perhaps, but absolutely essential if he were to stand a chance of getting away with the boy beside him. 'Good luck to you all,' he whispered as the last boy disappeared. 'And if you've really had enough after a few hours, shout.' He let the slab carefully back into place and turned to the boy.

'So your name's Fernando?' he asked.

'Of course.' Wide dark eyes studied the adult in the dim light.

'Fernando,' Parton repeated. 'Good. Let's be on our way.' He gestured to Seward, put an arm round Fernando's shoulder and turned towards the door, exulting.

He had the boy.

Gabriela dared not breathe. Palafox was back and he was standing in the semicircular space at the end of the building. Gabriela watched as he went to the tradesmen's entrance and tried the door. Then he stepped back and looked upwards.

Gabriela stuffed her fist into her mouth. If Parton were to come back and open the door now . . .

Palafox turned and quietly disappeared round the far corner of the monastery. Gabriela relaxed a little and began to breathe again. He had noticed nothing suspicious, she told herself. And if he knew they were there, why had he tried the door?

Then the granary door opened a few inches and Parton looked out. Gabriela found herself desperately wanting to call out and warn him, but Palafox could not be far and he would hear. Worse still, Parton might misunderstand, might take her shout for the all-clear signal and climb down. She had to remain silent. It was what they had agreed on in case of danger and it was what she must do.

The granary door closed silently and she could no longer see Parton's face. She shrank into the bushes and waited.

Parton cursed silently and held the door shut. He had neither seen or heard anything suspicious out there. Still, if Gabriela had not given the agreed signal, there was something wrong. Damn it, everything had gone well up to now and now he had the boy. . . . 'All right, Fernando?' he asked softly.

'Yes.'

There was little more to be got from him, but it was understandable. Parton tested the noose he had made at the end of the rope. It must not slip when weight was put on it. He went back to the door and listened. All was silent outside. He opened it a crack and peered out. The darkness was so thick he could not see the precinct wall. The semicircle below was empty. He looked towards the dark patch of the herb garden, but there was no sign of Gabriela. He had been inside the monastery for the best part of an hour. Could she have decided that he wasn't coming out, had she left as he had told her to if that happened? Or – he didn't want to admit the possibility, to face it – had she been captured, had he put her into Palafox's hands?

The slightest of sounds, not so much as a whisper, reached

him. It had come from the herb garden. It came again, then a third time. Parton breathed out. Gabriela was there after all and she was giving the signal. He opened the door wider and slipped the rope over the hook as it had been when he had climbed up. Fernando had already been drilled in what he had to do. Parton brought him out on to the threshold and pointed to the herb garden. Fernando nodded to show he had understood. He put his feet in the noose at the end of the rope as if it were a stirrup, held himself steady with his hands higher up the rope and Parton paid out the rope and lowered him gently to the ground. He watched as the boy took his feet from the noose and raced to the herb garden where he disappeared. Parton brought the rope back up and let Seward down in the same way.

'Quickly!' Gabriela's whisper was clear and urgent.

Parton stood on the threshold, pulled the door to, sat down, and let himself drop. He landed beside Seward and although he scarcely brushed him, Seward fell back. Parton helped him up, pushed him on his way towards the herb garden, picked up the fallen rope, and sprinted after him. He caught Seward before he had reached cover and helped him on his way. The two men slipped in among the herbs and lay flat.

Parton listened as he caught his breath. There were no suspicious sounds. He crawled forward, bringing Seward with him.

'Here,' breathed Gabriela.

Fernando was with her. Parton slid forward until his head was by hers. 'What's wrong?'

'I think it's Palafox who keeps coming and going. And there are sentries all along the wall. I heard him talking to them. I can't help feeling it's all a trap!'

Parton closed his eyes. So the calm inactivity of the monastery was only a show, as he had been tempted to fear several times. Each time he had chased the thought immediately from his mind. Now he had to face it. Palafox was playing his easiest card: let Parton come to the monastery and identify the boy, then move in and kill two birds with one stone. That meant there would be men all along the precinct wall and doubtless out in the surrounding countryside, waiting for the order to close in.

'Do you think he knows we're here?' he breathed into Gabriela's ear.

'I don't know. He walked past me as if he didn't know I was here. And he tried the door and looked up at the granary and why do that if he knew for sure?' she whispered back.

The guard at the refectory door hadn't behaved as if he had been sure, either, thought Parton. There was a chance – a very slight one – that Palafox was unaware of their presence. How long would it be before one of the men Parton had put out of action came to and gave the alarm? Until then, perhaps they had the advantage of surprise.

'This is Fernando,' he whispered to Gabriela, realizing that he himself would have to look after Seward. 'Fernando, this is Gabriela. I want you to stay close to her and let her help you.' Gabriela reached out among the bushes and gave Fernando's hand a reassuring squeeze. Parton fumbled for his boots and pulled them on. The rope could remain where it was, hidden by the bushes, he thought. He took Seward by the arm and helped him crawl forwards.

They left the herb garden and crossed the rougher bushes beyond without incident. Fernando, with Gabriela, seemed to be doing well; he moved neatly and quietly and Parton thought that of course a boy was better at sneaking through the dark than an adult. But Fernando could have been frightened, nervous, irresolute, and he wasn't. Seward was more of a problem. He was quiet, but slow. Either his nerve had gone or he was exhausted and perhaps in pain and too proud to admit it. Parton wondered, for a fleeting instant, what he should do if it came to a choice between the boy and Seward. He dismissed the question out of hand. He would

176

leave neither of them behind for Palafox to take vengeance on.

Parton looked out quickly. The precinct wall was close, the breach a little way to their right. There might be a sentry there now. He stopped the three others and crawled ahead towards it.

The darkness was a friend, but it was also an enemy. If he was well hidden, so were Palafox's men. Parton edged round the breach soundlessly. He could make no mistake now. If there was a sentry, he had to find him and dispatch him in silence.

He was there, five or six yards to the right of the breach, alone, huddled at the base of the wall, his face a paler mark in the thick blackness. Parton was sure no sentry had been as close to the breach as that when they had climbed in. He was going to be difficult to take with his back to the wall like that. Perhaps he could be decoyed away. Parton snapped a twig and crept silently off to the right. The pale blotch of the face moved. The man was standing now, he was moving forwards – Parton heard the slight dry crunch of a footstep on the rubble below the breach – then he had stopped and was surely staring into the darkness towards the spot where the noise had come from. Parton could just make out the vague outline of the upper part of the man's body against the greyness above the breach. He crept forward, judging the distance, planning his movements, picked up a chunk of rock, took three long strides, and he was at the man's back before the head began to turn – too late – in surprise. Parton's hand gagged him and the rock thumped down, once only, on to the skull. Parton lowered him gently to the ground, listening, scanning the surrounding darkness. The attack seemed to have gone unnoticed. He left the limp body and crawled back to the others.

'The way's clear,' he whispered. 'Fernando?'

'Yes?'

'We're going to climb over the wall now. We have to be

very quiet and very careful. Let Gabriela help you. Understand?'

'I understand.'

'Good. Let's go.'

The sentry was still lying at the bottom of the breach. Parton helped Gabriela up first then handed Fernando to her. The pile of rubble on the outside was high and she would need no more help. Parton turned to Seward.

'There! On the wall!'

The shout came from some way back inside the grounds. Parton pushed Seward up into the breach and followed, looking back. The shadows were moving. Feigning exhaustion, Seward hesitated. It would be so easy now to melt away into the darkness and be done with it. 'Get over and *run!*' came Parton's urgent voice from below. No, thought Seward, he's capable of seeking you out in the dark and nobly saving you. And Palafox had ordered: 'If he escapes, you must stay close and do nothing to make him suspect you.' What pity or forgiveness could Seward hope for on the Inquisitor-General's part if he failed? None. There was no escape. Parton was pushing him now, forcing him over the breach.

'On the wall! On the wall!' Men were running, shouts coming from all around and flaming torches, one after the other, began to appear from the front end of the monastery as Parton looked back. Above him, Seward rolled over the breach and Parton scrambled up to take his place. In the torchlight fifty yards back he saw the tall black figure of Palafox gesturing towards the wall. Something in the jerkiness of his movements gave Parton hope as he dropped over on the outside, helping Seward up and on after Gabriela and the boy, already running. Somewhere, there had been a hitch in the Inquisitor-General's plan. They had succeeded in surprising him. They were still in with their slim chance.

Hope lent wings. Even with Seward to help along, Parton

covered ground quickly, catching Gabriela and Fernando as they ran out of a belt of trees and into open country. 'Straight on!' yelled Parton, glancing back. Torches were waving and bobbing back there and he could imagine men pouring over the breach to take up the pursuit. For the moment, they were not close enough to be dangerous. Whether there were other men lying in wait somewhere out ahead was another problem.

Crack. That was a pistol shot. Cra-crack. There were more. Pistols were not really worrying, but muskets could be. There were musketeers among the soldiers and Palafox was unlikely to have overlooked the fact. The night was dark, but here on open ground visibility was just good enough for expert shots to be dangerous. It would be wiser to run for cover.

Ahead and to the right were trees. To the left, the open ground sloped up gradually towards a hillside. As Parton recalled it, the hillside at this point offered little more than the occasional dry bush or rock as shelter. The direction the hillside was in was the right one, because it led away from the Indian ruins and he did not want to make for them openly at this stage. But the lack of cover was decisive. They would make for the trees.

He called to the others, pointing, wheeling Seward round. Shots were coming faster now and one or two louder bangs suggested musketry. Parton was glad to see the trees looming closer. The torchlight behind them was surely picking them out as targets. Once into the wood and perhaps out on the far side, they would have clearer options. He sprinted on.

Then he saw the friars.

There were about half a dozen of them and they were breaking cover, coming out of the trees at a run, fanning out to cut off the fugitives' path. Parton sized them up. One each for Seward, Gabriela, and Fernando – that left three for him. They were certainly not true clerics, but some of

179

Palafox's tough mercenaries. All the same, three men surprised at being attacked by one made better odds than being picked off by marksmen in the open. . . .

'Run straight at them—' he began, then broke off. Torches flamed up among the trees. The six ahead were no more than the vanguard. The woods were crawling with Palafox's men. The trap was massive, the surprise effect of the breakout reduced to nothing. Now there was no choice but to head for the hillside as slow-moving targets for the musketeers.

Gabriela, Fernando's hand in hers, had already changed direction. Parton dragged Seward with him, following the first two. Behind them, their pursuers approached and ahead, the torches were spreading, moving from the trees towards the hillside as Palafox's men cut off their escape. Firing broke out afresh. With torchlight in front and torchlight behind, they would be easier and easier to see and the musketeers would not be long in getting sights. Would they have orders to choose their targets? The boy was an obvious choice. Parton slanted his course even further to the left in hopes of bringing some of the torchbearers themselves under fire and slowing them. The ground began to slope more steeply upwards and Seward, weakened, was struggling. The boy, too, was beginning to stumble and the moment would come when he would have to be carried. Running uphill was suicidal. They had to get past the line of cowled mercenaries coming from the right and the only way to do it was to sprint straight ahead, parallel to the hillside, while there was still some sprint left in their legs.

'This way!' panted Parton, pushing Gabriela and Fernando forwards along the foot of the slope, forcing the pace. A musket ball whirred through the air not far over their heads. Before the shooting got murderous, the fugitives had to be beyond the line of torches and out of range. But the new direction brought them automatically closer to the friars running towards them and into the light cast by the torches. A shout went up. They had been clearly sighted. A musket ball smacked into a rock just in front of them, setting a tuft of dry grass alight. Parton urged the others on, bundling Seward forward, taking Fernando's other hand, telling them it was now or never. Between the steep slope of the hillside and the advancing line of mercenaries there was an ever-narrowing gauntlet to be run, a gauntlet streaked by following fire. All that mattered now was sheer speed, was outflanking that advancing line, was staying on your feet and running to save your life.

Only yards now. The first group of friars – no doubt the half-dozen who had been the first to break cover – was almost in a position to cut them off. Between them and the torches of the following group was a gap of perhaps twenty yards. 'In between!' called Parton, turning and charging for the gap. They were there in seconds, running in between the two groups, the first friars yelling and milling round to come back on them. One of them fell abruptly and Parton realized that Palafox would not hold his musketeers' fire to protect his own men. That wasn't a bad thing, it was adding to the confusion and the torchbearers were only yards away now. He could see that there would be fighting. He urged the others on into the gap and turned to charge the torchbearers, defying them, refusing the boy's capture, and Gabriela's, and Seward's, and his own. He caught the first with a swinging blow that sent the man sprawling, ripped the firebrand from another and poked it into the man's eyes, flung it at two others who ran up and tore away from the group and after the stumbling Seward.

Gabriela and Fernando were through, but the first group on their way back were closing on him and Seward. Seward wasn't going to make it. Parton drew a pistol, cocked it and fired on the cowled assassin who was only feet away from Seward. The friar went down with a scream and Parton rushed on, taking Seward's arm, hauling him on with him. There were shouts and curses just behind him and Parton felt a hand clutch at his back. He turned and struck out with the pistol and the man slid down his back and grabbed him by the leg. Parton swivelled round and booted the face with all his force and then he was free and running on with Seward and Gabriela and Fernando. They were leaving Palafox's trap behind them, only yards behind them, but the jaws of the trap closing on nothing.

Then there were bushes and a field of maize, and trees, and no henchmen of the Inquisitor-General waiting in ambush. The four of them staggered on and disappeared into the welcoming shadows.

Parton struck a light with the tinderbox, found the candle-stub on the floor, lit it and took out his pocket-knife. There was no time to be lost. 'We can drink and catch our breath, then we must go,' he said, cutting the twine at Maria-Dolores's ankles.

'They *can't*,' said Gabriela between breaths, indicating Fernando and Seward. The boy stood beside her, rigid, a fist knuckling a dirty, tearful eye. As for Seward, pale, he sat slumped back against the wall, his eyes closed.

Parton untied Maria-Dolores's gag and passed her a canteen as she gulped in air. 'No choice,' he said briefly. 'We shook them off, but we can't wait now for them to pick up our trace. We have to disappear.' He took the canteen back and drank himself. There was not much water left. He crouched over Seward and handed him the canteen. 'I need your guiding light,' he said.

Seward drank a little and breathed out wearily. 'Which way do we go from here, is that it?' he asked.

'That's it. Given that Mexico City's out.'

Seward stared. 'Out? Why? It's the only way!'

Parton ticked off the reasons on his fingers. 'Because it's too obvious. Because the road there will be swarming with

Palafox's men. Because he'll have sent word there to search for us. Because the Mexico City Inquisition is all too powerful.'

Seward was silent for a moment, thinking. Then he said, 'We could go south from here – strike across country – and round the southern end of the range of volcanoes. Then we could cut across east towards Puebla and pick up the main road there. If that's the right general direction, that is.'

Parton nodded. 'The main road at Puebla, or better, after Puebla, all right. But not south from here. South means crossing rolling, open countryside for mile after mile. We'd be right in the middle of it at dawn. At dawn, they'll have the lancers out. They'd round us up like cattle before the end of the morning.' He paused. 'You talked about an old Indian road up there in the mountains.'

Seward looked at him with something like panic. 'We can't go up there!' he protested. 'Not in the state we're in! It's . . . it's damn high up there, it's difficult, for God's sake, there's snow! I don't know if there's any more than a rough track left of the road. We could get lost on the mountain, we could get caught in the snow . . . Anything could happen to us!'

Parton did not reply immediately. He alone knew of the rendezvous on the night of the tenth, four days away. He alone knew that, as soon as Palafox learned the identity of the kidnapped boy, he would send out riders to carry the name to wherever the father was, and that those messengers had to be beaten to it. The Indian road through the high pass was the straightest and shortest way from Tepoztlán to Puebla.

'North and south are out,' he said, standing. 'I'm afraid we have to go through the pass.'

'But—' began Seward, then clamped his mouth shut. Stay close, he thought. Hinder him, but stay close.

Parton looked at Fernando. The boy seemed better for a few minutes' rest and candlelight. He was nibbling at a *tortilla* which Gabriela had magically whisked out of one of the packs for him. Behind him, Maria-Dolores sat rubbing life back into her wrists and ankles. Parton looked at the stained, crumpled remains of the sumptuous lace gown and the tatters of her fine silk slippers. She could still be useful in a standoff, he thought, but how could she keep up with them attired like that?

Maria-Dolores caught his glance. 'I told you the truth about the monastery,' she said challengingly. Was she afraid he was about to get rid of her, wondered Parton? 'And I came back to free you,' he replied. 'You're coming with us, tonight at least. You might still be of some use.' He turned to Seward. 'Is there a place on the way where we could buy provisions and perhaps even find horses?' he asked.

'There's a town called Amecameca at the foot of the volcanoes,' said Seward briefly.

'How soon can we be there?'

'In this state, not before mid-morning.'

Parton slung his pack over his shoulder and picked up the flickering candle to light them to the door. 'We're going to have to do better than that,' he said. 'Come on.'

For Anselmo, the hatchet-faced tutor, whose incompetence at the refectory door had, according to Palafox, put Parton on his guard and sent him off in another direction with the boys, the reckoning was swift and harsh. Anselmo was locked up in a cell, awaiting his transfer to Mexico City where he would provide the Chinese executioner with subject matter. As Brother Lazaro, deep in the night, came to the Inquisitor-General's apartments to bring his report, the idea was making him ill. Palafox had still not announced his intentions concerning his aide. What will he do to me? worried Lazaro, waiting for the signal to speak.

Palafox turned to face him. There was nothing to be read in the Inquisitor-General's features, the line of the mouth non-committal, the pale eyes now totally expressionless.

Lazaro knew that that was a bad sign. When you could *see* the man's anger, it was little more than skin-deep. . . .

'The boys, Lazaro,' began Palafox. '*Which boy?*'

Lazaro's heart sank. The bad news would have to come first. 'I'm afraid . . . eighteen boys are still missing, Excellency, in spite of a thorough search.'

'*Thorough*? They haven't disappeared into thin air, Lazaro. We watched the Englishman escape with one boy, just one. The others are here somewhere. The matter is urgent and I suggest you find them quickly.' The suggestion had been proffered in a near-whisper. 'What else have you to report?'

Lazaro, relieved, hurried on to his good news. A rope had been found in the bushes and the mystery of the granary door had been solved. The duty friar on the back door, who had let the baker's wife and the girls in the morning before, had told of seeing the black-haired girl on the staircase. The baker and his wife, rousted out and questioned, had given a description of the girl who had come looking for work and then had disappeared from the town. 'So not only do we know how the Englishman got in so easily and silently, but also that there were no traitors on the inside,' concluded Lazaro, glad to be able to stress both points.

Palafox's smile was thin and Lazaro felt no better. 'Lazaro,' said the Inquisitor-General tonelessly, 'you and I have worked together for many years and perhaps this disposes me to leniency in your case, which is less clear than Anselmo's. Perhaps we can concede that your placing of the sentries was not entirely blameworthy – although I did find it necessary to reposition them when I had the good idea of going the rounds. By that time, of course, our man was already inside.' His eyes narrowed. 'The granary door was clever. It allowed him to break in soundlessly, which we didn't expect. And all thanks to this . . . baker's girl. We can be sure she is the one we saw running with the boy. Add her description to all new messages going out.'

'Certainly, Excellency.' Lazaro was beginning to breathe again.

Palafox caught his eye. 'You're under stay of execution, Lazaro,' he hissed. 'Do you understand?'

Lazaro's breathing stopped. 'Yes, Excellency.'

'Now.' Palafox began to pace up and down. 'There are two lines along which we are going to work. The boy's father is one, hence the urgency of finding the boys. Are Porfirio and Bernardo ready?'

'Yes, Excellency and awaiting orders.'

'As soon as we know the boy's identity, they will leave with the name and they will ride day and night, take ship if need be, until they reach the traitor. Needless to say, I want him alive if possible.' Palafox turned. 'The second line is obviously pursuit of the fugitives. We don't know which way they'll try to go but the Inquisition in every major town is on the alert. The road to the capital is being watched. As soon as light permits, the lancers will be out and their orders will be to sweep the plain in all directions around Tepoztlán. Until then, keep as many men out with torches as you can – without forgetting that you still haven't found the boys.'

'Very well, Excellency.'

'We'll stay in Tepoztlán for the moment. The fugitives may be found locally, or somewhere out in the countryside, before the day is through. If not, we may well move back to the capital – have horses kept saddled and ready.'

There was a knock at the door. Lazaro hurried across and opened it. After a brief exchange, he shut the door and came back towards Palafox, radiant. 'They've found the boys, Excellency! They were all fast asleep in the crypt under the oratory, there's a heavy stone slab and—'

'For God's sake, man!' Palafox gripped Lazaro's arm so hard that he cried out in pain. '*Which boy?*'

'To – Torres Mendieta!'

Palafox stiffened. '*Torres*?' His brow creased as he stared down at the pattern of the Oriental carpet. 'It could hardly be worse, Lazaro,' he murmured at length, looking up. 'The British have been closer to our secrets than we have suspected over these last years. Does the name mean nothing to you?'

'I . . . perhaps the *Casa de Contratación*?'

'Yes, yes, but within the *Casa*! The Cosmography Office, Lazaro, the chartmaking department of the oldest and most respected school of nautical studies in the world!' A long forefinger drilled into Lazaro's chest. 'Torres is one of our best chartmakers. He has charted most of our Pacific coastline, he knows the slightest detail of each port, approaches, gunnery, fortifications, treasure houses . . . If he takes all that to the English, they could make a killing even in peacetime and in case of war, Lazaro, it would be a major disaster for Spain!'

'But why should Torres betray?'

'If I were alone to decide in these affairs,' snapped Palafox, 'nothing of the sort would happen. Merit should be rewarded and Torres was not treated according to his merits. He was set aside three years ago to make way for a less able man who has favour at court.'

'We were also . . . withholding his son . . .'

Palafox's eye stopped banefully on Lazaro's for a second before he decided to ignore the insinuation that he, the Inquisitor-General, might bear some responsibility for Torres's disaffection. 'The mother died in childbirth,' he said with a shrug. 'The father in such cases may hate the child, or on the contrary find himself all the more attached to it. I suppose we must now assume that, between Torres and his son, there are stronger links than is generally the case – to the point where the father has set his son's freedom as the price of his defection to an enemy of Spain.' He moved. 'Get down to Porfirio and Bernardo and send them on their way. Veracruz is the place they must go to. With them on the road, we shall be able to concentrate on catching our fleeing quarry.'

'Yes, Excellency.'

Palafox smiled briefly. 'Do I hear doubt in your voice? Do you not think we shall?'

The greying assistant took courage. 'Perhaps it will not be easy.'

'Perhaps. The Englishman is indeed determined and intelligent and he surprises us at each turn of the road. We must be vigilant. But consider what he has to do and with whom. The child will not help him. He will be a burden to bear.' A shadow briefly crossed his face. 'If Doña Maria-Dolores is still his prisoner, he will have, as well as the child, an unwilling hostage to carry. And don't let us forget his guide and helper, the younger man from *Rodriguez y Cuevas.*' The voice dropped to a whisper. 'We watched Parton earlier as he did his utmost to rescue his companion. It was touching. He has no idea that, by his noble obstination, he has tied a traitor to his back – a traitor who has, need I mention it, precise instructions as to what he is to do. Parton has all my domains to cross, Lazaro, the concentrated might of the Inquisition against him—' The smile flitted back. 'And no one but a baker's girl to help him on his way . . .'

CHAPTER TEN

A solitary bell in Amecameca tolled eight. Parton put down the second of the pistols he had been cleaning and repriming and looked up. Gabriela should be back soon. A few yards away in the clearing near the stream where they had filled their canteens, Seward lay sleeping on his back. Between Parton and Seward lay Fernando, curled up and also fast asleep. Let them get what little rest they could, thought Parton. It was the first time he had been able to see Fernando clearly in daylight and his eyes came back once again to the boy. Like the other boys at the monastery, he was wearing a slate-grey jacket over a heavy linen shirt, knee breeches, grey worsted stockings and buckled black shoes. He was slim, almost slight and his dark features were fine and perhaps even a little girlish. On the long hike through woods and countryside during the night, he had been brave, he had walked until he had been ready to drop and then Parton had carried him. The fighting spirit was there and so was the desire to get away from the prison-like school and back to his father. Parton's only fear was that lack of sleep and exhaustion would take their toll on Fernando's willpower. If Gabriela found a horse or a mule in Amecameca, thought Parton as he looked above the trees to the mountain slopes, that would be an enormous advantage – although she must avoid attracting attention and, as it were, leaving a sign pointing to the old Indian road through the pass. The improbability of their choice of route was a vital joker in the tight game they had to play against the Inquisition.

And what was to be done with *her*, thought Parton, looking at Maria-Dolores by the stream. She had washed and was binding her feet up with strips of her gown – what had been left of her slippers had disappeared somewhere during the night. Parton wondered at it. She had not complained, although her feet must have been painful. And now what? Her possible usefulness seemed to him to lessen as they left the immediate area of the monastery and Palafox, even though he could still foresee situations where a hostage of her importance would be a guarantee. If their pursuers were to come upon them now, for example . . . But the road ahead, the mountain pass, perhaps snow and ice, Fernando to carry, Seward ailing . . . How could he and Gabriela drag the weight of a captive who would have to be watched at all times, who could betray them and who, perhaps worst of all, was dressed in the tatters of a rich gown and had no shoes?

Maria-Dolores looked up as if she had felt Parton's gaze on her. Her hair hung wet on her shoulders and the pale gown clung to her skin. Parton stood up and went over to her. 'This is where we part company,' he said quietly.

Maria-Dolores finished tying a strip of cloth and looked up slowly. 'What does that mean exactly?'

'Don't worry. I'm not going to murder you.' Parton smiled. 'Just let you go, that's all.'

Maria-Dolores closed her eyes and remained still for a second. Then she opened them and shook her head. 'Don't send me back to him,' she said quietly, desperately. 'Take me with you.'

Parton leaned forward and bent over her. 'What did you say?'

'Please, listen to me, please. Don't think I'm trying to trick you, I'm not, oh God, I'm not. I want to get away from him. I *must* get away from him. Oh, I wish I knew how to explain it. My life depends on it, that much I know. Can you understand that?'

Parton shook his head. 'No, I can't. Do you mean he'll kill you?'

A bitter smile trembled on Maria-Dolores's lips. 'That he would not do! Show mercy, Palafox? No, keep me alive the better to rot me, to take me down the same old paths to share his private hell, that, yes!'

Her voice was rising raggedly and Parton held up a hand for quiet. When she spoke again, it was in a fierce whisper. 'Do you know what makes me special among his mistresses? He bought me from a whorehouse in Mexico City – my mother practised there and that's where I was born – when I was only ten years old and he brought me up to be his mistress, to know nothing else, to share his taste for pain and blood, to haunt the dungeons with him and excite his jaded appetites – oh, how can I make you see! He made me what I am, he fashioned me, his plaything, his cruel doll! And I don't want to be his creature any more, I don't want to play for him and work up his deadened senses, I want to live another life, *my* life, do you see!' She caught Parton's sleeve, her eyes locked in his. 'You did what no one else could have done. You took me away from him. Now I want it to go on. I must not go back. I want to go on with you.'

Parton looked into her eyes. She was not play-acting. Her face, washed of its makeup and grime and tears, was fresher, younger, and her eyes, still golden brown, had changed. They were no longer vague, glassy, wide-pupilled. They were clear and purposeful. She was remarkably beautiful like that, he thought; but finding her charming now the mask had fallen was no reason for jeopardizing his mission. He shook his head. 'I have to take the child over there and my friend, and get out of New Spain. Palafox is not going to let me do it if he can stop me. How can I take you with me?' He gestured towards her feet.

'I could go through hell barefoot if I had to,' she replied. 'And I can help you! I'll tell you whatever you need to know – I know the Inquisition – and I'll do

191

whatever you want, *anything*, but please God take me with you!'

'I'll let you go and it's none of my business afterwards where you go or what you do. But I can't take you with me.'

Maria-Dolores paused, then said softly, 'I know which way you intend to go. If you abandon me now, I'll tell them where to look.'

There was a crashing among the trees upstream and Parton turned to see Gabriela running towards them. He looked back quickly at Maria-Dolores. 'I can't let you do that,' he said.

'I'm giving you a choice. Let me come with you or kill me so I won't be able to betray you.'

Parton pushed her away in anger and stood up. Gabriela ran into the clearing and Seward sat up in surprise. She was carrying black-and-white striped blankets over her arm and she was breathless. 'We must run from here!' she gasped. 'Amecameca is crawling with them, Inquisition all over the place! I managed to buy these blankets and some *tortillas*, but I couldn't get near the stables for priests and their friends. Anyone from out of town is quickly noticed. Come on!'

Parton was already handing a pack to Seward and taking his own. Fernando had heard nothing and was sleeping on. Parton picked him up gently and the boy's eyes flickered open for an instant, then closed again. 'The canteens!' remembered Parton as he crossed the clearing.

'Here.' Maria-Dolores, behind him, held the two canteens out and looked at him questioningly.

'Carry them. And don't hold us up.'

'Isn't it time we stopped dragging her along and left her for her loathsome Inquisitor?' Gabriela was looking back over her shoulder from the edge of the clearing, her black eyes challenging.

Parton shook his head. 'She knows which way we're going,' he said softly as he came up with her and they moved ahead with Seward.

'But you know she could betray us at any moment!'

'If we leave her behind, she's certain to betray us.'

'And if you take me with you, I swear I shan't,' said Maria-Dolores, pushing in deliberately among the trees behind them and following.

High above Amecameca, the rough track zig-zagged its way towards the towering, snow-capped peaks of Popocatepetl and Ixtaccihuatl. It had wound over the miles-wide shoulder of a massive outcrop and now, hours further on, it meandered halfway up the mountain across a bowl-shaped wilderness of grey stone, dust and grit, cut off from the inhabited world below. The track was obviously little used and there were few landmarks. There were no more trees. The last few leathery plants survived there in the shelter of the rounded boulders and yellowing scrub, and tumbleweed sizzled in the afternoon sun. Predators lived there, snakes, lizards, scorpions, spiders; kites and buzzards circled high, their thin cries cutting stark through the clear air. Parton wondered what prey they could possibly find in such desolation apart from each other. Eat or be eaten, kill or be killed, catch or . . .

Almost by reflex, he looked over his shoulder. The great outcrop cut off the view downwards to possible pursuers. At least, Parton consoled himself, they themselves could not be seen from below as they climbed. Behind him, no one spoke. Breathing was becoming more difficult and there was no relief from the burning sun. Gabriela walked steadily, although her face was drawn and tired and Parton felt sure she was struggling not to show her disapproval of the decision to keep Palafox's mistress with them; Maria-Dolores followed her, breathing raggedly, and fight as she might to hide it, her face contracted in pain at every step. As for Seward, his face still bruised, his shirt wringing with sweat, he walked with his hands on his stomach as if to hold it in place.

193

It was not a reassuring sight, thought Parton, looking down at Fernando, dozing in his arms, a blanket hooded over his head to shade it. At least, for the moment, fear was spurring them on and they were wasting no time. Parton looked up ahead. The track began to rise more steeply a few miles on, looping up the side of the bowl they were crossing. From there on, the trail would be even rougher and more tiring. How far, how high would they be when night fell? If they could get through the pass, it seemed to Parton that they would have put a wall between themselves and their pursuers. More important yet, the next day, the eighth of July, would see them on the Veracruz road, on horseback and with a serious chance of getting to the coast in time. If they could get through the pass. . . . There was a long, hard climb still ahead. Perhaps Fernando should walk for a while before the trail became too steep.

Higher, when it did get steeper, the trail became haphazard, difficult to follow, sometimes disappearing among the littered rocks or into ravines and fissures in the grey, dust-covered mountainside. Nothing grew there now and even the scorpions seemed to avoid the place. Dust flew in clouds, although the heat was less of a problem. As the altitude grew and the sun slid westwards, the air grew cooler.

And thinner. There wasn't enough of it. Parton inhaled sharply and looked down at Fernando, walking beside him. Thanks to his long rest, the boy was keeping up for the moment. But he was blowing and the dust was troubling him. He would soon have to be carried again. That, plus the thinning air, plus the growing difficulty of the track, meant that their progress would become slower and slower as nightfall came closer.

Parton looked up. They were winding through a narrow ravine-like fold in the mountain's crust, its floor rising sharply ahead of them. Above, framed by the black lopsided 'V' of the flanks of the fold, he could see the snowfields of

Popocatepetl, glistening in the sun, scaling away almost endlessly to the cone of the peaceful volcano. Ixtaccihuatl was far away to the left and invisible; as for the pass, they were so close in beneath it that it could not be seen for the rocks immediately above. It could not be far now, but Parton was sure it was a question of the difficulty of the climb, not of distance. It was time that mattered, not feet or miles.

He reached the top of the ravine and climbed the lower side of the 'V', looking out over the brim. The sun was well down in the afternoon sky. He shaded his eyes with his hand and looked down to the plain. It was too far to make anything out without a telescope. Finally, although they slowed progress, it was as well there were so many rocks and fissures to hide the fugitives. If an enterprising cavalry officer down there in the plain were to scan the mountain slopes with a telescope, the westering sun behind him to light the scene, he might well catch sight of them.

'Look!' Gabriela was lying beside him, a hand on his arm, the other pointing downwards. 'There, down among those loops.'

In the bends of the trail as it rose from the bowl they had left earlier, a lone horseman forced his mount.

'Everyone keep down!' called Parton, checking that no one was in possible view from below. He slid back down the slope with Gabriela. 'A traveller. Alone and on horseback,' he explained.

Maria-Dolores shivered. 'A scout or a spy of his. They've latched on to us.'

'No. If he knew we were here, he'd send an army, not one man. This man may be just a simple traveller.'

'So what do we do?' asked Seward, drinking from a canteen.

'We stop him and ask him.' Parton gestured to the narrow fold. 'Here. And whoever he is, we borrow his horse.'

'Oh good!' said Fernando, his eyes lighting up. 'I like riding horses! Can I ride this one?'

'Of course,' replied Parton. The boy's eyes were shining as much with nervous tiredness as with pleasure at the idea of riding, he thought. 'You can ride it over the top of the mountain and down the other side. I want it for you, Fernando. Now let's find a hiding-place for you and the girls.' He took Fernando's hand.

'What's on the other side of the mountain?'

'The trail goes down to Puebla.'

'I've been to Puebla. Is that where my father's coming to meet us?'

Parton led him in among the rocks strewn over the slope, Gabriela and Maria-Dolores following with the packs. 'I'm afraid we have to go further than Puebla to meet him,' he said guardedly.

'Why? Why doesn't he ever come for me?' asked Fernando, tugging irritably at Parton's hand. 'He *promised*, but he didn't come!'

'He can't,' said Parton, wondering how long it had been since Fernando had seen his father. And his mother? 'Far away', Cameron had said. What did that mean? 'Remember I told you at the monastery that they'd kill him if they could. He has to stay out of the way. That's why he sent me instead. They didn't know me beforehand.'

'They do now.'

'So they do. Now you stay here with Gabriela while I go back and see about that horse.'

Seward was behind him and Parton took him by the arm. 'I'll need help with the horse. Can you handle it?'

'Of course. What do you want me to do?'

Back at the top of the ravine, Parton chose hiding-places from which he and Seward could see each other across the trail.

'Wait until I move,' Parton said, hoping Seward's nerves would be steady enough. 'I'll see to the rider, you deal with the horse. Just take him by the bridle and lead him away. If there's trouble with the rider, don't worry about it, get the horse first.'

The sound of hoofbeats reached them, a distant but fast-growing drumming. Then it was louder, almost at the bottom of the incline and they began to hear the horse's laboured breathing. The thin air and the hard climb would take its toll on a horse pushed as hard, thought Parton, shrinking back and signalling to Seward to do the same.

'Hiyarrh!' The exhortation and the sharp smack of a riding stock came clear from the bottom of the ravine and the pattern of hoofbeats changed for that of a heavy, constrained gallop. Even on such a steep incline, the rider was forcing his mount to the utmost. This man was no simple traveller, Maria-Dolores had been right. A traveller might be in a hurry to get through the pass, but he would not risk his horse – and himself – like that without a much more urgent reason. The horse's breathing was louder now, Parton could hear the creaking of saddlery and he could hear the rider too, grunting with the effort of pushing on his mount.

The horse's lathered chestnut head, eyes starting from their orbits, nostrils blowing wide, came heaving into view. Then the broad Spanish stirrup and the rider's wide-trousered leg, a grey cloak above and the rider's face, dark-skinned and moustached. Parton leaped out of hiding, bent to the stirrup, lifted the foot high and toppled the man out of the saddle to the ground on the far side of the trail. The horse whickered and went on as Parton pulled a pistol from his belt and saw, from the corner of his eye, Seward reaching for the bridle, then he was on the winded rider rolling in the dust and he could see no more of Seward. He jammed the pistol under the man's jaw and cocked it. The man was instantly still, although he grimaced with pain and Parton supposed the fall had probably hurt him badly.

It was then that Parton heard the scream of a frightened

horse and the clatter of hooves behind him. He shoved the pistol harder under his prisoner's jaw and turned his head. The horse was rearing, hooves flailing, and Seward was hanging on grimly to the reins, trying to bring the head down and curb the horse. The more he pulled on the reins, the more the horse, panicked by the sudden interruption and the loss of its rider, struggled to break free.

An iron-shod hoof grazed Seward's head.

'Let go, for God's sake!' yelled Parton.

Seward let go and stumbled back. The horse turned and bolted with a scream into the rocks above, taking the opposite direction from the girls and Fernando. Seward swore loudly and ran after it.

Parton turned quickly to his man, looking into the pain-filled eyes. 'Palafox?' he asked softly.

The flicker of the eyes and the tightening of the jaw were confession enough. Parton ground the pistol barrel in under the clean-shaven jawbone. 'Written message?'

The rider grunted negation.

'Tell me the message.'

The man stared at him and said nothing. He's trying to choose between his fear of Palafox and his fear of me, thought Parton. He seized the black hair with his free hand, forced the head down into the rocky ground and levelled the pistol with the right eye at three inches. The messenger blinked. Parton lowered the pistol slowly until the barrel was touching the now-closed eyelid and saw the open eye watching his finger tighten on the trigger.

A touch more and it would blow. He squeezed a fraction.

'Torres Mendieta to be immediately arrested and held alive!' gabbled the messenger.

Parton released his pressure on the trigger but did not remove the pistol from the man's eye. Torres Mendieta would be Fernando's father. The messengers were out and on their way. 'Who's the message for?' he asked. The man had broken and he had to learn the rest quickly.

'Inquisition, Veracruz.'

'What are their instructions?'

'I have given you the full message.'

'Why Veracruz?'

'I don't know. I wasn't told. Please, Señor, I'm just a rider, a messenger, nothing more.'

He was telling the truth, thought Parton. Palafox had too great a love of personal power and of secrecy to give detailed explanations of his plans to his subordinates. The Veracruz Inquisition would have advance instructions on how to proceed on receiving such a message. Did that mean that the message would go on by ship to wherever in the Spanish dominions Torres Mendieta was, or did it mean that Torres was in Veracruz itself? Cameron had told Parton he was not to concern himself with that side of things. But Parton had also been ordered to move faster than the Spanish so as to ensure the traitor's safety. If the man were in Veracruz, the margin of safety was ludicrously narrow. That brief message, if it got through, would smash everything to pieces within minutes.

'What other messengers has Palafox sent?' asked Parton, settling back a little. The man had decided to talk and there was no need for further threats.

'He sent two before dawn *via* Mexico City.'

'Before dawn? But when did he send *you*?'

'Later in the morning when someone remembered this old trail and reminded Palafox it would be faster.'

'How much faster?'

'Going north round the mountains to Puebla takes the best part of two days, Señor. Even though I started later, I expect – that is, I expected – to be in Puebla several hours before them.'

'Did you stop off at Amecameca?' Parton was desperate to know if Gabriela had been noticed, if Palafox would think of the old Indian trail for other reasons than that of a quick route for a messenger.

The rider shook his head. 'I rode straight by.'

'Did Palafox send anyone else there?'

'Not with me.'

'What plans does he have for our capture?'

'I—' The man broke off, staring over Parton's shoulder. Parton wrenched round, alarmed.

Over them stood Seward, pale as death, a silver-chased pistol in his hand. He'd taken it from the saddlebags, thought Parton in a flash as he saw the pistol quiver. 'No!' he shouted, but already he was rolling out of the line of fire.

In the narrow ravine, the explosion was deafeningly loud. The ball went in just under the nose and blew out the back of the house messenger's skull. The head lifted sharply only inches from Parton's, then sagged back into the sickening debris and was still.

Parton scrambled to his feet, livid, all the irritation he had previously felt for Seward and repressed coming to the surface. 'Why did you *do* that? He was useful, he was talking, I wanted him alive, and *I'm* the one who decides, damn you, you jumped-up little bastard!'

Seward's shoulders drooped and the pistol slipped from his fingers and fell to the ground. He was trembling violently and his eyes shone feverishly as he looked up at Parton. 'His name is Francisco,' he said, his voice shaking. 'Like the saint, but he's no saint. When Palafox wasn't there, he was the one who conducted my interrogation. I didn't tell you how.'

Oh my God, thought Parton, the anger draining.

'Nothing refined. A wet cloth rolled and tied into a heavy knot. And again and again and again and again.' He broke off, breathed deeply, and looked beyond Parton to the messenger's inert body. 'Every time I move I remember Francisco,' he whispered.

Parton let himself slump back. 'I'm sorry,' he said. A pebble rolled above and he looked up. The two girls stood side by side, watching, while Fernando looked down frightened at the bloody remains, then turned to bury his face in Gabriela's skirts. Maria-Dolores reached down to stroke his hand, but the boy pulled it away sharply. Gabriela looked from Seward to Parton. There was pity for Seward in her eyes. If there was anything other than condemnation for Parton, Parton could not see it. He breathed out slowly and told himself it did not matter. His nerves were tightening dangerously. 'The horse?' he asked fatalistically.

'Bolted over a ledge and broke its neck,' said Seward. 'I took whatever might be useful from the saddlebags.' He handed over a packet of dried meat, some powder and shot and a telescope.

The glass at least was good news, thought Parton, weary, but it would not carry Fernando over the mountain. 'Then we'd better get the body off the trail and start walking again,' he said.

They camped in the bare, windswept zone below the snowline and the pass, where the trail was no more than a sketch in the volcanic grit which collected on the gentler gradients. Parton found a sheltered dip crowded with grey rocks, smooth and porous, tinged red by the dying rays of the sun. There was no point in trying to push on further. Better to settle for this poor shelter. There might be no more higher up.

They ate quickly and cheerlessly – dried meat from the saddle bags and a few *tortillas*. It was bitterly cold now. They wrapped themselves in blankets. It was literally freezing, in fact, thought Parton, taking the last of them. They huddled into the shelter of a rock which cut the icy wind. Fernando, tired beyond words and wrapped in two blankets, lay cradled for warmth between the two girls. Seward lay by Gabriela and Parton on the outside, closing off the little circle.

He was exhausted, but he was not sure if he could unwind

enough to sleep. He looked up at the sky, dark and almost starless. His eyes were burning as if salt had got into them. There were clouds up there. A sudden fear, a sailor's fear, of bad weather overtook him, but he shook it off. There had been clouds like that the night before, and the night before that. The sun dispersed them in the morning. It would be the same this time. A few hours' rest – Fernando above all needed it, a boy of his age, however spirited, couldn't be kept running day and night – and at the first glimmer they would be up and through the pass. Then they would be complaining rather of heat than of cold, he thought wryly, pulling his blanket round him.

If he slept at all, it was only fitfully between vague waking spells and wild snatches of nightmare. Palafox and Cameron drank one another's health in *aguardiente* in the Calle Alvarado building in Mexico City, Maria-Dolores in a white dress scaled the bell tower at the monastery, Parton was supposed to be conning a ship but he could never get on the quarterdeck and she was going to break up on a reef . . .

He woke up and was surprised to find himself on his back with no blanket over him. He had rolled away from the others in his sleep. Oddly, he wasn't cold. How long had he been half-sleeping like that? There were no stars to reckon by. He got up quietly and went forward among the rocks until he reached a point where he could look out down the mountainside. All was darkness. The wind was no longer icy. Had the thick clouds caused a rise in temperature since nightfall? It was not a bad thing. The freezing cold had made him fear for Fernando.

And indeed he should, he thought. It was not enough simply to avoid pursuit as they seemed to be doing for the moment. Getting an eight-year-old hundreds of miles across open, hostile country was not easy and was going to become more and more difficult as tiredness set in. A boy of eight was independent in some ways, wanted to show he knew how to do things – how well could Fernando really ride? for example – but, at times, exhausted, became a little one again, had to be carried, fed, warmed, cajoled, almost like a baby. Gabriela was so good with him. Fernando had taken to her at once and she looked after him, as the saying went, like a mother. She had lost a younger brother she had loved, remembered Parton and that surely helped to explain her immediate sympathy for Fernando. And Seward? Why did he seem to be reaching out to Gabriela – for comfort, or because she was desirable? Parton shook his head. After his angry outburst earlier, he was no longer sure he could think and judge coolly where Seward was concerned. The fact was that the two of them were from totally different worlds, Parton colonial American, dirt-poor, his family robbed and broken, while Seward was mother-country English, rich, from a solidly respectable background. Parton had been unable, right from the start, to understand Seward's feelings, his way of looking at life, his manners, even his gestures and inflexions – let alone reach a fair opinion of the man one way or another. And now, feeling responsible for Seward's beating at the hands of Palafox's thugs was adding to the difficulties. Twinges of annoyance at the idea that Seward was making up to Gabriela, or that she might feel sympathy for him, were no help either and Parton warned himself to avoid them.

Gabriela. Sensational, black-eyed, headstrong Gabriela. What place had she taken in his heart? Could he imagine sharing her life as he had, at times, with Mardi before she had announced her decision to fight on with the slaves in the mountains of St Domingue? No. Gabriela was searching for her way in life and the next steps – the return to Spain, to her unknown father and her gypsy origins – which she had traced out for herself, left no room for Parton. There had always been, he realized, a tacit understanding between Gabriela and himself as to the limits of their love – they were lovers by honest desire, by hatred of hypocrisy, by liking for one another's style and dynamism, but both of them knew that their commitment went no further than the sharing of the present moment, the brief journey together.

Parton heard a footfall and turned. Behind him, a blanket over her shoulders, Maria-Dolores came out of the darkness. 'I can't sleep,' she said. 'I can't stop imagining him catching up with us. Why didn't we go on?'

Parton stared at her and wondered what drove her forward. She had walked all day without complaint, with no more than rags bound round her feet. He wished he understood. 'I'd have preferred it if we had been able to keep moving,' he replied. 'If there'd been a moon tonight, we would have. But we can't afford to lose the trail and there's snow up there in the pass.'

'But don't you see! He sent a rider! He knows about the trail!'

'He doesn't know we're on it, or he wouldn't have sent the messenger alone. And look.' He took Maria-Dolores firmly by the arm and brought her forward next to him, pointing down the mountainside. 'If anyone were to try climbing that trail in this darkness, they'd need torches. Can you see any?'

Maria-Dolores shook her head and relaxed slightly. 'Forgive me,' she said. 'Now that I've decided to really run from him, he gives me waking nightmares.'

Parton couldn't make out her expression, but her accents were sincere. Was she lying to him? It occurred to him that her insistence on coming with the fugitives might have been motivated by her fear of the death which, in spite of Parton's offer to let her go free, she supposed inevitable if she were to be left behind. Was she waiting to get over the mountain, where there was help for her, a fanatical priest-ridden town like Puebla for example, where, having gained his confidence, she would betray him and make good her revenge? Or was all this a game, an amusement, a change for her jaded appetites? It hardly seemed to fit with her timid efforts to belong and to be useful. Parton remembered her hand on Fernando's earlier. Why make a gesture like that if she were false, hollow, lying? How to understand who she really was under the mask of the rich man's painted whore? He suspected, from the changes he had seen in her eyes and in her general manner, that Palafox, for whom the alchemy of poisons and narcotics would doubtless have no secrets, had used some kind of drug to keep her under his sway. She had said – and Parton found it hard not to accept her testimony – that the prelate had trained her, had literally brought her up from childhood, to live for his pleasure and to share his love of cruelty and bloodshed in the torture chambers. Did she really want to escape from that underground life, from the Inquisitor-General and his sick and devious world? Did she really hope that Parton could lead her to something new? Did she take him for some kind of saviour? What did she feel for him?

He had been avoiding that last question for some time. It led him on to dangerous ground because it begged another. He should mistrust her, he warned himself, she was Palafox's mistress, she had taken pleasure in torturing him, she was his prisoner and should remain so. He faced facts. He had the greatest difficulty in mistrusting her. From the beginning, their relationship, however dissonant, had been based on mutual attraction and frustrated desire. He was on the dangerous ground he had been trying to avoid, right on it. He stretched out his hand and touched her face. She sighed and, for a long, silent moment, reached up and pressed his hand to her lips. In the warm air, Parton smelled the last rich vestiges of the perfume, musk and nutmeg, that Maria-Dolores had worn in a previous life and he began almost to believe . . . Could it be that she was in fact capable of living a new one?

He reached for her. Under the tatters of the gown, she was naked. A gust of wind blew round them, warm and dust-laden. He unhooked the three or four fastenings which still held and pushed the gown aside, his hands brushing her heavy breasts. Gabriela? he thought. Gabriela believed in knowing what you wanted and taking it. She would understand. His hand slid between Maria-Dolores's parted thighs, his fingers unravelling the soft damp curls and she moaned and pressed towards him, imploring him as his fingertips caressed her and he bent and kissed her mouth her neck, her shoulders . . .

Thunder growled way off behind the volcano.

Parton broke away and looked off anxiously into the night.

'No!' pleaded Maria-Dolores breathlessly, clutching at him, 'Now, quickly, before it breaks, please . . .' Her hands, insistent, were unbuttoning his breeches, were inside and Parton caught his breath sharply. You couldn't stop a storm coming, he thought. He drew her to him and she arched forward, slipping the tip of his penis inside her. The air was hot now, dust whirling round them. Then the rain began to fall, great drops of warm rain driven by the wind and neither of them cared. As she came down over him, Parton thrust slowly, deep and she shuddered and cried out. The rocks darkened under the pattering drops, the dust fell and became mud beneath their feet, their skin began to glisten.

There was a lull as the wind soughed gently, carrying no rain. Maria-Dolores's golden eyes looked deep into Parton's as their bodies moved in unison again and again. Then a skittering, rustling sound in the rocks above and torrential rain rushed over them like a wall. Thunder growled closer, lightning flickered and Parton saw Maria-Dolores, in a blue-white flash, gasping for breath, her hair blackened and sticking wetly to her face, warm sulphurous rain pouring down between her breasts. She opened her mouth even wider and screamed to him 'Now, now, *now*!'

'Now,' said Parton, and he raised her from her feet and thrust deep for the last time.

*

Lightning split the night like the ripping of silk, the flash blinding, the great shattering crack of thunder ramming at them, inconceivably loud, paining their ears like a blow from a fist, shaking them physically as if the mountain itself had broken apart. For a second, still holding Maria-Dolores close, Parton thought: the volcano, but no, he knew it was the heart of a storm. The thunder rumbled and echoed away across the mountainside, leaving an acrid tang in the air that Parton knew from electric storms at sea, when St Elmo's fire played in the mastheads and along the yards and seasoned sailors hid their heads in their hands and prayed. It was the smell of lightning, the smell of sudden death and never had he smelled it as strong. The bolt had struck close, very close.

'The others!' he shouted, breaking away and running back among the rocks, Maria-Dolores with him, fastening her tattered dress. Lightning flashed repeatedly now over the slopes, thunder pealed deafeningly and the downpour was a continuous hissing sheet, water gouting down between the rocks, sweeping mud and small stones underfoot. Parton splashed ahead into the clearing, peering into the momentary blackness. 'Gabriela!' he yelled. 'Fernando!'

A huge fork of lightning stood overhead for a long fraction of a second. Parton scarcely felt Maria-Dolores's fingernails dig into his arm. In the flickering light, he saw what looked like a striped tent in the shelter of a rock. Then the darkness came back as thunder crashed, smashing into the mountain like a massive hammer blow, shaking the ground as Parton, Maria-Dolores clinging to him, ran across the muddy clearing. He scrambled down into the lee of the rock, pushing her ahead of him. Lightning flared again and he saw Gabriela and Seward holding a blanket over their heads as a flimsy roof against the torrents of water, while Fernando, surrounded by the packs of blankets in a hastily built pile, sat between them. He stared at Parton and his mouth opened, his lips moved, but Parton heard nothing over the beating of the thunder and the rain. The boy's legs, he noticed, were under water as he sat, and the packs were bathing in a stream of liquid mud. Fernando couldn't stay there, he thought, and neither could the packs which contained their last food and provisions and their only clean drinking water.

'What shall we—' yelled Seward. Thunder clapped and carried off the rest. Parton waited as the thunder rumbled away. There was only one thing to do. If this rain went on, what were now freshets would become torrents and they would all be in danger. It was no use looking for a cave or other shelter, not on this mountain.

'Climb on a rock!' he yelled as soon as the thunder abated.

'But the lightning!' That was Gabriela.

Parton pointed down at the rising water and shook his head. The water was a greater, more immediate and certain danger than the lightning. In the next flash, he stood up and looked round hurriedly. The rock they were sheltering under was too small for five. But Parton glimpsed in the bluish light a larger rock beyond, leaning in its turn against a higher one which might provide them with a little shelter from the cascades of water the storm was pitching down on them. He bent to Fernando.

'Hang on round my neck,' he said into the boy's ear, lifting him and taking a pack with the other hand. He made for the rock behind as lightning streaked the sky again. 'Up you go!' he said to Fernando, lifting him. Of course, Fernando wouldn't. Thunder banged and he clung desperately to Parton's neck. Then Gabriela was there, climbing up on to the rock, Maria-Dolores and then Seward helping her. Parton passed Fernando up, then helped the two others, passed up the packs and blankets and climbed up himself. Lightning forked and splattered into the mountainside and thunder boomed as Parton crossed the top of the rock bent double to the back, where Seward and

Maria-Dolores were struggling to spread a sodden blanket over Gabriela and Fernando's heads. Parton grabbed Maria-Dolores's end and tautened the blanket with Seward, adjusting the makeshift roof to the slight overhang of the higher rock behind. Maria-Dolores dragged the packs feverishly under cover and crawled under herself. Water poured down the front edge of the blanket and away down the sides of the rock. Parton stuck his head under. Water was pouring down on the inside too, but it looked as if the blanket was holding off about half of what was coming down and the gap between the two rocks was acting as a gutter. The water running where the girls crouched with Fernando was nothing compared with the streams flowing on the ground below.

Lightning flickered unceasingly now and thunder crashed close overhead. Parton saw Fernando's mouth wide open in a scream, his hands covering his ears. If it hits us, we won't know anything about it, Parton thought. The sheer noise of the storm was worse than anything he had heard, even at sea. The mountain magnified the thunderclaps, rolled them round, the echoes clattering away over the slopes. All that could be heard in an occasional brief lull in the rolling of the thunder was the beating of the downpour on the blanket and the gurgling and rushing of the spates it had created. Lightning spat and spat again and an acrid odour filled the air. A fresh detonation of thunder beat at their eardrums. They had to stay there, they must not move, their only chance was to wait and let the storm pass over them. He could hear the rain sheeting down again. Fernando's head, buried in Gabriela's lap, came up again. Was it wishful thinking, or was the rain lessening? Water was still pouring in a cataract over the thick, sodden blanket, lightning was still playing all around them, thunder rolling, but it seemed to Parton as if the force of the storm was diminishing. Perhaps they were simply getting used to it. They must stay put, they must wait.

'It's gone,' came a voice, unexpectedly loud, Parton could not tell whose. He listened carefully. It wasn't wishful thinking, the noise of the storm was abating. The beating of the deluge was lessening and the thunder was clattering away little by little over the rocky flanks of the mountain towards Ixtaccihuatl. The storm, weakened, would hit Mexico City that night, thought Parton, and with the thought he realized that the centre had gone over them and that they were still alive.

It rained for an hour longer, then it stopped. With the end of the storm came darkness and bitter cold. Their only resort, after stamping round the rock to get blood flowing again into cramped arms and legs, was to wrap themselves in the waterlogged blankets and huddle together for warmth. Parton huddled in with the others, but he did not cover his head and try to sleep as they did. He watched the sky.

The clouds thinned slowly. Mist rolled over the mountainside, but it was patchy. Eventually, through a gap in the mist, he caught more than a glimpse of the stars, enough to make out the constellations and reckon time from their position. When he had done so, he relaxed and rested. Dawn would come soon enough for them to survive the cold.

Just soon enough.

When it came, dawn was a dirty iron-grey streak high over the pass above and behind them. Parton pulled out of the huddle and stood up, muscles protesting. The group looked like a thickly draped statue carved in stone. He pulled back blankets and shook shoulders. Fernando, wedged into the middle, was sound asleep in spite of the mud and wet. Parton hoped that that was a good sign.

They breakfasted as they went on soggy, gritty *tortillas*. There was no time to waste. The light was scant as yet and the world was made of folds and creases in varying shades of

grey, mist rolling at the bottom of the hollows. Even the
fugitives were grey – the rain had washed dust and grit from
the mountain all over them, leaving silty deposits on their
clothes and skin. The track led upwards steeply, washed
clean and wet in places, but slimy and dangerous where
mud had collected. Within a hundred slithering yards they
were fighting for breath in the thin, cold air. Parton took
the lead, carrying Fernando, setting as fast a pace as he
dared.

The boy was still sleeping, or at least, keeping his eyes
closed. Some night's rest he had had, thought Parton. He
wrapped the trailing, heavy blanket closer round him.
There was a sharp little wind blowing from above, carrying
with it the smell and chill of snow, and it was getting
stronger as they climbed. Above, the horizon, sharply
etched against the paling eastern sky, ran swooping from
the tremendous cone of Popocatepetl before rising steadily
to that of Ixtaccihuatl, and there, in the hollow, was the
saddle they must go through. He turned to the others and
nodded upwards. They all stared silently up and no one
spoke. 'It's not as far as it looks,' said Parton, as much to
convince himself as the others and he moved on.

The trail was less steep now, its winding loops gentler and
Parton felt his cramped muscles easing as he walked. He
increased speed, his mind racing ahead of his steps. They
were already close to the snowline. Mid-morning on the
other side of the pass was well within the bounds of possibility. By late afternoon – it was the eighth – they could be
near Puebla, horses, the Veracruz road . . .

There was slush underfoot now and the wind bit sharply.
Parton hooded Fernando with his blanket like a little monk.
They splashed on through the rivulets of meltwater which
crossed the track under their feet. Patches of snow littered
the slope and, in the uniformly grey light, the landscape was
dull, chilling, sinister. The sun would not touch these
western slopes until later in the morning. If they wanted its

warmth, he thought, that was yet another reason for climbing fast. He hurried along the last loop and stepped into the first drifts, cutting across them easily.

'Can you see that?' gasped Seward from behind.

'What?' Parton turned. Seward gestured at the snow. Parton stared at it. 'Last night,' he said at length. 'Rained below, snowed up here.'

'Fresh snow,' said Seward. 'We'll never get through that.'

Juan Mendoza and his son Pedro were out at first light on the lower slopes of Popocatepetl, herding cattle which had scattered and fled down into the woods during the night's storm. It was Pedro who saw the vultures as he came out of the mist at the top of a neck of woods. He waited for his father and pointed upwards to show him. 'Must be something big,' he said.

Juan agreed. There were a lot of vultures high up there on the mountain, wheeling and dropping and squabbling. But he had been a herdsman in the area for far too many years to agree with his son's suggestion that cattle had strayed up there and been struck by lightning. 'Too high,' he said simply. Anyway, at the first whiff of a storm, cattle came lumbering down the slopes to seek shelter.

'Looks as if it's on the old Indian trail,' hazarded Pedro.

His father's brow furrowed. So it was. As high as that, it could only be human, he reasoned. A traveller or travellers on the old trail who had come to a sticky end. And the Inquisition on the jump for the last two days, searching for some kind of outlaws or runaways . . .

There might be no immediate advantage for him, he thought, but a poor herdsman could never afford to let a chance pass him by. And it was always advisable to stay on the right side of the Inquisition. . . . Juan left his son with the cattle and went into Amecameca to report.

The priests wasted no time. Father Agustín, the parish

212

priest, and two Dominicans from the Inquisition climbed up into the bell tower with Juan. Juan pointed out the vultures high above. One of the Dominicans took out a telescope and trained it on the spot.

'A horse,' he said at length. 'Saddled.'

'No sign of the rider?' asked the second Dominican.

'No. There are rocks. The vultures are after something else I can't see.' He panned the telescope across the slopes.

'That'll be the rider. Anything else?'

'No.' He lifted the glass. 'Oh! Up there, at the snowline!' He turned, grinning and passed the telescope to his fellow.

The second Dominican looked through the glass for a moment, then nodded. He turned to the parish priest. 'A fast horse and a messenger!' he ordered. 'To the monastery at Tepoztlán, quickly! The message is for his Excellency himself. Tell him four travellers on foot have been sighted on the old Indian trail. Oh, and—' He looked across at the other and exchanged a satisfied smirk. '—inform him that they're on this side of the pass. And that it snowed during the night . . .'

CHAPTER ELEVEN

Parton glared at Seward but kept his temper. 'What do we do?' he asked woodenly. 'Go back?'

Seward inhaled deeply and looked away without replying. The two girls stared somewhat apprehensively at the snow-bound slopes above. Damn Seward, thought Parton, looking at their sodden, grimy coverings, Maria-Dolores's feet. . . . All right, Seward had always said that this was not the way to come, but he hadn't had to add to the difficulties by discouraging the girls and Fernando, now they were up on the mountain and had no choice but to fight through.

'We'll make it,' said Gabriela simply.

Parton looked at Maria-Dolores again. She was the one who would suffer the most. She caught his glance and returned it with a little smile and an affirmative nod. She was not going back.

'Come on,' said Parton, leading the way. The trail disappeared into the snow, but it was easy enough to make out its hollow trace. The snow was soft, wet, clinging. Parton's feet sunk into it for several inches and his boots came back up coated and dripping. It was cold and unpleasant, but it was no worse than anything they had already gone through. The layer of snow was far from being too thick to stop their advance. It was fair enough, thought Parton. If it was all the pass had to throw at them, they would be through to the other side by mid-morning, as he had hoped.

Half an hour later, he recognized that things were not so simple. The snow deepened as they climbed, which was only to be expected. But now, in the steep incline just below the saddle, it held – only just – on the icy crust of the old layer, the polished surface of which they had seen glinting in the sun the day before. Shoe leather slipped all too easily on it and bone-jarring falls became frequent until Parton found that he could kick into the frozen crust and make steps for the others to use in their turn. There were no more falls, but their progress slowed. The trail was harder to make out now and Parton chose wrongly several times, wasting time and effort. A chill set in between them. The western side of the pass, still in shadow, was icy cold, and the wind, if anything, stronger. Fernando, wide awake now, was silent, out of sorts, no doubt, thought Parton, because he was exhausted.

'Where's the trail from here?' asked Gabriela, panting.

The whiteness ahead of them seemed unbroken. No one spoke and the only sounds were the soughing of the wind and their own ragged breathing. Parton pointed. 'It loops round. Up there.'

The silence between them was bitter. The loop was long, perhaps an hour long and it was deep in shadow all the way. An hour's struggle in the piercing cold was more than any of them wanted to face.

'Why not go straight up?' suggested Maria-Dolores, pointing at the steep slope beside them. It was the most direct way to the saddle above, but it was icy and almost sheer. Parton handed the boy to Gabriela and took a closer look. He kicked at the ice with the toe of his boot until he had formed a foothold. He tested it. It took his weight and he kicked another beside it. The steps would hold them, he decided, but the climb would still be perilous. He turned back towards the group, seeing them breathless and shivering, hoarfrost forming on their wet clothes and hair, and glanced back at the long loop which was the safe way up. Perhaps the short way, however dangerous, would help them steal a march on Palafox. He nodded.

'Kick steps – like a ladder,' he said. But he would not be kicking them, he thought, looking round questioningly. He would not confide Fernando to anyone else on a dangerous climb like that. Seward stepped forward in response to Parton's look.

'I can try,' he said.

It was fair enough, thought Parton, watching him as he began the climb, kicking footholds at regular intervals. 'Make them wide,' he called, thinking of Maria-Dolores whose feet were still bound with rags. She had said she could go through hell barefoot if she had to. Perhaps now she would find out if it were true.

When Seward had made about twenty feet, Parton tested the ladder. The footholds were solid. 'Keep going!' he shouted up to Seward, swinging Fernando up on to his back and telling him to hold on tight. He led the way, Maria-Dolores following and Gabriela bringing up the rear. Parton took his time, leaning into the slope and using his hands, conscious of the weight on his back and not wishing to hurry Seward and push him into a mistake. If Seward slipped, Parton would have to anchor himself, keep hold of the boy and try to stop the falling man. He didn't want to have to attempt it.

'I'm cold,' complained Fernando by Parton's ear.

'Not long now,' said Parton, watching where he put his feet. 'Sun at the top.'

'Go faster!' The boy shook Parton's neck.

'Stay still!' Parton steadied himself. 'D'you want us to fall?'

The boy looked back. 'No!' he said immediately and was still. Parton glanced back too. The drop was impressive now. Far down, somewhere above the rocky slopes, vultures wheeled slowly. Even if the incline was not absolutely sheer, a fall would mean sliding faster and faster down the ice and would end in certain injury and perhaps death. He turned back, glimpsing the two girls some way below him and in no apparent difficulty, and concentrated on climbing.

*

Seward, panting, kicked the last few steps hurriedly and disappeared over the top of the slope. He would just have a minute or two, he thought feverishly. Parton had been delayed by the traitor's brat, but he would soon be up into the sunlight. Shading his eyes with his hand, Seward made out a knoll some yards away which would provide him with a vantage point. He ran to it, pulling from his jacket pocket as he went the polished brass disc which he used as a mirror. From the top of the knoll, he looked back down into the plain. Tepoztlán was off in the haze, he judged, but Amecameca, much closer, down to his right, would be both in clear air and in the shadow of the mountain. This was his first opportunity and it was a good one. He caught the sun's rays on the disc and began to signal.

He had no idea if his signals would be seen. The disc was small and the distance considerable. Answering signals would be impossible because the town was in shade. He could do no better, he consoled himself. He was doing what he could, he was staying close to Parton, remaining undiscovered, he was hindering the fugitives' movement when it was possible. Now he was signalling back, obeying orders. He glanced nervously over his shoulder at the top of the slope, terrified of seeing Parton already up and about to catch him. Terror had become part of his life. The glory of the noble blow he was to strike for the cause had somehow seemed to fade as time had gone by, leaving him driven on by fear, miserable, treacherous, trapped between the threat of his master's punishment if he failed and his victim's revenge in case of discovery.

Pull yourself together, he told himself, still signalling and watching for the first sign of Parton's arrival. Palafox was not his master, but his ally. And the cause was just. Which soldier did not know fear as he went into battle? He must steel himself, he must remember. Remember the true King by divine right, despised and banished. Remember the true faith thrown down by vile heretics. Remember his family, father, mother, uncles, brothers, all humiliated, forced to abjure and mouth the filthy heresies of Anglicanism, to swear loyalty to the German swineherd who sat in power in London. Remember, remember. And fight on.

How well had he succeeded up to now? Well enough, he thought. The messenger had been a terrible risk – the man had seen him speaking to Palafox on friendly terms and could have said as much to Parton. Killing him – the first man Seward had ever killed – had been a drastic but necessary decision. And Parton had been fooled by the torture story he had trotted out, had even apologized, thought Seward with a sudden grin – when all the harm Francisco had ever done him had been to bring him a meal and a flask of wine! Maria-Dolores was another cause for congratulation, although she was an apparent traitor to Palafox. The vital thing was that she knew nothing of Seward's duplicity, as the Inquisitor-General had sworn she did not. Gabriela? Ah, Gabriela didn't suspect him at all. He wished he could see more than pity in her eyes. He wished . . . He checked his thoughts, surprised by the force of his feelings. When had this begun? How long—?

The sound of ragged breathing came to him and he slipped the brass mirror into his pocket. Shivering with cold and renewed fear, he turned and looked out across the mountain pass.

'Excellency!' The grey-cloaked mercenary trained the telescope unshakingly on the pass. 'Signals!'

Palafox crossed the crowded space at the top of the Amecameca bell tower in a stride, pushing Brother Lazaro aside. 'Show me,' he commanded, putting an eye to the glass as the mercenary held it.

The rapid flashes, filling the circular lens, dazzled brighter than the white glare of the snow. Neither the sender of the signals nor the other fugitives could be seen, but the Inquisitor-General did not hesitate. 'Our young ally is proving his worth,' he said softly, turning to Lazaro with a grim smile.

'Excellency?'

'Now we are sure, Lazaro, that the travellers sighted earlier are indeed our quarry. We shall not waste our time in a vain search on the mountain.' He moved towards the rickety ladder which led down. 'Better still, we can be sure that they are trapped by the snow on this side of the pass.' He was hurrying ahead, his Dominicans and hired soldiers bustling to follow down the ladder. 'All we have to do is pick them like flowers! We saddle our fresh horses, gentlemen, and we ride at once!'

Parton took the last footholds carefully and clambered up into the glare, swinging Fernando down from his shoulders as soon as he was well over and on to the flat snow beyond. The wind was chill but the sun felt wonderfully good for all that. Seward, from the vantage point of a knoll some way off, was looking out across the pass in the direction they were to take, his eyes shaded by his hand and Parton imitated him. Maria-Dolores then Gabriela joined him. The silence as they stared was long.

Cortes had come through that wide expanse of snow with a small army, thought Parton, astonished, and the Indians had used the pass regularly. Of course, it was the fresh snow that had fallen during the storm that had blanketed everything like that. On an average day, the trail would be visible and perhaps even quite easy to follow. This wasn't an average day, that was all. He looked at the sun. It would soon be nine o'clock. Through all this snow and out on the other side of the pass by mid-morning was beginning to look unlikely. He shook himself and called Seward over. In few words, it was agreed that, since the trail could not be seen under the snow, they would walk in a straight line eastwards. Parton bent for the boy and led the way off into the thick snow.

If the sun was a slight comfort, warming them a little, it

was also a blinding light directly in their eyes, reflecting from the vast field of snow and ice, while the wind whistled uncompromisingly through the pass, whipping spirals of powdery snow into their faces as they advanced. The only way to be sure they were moving due east, Parton decided, was to go straight towards the dazzling sun. But the drifts, into which he plunged waist-deep, soon forced him to pick out a meandering path, coming back to face east as often as he could. His eyes slowly adjusting to the glare, he began to make out the differences in the landscape ahead of him. The drifts were fresh snow, matt white, while yesterday's icy crust – ironically, the safest passage – gleamed where the wind had uncovered it. Where it was flat, they could move ahead a little faster, but on the slightest gradient, steps had to be kicked to avoid falls. Their progress was painfully slow and exhausting in the rarefied air.

They did not draw breath, they heaved, as if they were constantly on the point of suffocating, the thin air burning as it passed. They were bedraggled, powdered with the snow the wind was spinning. The snow melted in the sun and kept their blankets, the only efficient protection they had against the wind, sodden and heavy. Seward looked particularly pale, shaking with cold and tiredness, no doubt from his effort on the climb. Parton looked ahead. Things would be better when they were through the saddle, he thought. They seemed to have covered so little ground and time was going by, that was for sure. The sun was higher in the sky.

Of course, he realized, the sun would get warmer as the morning went on. Was he numb, or was the cold really less intense? He looked at the others. It was true, they seemed less frozen. When his feet began breaking through the icy crust without him having to kick at it deliberately, he was hardly surprised. In a sense, it was a good thing. There was no more skidding on the ice and the snow underneath was firm. But the crust cut into his shins, dragging on his legs, tiring them, slowing him. By the sun, it was at least ten. He looked back over his shoulder. Time was working against them now. If Palafox, with the thoroughness which could be expected of him, had sent searchers on horseback up the Indian trail, they would come upon the fugitives suddenly, caught in the snowbound pass. There would be no escape. How much further did they have to go? It was hard to say. The snowfield seemed endless.

Fernando appeared to be asleep again. So much the better. Parton plodded on, the girls behind him, stumbling, Seward at the rear, haggard, like a man in another world. The sun burned now because it was high. Parton looked up. Eleven o'clock. He urged the others on, trying to shake them out of the torpor that was overtaking them all. As long as they were in the snowy pass, they were an easy prey for Palafox. They had to get off the damned mountain and away. There was still snow to be crossed in the wind, and still the trail could not be seen. The ice gave way beneath their feet, tiring them, holding them back. Their progress was agonizingly slow and Parton looked back often, automatically, fearing pursuit as the minutes went by and noon approached.

The endless, rolling expanse of the mountain saddle went on to the very edge of the eastern slopes of the range. At one moment, Parton was in a dip, avoiding the soft snow and studying the opposite slope for the best way up; the next, he was at the top of a steep escarpment dropping away beneath his feet. To his right, the escarpment shelved down more gently, then the snow ended and the trail picked up again, clearly visible from above. Parton would have laughed if he had had enough breath to do so. They had surely been following it little short of exactly all along.

The snow on the slope, under the sun since dawn, was slushy and it soaked them afresh, but they didn't care. They splashed down the escarpment on to the rocky track, completely out of breath but so relieved they were almost happy.

'Dry land!' gasped Gabriela, stamping her foot on the rock, spattering meltwater all around and making Fernando giggle.

Parton looked down the slopes. They looked as dusty and rocky as on the other side. To the east, ahead of him, the country lay wide open, grey and green and the colour of dry grass, with dusty haze on the horizon and a dark smudge deceptively close on which he trained the telescope. Cathedral spires and towers. Puebla de Los Angeles, City of the Angels. He panned the telescope back to the slopes below, searching. Among the trees, he caught sight of roofs and brought the glass back on to them. There was a small hamlet nestling far below in a valley. He pointed to it. 'Let's get down there to that hamlet,' he said. 'We can surely get food there and perhaps horses. Come on.'

They needed no prompting. Over the next few hours, they moved quickly down the winding track through the grey rocks. The track soon became dry and although wet leather chafed their feet and Maria-Dolores in particular was suffering, it seemed easy to walk after the ordeal they had gone through. Out of the snow and wind, the sun was hot and their clothes dried out at last. Each downward step took them into richer and warmer air. Instead of tiring as they advanced, they felt stronger. Seward began to look less pale and, to his joy, Fernando no longer needed to be carried. They passed the first bushes, pointing to the first lizard scuttling away. Good humour began to flow through them, growing with the richness of the air and the heat.

They reached the treeline by mid-afternoon and went past the first trees at a good pace, the energy-filled air giving them wings. The gurgling of a stream drew them aside to drink and wash away the grime and dust of the mountain. They shook and brushed down their clothes, threw away the filthy, grit-laden blankets and began to feel light and clean and human again. It was wildly elating to breathe normally, to feel warmth and strength running through their limbs. In the hour which followed, they simply ate up the miles of trail which led down into the deep valley.

The roofs were clearly visible now, not far below, perhaps

half an hour away and Parton was delighted to see that there was no chapel in the tiny hamlet. No priests to meddle. That would be a change. They crossed a clearing and he could see the mountain back up there from the corner of his eye. He stopped for an instant to look back at the terrible place which they were, only a few hours later, so quickly forgetting. He frowned and took out the telescope.

As he trained it on the saddle between the two volcanoes, his blood ran cold.

High in the pass, clearly outlined by the westering sun, was a large group of horsemen. Parton watched them. No group as large had any possible business in the pass as late in the day unless they were Palafox's men. This time there was no doubt.

Their pursuers were on their track.

Palafox, his fine grey mare at a stand, pulled aside his black riding cloak and cursed silently. The birds had flown, the tracks which led to the eastern edge of the snowfield proved it. How dear a price they had paid, the Inquisitor-General could only surmise. On foot through those miles of snow and ice. . . . He shook his head. The Englishman had won another round.

But now the chase was truly on, thought Palafox with a surge of bloodlust and the scent was fresh. Whatever his aversion for the heat and glare of the sub-tropical sun, he had to stay in the saddle, lead the pack, stick close to the quarry and be in at the kill. It was bound to come. Parton could not win every battle and he had only to lose one to lose the war. . . . The fugitives could not be far ahead, they were on foot, they were exhausted – and Seward was with them.

Palafox stared out across the hunting ground below, dry hills and partly wooded valleys across to Puebla and the high mountains beyond, hazy in the late afternoon. Seward was even more important now that Parton had succeeded in escaping from the Mexico Valley, he thought. The

Inquisitor-General had had two fears concerning his ally. The first had been that, young and inexperienced, Seward might have flinched before the danger his role was to lead him into and that his Jacobite faith might have been weaker than his fear. The signals from the pass that morning had been reassuring on that score. Seward had not wavered. But now – this was Palafox's second fear and he had attempted to drill it into Seward in Tepoztlán while preparing the young Englishman for his possible rescue by Parton – the traitor must not give way to the temptation of rashly seizing any opportunity to force the issue and bring the game to an end. Parton had shown his ability to cheat or fight his way out of the most difficult situations and Palafox had little confidence in Seward's chances of trapping him. It was essential that Seward remain cautiously under cover and hence able to signal back. He was not to play the hero, but the traitor.

The word brought Palafox's thoughts to Torres and he compressed his lips with irritation. By the most optimistic reckoning, Bernardo and Porfirio would not be in Puebla before that evening, while the messenger who should have been through the town and down the Veracruz road by now, was lying dead on the far side of the mountain. Palafox looked eastwards towards Veracruz, the horizon barred by the high Orizaba volcano. Torres would be stopped, must be stopped, from carrying his precious information to the English. Bernardo and Porfirio must get through. But who would stop them? The fugitives on foot? No chance of that.

'No sign of them on the slopes, Excellency.' Lazaro reined in beside Palafox, a lean, scar-faced mercenary beside him. 'Modesto here knows the area down there. He says there are deep, forking valleys and woods it would take days to search.'

Palafox reached out without replying and took a telescope from Lazaro's hand. He trained it on the lower slopes and woods below, scanning right and left. Then he stopped, held the telescope still for a moment and looked through it carefully before shutting it with a click. 'In their place, what would you be looking for?' he asked, glancing from Lazaro to the mercenary.

'Food and rest?' ventured Lazaro, looking round at the snowy pass.

'Horses,' said Modesto and spat affirmatively.

'Right,' said Palafox, looking at him appreciatively. 'In Parton's shoes, I'd be desperate to find horses.' He handed the glass to the mercenary. 'Look down there,' he said, pointing. 'Tell me what you know about the place, if you know it.'

'I know it,' said Modesto with a grin, looking through the glass. 'It's a lousy little hamlet of half a dozen poverty-stricken homesteads. It's called Dos Caballos.'

Palafox smiled briefly. 'How very apt,' he said. 'And what are their chances of finding them there? The two horses, I mean?'

'Not a hope,' replied Modesto, shaking his head and passing the telescope back. 'The name's a standing joke in the area.'

'Perfect.' Palafox stirred in the saddle. 'But whatever happens, that hamlet is our first port of call. We must waste no more time.'

'Nightfall will slow us before we're down from the mountain,' proffered Lazaro.

'All the more reason to be on the move,' rejoined Palafox, pushing the mare forward at a brisk walk down the trail.

Parton strode down through the trees, forcing the pace, but saying nothing of what he had seen. They're sure to be on to us, he was thinking. They'll have found the messenger's body, they'll have seen our tracks in the snow, they'll know we're on foot. However, the screen of trees seemed to him thick enough to give them cover for the moment. For a moment, he toyed with the idea of branching off into the woods and not showing themselves at the hamlet below, but they had no more food and they could not pass up the chance of perhaps finding horses. They could not go on on foot. Horses were now their only chance of getting to the coast in time.

The track dropped to the valley floor where a narrow stream bubbled between meagre strips of maize. A boy with a stick was guarding them from two thin and determined-looking cows and he looked up in surprise as the fugitives appeared. Parton tried to speak to him but he hid in the maize. The hamlet was not much further on. It didn't look promising, thought Parton as he looked at the first three or four very poor houses of unhewn stone and clay. There was a movement in a doorway and he went over to it. A peasant in rags watched him suspiciously from within. He did not reply to Parton's greeting. There was no time to waste. Parton took a coin from his pocket and let it be seen. 'Can you help me, Señor?' he asked. 'Can we buy food?'

The man looked at the coin, came forward and nodded. '*Tortillas*,' he said. 'Nothing else.'

'Fine,' said Parton, trying not to think of better food. The peasant disappeared and came back a little later with a woman, a half-breed like himself, carrying a pile of *tortillas*. Parton handed over the coin and took out another. 'Do you – does anyone here – own horses which might be for sale?' he asked, taking the pancakes.

The man and woman both looked at him as if he had fallen on his head. 'No,' said the man simply. 'The cows do the ploughing and if we want to go somewhere we walk.'

'Where might I find horses?'

The peasant shook his head. 'Between here and Puebla, Señor, there is nothing. In Puebla there are stables. You must go there.'

'How far is Puebla?'

'If you walk quickly, four hours.'

Parton despaired. They were in no condition to walk quickly after two nights and days of scrambling over hills and mountains. Night would fall long before they reached Puebla, slowing them even more. Four hours would become six. And behind them were the horsemen – not that they could gallop down the twisting, rocky trail. Night would probably slow them too. They would surely have torches, but they would have to walk their horses by their light. In all, Parton reckoned that the fugitives had a three-hour lead. It would quickly reduce as the road bettered nearer to Puebla. In all likelihood, they would be caught before they got there.

'Thank you,' he said flatly, giving the peasant the second coin.

'Come and see!' called Fernando, running up and taking Parton by the hand. Parton realized that he had not noticed the others moving on in the hamlet while he had been speaking. Now, round the corner of a house, he saw Gabriela and Maria-Dolores, Seward watching them, in conversation with a bearded man by a cart. Maria-Dolores seemed to be holding a pair of shoes in her hand.

'He sells everything!' said Fernando excitedly. 'Clothes and blankets and everything! He's a hawker!'

Parton saw two horses harnessed to the cart and turned angrily to his informer. 'There are horses over there!' he protested.

'Si, Señor!' called the man apologetically, running up in hopes of more largesse. 'But they do not belong to anyone here. They belong to Gomez and I do not think he will sell them to you. He needs them to get back to Puebla. Oh!' His eyes shone and he caught Parton's arm, sure now there would be a reward. 'If you pay him enough, he will make room in his cart and drive you into Puebla with him . . .'

Gomez would have been talkative, but Parton followed the others' example and lay back on the piles of blankets and rolls of cloth in the bottom of the cart and closed his eyes. For the extortionate fee they had paid for the ride, they had a right to some quiet and rest. But, unlike the others who had fallen asleep immediately, Parton watched the hawker through closed lashes. The man must have realized that he was transporting queer fish. Who were these people who had come down off the mountain in rags – rich woman's rags, in one case at least – and had made his day by buying half his stock of blankets, a cloak for the child, a dress and shoes for the one in rich rags? And Parton had bought powder for the pistols, their stock having been ruined by the rain. Gomez, black-bearded and dark-eyed, looked back at the sleeping travellers every now and then and Parton would have given a lot to have been able to penetrate his regard and know what he was thinking. There was no trusting him, Parton knew.

But the ride in the hawker's cart was a godsend. They would get to Puebla in less than half the time it would have taken on foot, and, although they were travelling no faster than the horsemen who would still be riding down the mountain trail, they were maintaining their lead. And into the bargain, the cart was giving them some unhoped for rest.

Night fell as they came into the approaches to Puebla. This town would be difficult and dangerous. Parton contrived to raise his head and look out over the side of the cart without arousing Gomez' suspicion. They were riding through poor Indian quarters as there were on the outskirts of all New Spanish towns, squat mud-walled buildings and lean-to plank shacks on either side. Gomez drove straight on up the road, but it seemed to Parton that he was nervous and looked back at his passengers more and more often. However, he showed no sign of wanting to wake them and ask them where they wanted to get off. On the contrary, he appeared more concerned with letting them sleep on. Then, some way ahead, Parton saw the reason. Two priests were standing by a house wall at the beginning of the Spanish town. They were talking to someone on foot who was now leaving them and walking on into town. The Inquisition had been alerted and was watching the roads in and out of Puebla. Gomez undoubtedly knew it and he was about to finish a profitable day by turning the fugitives over. The priests were little more than a hundred yards ahead and it was no use getting down and trying to slip off unseen into the Indian *barrio*. There was only one way through.

Parton slid forward in the cart, keeping low, pulling out a pistol. 'Not a false movement and not a sign to them,' whispered Parton in the hawker's back, prodding him with the pistol. 'Believe me I'll blow you apart if you don't do as I say. Slow your horses gently but don't stop.' Gomez, with a sideways glance of terror, obeyed. Parton kicked out at Gabriela, closest to him. 'Keep down! Wake the others and hide under the blankets!' he hissed. 'Inquisition ahead!'

He leaned back, took a couple of blankets and pulled them over himself, pushing some of the assorted hardware at the front of the cart back over his friends. They looked well hidden, he decided. He prodded Gomez again. 'I'm right behind you,' he whispered. 'Don't try anything, just ride in normally and take your usual road. Any tricks and I'll shoot you.' He pulled a blanket over his head and lay flat. He could just see Gomez' back above him. The priests could not be far now. He pulled out a second pistol and held it ready in his left hand.

'Halt!'

The cart came to a stop. Parton watched Gomez and hoped the priests would not search.

'It's Gomez,' said one of them, close by the side of the cart. Parton imagined him giving a quick look into it.

'Evening, *padres*,' said Gomez.

Seward stayed still under the blankets and held his breath. Parton was on the alert, with two loaded pistols, and he was quite capable of turning the situation to his advantage if Seward called out. Now was not the time. Perhaps the stables would provide a better opportunity.

'Drive on,' said another voice. The cart shook and began to move and Parton breathed out slowly. He lifted his head slightly the better to watch the hawker. The man sat looking stolidly forward. 'Take your usual way back to your house or wherever you usually go,' whispered Parton. 'Don't stop until we're in a safe place.'

The cart went uphill then turned right and through narrower streets for half a mile. It stopped in front of double doors in the stone wall of a two-storeyed house. 'I have to open the doors, Señor,' said Gomez unhappily.

The street was dark and apparently empty. 'Go on,' said Parton, raising himself on one elbow to watch.

Gomez unlocked the doors, opened them, climbed back up and drove the cart in. Parton stood up and gestured the hawker down again with the pistol. He called the others out of hiding. 'Look out into the street,' he whispered.

'No one in sight,' said Gabriela.

'All right. We're on our way. Gomez?'

'Señor?'

Parton hit him as he turned, a blow full on the jaw and the hawker crumpled to the floor. The big key to the doors was in his pocket. They slipped out into the street and Parton locked the doors behind them. 'Let's get away from here,' he said.

They walked silently through several dark streets until Parton called a halt. 'Now we need horses,' he said, 'and while we're about it, the best.'

'The stables are higher up, that way,' said Seward.

'That's right,' said Maria-Dolores.

Parton turned to her. 'You know Puebla too?' Of course she does, an inner voice warned him.

'Quite well.'

'Do we have no choice of stables?'

'Not after sunset. Even the main commercial stables have a hard time staying awake for travellers,' said Seward.

'And if there's an alert on, the Inquisition will be having them watched,' added Maria-Dolores.

Parton had already thought of that a thousand times. They had no choice. They would have to slip through the net as they had earlier. 'Fernando?' he whispered. 'Are you awake now?'

'Just about,' said Fernando, rubbing his eyes.

'Listen. We're going to sneak through the streets and we don't want to be heard. Are you ready?'

'Ready!'

Parton let Seward and Maria-Dolores lead the way. The streets were strangely empty and echoing. When they were several blocks higher, bells began to toll above.

'Compline,' whispered Maria-Dolores. 'A good thing because most of the clerics will be shut away in church for the next half hour.'

'And the people who aren't in church?' asked Parton, whom the clanging bells were beginning to irritate.

'They'll be out later for the evening walk on the *paseo*, but now they'll be having supper. We could hardly have chosen a better moment.'

Higher, they stopped in the shadow of a house wall. 'The stables are up there at the top of the street,' whispered Seward. 'This side is the back.' If only Parton goes in there without me, he was thinking, I might be able to do something.

Parton pointed out a porch on the far side of the street, closer to the stables. 'That might give us cover,' he breathed. They crept along the foot of the wall, relieved that the echoing bells drowned whatever noise they were making. Parton slipped quickly across the street and checked that the wide porch was empty, then beckoned the others across into its deep shadows. Looking out, they could now see clearly the long, low wall of the stable building at right angles to the street they had climbed. At the far end was a door and a window, light creeping from between the shutters. 'The stableman's quarters,' whispered Seward. Go on in there, he willed. Leave me free for a few minutes with the boy.

Parton searched the shadows for hidden watchers. He could see none, but there was no doubt that some kind of watch was set. Wouldn't it be logical to watch the main doors on the far side? In any event, the back door was the way in. He turned to Seward. 'We'll go in together,' he said. He was about to move forward when Maria-Dolores touched his arm. 'Let *me* go,' she whispered. 'I'm the only one among us who stands a chance of succeeding.'

'What did you say?' broke in Gabriela stiffly, wondering if she was dreaming. Maria-Dolores had been a hostage, then a fellow traveller, and now she was proposing to go out on a difficult task as Gabriela herself had when she had opened the granary door at the monastery. 'Why shouldn't *I* go?'

'Because your description has surely gone out by now,' replied Maria-Dolores quietly, 'and I'm certain the stables are being watched in one way or another. If the priests lay their hands on any of you three, it's all up for you, whereas I'm not wanted for arrest. I'm Palafox's mistress and that gives me power over them, believe me.'

There was something in what she was saying, thought Parton. There might be treachery too, the warning voice told him. Could he really trust her? Had she made love with him so as to gain his trust, the better to betray him? 'But they'll let you ride off with horses for all of us?' he asked. 'I find that hard to believe.'

Maria-Dolores held his gaze through the darkness. 'I can try. I stand a better chance than any of you.'

'We can't trust her,' said Seward to Parton, cursing Maria-Dolores but hoping to use her. 'We can't let her go in there alone.' Whether or not she had sincerely gone over to Parton's side, she must not get in his way. Parton had to go in there with her. 'What's more, we need the finest mounts in the stables if we're to cover ground quickly.'

'I'm a horsewoman and I know how to choose the best,' retorted Maria-Dolores quickly. 'As for trusting me, I'm not sure that you've much choice. You must avoid showing your faces.'

'Once she's in there,' whispered Gabriela, turning to Parton, 'she only has to say the word to have us caught like rats in a trap.'

Parton found Maria-Dolores's eyes again. 'She won't,' he

said. 'She's right she has the best chance of succeeding.' This may be the biggest mistake you've ever made, he was thinking. 'I'll be watching,' he went on. 'Go ahead.'

Maria-Dolores turned and disappeared among the shadows of the street. Parton caught a glimpse of her, outlined by the weak light, as she limped to the door by the window. The memory of her feet bound in rags, of her determination, helped to reassure him. Her soft knock was scarcely audible at that distance. The door opened – a yellowish gleam from within – and closed behind her.

In the porch, there was a long moment of constrained silence. Gabriela sat back against the wall, Fernando drowsing, his head on her shoulder. 'I hope you're right,' she said finally.

'So do I,' said Parton, watching the stables.

'If you're not sure,' muttered Seward, settling next to Gabriela and hoping she would take sides with him, 'we shouldn't have let her go in there alone.' If only Parton were to follow Maria-Dolores, Seward would be alone with the child in a stronghold of the Inquisition and his ordeal would no doubt be over. Alone? There would be Gabriela too. The thought shot through his mind with a blend of pain and excitement. Could he get Gabriela to listen to him, even to go with him? Even to love him? Wasn't that what he wanted? He hardly dared admit it to himself, but it was true, he realized, and he wanted it intensely.

'Perhaps not,' conceded Parton, his eyes riveted on the building. Perhaps he had allowed his physical passion for Maria-Dolores to distort his judgement. Gabriela – he remembered their first night together outside Cordoba and was surprised to find that his feelings for her were still as strong – was perfectly within her rights in showing her suspicion. He narrowed his eyes. The back door of the stables had opened and a dark figure – a woman, it seemed to him, but certainly not Maria-Dolores – had slipped out and hurried round the end of the building. Who had sent her and on what errand?

Was his confidence in Palafox's former mistress justified? 'If I do have to go,' he said softly, 'the two of you must look after Fernando and the packs. Stay here and stay hidden. This porch will be the meeting-place whether we find horses or not. Agreed?'

'Of course,' replied Gabriela.

'Agreed,' said Seward, masking his excitement.

Parton took out and checked his pistols. At the stables, the woman was already back. Behind her, outlined for a second as the door opened and he went in, unmistakably dark-frocked, was a priest.

'I'm going in there,' said Parton, and he stepped out into the street.

CHAPTER TWELVE

Parton walked softly up the dark street, alert for signs of danger. The watch on the stables might simply have been organized on the basis that the stableman would send a message to the Inquisition if any suspicious customers came his way. But other precautions might well have been taken, and if Maria-Dolores had decided to betray . . . As Parton crossed quietly to the door, seeing no hidden watchers, the compline bells ceased abruptly and the night was reassuringly silent. Through the window shutters, he could see little apart from a glowing fire in a small hearth. He tried the door and opened it soundlessly. Watch out for the woman who had run the errand, he thought, looking in.

The room was a kitchen cum living quarters for the stableman. A half-eaten meal lay on the table, no doubt the man's interrupted supper. There was no one in the room. To the left, light came through an open door which led into the stables themselves. Parton closed the street door, bolting it to prevent fresh interruptions and went over to the open door and listened. He could hear voices, one of them Maria-Dolores's, but they were muffled. He took a pistol from his waist and moved stealthily forward.

The stables were large, with a long line of stalls on either side of a wide passage running down the middle of the building. In the passage stood the priest, fat and self-important, his back to Parton and Maria-Dolores, partly hidden by the priest. A man and an old Indian woman – the messenger, thought Parton – were preparing saddles and bridles further down. Parton crept forward towards an empty stall and slipped into the shadows. The priest was not far from him now.

'And so you understand, Father Obaldes,' Parton heard Maria-Dolores say, 'my need for several horses. I must ride to Mexico City immediately to rejoin His Excellency and I shall go escorted by the people who saved my life. I intend to have them recompensed.'

Parton's relief was immediate. She was lying. He had not misjudged Maria-Dolores.

'Of course, Doña Maria.' Parton could see a greasy smile on the man's face. There was something false about it and there was danger in the air. 'But, Doña Maria, there was a man – the man who abducted you – whom His Excellency was most anxious – he emphasized it strongly in his message – was most anxious to capture dead or alive.'

'I believe I told you, Obaldes, that he was killed by my rescuers. You will find his body where the fighting took place, near the hamlet I told you of.'

Maria-Dolores and the priest knew each other, thought Parton, which meant that the man was no minor official in the Puebla Inquisition. He spoke of only one message about Maria-Dolores and her kidnapper, and that was vital news because it meant that the riders for Veracruz had not yet reached Puebla. If only Maria-Dolores could succeed in bluffing her way through the priest's questioning, the fugitives could be on their way with a chance.

The priest laughed almost as if he had understood Parton's thinking. 'The trouble is, Doña Maria,' he said, moving forward and redoubling his greasy smile, 'that I don't believe a word you say. And even if I did, it would make no difference. I fancy I know when a favourite of His Excellency falls into disgrace . . .' He was close to her now, his eyes on her breasts which tautened the cloth of the unbleached calico dress bought from the hawker. 'You see, His Excellency's orders were, if we found you, to hold you awaiting his pleasure.' He smirked. 'I do believe holding you will be more my pleasure than his . . .'

As the fat priest laughed at his own joke and the stableman

and the old woman stopped their work to watch, Parton cocked the pistol and stepped out of the shadows.

'Nobody move,' he said.

Seward sat in the porch in the darkness, thinking furiously. He had only to hand the boy over to the Inquisition to sabotage Parton's mission and bring an end to the nerve-racking game he had been playing for what seemed to have been an eternity. But two things were worrying him. One was that he had to be totally sure of succeeding. Palafox had ordered him strictly to avoid rash attempts which would only serve to reveal him as a traitor and, if Parton were to catch him now, it would be catastrophic.

The second was Gabriela's reaction. Seward's feelings were clear now. Without him realizing or admitting it, Gabriela's passionate, dark-eyed beauty had been stirring him for some time, perhaps even longer than he thought. He wanted her and he wanted to take her with him. The problem was that she must not resist. How deeply did she love Parton, how loyal to him would she be? Wouldn't she try to stop Seward, wouldn't she fight him? And in that case, Seward was far from sure if he could persuade the Inquisition to treat her with leniency. How much influence could he have on Palafox and his brutal followers? He reminded himself yet again that the Inquisitor-General was his ally and not his master, but the memory of those lifeless eyes brought back misgivings. Whatever happened, Seward could not face the idea of Gabriela suffering the kind of dreadful punishment which Palafox and his thugs might take pleasure in devising for her.

But if Gabriela agreed to go over to the Inquisition with him, Seward could say that she had helped him and obtain her pardon. And from there on . . . What he now had to do was to explain to Gabriela, to turn her against Parton, to win her over.

'Gabriela?'

'Yes?'

Already he was hesitating. He had to be careful not to say too much. He could imagine Parton coming back to the porch unexpectedly and Gabriela saying to him 'You won't believe what Seward's trying to persuade me to do!' Perhaps the first thing to do was to lure her away from the meeting-place. Seward stood up and peered out into the street. There was no sign of Parton's return, but the street would all the same be risky. And inwards, what did the porch lead to? While starting to speak to Gabriela, he began slowly and methodically to feel his way along the wall opposite her. 'There's something I wanted to tell you now we're alone together.'

'Yes?' Seward's tone was strange and Gabriela had a sudden premonition that he was going to surprise her.

'Your mother, first of all.' Pilar was an obstacle that had to be removed quickly, thought Seward. 'I want you to know that I only did – what I did with her because Parton wanted it, ordered me to mix with your family because he needed it as cover along the road.'

Gabriela laughed quietly. 'If that's what you call mixing with my family! But I can't say it ever bothered me. Why should it?'

'I'm glad to hear that. But I swear it was Parton who gave the order. At the same time, he told me he was going to seduce you so as to use you.'

Gabriela's laughter died. She knew perfectly well that what Seward was saying was utterly false.

Seward thought that he should stop there. If Parton came back now he could explain what he had said by his love for Gabriela, but he should not go too far. Perhaps he should try another approach. He would say more against Parton if he managed to get Gabriela away from the porch. 'I want to tell you something else, Gabriela. When they . . . made me talk and I told Palafox everything I knew.' There was an opening behind him, a draught flowing through it. Since there was no

238

door to close it, it was probably the way through to an inner courtyard or garden. It would be a first step. 'There was one thing I didn't say,' he went on, crossing back to the opening which gave on to the street. 'I told them nothing about you. I didn't mention you.' Still no sign of Parton. Seward went on speaking while trying to think of a way to induce Gabriela to go through the passage and, if possible, further. 'Whatever happens, I don't want you to be hurt. I'd do anything to protect you from that.'

'That's – it's kind of you,' said Gabriela, slightly bewildered. What was this man doing, prowling around in the dark and making what was tantamount to a declaration of love? She hugged Fernando instinctively closer. The sound of footsteps came from out in the street and she jumped. 'What's that?' she asked softly.

Seward looked out. Lower down the street, a man and a woman were crossing. As far as he could judge, they were evening strollers. He turned and crossed quickly to Gabriela. '*Priests*,' he hissed, taking her by the shoulder. 'Quickly! They're coming this way!'

Gabriela held Fernando to her and scrambled to her feet. 'We're trapped,' she whispered, shrinking back against the wall.

'No! There's a passage over here! Come on!' Seward helped her forward to the opening, then led the way into the blackness of the passage. They came out into the open air. There was just enough light to make out bushes and an arbour. 'We must go as far as we can,' whispered Seward urgently.

Beyond the arbour, they were halted by a wall. Gabriela's arms were aching as she cradled Fernando, willing him not to wake up and betray their presence by a sound. 'There's a gate here,' breathed Seward, unlatching it carefully. On the far side of the wall, all was darkness and silence. Perhaps there was some kind of yard or another garden. 'They won't find us here,' he murmured close to Gabriela's ear, leading her through the gate and closing it quietly behind them.

And neither will Parton, he thought triumphantly as he helped Gabriela to sit with her back to the wall in the deep shadows – neither will Parton.

'Stay where you are, whore,' Parton said to Maria-Dolores. 'And you, priest, not a sound. Stableman, come here. The woman too.' He took up position in the middle of the passage between the stalls and drew his second pistol. 'What's behind that door?' he asked the stableman, pointing to a door at the end of the stables.

'Tack, Señor.'

'Go there. All of you. *Slowly*.'

At the tackroom door, the stableman turned questioningly. 'Open it wide,' said Parton. 'Then you all go in.'

The room was small and cluttered. There was a window. Parton thought that he couldn't risk leaving them conscious. 'Face down on the floor,' he ordered.

Maria-Dolores threw him an uncertain glance and he said: 'You too, whore.'

He hit the stableman first, then the priest. The woman was a problem, but he wanted no witnesses. He hit her more lightly. He leaned over Maria-Dolores. 'Go on,' she said, choking, her eyes turned to his. Pain and fear swept across her features as he leaned closer.

He raised her head and kissed her.

'Oh my God,' she said, burying her face for an instant in his shoulder as he helped her to her feet, 'I thought you'd really decided to get rid of me this time.'

Parton looked into her eyes and shook his head. 'I'm beginning to think I can trust you,' he said. 'Let's see to the horses.'

'I've chosen four,' said Maria-Dolores as Parton locked the tackroom door behind them. 'They're good.'

'Why not five?' He lifted a saddle.

'Can you really see Fernando riding at night?' Maria-

240

Dolores led a fine black mare out from her stall and finished saddling her.

'No,' acquiesced Parton. 'Which one do I saddle?'

Maria-Dolores had chosen a piebald and two bay geldings apart from the black mare. She really did know horses, he thought. These four looked fine – and there was an advantage in choosing at the main livery stables of a large town. Later, they might find it hard to get mounts as good. He saddled the piebald and decided it would be his.

'Do you think they'll see us riding out?' asked Maria-Dolores. 'There, I've finished these two.'

'No way of knowing,' said Parton, helping her with the last horse. 'The old woman went to fetch the priest. Perhaps there's no watch in the strict sense.'

'Obaldes will be missed. He's important here. We've little time.'

Parton went to the big main doors, opened them a little and peered out. 'No one in sight,' he said, pushing them wide. Maria-Dolores was already up on the black mare, one of the bays attached to her saddle. Parton followed her out, leading the piebald and the other bay and closed the doors. Then he mounted and they rode smartly round the corner of the long building into the dark little streets behind. The porch was only a few yards down. The street appeared to be empty. 'Psst!' Parton called towards the porch. There was no reply. It was strange. They must surely have heard the horses arrive. He dismounted and went into the porch.

He found nothing but the packs and stopped dead for a moment, staring into the darkness as if he could cut through it. Then he looked out into the street again. 'There's no one here,' he said.

Bernardo and Porfirio were among Palafox's toughest and most professional soldiers. They knew the urgency of their task and they had no time for creature comforts. As soon as they had reined in in front of the building in a courtyard behind the bishop's palace which was Inquisition headquarters in Puebla, they had dismounted and unsaddled their horses themselves to save time and they were now eating and drinking standing while fresh mounts were prepared.

'Gentlemen!' The newcomer was a small, swarthy man in Dominican black and white. 'I understand you won't come in to take a little rest?'

'No time, Father,' said Bernardo, the taller of the two messengers. In spite of his position as one of the Inquisitor-General's most trusted hirelings, he knew that some respect was due to this man, Costilla, chief of the Puebla Inquisition. 'Please listen carefully, Father,' he went on. 'His Excellency expects the greatest vigilance on your part – you are to leave all other business and to neglect nothing in the search for these fugitives: the man described by the first message and the young woman Maria-Dolores and now also a second Englishman, younger than the first, a second young woman with black hair, and above all a child. A boy of eight by the name of Fernando Torres Mendieta. If possible all these persons are to be taken alive, although they are to be stopped at whatever cost. If you were to fail – I may speak freely, Father?'

'Of course,' muttered Costilla unhappily.

'I believe His Excellency would punish the person responsible with the same punishment as he is devising for the Englishman named Parton.'

'Ah!' Costilla licked his lips nervously. 'We have men out on every road in and out of Puebla. We have sent men out to the surrounding towns and villages, but there has been no sign of these criminals, no sign at all.' He spoke quickly, self-defensively.

'We rode into town easily enough,' broke in Porfirio. 'Two men are not sufficient. No one must move in this town without your knowing it. Put twenty men on every road, not two. Let them see without being seen. And please don't forget important places like stores and stables where runaways might try to help themselves, or even buy horses and provisions. We know they have money.'

'Precautions have already been taken, gentlemen, but I will immediately order their reinforcement as you suggest. Ah, I see your horses are ready. Are you sure you do not wish me to replace you in forwarding your message so that you can rest?'

Useless trying to get round us, Costillo, thought Bernardo as he swung into the saddle, it's Palafox you'll have to deal with if you don't do your job. 'No thank you, Father,' he said politely. 'His Excellency has entrusted us with a particular mission and we shall see it through ourselves. *Adios*.'

Costillo mopped his brow as the two men rode out of the courtyard and took the direction of the Veracruz road. He could scarcely believe it. He had been threatened with torture and death, he, the head of the Puebla Inquisition, and in view of the quarter from which came the threat, he decided he would put fifty men on every road, not twenty. He would seal the district off like a prison. He went inside the building to give orders and ran into one of his younger colleagues.

'Father, I was looking for you!' gasped the younger man. 'There's Gomez the hawker here and he says four individuals with a child forced him at pistol-point to hide them in his cart and bring them into town from Dos Caballos and the description made me think of the Englishman and the young woman in rich clothes—' He broke off, breathless.

Ice seized Costillo. 'And where are they now, fool?' He shook the young priest.

'He doesn't know, Father. They knocked him out and left him locked up at his house and he came to us as soon as he could.'

'Mary Mother of God,' gabbled Costillo. 'They're *here*! Where's Fuente? We're going to have to cordon off the town, there's not a minute to lose! And where the devil's Obaldes?'

'The old woman from the livery stables came to fetch Father Obaldes,' said the younger friar. 'About a quarter of an hour ago.'

Costillo's eyes widened slowly. Then he snapped: 'Get every man available and let's be down at the stables before it's too late! At the double!'

'But don't you see, Gabriela!' Seward was beginning to feel desperate. He was doing his utmost to win Gabriela over, but she had remained coldly unresponsive throughout his declarations of love. How far could he go without revealing all his cards? 'You shouldn't be mixed up in all this, a girl like you shouldn't be running from the Inquisition! You've done nothing really wrong and neither have I. Parton's in this business up to his neck and so is *she* because she's Palafox's woman, but we're not, we're just people he's using and we could refuse, can't you see that, we could get up and walk away!'

Gabriela's first reaction to Seward's passionate outbursts had been shocked surprise, but shock was now turning to anger. What she had done, she thought heatedly, remembering the granary door, had been to help rescue Seward from the clutches of the Inquisition. And now the same Seward was pouring out his love for her and trying to persuade her to go off with him as if the Inquisition didn't exist! How could she tell him she didn't love him, didn't even like him, that she had only felt sorry for what he had suffered?

'Gabriela . . .' His hand pressed her arm.

If only he'd stop pawing me, thought Gabriela. How much longer would they have to hide in the pitch blackness of the garden? Had the priests searched the porch had they found the packs and blankets? If so, wouldn't they search further, wouldn't they come back with reinforcements? She strained her ears to catch whatever sound might come from back there.

'Please try to understand—'

'Be quiet! Listen!' The sound had been muffled, but it seemed to Gabriela that she had heard hoofbeats out in the street.

'Listen to what?' said Seward deliberately. He had heard the sound too and he was suddenly afraid of Parton's return. They were hidden in the garden, but time was running out and he had to get Gabriela and the boy further away before Parton began to search. 'I can't hear anything. Unless—' He dropped his voice to a murmur. 'Unless the priests are back.'

'No. It was hoofbeats.' Gabriela listened again. This time she had to admit that there was not a sound.

'You see? You must have imagined it.' Seward prepared himself for a last-ditch attempt. 'Gabriela, come with me, let's leave all this dreadful business behind. Can't you see he's just using you? All you're good for is looking after the boy like a baby-minder or a nurse while he goes off with the priest's whore!' Seward clutched at Gabriela's shoulder and launched his final attack. 'Didn't you wonder what they'd both been doing together last night when the storm broke? I didn't. I was awake. I heard her screaming while he—'

'That's none of your business, or mine!' broke in Gabriela furiously. 'I'm not married to him!' Of course Parton had sworn no oaths to her and of course he was free, as she was, to do as he wished. If the growing attraction for Maria-Dolores which she had noticed in Parton pained her, she was certainly not going to discuss it with Seward. The man disgusted her now with all this disloyal and spiteful nonsense he was talking. She—

Disturbed by the angry exchange, Fernando stirred in her arms and looked around. 'What are we doing?' he asked.

Gabriela's indignant thoughts calmed abruptly as she realized that it was Fernando who was asking the right question. Perhaps Seward, in his apparently confused state of mind, believed that he and she could just wander away with no fear of the consequences, but what was supposed to happen to Fernando if they did? How could Seward imagine that they could abandon the boy in the dark, or, worse still, take him with them? In either case the Inquisition would be likely to recapture him, and then . . . For the first time, Gabriela fully realized the threat which hung over

Fernando's head. If he were caught, Palafox would not hesitate to use him – would go to any lengths including torture and murder – in order to capture or at least silence Torres. The only way to avoid that was to get the boy away to his father quickly enough and that was what Parton had gone to the stables for. And instead of waiting at the meeting-place for the horses they so vitally needed, what were they doing? Hiding in the dark where Parton could not find them. She hugged Fernando closer to her and stood up.

'I'm going back to the porch,' she said. 'I don't think the priests you saw are there and I'm sure I heard hoofbeats.'

Seward stood up beside her, humiliated and rebuffed, fearful of discovery and of Parton's revenge, but still impatient to get away with the boy and end his long ordeal. 'I can carry Fernando if you like,' he whispered, reaching out.

'No!' shouted Fernando, wriggling from Seward's grasp.

'Ssh, Fernando,' warned Gabriela. 'No noise!' She turned to Seward. 'If you want to make yourself useful, open the gate.'

Seward hesitated. He had seconds in which to decide. Only violence could serve him now. Could he force Gabriela to come with him? It was unthinkable, she would struggle, the brat would scream . . . Then could he seize Fernando and run? The same thing would happen, and he would be hard put to it to find his way quickly in the dark. There *had* been hoofbeats and Parton was unlikely to be far. The chances of success were all too slim. Palafox had forbidden him to run the risk of discovery unless he were certain to succeed. There was nothing for it but to go back, to go on playing the game. Worse still, now he would have to show diligence to turn away Parton's hostility and suspicion when he learned what Gabriela would tell him. Damn it and damn it again. He was trapped in his treacherous game and the glory of it had long since disappeared. With a heavy heart, he unlatched and opened the gate in the wall.

Gabriela felt her way forward past the arbour until she

found the beginning of the passage. 'Not a sound,' she breathed to Fernando, creeping through to the porch. All was quiet. She crossed to the far wall and, surprised, felt around on the ground, turning as Seward came into the empty space behind her. 'The packs and blankets have gone,' she whispered.

Maria-Dolores and Parton walked the four horses as silently as they could through the streets which sloped down from the back of the stables. Starting from the porch where they had loaded the packs and blankets in order to save time, they had searched all the streets around, systematically but quickly. Parton knew that they were walking on the edge of a precipice. At any moment, one of the three in the tackroom could wake up and begin to shout. In future, he warned himself, he must show no mercy in situations like that. If there were to be a future, he countered mockingly. Where had Gabriela and Seward gone with Fernando, why had they left the porch?

'Nothing and nobody,' said Maria-Dolores at the end of the last street.

There was one place where they might be, thought Parton grimly. 'We may have to assume that the Inquisition's caught them,' he said. 'Where are they likely to be in that case?'

'Headquarters are behind the bishop's palace. But if they're locked up in there, I don't see how we can get them out.'

Parton shrugged. He would have no choice but to try. 'Explain to me how to get there, tell me whatever you can about the place,' he said.

Maria-Dolores hesitated. 'Can't we go on looking just a little longer? Can't we try the porch one last time?

'The stables are getting more and more dangerous by the minute. But yes, let's try.' Parton led the way, looking carefully ahead. The streets were still quiet. Why had he split them up, why hadn't he taken them all in with him when he had gone into the stables? It was ridiculous blaming himself for that, he told himself. He had gone in blind and there had been every good reason for leaving them in hiding. Perhaps he should simply have kept Fernando with him. Because now, he asked himself caustically, you'd go off and leave Gabriela and Seward to their fate?

They were almost halfway up the street when shouting broke out on the far side of the stables. It wasn't simply the stableman or Obaldes. There was a crowd. Light was outlining the black edges of the low stable building.

'Get back!' said Parton to Maria-Dolores. There was nothing for it but to retreat into the darkness and make fresh plans – not that many plans were available. It was as he turned that he saw a head leaning out of the porch higher up the street, profiled by the light. He recognized it immediately. '*Gabriela*!' he called, overjoyed.

Fernando was already coming, Gabriela running beside him, Seward following. Maria-Dolores was up on the black mare and Parton handed Fernando quickly up to her, sure by the flair she had shown in choosing the horses that she would be capable of looking after the boy. Parton himself needed his hands free.

'The packs!' said Gabriela. 'They've gone!'

'We've got them!' Parton helped Gabriela up on to her bay and mounted the piebald as Seward clambered on to his mount. The noise back at the stables was increasing. 'Quickly now!' called Parton, turning and spurring up his horse.

At the bottom of the street, Maria-Dolores took the lead, Fernando perched in front of her. Parton glanced back. People were opening windows and coming out into the street to see what the fuss was about and a torch flickered up at the top behind the stables. But it looked as if they were away without having been clearly seen. They rounded a corner and rode on at a brisk trot. Parton rode up beside Maria-Dolores. 'There'll be priests on the way out,' he called. 'Let me know when we're on the right road and I'll take the lead.'

They came out into a wider street and Maria-Dolores

gestured ahead. Parton fell in beside Seward and beckoned him on ahead with him. He pulled out a pistol. The two of them were leading the way now, the girls right behind them. They were coming to the outskirts. Ahead, the houses came to an end and the Veracruz road ran on. Parton remembered the spot now. Some way further on was . . .

Oh my God, he thought, remembering clearly.

Some way further on, at the edge of town, the Veracruz road went through a fortified toll house.

CHAPTER THIRTEEN

The night was too dark to see the archway of the toll house clearly ahead, but it could not be far now. Parton decided to approach gently, reining in slightly and signalling to the others to do the same. There would always be time to spur up at the last minute if need be.

He could see it now, a massive stone block flanked by high walls, only a hundred or so yards ahead, and it seemed to him that the gates were open. Seeming was not enough, however. He made the pistol ready in his hand. If the gates were shut, they would have to stop. If not. . . .

No. Now he could see the road going on through the archway. The priests were there, only two of them, one coming forward to stop them. Let them think we're going to stop, thought Parton. He half turned and spoke softly to the others. 'When I give the signal, spur up and ride straight at them,' he said.

'Halt!'

The second priest back under the archway still had time to close the gates quickly if he wanted to, thought Parton. Just a little closer before we move.

The first priest was in front of them, waving his arms and shouting 'Halt!' again.

'Now!' said Parton, firing his pistol towards the archway and digging his heels into the piebald's flanks at the same time. The powerful animal leaped forward and Parton saw the priest dive for cover with only seconds to spare. They were at the archway, they were thundering through and the other priest was nowhere in sight; he must have jumped for cover too. Parton glanced aside. They were all there. They had horses and they were out of Puebla.

The road twisted, pale strip against dark surrounding scrub, and they slowed now that they could no longer be seen from the town.

'What now?' asked Gabriela. She had decided that she would wait to be alone with Parton to tell him what had happened with Seward in the garden.

'We try to find out how quickly we can get these horses down the road in the night without breaking our necks,' said Parton. 'As soon as they've realized in Puebla exactly what's happened, they'll organize the pursuit.' He said nothing about the riders in the pass, who would soon arrive in Puebla themselves – and among whom Palafox was certain to figure. It was enough for Parton alone to be aware of how pressing was the danger behind them.

Riding in the dark was no easy business. They could see the road, but there were ruts to be avoided and people too – the Indian carriers slept out on the roadside with their families and their burdens. However, close to Puebla this was less of a problem and the road was in fair condition. They were able to move quickly for the first half hour. The horses were fast and sure-footed and eager to move. The best thing was to let them go ahead at their own pace and not try to push them faster. When the road became really much more difficult and dangerous, they had to be slowed and held to a cautious walk.

No use wishing for moonlight, thought Parton. Their pursuers would benefit from it as much as themselves. All that could be done was to put as much ground as possible between them and Puebla. Their lead over their pursuers, he estimated, could be no more than an hour now, no doubt less. They rode through the small town of Amozoc in the late evening. Strollers were still taking the air before retiring and they turned to look in surprise as the four horses clattered through. After Amozoc, Parton remembered, the road wound in a long stretch with nothing but tiny villages until the town of Los Reyes. It would take them the rest of the night to get there safely.

The night was long and wearisome. Fernando spent it

jogging uncomfortably, gripping the pommel or the horse's mane, in front of Maria-Dolores or Parton or Gabriela – with Seward he would not go. They tried mounting him behind to see if it was more restful for him and it was, but when he began to drift off to sleep he almost fell and they had to sit him up front again. Maria-Dolores had been right, thought Parton, the boy was just too young to hold his own on the dangerous night road, with one of the big, powerful mounts they were riding. The more was the pity, because the journey was becoming a terrible ordeal for him. 'Hold on, Fernando,' Parton whispered several times in his ear, 'don't forget who we're going to see.' Each time the boy had nodded wearily and had gripped the pommel afresh.

Just before dawn, the road began to wake up. The *tamemes* bent to their loads, no time to waste. Travellers set out from the towns and villages. By dawn, the road was already busy and other riders, mule trains, carts and the occasional carriage or sedan chair added to the obstacles. The fugitives did not push their horses to a gallop, partly because of these obstacles and partly because their horses had to last. Parton had decided that they would change horses only in towns which were big enough to have a reasonable choice of animals. Whatever happened, they had to have mounts which were capable of putting on a spurt if the circumstances called for it. Their pursuers were mounted on the best. The Inquisition only had to crook a finger to obtain the finest livestock in the country. The fugitives could not afford to find themselves mounted on the worst.

Los Reyes, in the early morning, was a large enough town. The stableman eyed the fine horses from Puebla and immediately tried to exchange them for old nags, but Parton cut him short with a generous bribe and they chose the four best horses in the stables. While they were saddling, Gabriela and Fernando bought food and they ate as they rode out of town.

They pushed the horses faster that morning down the long straight stretch which went down through the town of

Huixcolotla, which they passed at mid-morning. It was hot and getting hotter and the horses had to be pushed. They could afford to tire them, however, thought Parton, knowing that they would be able to change them soon. They rode through several small villages before, in the early afternoon, they reached a small town at the head of a rocky valley, baking in the sun. Its three or four belfries, its whitewashed houses and the dusty square in front of the stables where Parton called a halt, were sleeping in the heat.

Esperanza, thought Parton as he banged on the stable doors. I owe this town a lot. A sleepy stablehand opened up and let them in with their horses. He was a lad of about fifteen with dark down on his upper lip. Parton took out a silver dollar and showed it to him. No point in wasting time as at the last stop. 'We want the best you have,' he said to the boy.

'You can choose, Señor,' said the hand, delighted. He watched as the fugitives set to examining the more obviously powerful mounts for injuries or hidden flaws. 'You're lucky,' he said conversationally, perhaps thinking that he had better be civil to earn the dollar Parton had given him. 'I thought the two who went through not long ago were going to take my best, seeing the beautiful beasts they were on.'

'This one looks good to me,' said Parton to Maria-Dolores. 'Have a look.'

'But no worry,' went on the stablehand. 'Then I saw them closer. *They* don't change horses in no common livery stables, not them.'

Parton looked up. Something in the tone the lad had used in speaking of *them* alarmed him. There had been fear in the boy's voice. 'Don't they?' he asked, crossing to look at another horse.

'No, they don't.' The boy looked around, then ran his eye over his customers again as if to be sure of them. 'Inquisition,' he whispered.

Everyone looked up at that and the boy faltered. 'I – I didn't say anything wrong,' he protested. 'Did I?'

'No, not at all,' reassured Parton, closing with him quickly. 'We're not Inquisition.' He took out another dollar. 'This is for you if you answer my questions. . . . Sorry, what's your name?'

'Paco.'

'Paco, did you see *two* riders? And are you sure they were Inquisition?'

'Yes, and I'm sure. When you see faces like that, hard and cruel, men dressed in black like priests but not priests, mounted on rich men's horses but not rich men. . . . Everyone looks away and hopes they'll go by quickly.'

Parton took him by the arm. 'How long ago, Paco?'

'Not long. With those horses, they'll be at the top of the loops by now.'

Parton remembered the loops. More than twenty miles of bends down the steep flanks of the mountains before the road reached the huddle of small towns at the bottom, Nogales first, then Rio Blanco, Ciudad Mendoza and finally the big town, Orizaba, the last important town before Cordoba and certainly an Inquisition base. How could the messengers have got through this far? The fat priest Obaldes had only spoken of one message from Palafox. But what if the two riders had arrived in Puebla at that very moment? They could have ridden on before the fugitives had – and would be several miles ahead of them, as Paco claimed. In any event, the lad's sincerity could not be doubted. The men he had seen were almost certainly Palafox's riders.

They had to be stopped. They were carrying the message which would denounce Torres Mendieta, throw the whole British plan overboard, cause multiple arrests and torture and make an orphan of Fernando. And they would alert the Inquisition in each major town as they passed, making it impossible for the fugitives to get through. Orizaba would be their next stop. They must not reach it.

'Let's hurry,' said Parton, tightening the girth on the mount he had chosen. 'Ready, Fernando?'

Fernando, who was stretching his legs at the far end of the stables, turned. His dark eyes flashed and Parton thought for a second that he was going to rebel. Then he swallowed, obviously making an effort to understand and be big and brave. 'Ready,' he said, coming forward.

They led the horses out. 'Oh and Paco,' Parton said, turning. 'You'd know better than to tell the Inquisition about the money I gave you and what you told me, wouldn't you?'

'Oh yes, Señor,' said Paco fervently. 'No fear of that.'

He would go off and hide his two dollars, thought Parton as they rode out of Esperanza and down its rocky little valley. The valley widened into a plain. To the northeast was the snowy peak of the high volcano over Orizaba. Ahead, the road crossed the plain, then the higher mountain plateaux began to drop away to the loops. The riders would be somewhere there, slowed by the seemingly endless bends in the road.

Before they had crossed the plain, Parton called a halt for which Fernando at least was grateful. There were the pistols to be carefully checked before riding on. He rummaged in the pack on Gabriela's horse and took out the pistol he had taken from the guard at the monastery door. He handed it to Seward. 'Check it, and the silver one from the saddlebags too.'

Parton examined his own pistols, wondering how much help Seward would be. Since the escape from the monastery, the man had seemed nervous, changeable, brittle, as if something had snapped inside him. Of course, Parton told himself once again, the pain and humiliation of the torture he had undergone at the Inquisition's hands explained it. But was that enough to explain the kind of resentment which he thought he sometimes saw in Seward's eyes? And hadn't the man's physical recovery been remarkably fast? Parton brushed the unworthy thoughts aside. You've never liked him, you've never been able to fathom him and get close to him, he told himself and so you have a distorted view of him, you exaggerate his failings. He looked across at Seward with a deliberately conspiratorial grin. 'You enjoy shooting Palafox's messengers,' he said, 'and these two must absolutely be stopped.'

'It'll be a pleasure,' said Seward simply, his eyes on the priming of his pistol. He knew that he had to stay close and show eagerness to help. But would no opportunity to turn the tables occur? He was going to have to play it tight. He stuck his pistols into his belt and walked his horse forward as if impatient to go.

Parton spoke quickly to the girls – Gabriela seemed troubled, but there was no time for discussion – telling them to follow as fast as they could with Fernando. He wheeled his mount round, fell in beside Seward and dug his heels into the horse's flanks. The two horses, fresh and fleet, took the rest of the plain at a rapid full gallop. The road ahead dipped away on the first slope towards a wide bend. Parton and Seward did not slow as they took it. Parton glanced across as they thundered down the hill and a muleteer, swearing foully, pulled his two beasts out of the way in the nick of time. Seward's face was set as he stared forward, a light in his eyes. Parton was reassured. Seward's aid would no doubt be vital.

The next bend gave on to a wide, flat shelf and they kept their horses at a gallop for half a mile before the long series of winding loops began. The road disappeared over the edge of the shelf – Parton remembered them camping there with the Andalusians on the way up – and they were forced to rein in, taking the hairpin bend which followed at a near walk. Below, the slope was steep and seemingly endless, dry and covered in scrub. Mile after mile, the yellowish road snaked down to the lower valleys where Orizaba and its sister towns lay.

Parton reined in to a stop and shaded his eyes with his hand. The road was busy and he was anxious to note in advance any particularly large or dangerous obstacles they might meet. There was a carriage lumbering halfway down

and that would have to be watched for. Further down . . .
He caught his breath. Coming out of a bend, a long way
below, dark and unmistakable, were two riders. Their
speed was perilous on the twisting, crowded road. Parton
pointed as Seward drew up beside him.

'That them?' asked Seward, breathless from the gallop.

Parton nodded and they spurred up their horses. The road
banked steeply, dusty and stony and they pushed their
mounts into a new gallop until they reached the next hairpin
bend, where they reined in as late as they dared to trot round
tightly, spurring up again as soon as the bend was over, other
riders and travellers on foot pulling over to the side at the
sound of thundering hoofbeats. Turn after turn, the straights
at a gallop, they wound their way down the mountain slope,
narrowly avoiding collision several times, fearing fatal slides
on close bends which overhung empty space. The horses
were clever, feeling the need for caution and sure feet in the
bends, responsive to the reins, and they had mettle, enjoying
the rush down the straight before they were checked again.
Maria-Dolores would have checked their hooves while he
had been talking to the stable lad, thought Parton. A shoe
thrown now could be catastrophic. He looked downwards
over the slope. The riders, cantering down a straight, still
looked far below, but Parton realized that, if he could make
out the gait of their horses, he and Seward had gained
ground. In fact, the messengers had no reason to suspect they
were being pursued and, although they were riding fast, they
were not taking the road at the breakneck speed their
followers were.

'Look out!'

Parton looked up at the cry. The carriage he had seen from
above, far from lumbering as he had thought, was at a
standstill in the middle of the road ahead of them, an axle
broken, and servants were trying to lift it to carry out repairs
while a lady and gentleman in finery stood by and watched. It
had been one of the servants, startled by the approaching

gallop, who had shouted in alarm. The gentleman reached for his pistols, no doubt convinced that they were about to be attacked by bandits. The only way through was on the outside, where a yard of road separated the carriage from the edge. 'Out of the way!' yelled Parton to a servant who was standing there, wide-eyed, as he rode for the gap, Seward following. The servant flung himself aside at the last minute and Parton was through, his leg brushing the carriage as he passed. At the next bend, reining in, he glanced back and saw to his relief that Seward was still with him. The gradient lessened as the road wound round an outcrop on the mountainside – they had stopped to camp there with the Andalusians on the way up, Parton recalled. The messengers had gone beyond the mass of grey rock and could no longer be seen. Parton remembered the slope which followed, steeper than the one they had just come down, a stark, interminable flank of the mountain, the zig-zagging loops of the road a mile or two long. He looked down, reining in at the top of the slope as they passed the outcrop and pointed.

The riders were only two long loops below them. Parton ran his glance over the loops. They were three or four miles long, while straight down the mountain was hardly more than half a mile. The scarp was steep and stony, but it wasn't a cliff. He looked at Seward and gestured down with his head.

'No!' gasped Seward, but Parton was already dismounting and leading his mount down over the edge of the road, picking his way through the rocks and low bushes. The horse was lathered and panting and Parton went cautiously, giving the animal time to breathe and to adapt. Rushing things would lead to disaster, because everything depended on the horse's surefootedness. He looked back and saw Seward following at a distance. It was better that way, better not to crowd each other.

A rattlesnake whirred a few yards ahead and Parton led the horse well wide of the sound. It was the kind of dry slope that might be full of the things. He stooped and picked up a large stone, wishing he had a stick. A rattler between the horse's hooves would be the end of the affair. He went on gingerly through the scrub, eyes peeled for movement. The horse slipped slightly at each step, but righted itself without difficulty. Parton reached the road, crossed it and began the second steep descent. Below, the riders could not be seen, but he knew they were off to his right, making for the next bend which was hidden by the swollen flank of the mountain. He led his horse on carefully, talking softly to it, coaxing it on, his eye attentive to the hazards ahead.

Then he was down on to the road again and the riders were still out of sight in the bend. Seward was still some twenty yards up, coming down very slowly. Parton flattered his horse for a moment, telling him he was the best, checking the girth, then remounting. When Seward was almost up with him, he set off down the road at a canter.

As he rounded the curve in the mountainside, the messengers came into view, leaving the tight bend and spurring into the straight. Parton reined in gently, signalling back to Seward to do the same, not wishing to alarm the two black-cloaked riders at that point. They crossed, the messengers on the straight below, their pursuers above and then Parton, followed by Seward, was in the turn, round it and Parton beat his horse's rump with the reins, whipping it into a gallop. The straight was over a mile long and they had to catch the riders on it.

At the halfway mark, they were clearly gaining. But, at that point, Palafox's messengers heard hoofbeats, looked back, realized they were being pursued and picked up speed. Did they think, as the gentleman with the carriage had, that they were under attack by highwaymen, or, as tough soldiers hand-picked by the Inquisitor-General, did they immediately understand the true danger? Parton had no way of knowing. Whichever it was, their horses were good, and it was proving to be harder and harder to gain ground on them.

The distance was now about five hundred yards. The messengers were going to reach the bend. Parton looked down. Coming out of the bend, the riders would be immediately below him for a second or two. He pulled out a pistol and waved it at Seward, now almost level with him, so he would understand. The range would be difficult, almost impossible, but it had to be tried. The messengers' horses, though less fresh than theirs, were far too good to risk a long-drawn-out race.

Then, as the men reached the bend, Parton realized that it was not going to happen exactly like that. The messengers, perhaps realizing the danger of being fired on from above, had stopped and were conferring, turning to face their attackers. They too had pistols in their hands. They were going to make a stand.

'Split up!' yelled Parton to Seward, taking the outside and leaving the inside of the road to the younger man. The messengers were at a standstill, which would allow them to aim accurately. Let them at least hesitate in choosing a target. The gap was narrowing fast and Parton made his pistol ready. 'You take the one on the left!' he shouted to Seward. I'll take *you* if I get a chance, was the thought which flashed through Seward's mind.

Two hundred yards separated them when the man on the left, Seward's target and the taller of the two, spurred up his horse and rode straight at them. Parton didn't understand at first. It was suicidal. Then, beyond, he saw the second kicking up his mount and galloping down the road hellbent, while the first shouted defiance and drew off their attention. No doubt the escaper had the better horse of the two. Parton fired down at him, but, from a galloping mount at a moving, ducking target, the shot had no real chance of success. He heard a bang behind him and understood that Seward had fired off a shot too. That was totally useless. Seward had even less chance of hitting the man than Parton. The messenger galloped on and away. Parton pulled out his second pistol and turned to the first messenger.

His ride was not as suicidal as that, he thought. The man was riding hard for the gap between him and Seward. Although two pistols were waiting for him, he had one to reply with, perhaps two, he was determined and he had a chance of breaking through and escaping in the other direction, back up the road. Palafox's soldiers were no fools. One way or another, the message now stood a good chance of getting through. The rider was levelling his pistol on Seward. Parton knew the man was too experienced to fire too early, but Seward, no doubt panicking, fired at him before Parton could yell at him to wait. The range was too great and the shot was wasted. The man turned his pistol on to Parton, grinning wildly. He had succeeded in making one of his attackers fire a wild and useless shot and meanwhile, his colleague was escaping down the road. Parton could see the man's eyes now, glinting dark. The pistol was levelled on his chest and he knew that he still had to wait. The eyes were on him, judging the distance as he himself was doing.

Seward wondered frantically what he could do. He had narrowly missed Parton with his first shot and had deliberately wasted his second, not wishing to shoot the messenger and not daring to fire on Parton openly. But now Seward himself was risking death at the messenger's hands and he desperately needed to show that he was an ally. As Parton pulled slightly ahead of him, he raised the empty pistol in his hand and made ready to throw it at Parton's head.

The missile never left his hand. Parton fired at the very instant he saw the messenger's eyes flicker away towards Seward, and the man jumped clean back from the saddle and crashed to the ground. His horse careered on, ears back in fear, and galloped between Seward and Parton. As they passed, they looked down. The dark eyes that had been determinedly estimating the distance to Parton's chest were now staring up at the clouds above the mountain tops. This rider would carry the message no further. Without a glance towards Seward, who, trembling to think of how close he had been to disaster, was hanging back, Parton checked his horse into and round the turn and out again on the track of the escaping rider.

He had gained, in the confusion, almost half a mile and his horse was visibly powerful. He was armed and Parton and Seward had both emptied their pistols. In a few more miles, at the foot of the slope and down the valley, he would reach the safety of the string of towns and Orizaba, he would alert the Inquisition and all would be lost. Parton whipped his mount with the reins and launched forward into a desperate race.

At the next bend, he thought he had gained a little. His horse, after all, was fresher. He glanced back and saw Seward fading, either because his horse was slowing, or because he no longer had the stomach for the kind of risks Parton was taking – scarcely reining in for the bends, letting the escaper clear the road for him and riding hell for leather after him, giving the other travellers no time to move back into the way and obstruct him. At the end of the second straight, he knew he was gaining and the escaping rider, as the occasional backward glance proved, was well aware of it too. He urged his horse on frantically, lashing it with a riding whip, and Parton forced his mount on faster in his turn.

The gap narrowed to several hundred yards. Without Seward, now far behind, and without a pistol, Parton began to consider how he would stop the messenger and avoid getting killed. What would the man decide to do? Ride on in hopes of winning the race to the towns, or make a stand, one against one? As the rider flung himself into the next bend, Parton reckoned the gap at about three hundred yards. The man would have no choice but to make a stand, he could not hope to win the race. He had fired no shots and he was probably armed with a brace of pistols. Did he realize that Parton was unarmed? He would be looking, beyond the bend, for a suitable place to stop and shoot Parton down. Parton could only give him time to fire the first shot, and that shot had to miss.

There was a scream and Parton looked over the edge as he

approached the bend. Just below, coming out of the bend and spurring his horse to a gallop, the messenger had found himself face to face with a family of Indian carriers, two men with burdens, a woman with a baby in her arms, three or four children. A girl was sitting by the roadside, resting. The scream was coming from the woman with the baby and perhaps from the girl too.

The rider did not flinch. He rode straight at the barefoot Indians. The children scattered but the men were too heavily laden to react quickly and the woman, paralysed with fear, stared at the on-coming horse, her mouth open in a now-silent scream.

The horse and rider were only yards from the Indians when one of the men swung the huge pack from his back, flinging it down in the horse's path and staggered desperately towards the woman. The horse started and reared up, screaming in its turn, and as the Indian pulled the woman and baby aside, its hind legs lost their grip. Slithering across the dusty road, it slewed round, falling, bucking in its fight to straighten up and stand again, losing the fight and rolling on to its back, the rider pinned beneath, then back again on to its flank. The horse slid past the seated girl, transfixed, and went over the edge of the road. The messenger, his foot caught hopelessly in the stirrup, followed, his head beating the ground as he went, and Parton was sure he knew nothing of the long, rolling fall which took them, man over beast, beast over man, down hundreds of yards of steep slope, until there were more bones broken than intact and the two corpses lay trapped between two rocks just above the next loop in the road.

As Seward came up with Parton, who had reined in on the bend, they rode slowly forward together, the girl by the side of the road looked up at them in terror and screamed again. She had been inches from death.

Some miles on, in the shade of a rock, Parton and Seward hid and waited until the girls and Fernando had got through the fuss on the road – travellers had wanted to hold them back from following too closely on the heels of the cruel *bandidos* who had just savagely murdered two men – and caught up with them. They rode on together into the string of towns and, as the sun set, changed horses (Parton's and Seward's were completely blown) in the town of Rio Blanco, which seemed to have the best stables in the valley. Night had fallen by the time they left the town and set off, all of them weary and dispirited at the idea of another night in the saddle, down the ten-mile stretch to Orizaba.

It was a severe blow, thought Palafox, the lines of tension and fatigue tightening in his face as he looked at the crumpled body of the man who had been one of his most trusted mercenaries. Neither of his messengers had got through. The Englishman was proving to be even more stubborn and resourceful than he had at first suspected. Not that he had seriously underestimated Parton. Any man who could bluff his way out of the Calle Alvarado as that man had was worthy of respect right from the start. But now the English agent was not just proving himself daring and versatile.

Now he was ripping Palafox's system apart.

The Inquisitor-General sat on a rock by the side of the road and wiped the dust and sweat from his brow. Patriotism pure and simple was hardly his driving force. There was hatred of foreigners and ingrained religious intolerance in him, but little in the way of positive love of his country. However, when he thought of the harm Torres's information could do to Spain if it fell into the hands of the British Admiralty, he blenched. And the carefully constructed system of checks and balances, the intricate network of fear and constraint which he, Palafox, had built up over the years as he had founded his personal empire within the inefficient, crumbling Spanish empire, would lose its equilibrium, totter and fall. A first-rate defector would succeed in going over to a major foreign power and that would be a mighty incentive to other would-be sellers of secrets. Of them, in a corrupt and unjust administration, there were all too many, as it was his job to know. The Inquisition would fall down on its task of constraining them to silence, now, when the system seemed perfect, when even the viceroy himself quailed before Palafox's personal authority and – who knew? – might even be persuaded to step down in the Inquisitor-General's favour. It was a distant possibility, but one which Palafox occasionally liked to dwell on in the secret of his private thoughts.

Parton did not know it, but he was there now, thanks to his particular combination of unpretentious intelligence, of courage, of tenacity, there in Palafox's secret mind itself. He was shooting down the prelate's almost unavowed dreams as a hunter shoots down larks. And he was running with Maria-Dolores.

Maria-Dolores. Palafox gripped the rock on which he was sitting and stared into space in front of him. He had been angry – was still angry – at the foolishness Maria-Dolores had shown in virtually handing herself over to Parton as a hostage. He had indeed ordered that she be arrested and held awaiting his pleasure. But what was that compared to the fate of his colleagues who failed in their duty, Anselmo, Obaldes, Costillo, on their way to give the Chinese executioner practice? Of course he would have taken pleasure in chastising her . . . before taking her back again and making of her an even greater splendour, a royal whore, a demon queen, a scarlet-lipped, naked, sweet-scented, wet-sexed bloodcutter—

Palafox grimaced and shook himself back to clearer thoughts. Rationality disappeared when he thought of Maria-Dolores. The tiny suspicion, the breath of jealousy, at the idea that she might be more Parton's than his, had to be banished or it would cause utter chaos. Parton was running her on with him, forcing her, even in Puebla where she had appeared to lie for him, he had been there in the shadows threatening her with a pistol, he had insulted her before witnesses and the hawker who said she seemed under no constraint was a liar and a fool . . .

In these arid, shit-ridden mountains, he thought, casting an eye around him at the sun-baked rocks of a landscape he had always hated, lived lions they called pumas, terrible fighters but never more so than when they were wounded. He stood up. He would be like the puma, he would fight back – but he would remain cool even in the heat of the action. The fugitives were deep in his domain and he still held all the most important cards. Capture them, use the black-haired girl – what did *she* mean to Parton? Above all use the boy, the key, make his father talk, make Parton talk . . . Yes, Parton was the kind of man who would hold out under torture but talk at once to save a child from suffering. He had far more weaknesses than Palafox. Palafox almost laughed. Capture them, break them, follow up the leads they would give, arrest their accomplices, penetrate the British Secret Service. A warning to would-be traitors, a severe blow to the English, the consecration of Palafox's system, his present and future power . . .

He looked towards Brother Lazaro and thought: no, you won't do any more, you're too old. I won't have you killed but I'll put you well out of the way. And the group, he decided, now a hundred strong with reinforcements from Puebla, was ridiculously large and heavy to move.

'Lazaro,' he called. The elderly priest came over. 'You will take charge of the Puebla faction,' Palafox told him. 'I am going to ride ahead with some of the musketeers and my own men. You will follow and support if need be.'

Lazaro acquiesced, half afraid of disgrace, half relieved to be taken from the heat of the action.

'Modesto!' called Palafox, walking over to the scarred mercenary who had, on reflection, impressed him since the moment up in the pass.

'Excellency?'

'I want you to take charge of the advance squad under my overall leadership. We need a tough, fast-moving group. Choose your men quickly – anyone who doesn't meet with your honest approval as a rider and fighting man can stay with Lazaro. We'll also take the ten best musketeers, no more. We're to have the best of the horses.' He gestured to Porfirío's body which two men had carried down to the roadside. 'This happened perhaps two hours ago. They can't be far down the road. We have to catch them, Modesto, it's essential. What do you think of our chances?'

The mercenary rubbed his deeply tanned cheek thoughtfully. 'If we lighten our group as you suggest, Excellency and if they keep riding down the road in the same direction, we'll catch them without a shadow of a doubt because we'll always have much better mounts than they and they have a child to carry. But what will happen if they leave the road, if they branch off somewhere? We'd be none the wiser and we'd just go riding by.'

Good, thought Palafox, appraising him coldly. If Modesto proved himself now, there was a future for him and no doubt he knew it.

'Listen,' he said with a brief laugh, 'I'll tell you a secret.' He leaned towards the mercenary and whispered.

'And he can signal back?'

'He's already done so once.'

'The poor devils.' Modesto turned in the saddle and spat. 'If only they knew it's not worth their running. They don't stand a chance.'

CHAPTER FOURTEEN

Parton said nothing to the others, but, as he leaned his head back yet again to listen to the murmurs in his back, he told himself that there was absolutely no doubt about it. Fernando was ill.

The night had been long and hard. They had ridden through Orizaba, dark and still, and had begun the tiresome descent to Cordoba. The two towns were twenty miles apart as the crow flew, with a difference in altitude of over four thousand feet. The result was fifty miles of twisted, looping road which would have taken hours even in daylight. They had made the best time they had been able to along it, knowing that their pursuers would not stop for an instant and that they could not be far behind. They were all exhausted, eyes burning, nerves strained from the constant watching for obstacles and danger ahead and the anxiety bred from the feeling, as in a nightmare, that the monster was breathing down their necks and that they couldn't move forward quickly enough to get away. But it was Fernando who was reaching the point of no return.

Lack of sleep – seven or eight hours in three nights and days, and over twenty-four hours since his last sleep – and violence and murder around him had left him brittle, ready to break. And for Fernando, riding was the sheer physical problem, hour after miserable hour, of staying on the horse, jolting, clutching the mane, legs too short to grip. The fight was too much for him. If he began to drowse, he began to slide from the saddle; if he fought to cling on, he was desperate, weeping, tense. Neither Gabriela, nor Maria-Dolores, nor Parton had been able to make him comfortable until Gabriela had remembered the way Indian women tied their children to their backs and suggested that they use a blanket to do the same for Fernando. He had been hitched to Parton's back and had immediately gone to sleep.

Parton's relief had been short-lived. After about an hour of quiet sleep, Fernando had begun to move, to wriggle, to mutter snatches of delirious nonsense. That could have been simply troubled sleep, but the delirium had increased and now, as Parton clasped the boy's hand behind his back, he felt it burning, hot with fever. How serious it was, Parton had no idea. He detested illness. When he had been nine years old – little more than Fernando – he had survived an epidemic of fever that had carried off his grandfather, his father and his younger brother Matthew. His memories of the illness were vague, but the episode had had dramatic consequences for his family and it had left him with a hatred of the virulent fevers which came and went in the tropics, and of the doctors with their patent and useless remedies. Fernando, let it not be that, he prayed. Bear up, hold on. Not even twenty-four more hours to go, Fernando. For God's sake hold on.

Cordoba was ahead and it would soon be dawn. Parton remembered the town and the dangers he had met with there. He would happily have avoided it, skirting round it on the mountainside, had it not been for the time that would waste – and the fact that they had to change horses. The mounts they had were far from blown, although the night had tired them – but Parton, and he alone, knew that the fugitives would be leaving the Veracruz road between Cordoba and the next stage where horses could be hired. Cordoba was hence their last chance to get fresh horses before reaching the coast. There was no choice but to ride into the town and hope that the Inquisition, Palafox's second wave of messengers not having succeeded in getting that far, would not be dangerously vigilant.

Day was dawning as they clattered into the top end of the town by the stony main road that the pilgrimage had taken

269

almost three weeks before. There were no priests checking travellers and no sign of watchers. Behind him, Fernando was quiet. He seemed to have fallen into a heavy doze, although he was still as feverish. If only he could stay like that while they hurriedly changed horses and rode out of the town, thought Parton. The stables were near the tavern where he and Seward had taken rooms. He led the way, branching off downwards to skirt round the high town.

The road leading down was familiar. Parton recognized the small square with the fountain and the steps he had climbed to shake off his Inquisition shadowers, the twin towers of the church above. He remembered the priest and the Indian unconscious in the alleyway. He was known to the Inquisition in this town. He nudged his mount forward a little faster. The sooner they were quit of the place the better.

'This is Cordoba!'

Parton glanced back over his shoulder to see Fernando, dark brown eyes wide, looking round. 'This is Cordoba!' he repeated. 'Is this where my father's coming to meet us?'

'I'm afraid not, Fernando,' said Parton softly. 'We have to go further. It'll soon be over.' He signalled to the others to ride on.

'Then are we going to see Margarita?'

Parton's heart sank. 'We would, but she doesn't live here any more,' he lied, riding on.

'Yes she does! She lives down there!' said the boy sharply, pointing down a sidestreet. Parton looked at him carefully, reining in. His cheeks were flushed and his stare was unnaturally harsh. He was ill, but he had been quite right about the street. 'I want to go and see her,' he said.

Parton looked helplessly towards the others, who had stopped and were waiting a little way ahead. One or two early passers-by were turning their heads. Parton eased his horse forward. 'You're right that she used to live down there,' he said, 'but not any more. She doesn't live in Cordoba now.'

'*Yes she does*!' This time it was a cry of defiance. Passers-by were stopping to stare.

'Fernando, don't shout like that,' said Gabriela soothingly. 'Do you want to come with me for a while?'

'We have to keep going,' added Parton gently. 'We have to change horses. You're big enough to understand that. We're going to your father, don't forget.'

'No!' shouted the boy, struggling to free himself from the blanket which tied him to Parton's back. 'I don't *want* to keep going! I want to see Margarita!'

'Fernando, please!' Parton halted again, twisting round to catch the boy's eye, speaking urgently but quietly. There were half a dozen watchers on the far side of the street. What kind of spectacle the fugitives made, Parton didn't like to think. 'Fernando, you know we're having to run from that priest, the tall one with the pale face and all his men. They're following us. If they catch us, we'll never get to your father. We can't stop now. Do you understand?' It was useless, he knew it as he spoke. There were bright fever spots in Fernando's cheeks. He was too far gone to want to understand.

'Take me to Margarita!' shrilled Fernando. 'Take me to my nurse!'

'This is dangerous,' said Maria-Dolores with a glance across the road. 'We look like highway robbers.' The group of passers-by was growing and, although one or two moved on with a shrug, others stayed to watch the shouting, struggling child at the hands of the four dirty and sinister-looking adults. Parton set his horse moving. 'Let's get down to the stables and out of here,' he said.

'No, no, no,' sobbed Fernando. 'I don't want to! I want to go to Margarita, to Margarita!' With a desperate twist, he slipped out of the side of the slung blanket and slid from the horse's crupper, his leg catching in the blanket and his head going down first, making him scream. Parton leaned down quickly and pulled him upright. 'For God's sake stop it, Fernando!' he whispered.

'*No!*'

Murmurs came from the growing group of watchers as Fernando struggled to free himself from Parton's grip.

'Look down there,' said Gabriela softly, nodding down the street.

Fifty yards away and walking towards them quickly was a Franciscan friar. He would be up with them soon.

'That settles it,' said Parton. He wheeled his horse round and led the way down the side street towards Margarita's house.

'Thank God you've found him!' Margarita stood on her doorstep and clasped Fernando to her. 'But he's hot and feverish!' she said, kissing his forehead.

'Will you let us in?' asked Parton, looking back nervously into the courtyard where the horses were hitched. He could not forget his first visit to this house. It was indeed possible that it was watched. 'Please, it's important.'

The old woman made way, carrying Fernando, and Parton followed Seward and the two girls into the one small room. He shut the door behind them and went over to the window from which he could watch the courtyard.

'They said you didn't live here any more,' said Fernando, his arms tightly round his nurse's neck. The old woman looked with surprise and no little apprehension at Parton, now with a pistol in his hand, and his unsavoury companions.

'Señora . . .' Parton caught the old woman's eye. 'Fernando is tired and perhaps ill, but he has to calm down and accept that we must move on. It's desperately important.' He dropped his voice and gestured outwards. 'They're right behind us.'

Margarita's dark eyes held his for a moment, then she nodded. 'I understand,' she said. 'I think I can help.' She carried the boy across the room to the bed and laid him on it. 'Now, Fernando,' she said quietly, 'you're going to be a good boy and take your medicine. Do you remember, when you were small, you were sometimes poorly?'

The child nodded, but grimaced. 'Do I have to take my medicine?'

'Of course. You're not well, are you? And I've still got your old bowl, you know, the red-and-blue one.' She left the room by the courtyard door. Parton watched through the window as she went in to another door opposite. The horses' tails were busy chasing flies. All was quiet. The nurse came back after several minutes, carrying the promised bowl, steaming with amber liquid. 'This will bring down the fever,' she said to Parton. 'Fernando?'

Fernando sat up and looked seriously at the red-and-blue bowl before beginning to sip from it. The nurse sat by him on the narrow bed, her arm around his shoulders, watching him lovingly.

'What are you giving him?' asked Parton.

'An infusion made with herbs. It's good against fevers.'

Parton felt his hackles rising against sickness and remedies and . . . He controlled himself. 'Will it take long?' he asked.

'It doesn't work in the twinkling of an eye,' replied Margarita. 'If you take him away immediately it'll do no good at all.' She took the empty bowl from Fernando's hands. 'Good boy.' She turned to Parton. 'Will someone go and fetch some more? I'll stay by him.'

Gabriela took the bowl and asked: 'Where should I go?' and Parton said: 'I'll show you.' He was anxious to go out and take a precautionary look round. As Gabriela crossed the courtyard to the door he had indicated, he went out beyond the horses to look along the back of the houses. On the terraces below, the maize had grown by a foot or two since his last visit. All seemed calm and no one was in sight, but the sooner they were away from there, the better. He turned to see Gabriela beckoning urgently from the doorway.

'I must talk to you,' she whispered as Parton went over. Taking him by the arm, she pulled him through the door and closed it on them. The room was a small kitchen and, in a pot over a desultory fire, the Indian nurse's herbal remedy was beginning to simmer. 'I must tell you what happened in Puebla and there's been no time on the road,' went on Gabriela hurriedly and explained Seward's singular behaviour while Parton and Maria-Dolores had been at the stables.

Parton was silent. 'He wanted to leave and take you with him?' he asked at length.

'He did nothing else but try to persuade me.'

'The fool.' Parton shook his head slowly, pausing before saying: 'You see, Seward only came on this mission as a guide. He's not an officer and he's no experience of this kind of business. Worse still, he took a beating at Tepoztlán and that must have done something to his mind.' He grinned, taking Gabriela by the shoulders. 'And perhaps he really has fallen in love with you. Who could blame him?'

'Listen, he tried to turn me against you!' Gabriela wasn't ready to smile. 'He said he went with my mother because you ordered him to, he said you only wanted to use me, that I was the baby-minder while you were with Maria-Dolores –' She broke off, looking away. 'Please don't think I'm asking you to explain. There's no reason why you should. But I was so angry at the false way he served all that up.'

'Damn him!' Parton turned, furious. 'I've half a mind to drag him over here and find out what the devil he thinks he's playing at!' He checked himself. 'But no, there'll be time for that later, if we ever get out of this alive. Whatever happens, Gabriela, my orders are to get precious Mr Seward back safely to his loving family. If we have scores to settle, we'll settle them then. Right now, if there are only minutes to spare, I'd rather give them to you.' He hesitated. Explaining was not going to be easy, but he owed it to Gabriela. He took the plunge. 'It's true I . . . well, about Maria-Dolores. She attracts me and I suddenly realized how strongly. The rest isn't hard to guess.'

Gabriela nodded, hiding her feelings with a quick smile. 'You were right.'

'She's not who she seemed to be at first, Gabriela. She really

274

does want to escape from him and change her life. She's with us, she's not a traitor.'

'I know that now. She didn't betray us in Puebla, she didn't try when you and Seward were ahead of us on the road after the messengers. I think I've seen enough of her . . . to understand.' Her black eyes were fixed on Parton's. 'And is it she who moves you now?'

Parton looked into the dark depths of Gabriela's eyes and felt the same tightening of the throat he had known when he had first seen her. He shook his head. 'You move me too,' he said simply as she rushed into his arms.

'It's going to boil over,' he said a moment later, glancing at the pot. As Gabriela, looking down studiously to hide the brightness of her eyes, poured the mixture into the bowl, Parton opened the door and looked back towards the high mountains they would soon be leaving behind. While trouble was riding down towards them as fast as the finest horses could travel, they were trapped in Cordoba with a sick child. 'Let's give Fernando that medicine,' he said.

As Palafox rode beside Modesto at the head of the score of hand-picked men who formed the advance group, down the last stony miles to Cordoba, he thought: we've ridden fast and now we're closing off the bottleneck. Cordoba held the passage between the uplands and the coast. Ahead were the foothills dwindling to the jungle-covered coastal plain – and the sea.

Logically, the fugitives were making for the coast. But where? Veracruz stood out as the most obvious choice because Torres was stationed in Veracruz and Parton was taking his son to him. If things were as simple as that, and in spite of Bernardo and Porfirio's failure to get the message through, Palafox felt optimistic about the end result. The first alert he had sent out, after Parton's escape with Maria-Dolores, had required the Inquisition in all ports, above all Veracruz, to implement a pre- arranged plan which blocked all ships in port and prohibited all embarkments and disembarkments. So, even if the fugitives succeeded in getting into Veracruz with a short lead and joining up with the traitor, they would quickly find themselves trapped with their backs to the sea and no time to find another way out before Palafox himself was on them.

But that, thought the Inquisitor-General grimly, was the comfortable way of looking at it. Other possibilities nagged at his mind. The British had obviously given thought and preparation to this mission and they would have carefully considered the problem of how to get Parton and the traitor out of New Spain. Seward had been unable to inform him on the subject, but Palafox could imagine several ways and means. Other English agents might be waiting to take the boy off Parton's hands, or to draw off pursuit. A rendezvous with a ship in some isolated spot was not impossible – or Parton might have a small craft hidden somewhere along the coast. Any of these possibilities would mean either a sudden change in direction or a change in the guardianship of the child. Seward was there – and for God's sake, willed Palafox, let him not reveal his true colours by some impatient move – to signal back in case of a change in direction, should it take place before nightfall. The boy changing hands was the hypothesis the Inquisitor-General feared the most because it was the one which laid him open to surprises and gave him the least control of the situation. Seward would have to find a way of alerting him – perhaps by using the distress signals they had agreed on previously. And perhaps Maria-Dolores might at last succeed in doing something to help . . .

The group of horsemen roared down the tree-lined avenue in front of the church and Palafox almost winced at the thought of his mistress. If only he could be sure that she could free herself sufficiently to do something decisive at the right moment, if would be two against two among the fugitives – Seward against Parton, Maria-Dolores against the other girl. The fear that she might not *want* to do that was as

276

irrational as a child's fear of the dark. As he recognized the entrance to the Dominican priory which was Inquisition headquarters in Cordoba, he dismissed it. There was work to be done, and quickly. The thin, bald man coming out of the door in haste as the group reined in was Father Javiero, the local Chief Inquisitor. An end to it, thought Palafox, dismounting. Down to practical matters. He cut Javiero's effusions short.

'Modesto here will tell you our needs in fresh horses and provisions,' he said, walking into the priory. Its coolness was refreshing. As Javiero rejoined him he queried: 'Have you anything to report concerning my last message?'

Javiero's hollow eyes and stark features concealed ill his inner jubilation. 'Somehow, I was not surprised to see you, Excellency,' he said. 'Something came up only a few minutes ago. There's a Franciscan here – he came to us when he realized that what he had seen might well have to do with the outlaw we were told to look out for.'

Palafox wheeled. 'He's seen the man?'

'No doubt. Here in Cordoba, an hour or so ago.'

'Bring your Franciscan here! Quickly, man!'

When the friar had been called and was shuffling forward, Palafox said: 'Tell me what you saw, Brother.'

The friar stared at the great man humbly. 'Excellency, I was walking up the Avenida San Juan when I saw a gathering. People were stopping to watch four individuals on horseback. They rode off before I could see them closely myself, but people in the crowd gave me a description.'

'Was there a child with them?' interrupted Palafox.

'Exactly, Excellency, that's why there was a crowd. There was a boy, apparently ill, and he was protesting that he didn't want to go with them – they were a dirty-looking lot, two men and two young women, obviously on the road and little good to be said for them. Well, the boy was shouting that he wouldn't go with them and that he wanted to go and see someone called Margarita.'

Palafox felt a surge of triumph. The boy was ill, that was good news and he was giving Parton trouble. With luck, the balance of power within the fugitive group would soon be three against two. He glanced at Javiero. 'Who might this Margarita be?'

'I'm afraid she could be one of many. All we know is that they rode off down a sidestreet in the direction of the poor quarters in the lower part of town.'

Palafox stared at him. 'If the boy's ill, they might still be in Cordoba,' he said.

Javiero nodded. 'I've had a watch set on the livery stables since I received your alert. No one has changed horses there since yesterday afternoon.'

Palafox stepped forward. 'Get a score of men out on to the Veracruz road at the edge of town,' he snapped. 'Tell them no one and nothing is to get through. Any other men you can muster are to come with us. Modesto!' He called to the mercenary from the priory door. 'Call the men together! We're going to search the lower town!'

Then it came back to him and he wheeled round.

'Javiero! The boy lived here before we took charge of him! It's the Torres Mendieta boy!' He turned to the friar. 'He did his schooling with the Franciscans here!'

The Franciscan looked at him dubiously for a moment, then his eyes widened and he burst out: '*Torres*! Of course, now I remember! He took his lessons with Damiano and—' He looked across excitedly at the Cordoba Inquisitor. 'He had a nurse named Margarita! You know her, Father, an old *mestiza* who lives down in the *barrio* Trinidad – and that was the direction they were taking when I saw them!'

'Come on!' said Palafox, leading the way forward.

Parton touched Fernando's forehead and said: 'The fever's going down.' Half an hour before, the boy had been staring, red-cheeked, at the ceiling, and now he was dozing, apparently peacefully, his colour normal. How much had been due to the infusion the old woman had prepared – although people said that the Indians knew more about drugs and medicines than the doctors, and *that*, thought Parton, wouldn't surprise him – and how much to her simple presence, reassuring, calming, soothing the exhausted child? An academic question, he thought. 'We'll have to be leaving,' he said.

The old nurse nodded and leaned over Fernando, kissing him. The boy opened his eyes and smiled at her. 'Listen, Fernando,' she said, 'you're a lot better now. I want you to go with these people and I want to know that you're going to be strong and brave. When you see your father, you'll tell him and he'll send me a message so I'll know and I'll be proud of my big boy. Will you?'

The boy looked at her, dark-eyed and nodded. He sat up. 'Are we going now?' he asked.

The old woman laughed, her eyes shining. 'You can take your red-and-blue bowl with you,' she said, holding it out.

Fernando looked at it and said solemnly: 'I can't carry it on horseback,' and swung his legs down from the bed. Margarita laughed again rather loudly, the better, it seemed to Parton, to blink back tears. This time she knew that she would not see Fernando again.

They slung the boy to Parton's back with a blanket again so that he could rest as much as possible and hurried out into the courtyard. The nurse, still clutching the red-and-blue bowl, gave careful directions to Parton on how to get to the stables by the shortest route and Parton and the others mounted. He looked down at the old woman and felt a twinge of fear for her. She must have read it in his eyes because she said: 'You came and you went, what more do I know? What can they do to an old woman like me? I don't fear them. I am going back to my prayers.'

They rode cautiously round the back of the house and out into the street. Opposite, a long, narrow street rose diagonally towards the commercial section of the mid-town where the stores and taverns and stables were to be found. Parton took the lead, edging his mount into the street at a walk.

The streets were busy at this time in the morning, but the passers-by took no particular notice of them. All the same, Parton's eyes and ears were alert. Cordoba left ringing memories in his mind, memories of danger. As they reached the top of the street, he could see light and people moving. He remembered the small *plaza* and the Three Reals tavern. The stables were on the far side of the *plaza*. He half turned to the others, holding up a hand to check them and walked his horse on softly to the end of the street, looking out into the busy square from the cover of the corner wall.

People were going about their everyday occupations, fetching and carrying, harassed women with children shopping, a man leading a mule-cart crossing the middle of the square. Everything seemed normal at first sight. Opposite, the stable doors were wide open, but there was no sign of activity. Parton scanned the sides of the square. A man in the tavern doorway attracted his attention, but the man turned and went inside and did not come back. On the other hand, opposite the tavern, a squat individual crouched at the foot of a wall, his chin sunk into a blanket and a hat pulled down over his eyes. He could be sleeping, he could be watching the stables, thought Parton. Was it worth trying a roundabout way? There was no time for it. The individual would have to be watched. If he as much as moved an inch to prove he was with the enemy, he would have to be dealt with. Huddling to the wall, Parton pulled out a pistol, cocked it and held it hidden under his jacket while he held the reins with the other hand. He would go out first and alone. He walked his horse out into the open.

It was as he did so that the squat individual raised his head and Parton saw that his face was bandaged. But it was when he turned to face Parton, that Parton recognized the Indian whose jaw he had broken three weeks before.

*

Father Javiero was not overweight, but he was finding it a struggle keeping up with Palafox as he strode down through the streets, followed by half his men and a score of Cordobans, the others under Modesto having been sent off in a downward circling movement to cut off escape across the mountainside below the town. However, the Cordoba Inquisitor knew that he had done excellent work and that it was time to press home his advantage. He found the breath he needed as they rounded a corner. 'Excellency,' he puffed, 'when we received your message concerning the man you were looking for, the description reminded me of a man involved in an incident here three weeks ago. Tall, dark-haired, grey-eyed, about thirty years old . . .' He broke off to point down a filthy alley. 'This way will save time, Excellency.'

Palafox's nose wrinkled in disgust as he plunged into the alley. 'I know of the incident,' he said. 'It was our man. His companion alerted you, but you lost his track. How did that happen?'

'He left one of my men unconscious in a corner and disappeared. Across the avenue now, Excellency.'

'Quite like him,' allowed Palafox, crossing the wide avenue.

'Broke the man's jaw. One of the best men I've got for that kind of work. Fortunately he's back at work. He's the one I've got watching the stables. Down that way, Excellency.'

Palafox was walking quickly and looking ahead towards the poorer, single-storeyed houses which were appearing lower down the street. It took several seconds for Javiero's remark to penetrate his consciousness and for its significance to come home. When it did, he stopped dead and wheeled round on Father Javiero. 'Do you mean to say that the man you've set to watch the stables can be recognized by the outlaw? By Parton?'

The Cordoba Inquisitor stood still and went pale. All his good work crumbled to nothing and fear seized him. 'He's a very good man, Excellency and he has orders to be discreet,' he proffered lamely.

Palafox stared at him murderously. At the stables, the watcher might well be dead and the fugitives gone on fresh horses, while he and his men were wasting time wandering round the foul back streets of Cordoba. He swallowed back his rage and hissed: 'Which way are the stables? Lead the way, man!'

Javiero pointed back up the street with a bony finger and the two men pushed rapidly through the following group, Palafox calling them as he went, forcing the pace. They turned into the avenue above and crossed the mid-town of Cordoba, passers-by seeming to melt out of the way as they arrived, hurrying now, almost running. Palafox was furious. If the stop in Cordoba turned out to be a hideous waste of time, Javiero was finished. He quickened his pace to a trot as the Cordoba Inquisitor, breathless, pointed to a busy square at the bottom of a short thoroughfare.

Palafox burst into the square from above, the first of his men overtaking Javiero and coming out into the open beside him. In a sweeping glance, Palafox took in the stables, the tavern, the stores, the people busy on errands, the dogs, the children. His eye stopped on a man on horseback, riding forward into the square, tall, ragged, grey-eyed, turning to face the newcomers. On the horseman's back, held by a striped blanket of indeterminate colour, was a dark slim boy and the boy was staring round-eyed straight at Palafox.

The moment lasted no more than a split second.

'It's him!' said Fernando.

'Seize them!' shouted Palafox, waving his men forward.

Parton had been watching the Indian's slightest move, not sure if he would have to shoot the man or if there weren't some other way of handling him, when the Inquisitor-General and his men ran into the square. Now, as Palafox shouted orders to his mercenaries and Fernando buried his face in Parton's back, he took his pistol, ready to fire, from under his jacket and aimed it at the dark-cloaked prelate. The expressionless blue eyes stared back at him as, tugging the rein with his free hand to bring the horse round, Parton fired and saw Palafox disappear at the same instant, dragged to the ground by the man next to him. There was a scream of pain from further back as the ball went on and hit one of the mercenaries behind. Parton wheeled the horse right round and kicked its flanks desperately, winging it forward across the square as the crowd scattered, screaming, dogs yelping and crawling belly to the ground for shelter. One of the faster of Palafox's men was sprinting madly beside him and Parton took a foot from the stirrup, stuck his leg out and dug his heel into the man's face.

'Ride for it!' he yelled to the others as he reached the corner. A shot rang out behind him and he felt Fernando in his back and feared for him, then he was round the corner and into the narrow street, bundling the three others on their way down, shouting at them to ride faster. All Palafox's men were on foot, he had seen it in the square, and the fugitives had the meagre, tiny hope of gaining a few minutes now, if they rode fast and well and escaped from Cordoba. A few minutes and that would be all. He glanced back and saw the first running figures outlined at the top of the street. Shots would soon be fired and Fernando was directly in the line of fire. 'Turn!' shouted Parton to Maria-Dolores, riding ahead, and watched her as she guided her mount expertly into the right-angled turn, Seward and Gabriela following only a little less expertly, then Parton himself as the first shots rang out.

Palafox and his men would now scramble for their horses – how far away were they? The fugitives' only margin of safety lay in the lead they could establish in the meantime. Parton urged his horse on faster, whatever the danger in the narrow streets where the sun scarcely penetrated to dry the filthy ground, where passers-by shrunk to the walls and where other horses or carts would be fatal obstacles. They had to get out quickly on to the Veracruz road.

But if Palafox was in Cordoba and had been for some time, then the way out to Veracruz would certainly be blocked, and efficiently so. They must not go that way.

They rode out of the back streets and into a wider, sunlit road where there were indeed other riders. A smart gig flashed by in the opposite direction as they took the middle of the road at full gallop, shouting frantically to clear the way ahead of them. Maria-Dolores was making for the Veracruz road. She had to be stopped. Which way should they go?

A narrow street dipped away to the right some way ahead, going down towards the bottom end of town. Parton remembered the flat terraces where maize was grown. Might there not be a way out across the mountainside? He spurred up and took the lead, calling to Maria-Dolores to let him through, crossing the road towards the street, waving the others into it. As he led the way, Parton turned to glance back up the road. They had left the enemy behind.

After several hundred yards' descent, the street swept back round in the wrong direction, leading back towards the part of town where Margarita lived. Between two houses as he slowed, looking for a way out, Parton saw the stone wall which edged the top of the terraces and pointed. He reined in sharply, walked the horse between the houses, stopped at the wall and looked down as the others followed. The wall itself was low and could be jumped quite easily, but the drop to the first terrace was over six feet and was unthinkable. However, the terrace ran out, following the contours of the mountainside, below the Veracruz road, the lower terraces parallel to it. It might not be easy, but it was probably the only way out of Cordoba. Parton scanned it, looking for the way down. There had to be some kind of track for mules and carts, unless the dirt-poor farmers carried everything up the stone steps on their backs.

Shouting broke out behind them and Parton swung round.

Back among the houses and along the terraces ran dark figures, calling and pointing. The fugitives had been sighted.

Maria-Dolores was already moving ahead along the narrow path between the houses and the terrace wall. She was right, thought Parton. It was the only way out. He took up the rear, pushing the others on, leaning out a little from the saddle to look along the wall. He could still see only occasional flights of steps going down. Ahead, the wall swung round to an end against a house. The horses in front of him were blocking his view and he could not see if there was a way through between the wall and the house. He thought of the jump and the six-foot drop and glanced back. Palafox's men chasing them had no hope of catching them as long as they rode quickly away, but if they had to stop and ride back, it was all over. He looked ahead again and did not understand what he saw.

Maria-Dolores had disappeared. Only Gabriela's head was visible. As Seward reached the end of the wall and disappeared in his turn, Parton understood. A long ramp, rutted by cartwheels, led down to the terraces below, zigzagging from one to the other. As he began to ride down it, Parton looked ahead and out of Cordoba.

The Veracruz road was above them, shored up by a long buttressed wall. It was crowded with travellers and vehicles for over half a mile at the edge of town. There were black-frocked figures everywhere. Parton had been right that Palafox had had the road efficiently blocked. The fugitives would never have got through. He shouted to Maria-Dolores to take the third terrace. The top two were really within too easy pistol range from above, but going any further down would take time and give the men chasing them time to close. Maria-Dolores led the way skilfully down the tight turns of the ramp, the other horses adopting the leader's gait and making the task easier for the following riders.

They wheeled from the ramp into the third terrace, urging their horses into a full gallop to escape from the men behind them before shots were fired. Above, travellers held up by the roadblock were staring curiously over the walled edge of the road at the four riders galloping desperately through the maize below. Parton saw some of them pushed aside as figures in black took their place.

'Faster!' yelled Parton, whipping up his mount, feeling the weight of the child on his back. They were within bad pistol range, but downward shooting was always dangerous and the Inquisition men were directly above them. Shots began to clatter. The fugitives had to move quickly so as to be difficult targets and to increase the range rapidly. A ball crashed down into the maize a few yards away and Parton heeled even more speed from his horse, drawing level with Seward, stirrup to stirrup.

Another shot fell close and Seward's mount sidestepped in fear. The stirrups touched and Parton eased away, giving room. Seward's foot slipped from the stirrup and he lurched from the saddle with a cry.

Parton's hand shot out and grabbed Seward by the arm as he slid over the far side of his horse. The two horses pounded on, side by side, Parton desperately holding Seward's weight with his outstretched arm, while fending off the now unchecked horse which threatened, in the narrow space, to come hurtling into collision. 'Hang on!' he called to Seward as they crashed on through the flags of corn beaten down by the horses ahead. A pistol ball whistled off the containing wall. Parton freed his boot from the stirrup and pushed the other mount firmly away, heaving Seward up and into the saddle in the same movement. Seward clutched at the reins, white-faced and took control of his mount again. 'Got to get you back to Jamaica!' yelled Parton without the trace of a smile.

He looked up. They were out of pistol range. The Inquisition men were fighting their way along the wall, hindered by the roadblock they themselves had set up. Ahead, Maria-Dolores was at the end of the maize. The ten-yards-wide terrace dwindled to nothing as the mountainside became steeper. The only way was straight up – the horses would slip and fall if an attempt were made to ride across as steep an incline.

'Fan out!' called Maria-Dolores as they reached the end of the terrace and turned their mounts towards the road above. It was sound advice. If a horse were to fall back or dislodge a rock, no one should be behind it to take the consequences. The horses grunted and blew with the effort of the hard climb after the gallop. On the road nearer the town, the priests were shouting and pushing through the crowd. There might be more shooting, thought Parton, thinking of Fernando's safety and edging further away as he climbed. Maria-Dolores reached the roadside and dismounted to lead her mount over the last steep bank, turning to help Parton, hampered by Fernando, as soon as she had done so. The two others were up and over, the priests came running, a shot rang out, but the fugitives were on the move, kicking up their horses and galloping off down the road.

'They've got no horses!' sung out Gabriela and Parton glanced across at her and grinned. He began to think of the next contingencies and his grin faded.

They were out of Cordoba and on the road, but their lead was now little more than a matter of minutes. At best, Palafox and his men might still be delayed by re-saddling fresh horses, but that would not take long. Adding to it a few minutes for clearing the road on the way out of Cordoba, Parton concluded that the most favourable situation possible for the fugitives was a ten-minute lead and it was wiser to count on less. The real problem was that they had been unable to change horses, while the Spaniards would certainly have fresh mounts and, as always, the finest that were to be had. Logically, inexorably, the Inquisition would make up its lost ground.

Before it did so, Parton had to turn the tables decisively.

From Cordoba the road wound down into the lower mountains, snaking through greener and greener valleys, skirting peaks of a softer, rounder relief than the stark volcanic heights the fugitives had left behind them. Places where a traveller could see more than a mile or two ahead or behind were rare and Parton, looking back often as he rode, could not in fact see their pursuers closing on them. It was an illusory form of comfort, he thought bitterly. The only real hope came from his knowledge that they were going to turn off for the coast. If that were well done, the Spanish would be fooled into riding on towards Veracruz and the fugitives would be free. He forced the pace and recalled from memory the road ahead, seeking desperately the answer to the question: where will be the best place to turn off?

They would have to skirt north through the hills before crossing the unhealthy, low-lying plain to the coast. If they turned off the road too soon, they would find themselves still in difficult, mountainous terrain where their progress would be too slow to reach the rendezvous before dawn the next day. Too far down the road into the easier foothills, and Palafox would have time to catch up with them. Parton remembered the small village of Paso del Macho, snuggling into the head of the pass which marked the shed between the last mountains and the foothills. They would ride for Paso del Macho and turn off after it as soon as they found a suitable spot. Until then, they would have to flog their horses to try to maintain as good a lead as they could.

In this flat-out race, wondered Parton with a twinge of alarm, how was Fernando doing? He half turned to him. 'All right?'

'Yes. Is it much further?' The voice was small but calm.

'In a few more miles we'll slow down. It'll soon be over.'

'You kept saying that in the snow.'

'Well, we got through in the end, didn't we?'

'Yes, we did.'

'And we're going to do it again. You want to get to your father and escape from that priest, don't you?'

'Oh yes! Don't let him catch us!'

'That's why we have to ride quickly. Don't worry, we'll get

away.' Fernando was going to make it, thought Parton with relief. He was tired, but no longer feverish and agitated. He would be exhausted, he would need a fortnight's sleep to get over it all, but he would hold out. Just a few more miles' gallop and we'll twist aside and cheat them and they can spend days searching for us, Fernando. By dawn tomorrow we'll be out of the trap.

Unless we get there after dawn and the ship's gone and we're stuck here for good.

As Paso del Macho appeared in a dip below, Parton looked back. Over the hills behind them hovered a spreading cloud of dust of the kind only a large group of horses could kick up. 'Faster!' he yelled to the others, lashing his mount with the reins.

They galloped through the hundred yards of main street of Paso del Macho without stopping. Had the place been a little larger, there might have been livery stables, but they would have been of no use. There was no time now to change horses. Twenty miles further on, Parton knew, was the town of Soledad with its stables. If all went well, Palafox and his men would ride as far as that before learning that the fugitives were no longer on the road. Picking up their tracks again would take time and Parton had every intention of making it difficult. The turn-off point had to be on dry, rocky ground where the horses would leave no trace.

As the road plunged from the pass and down to the floor of a widening valley, Parton looked ahead for the way out. For the moment, the valley sides were too high and climbing them on horseback would take time during which they would be exposed to view. They would have to go further. The horses were blowing hard, lathered, eyes wide, and it was not clear how much longer they could keep up the pace. Something had to be found soon. The valley widened, turning and the road crossed the rushing river by a stone bridge before running under trees.

It was still no good, decided Parton. Above the trees was

open ground. They would be seen before they had made good their escape. He glanced back. The dust-cloud was hanging over the head of the pass. As the fugitives galloped under cover of the trees, Parton estimated their lead at two or three miles, no more.

Out of the trees, they were in the rolling foothills and Parton knew that he would have to find the turn-off point in the next few miles. He rejected a couple of possibilities before the road led over the broad back of a ridge, twisting to the right as it followed the slope down and disappearing into scrub and trees at the foot. This was it. The ridge would hide them as they left the road, the ground was stony and there was cover enough in the area to hide while the Inquisition rode by. He took the lead, flagging the others down, pointing left, dismounting and leading his panting horse off the road and in among the rocks.

'Walk them!' he told the others. They must avoid kicking up dust which would betray their passage. Five hundred yards on, an umbrella-like clump of treetops showed almost flush to the ground. There had to be a dip there, perhaps a valley. He pointed them on towards it, ignoring the surprise on their faces.

As they reached the edge of the dip, a vague rumbling from back up the road reached their ears. They hurried the horses over and down the incline beyond. The trees which could be seen from the road were rooted in a marshy spot around a small spring. They led the horses down, although they were blowing too hard to drink. The rumbling grew then burst into a loud roar and rolled over the ridgetop. The horses raised their heads nervously and one of them called in alarm. 'Keep them quiet!' hissed Parton. The thunder of hoofbeats rolled away and off down the road. Parton waited, listening.

When the rumbling had finally disappeared he closed his eyes for a second and let the feeling of immense relief flow through him. It seemed as if they had been running for weeks with the Inquisition behind them. Now they had thrown them off, now they had a fresh start. The escape route lay open.

'Now what?' asked Seward anxiously. 'We've got them on the road ahead of us now. How do we get through to Veracruz?'

'Do you want to walk for a while, Fernando?' asked Parton, turning his head away from Seward.

'Yes, please.'

Parton untied the knots in the blanket and set the boy on his feet. Then he looked up and said: 'We're not going to Veracruz. We're going that way.' He pointed north, took his horse by the bridle and Fernando with his free hand and walked off down the bed of the stream which flowed from the spring.

It was late morning. Through midday and the hot afternoon, they picked their way in silence through the foothills, following a northward-leading line roughly parallel to the coast. Of course, the Spanish would be looking for them, Parton had no illusions about that. Palafox would have called up reinforcements, would have spread his men out in all directions. In the end, the fugitives' tracks might be found, or they might be seen from afar through a telescope. A few miles below them, often visible, the coastal plain stretched green and flat. There were covering trees down there which could hide them. But the tropical forest was thick and wide rivers meandered through steamy, fever-bearing marshes as they neared the coast. The shorter the distance they had to travel across that kind of country, the better. The rivers were proving hard enough to ford as it was and twice they had to ride several miles higher into the hills to find a suitable crossing before being able to move on.

The third major river they came to, at about five in the afternoon, was the widest. It was no longer a mountain torrent, but it was quick-flowing and powerful, running smoothly level by level through a deep valley. The fugitives reined in at the rocky top of the valley side and looked down.

'I think we're in luck,' said Parton, pointing half a mile downstream towards a calmer level which seemed likely to provide a reasonable crossing. He looked across the plain below. The sea was visible now, pale and hazy in the heat. It was not yet time to plunge down into the thick forest, however. They were still several miles – exactly how many, Parton could not say – short of the rendezvous and those miles would be easier to cover among the foothills than in the jungle and along the marshy coast.

As Parton rode down the slope towards the river, followed by the two girls, Seward hung back. He was not sure whether Parton's thoughtful gaze towards the sea didn't mean that they were about to leave the hills for the jungle, or not. This might well be his last chance to signal back to Palafox, and this time he had to take it. Sweat pearled on his forehead. This was dangerous, desperately dangerous, but it had to be done. He watched the others begin to wind down the valley side, then dismounted quietly, bending to his bay mare's front hoof. He picked up a stone and hit the horse's fetlock lightly, drawing blood. The mare whickered and stamped, but the sound of the river drowned it and no one looked back.

Having prepared his excuse for holding back, Seward crept forward until the mare and a rock beside her were covering him from unwanted glances and took the brass disc from his pocket. He would use the distress code he had agreed on with Palafox – long, short, long, long, short. That would underline the urgency of the situation. He looked back the way they had come, seeing the hills and green plain stretching away southwards towards Veracruz and began to signal. The sun was going down in the sky, but the angle was still easy. He hoped, with an impulsive glance over his shoulder, that the flashes would be seen quickly. He would have little time before they noticed he was not following. His hands trembled. Parton had not mentioned the Puebla incident, although Gabriela would certainly have told him of it by now. What had been Parton's reaction? Gabriela's account must surely have sparked off suspicion in his mind. Damn it, why was there no reply from Palafox and his men? They were back there somewhere, searching in all directions, they had to be. These really were distress signals, thought Seward frantically as he plied the mirror. In a matter of hours, they could be down to the coast and off in a British ship and all would be lost. Would Parton wait for that moment to accuse Seward and force a confession from him? Come on, Palafox, come on – you know what to be on the watch for, we agreed on this system and you must be desperate to see my signals. Still no answering flicker, either from hills or plain.

'Drop it!'

Seward's blood ran cold and the mirror slipped from his fingers to the ground as he turned unwillingly to find himself staring into the muzzle of Parton's pistol. The moment he had been so long dreading had come. Parton had caught him in the very act of betrayal.

'What was he doing?' Gabriela, on foot like Parton, came over the top of the rise by the bay mare.

'Signalling back to Palafox,' said Parton, his eyes on Seward's as he took the brace of pistols from the other man's belt. 'I don't know how often he's done this in the past, but he's been working for the Inquisition since we left Tepoztlán.'

'What?' Gabriela's stupefaction was genuine. 'And you *knew* . . .?'

Parton stepped back, his pistol still on Seward and shook his head. 'I only began to suspect him yesterday after we'd stopped the messengers. When we changed horses after that, I noticed a fresh nick in the back of my saddle – a groove caused by a pistol ball. It could only have come from him when he'd fired at a rider below us and I couldn't believe he had aimed as badly as all that. I had to suppose he'd aimed deliberately at me, missing me by inches. The idea that he might be working against me seemed to explain a number of things, including his killing the rider on the mountain. Then, this morning, when you told me about Puebla, I was sure.'

'Then why didn't you accuse him? Or simply leave him behind, even kill him?'

Parton's grey eyes glinted. 'Because I wanted to get the

bastard back on to the ship that's coming for us and back to Jamaica, face to face with my commanding officer. The best way to do that was to let him come of his own free will, risky though it might be. Forcing him along would have taken all my attention and he would have found a hundred ways of making us waste time. So I said nothing, not even to you.'

Gabriela was beside Parton now, her eyes on Seward's. 'So . . . in Puebla, what you really wanted was to get away with Fernando and hand him over to the Inquisition,' she said slowly, disgust then anger taking the place of surprise in her mind. 'Do you know what Palafox would have done with him, how he would have used him? Do you? *Do you*, God damn you?' She stepped forward, her eyes blazing, took Seward by his shirtfront and shook him furiously. 'I hope he's paying you enough, you murderous little trickster!'

'No!' Seward struggled free, turning imploringly back to Gabriela as soon as he had done so. If anyone had to understand, she did. 'Don't you see? You're on the wrong side, you're with him—' he pointed towards Parton, '—instead of being with your country and your religion! You're Spanish, Gabriela and you were brought up in the Catholic faith. Do you know how things are in my country? If you hold to the true faith, you are persecuted and deprived of even the most elementary rights of a free citizen. And the King? The King is in exile, overthrown and banished by the Protestant heretics and a usurper rules in his place. Parton serves that fat German usurper. *I* serve the true King, the Stuart, His Catholic Majesty James III, and Spain and the Spanish Church are our closest allies!'

Gabriela shook her head disbelievingly. 'And for *that* you'd have helped Palafox torture a child?'

'Gabriela . . .' Seward's voice trailed away and his hands dropped in despair. Parton watched him, taken aback. Seward was a Jacobite. He had betrayed for principles, for ideals, not for money or promises of power. What did that change? Parton asked himself angrily. The effect Seward had been seeking had been the same, whatever his motives. All that changed was that he had been a traitor right from the start, that he had not been frightened and bullied into it by Palafox and his thugs as Parton had been several times tempted to think. He found himself looking at Seward's shirt, torn open by Gabriela and at the unblemished skin of his chest and stomach. He had never been tortured at all. He had been Spain's ally all along. My God, thought Parton with a kind of wonder, Cameron sent me into New Spain to fight the Inquisition with a Jacobite as a guide.

'I didn't know, I didn't realize, fool that I was.' Maria-Dolores spoke softly, close to Parton. Fernando had walked to the top of the slope with her, hand in hand. 'Palafox has secrets he keeps even from himself . . .'

Seward raised his head and faced her venomously. 'And so he should, surrounded by cheap treacherous whores like you.'

Parton hit him once, hard, in the midriff and Seward doubled up with a gasp. Parton withheld a second blow with difficulty. Fernando was there, watching and Fernando had seen enough violence over the last few days. Since Seward was coming with them – Parton was determined to get him back and face Cameron with him – it was better not to weaken the man.

'What's he done wrong?' asked Fernando, staring at Seward.

'I don't think he should insult Maria-Dolores,' said Parton, bending to the boy and picking him up with a grin. 'And don't worry. He *tried* to do something wrong, but he didn't succeed.'

'I'm not so sure,' broke in Gabriela. 'Look!' She pointed.

From several miles back on the edge of the plain were coming rhythmic pinpoints of light in response to Seward's signals.

CHAPTER FIFTEEN

Parton cursed under his breath, estimating distances. The flashes came from perhaps two or three hours' riding behind them. Even if Palafox were not with the group that had seen the signals, he would be rapidly informed and would bring his best troops on fresh mounts to the spot. The fugitive's tracks would be picked up and the unequal chase would begin. Parton knew that their own horses were too blown to go at more than a walk and the two or three hours' lead would melt like snow in the sun.

Was the jungle a way out? He didn't want to go down there yet, he wanted to avoid the difficulties which he was sure they would meet in following the coastline, but he had to admit that it might be their last hope. If they could slip down into that thick cover without leaving tracks which the Spanish would immediately see, they might yet keep enough lead to fight their way through to the rendezvous. He looked across the coastal strip below. It was perhaps a dozen miles wide at that point and the river they were about to ford could guide them to the sea. It might also help cover their tracks . . .

'Down to the river,' he ordered, pushing Seward forward at pistol-point. Having crossed the river on horseback, they chose the sturdiest mount, unsaddled the three others, letting the river carry off the saddles and drove the horses up the bank and away. Then they waded downriver in the shallows, leading the last mount with their packs and Fernando up, for several hundred yards. They left the water on stony ground and followed the riverbank down towards the plain.

Nightfall found them deep in the thickening forest. On Parton's reckoning, the Inquisition would not yet be at the point where the river had been forded and the darkness would help to deceive them into following the decoy tracks left by the freed horses. But he had no illusions. The true tracks would be found in time. What mattered now was to cross the plain as quickly as possible, in spite of the thickening vegetation and the blackness around them. The vital thing was to keep the river within earshot at all times so as not to get lost and go round in circles. Gabriela and Maria-Dolores worked unstintingly and uncomplainingly, alternately leading Fernando's horse by the bridle and clearing the way ahead with one of the heavy knives taken from their packs. As for Parton, his attention was divided between watching Seward, who stumbled ahead in silence, the pistol never more than inches from his back, and Fernando. The boy seemed to be doing well, hugging the horse's neck and keeping his head down under the branches and creepers, but Parton spoke to him often, encouraging him, anxious not to see him feverish again. If they could go on in that way, thought Parton, they would get there in time.

The going got no better, however, as they forced their way along by the riverside. As the ground became lower and flatter, it became more marshy and the river meandered in wider and longer loops. At about midnight, it became impossible to drag the failing horse further and they unsaddled the animal and left it to find its way back to the hills, carrying Fernando from then on. They stumbled into mud and fetid water, scrambled up again, fought through the clinging jungle, hacking at creepers with seemingly ineffective knives, Parton carrying Fernando on his back most of the time and taking care to keep Seward moving ahead of him.

About an hour after leaving the horse, they were confronted with a widening mangrove swamp. That was good news as well as bad. The bad side was that they could no longer go on following the river, while the good was that at least the swamp, formed around the estuary, betrayed the nearness of the sea. Their next move was simply to go round its northern edge until they reached the coast. It was sooner thought than done. Slimy, dangerous creeks cut across their path and sent them on detours, while apparently solid banks of silt jutted out into the water to lead them astray, wasting precious minutes by obliging them to retrace their steps and take a fresh direction. By the time they heard, muted but not so very distant, the soughing of waves on the shore, Parton reckoned that they had spent another two or more hours crossing from the river. The thick foliage cleared as they skirted round the last few hundred yards of the mangrove swamp and reached the low, sunken coastline. Parton stopped for a moment to get a sight of the stars between the clouds. According to his calculations, dawn was perhaps two hours away, barely more.

He stared along the coast, wondering how many miles were left to cover. According to Cameron's description, the rendezvous was off a rocky headland with a creek to the north of it. But here, there were no rocks, no headlands. As far as he could see, the shore was desperately flat and muddy, isolated thickets of mangroves building false land here and there. He hitched Fernando up on his back giving him the ritual, 'Not much farther now, Fernando,' hustled Seward forwards and led the way north at the fastest pace he could.

Over the next hour, they hurried along the low-lying coast, threading their way between trees and bushes where the earth was firmer, trotting over oozy mud flats which appeared, from time to time and for short distances, to be trying to pass themselves off as beaches, Parton staring constantly forwards and out to sea. In spite of his efforts to remain calm, he was beginning to feel seriously alarmed. There was no sign of the headland and time was running out. Thank God he was the only one to know that – it was hard enough keeping the fighting spirit alive without the others knowing that they had to find the ship by dawn. The girls were flagging, Seward had to be constantly prodded forward and Fernando, clinging tightly round Parton's neck, no longer replied to his encouragements. Keep moving, Parton told himself. There was still time, the night was dark and in another half mile they might come upon the headland almost without having seen it.

Half a mile further, the coast was as flat as ever. What would they do if they failed to make the rendezvous? Keep moving up the coast, Parton supposed, until they found some outpost of civilization where they could buy or steal a boat. It was more than shaky and he knew it. They had money, but no food and only a day's supply of water with the choice between salt water and fever-bearing swamp water when that was gone, they were on foot and too dog-tired to run much farther, Palafox and his forces were certainly right behind them and would not fail to be faster . . . The whitewashed walls of the dungeons of the Inquisition rushed into Parton's mind. He felt Fernando's weight on his back, the hands clasped tightly round his neck. He shook away the thoughts. Whatever happened, whatever else was at stake, Parton swore to himself that he would not let Palafox get his hands on the child. He moved ahead faster.

It was not yet dawn, but the night was definitely fading. To the east, the Gulf stretched flat and hazy grey. It was still not light enough, however, to see and to be seen from a distance. The ship, close in to a hostile shore, would not be showing a light, that was for sure. On that dark expanse of sea, she would appear as a blackish shape at a few cables. They would have to be practically on top of her to make their presence known. Parton was running now, pushing a breathless Seward ahead of him, hearing the heavy steps and ragged breathing of the girls behind him, and calling back to urge them on over the mud.

No. It was no longer mud. The ground was firmer, springier, the trees taller and more widely spaced. To his right, Parton began to hear the hiss and splash of waves breaking on a rocky shore. He stared ahead in the growing light, looking for a headland. He could see the whitish fringe of the sea against the dark rocks, but there was still no sign of either headland or ship. The sky was greying. Exactly when would the commander of the sloop decide that it was dawn and that he had waited long enough?

The calm surface of the sea paled under the light which came creeping from the east and suddenly Parton saw it. The outline of the headland was black against surrounding grey. The sight put fresh energy into his legs. Forcing Seward on, he ran up the long slope. Above the rocky top of the cape, he could now see masts and spars. The ship was there, on the far side in the mouth of the creek, a sloop as he had expected. He waved and began to shout. There would be a watcher up in the crosstrees, but would he see them in time against the dark background of the coast? Parton stopped shouting and saved what was left of his breath for running. It was still too far for voices to be heard.

He paid no attention at first to the new shapes which were looming out of the night as the pale light grew. He was focusing on the masts, sure that he could see movement up there, dark blocks of unfurled sail changing the pattern which was etched against the grey sky. The sloop was making ready to sail and still the fugitives were too far to be heard, still they had not been seen against the trees. Parton imagined the sloop making way and leaving them shouting and waving desperately on the shore, at the rendevous after hundreds of miles, but minutes too late. He forced his weary legs on into a mad spurt to the top of the slope, realizing as he went that the shapes coming out of the night and the forest were familiar. Overlooking the shore and the headland were Indian ruins, massive and gloomy, overrun with tropical vegetation. To Parton's left was a high pyramid. From up there he could make them hear . . . He stopped for a second, untying the blanket which slung Fernando to his back and setting the boy down making sure that Seward, lying on his back and fighting for breath, was incapable of doing harm, then he ran to the pyramid and began to bound up it, striding over the blocks of stone as if it were a gigantic staircase. Halfway to the top, he turned and hailed the sloop.

There was an answering shout from the ship, an exchange of voices from masthead to quarterdeck and Parton called again to be sure there was no mistake. No, the sloop hailed him again in return. He felt the energy drain from him and he almost sagged as relief filled him. It was over, they had succeeded. Now the commander would order the yards round, back the sails against the light easterly wind which was blowing in towards the shore and he would have the boat put down and sent ashore.

He did nothing of the sort.

The mainsail was run out, hanging for a moment listlessly while the yards were braced back. The canvas flapped and banged as the wind caught it and the sloop heeled slightly and began to make way. Parton could not believe his eyes. He had been seen from the sloop and now she was putting out to sea!

He opened his mouth to shout then saw, beyond the headland in the still uncertain light, the second ship. In a glance, he read the situation. She was a Spanish *guarda-costa* on patrol, and she was sailing in on the port tack towards the headland. A short starboard tack and a fresh port tack would bring her clear of the headland and just off the little bay formed by the mouth of the creek, sealing it off and trapping the British sloop, bottling her up in a hopeless position on a lee shore. The sloop commander had seen the danger and was hastening to put out to sea and get to the windward of the Spaniard, his only chance, whether he were to choose to fight or to run. Since he knew of Parton's presence, he would not do the latter. The *guarda-costa* was weatherly, fast and fairly well armed, but the sloop, attacking from windward, would be far and away the stronger vessel in a fight. Normally speaking, it was simply a question of waiting. The problem was that there was no time to wait. At the foot of the pyramid, the girls and Seward were lying exhausted. Fernando alone was standing, watching the sloop inch out of the bay. They could run no further and how soon would the Inquisition be there? The sloop would have to put down a boat for them and quickly. He cupped his hands round his mouth and yelled with all his might after the ship.

There was a moment's hesitation, then an answering cry.

Parton bellowed: 'Boat!' several times. The wind brought a reply of which he could not be sure. He yelled again. This time he had the satisfaction of seeing the profile of a boat being slung over the side of the sloop as she left the bay. Under cover of the headland where the creek flowed out was a tiny strip of sand and rock. The ship's boat would be able to beach there. The fugitives must make for its shelter. Perhaps it was the thought of shelter which made him turn his head and look back along the coast. He was still for a moment, every nerve taut. A group of over a score of dark-clad horsemen were splashing through the mud flats, almost at the foot of the slope. The fugitives' margin of safety had been slimmer than he had expected. The Spaniards would be up with them before the boat had rowed in to the beach.

He looked out to sea. The ship's boat was down and beginning its long row into the bay. The *guarda-costa*, close-hauled, was holding her starboard tack and racing the sloop for the wind. For the moment, no help would come from the sea. They would have to help themselves. He leaped block by block down the pyramid and raced towards the others.

'Inquisition at the foot of the slope!' he told them breathlessly, pointing back. Maria-Dolores scrambled to her feet, livid, followed by Gabriela, while Seward hid his head in his hands, not before Parton had seen the broad grin of relief he was trying to dissimulate. Parton, with some effort, ignored it and looked around. He could not see the Spanish, so the Spanish could not see them. What was more, the headland and its Indian ruins would conceal the bay and the beach from Spanish view for some time yet. If the Inquisition were delayed and kept on the blind side of the headland, the boat might have time to beach and take Fernando and the girls aboard. He himself would act as a decoy along the headland, forcing Seward with him – leaving him with the girls would entail tying him up and there was no time for that. Briefly, Parton outlined his idea to the others.

'It won't work,' said Maria-Dolores immediately. 'With only you two in sight, Palafox will be suspicious, especially as he'll understand immediately that, at this stage in the game, Seward's not with you of his own choice. But he's less sure of me. If I go with you perhaps we can make Palafox hesitate long enough to get Fernando away.'

Parton looked at the two girls, Maria-Dolores with her clear eyes, her skin now browned by the sun, her hair falling in a long riot of dark curls and Gabriela, the perfect matt sheen of her complexion, the liquid blackness of her eyes. Both girls were dear to him now, each of them had the right to claim the new life she was hoping to find. He desperately wanted to see them aboard that sloop and on their way to safety. But there was Fernando, watching him, exhausted and anxious. Parton's first duty was to the child he had brought so far and whom he had sworn he would not let fall into the Inquisitor-General's clutches. The success of the whole mission depended on these last minutes. If no one else left the New Spanish shore, Fernando must. Parton nodded to Maria-Dolores.

'I think you're right. Gabriela, you're in charge of Fernando. Hide with him down there among the rocks and as soon as the boat beaches, get aboard with him like lightning and make the men understand the danger, make them row for their lives. On your way!'

Gabriela's eyes held his for a second before she took Fernando by the hand and left without a word. Parton dragged Seward to his feet and pushed him on his way after Maria-Dolores who was already running towards the carved stones and ruined walls of the headland. The two men caught her as she climbed a narrow passage between broken-down buildings and as the three of them emerged on to the backbone of the headland, overlooking the long slope, they saw the first of the riders, a man in a black riding cloak who was no doubt Palafox among them, barely four hundred yards away.

'Quickly! Up there!' gasped Parton, pointing to a larger building further along the cape. As they ran, a shout went up. They had been sighted. Now they had to succeed in keeping the Spanish on the wrong side of the headland. They hurried into temporary shelter behind the ruined building, leaning back against the wall, panting. Parton looked towards the narrow beach. Gabriela and Fernando could not be seen, but that was normal because he had told them to hide. The boat, oars dipping in unison, was halfway to the landing place. Out to sea, the sloop was gaining on the *guarda-costa* and creeping out of the trap of the lee shore. It was just a question of time . . .

He took a fresh look at the Spanish from the corner of the building. The first riders were coming on fast and although they had changed direction towards the ruins on the headland, they would soon be at the top of the rise and would have a view down into the bay.

'We've got to find a way of keeping them on the blind side of the headland,' he said to Maria-Dolores. 'If they see the boat coming in, it's all up.'

'This is where I come in,' said Maria-Dolores simply. She pointed down among the ruins. 'If I run down there and towards them, as if I've managed to escape from you and want to get back to Palafox, that'll surely halt them and bring them in my direction.'

'And what happens then?' Parton shook his head. 'It's too risky for you. They'll capture you.'

The pressure of Maria-Dolores's hand on his arm was gentle. 'I'm not afraid of risks. Haven't you taken risks for me? Before they reach me, I'll fall among the rocks and you'll come and get me back.'

It was certainly a likely way of diverting the Inquisition, thought Parton, and there was no time to work out another and no other that did not entail risks. 'Go on,' he said.

Maria-Dolores broke away and ran, shouting for help, waving wildly. Parton watched as the Spaniards turned towards her, checking their horses, visibly waiting for orders. He had to add something to the subterfuge. He stepped out from behind the ruined building and levelled a pistol on Maria-Dolores as she ran down. The black-cloaked figure that was surely Palafax was pointing, shouting orders. Parton fired deliberately low into the rocks. The Spanish were riding towards Maria-Dolores now. The feint was succeeding. Maria-Dolores, you've done enough, thought Parton, willing her to fall as they had agreed. If she went too far, she would be caught. Surely she wasn't going to . . . No, thank God, she was stumbling, disappearing between two blocks of stone and she was still close enough for him to get her back.

Seward watched from Parton's side, screwing up his courage. Parton was momentarily absorbed in what Maria-Dolores was doing and the chance had to be seized. Palafax had to be warned that the whore was against him, that the traitor's boy was on the far side of the headland and about to be taken off by boat to a British ship and that all would then be lost. It had to be done, Seward told himself to quell his rising fear, it was his duty to the Stuart cause. But it would be hard. Parton would probably try to kill him. What did that matter? Better to risk death now, with a chance of reaching freedom, than to be dragged back a prisoner and to see his family ruined and disgraced, denounced as crypto-Catholics and Jacobite traitors, thanks to the errors of a foolhardy son . . . Only if Palafax won could the shame be avoided.

It was of his mother that Seward was thinking as he pushed Parton heavily aside and ran desperately towards the Spanish, shouting to gain their attention. Heads were turning and he waved and pointed towards the other side of the headland. Palafox had to understand. Seward pointed again frantically.

Parton picked himself up, drew a pistol, aimed and fired. Seward's waving stopped as he clutched at his arm, but he went on running through the ruins, not far now from where Maria-Dolores had disappeared. Parton ran forward several paces, took a third pistol from his jacket and aimed carefully. This one must not miss, or Seward would be out of range. He pressed the trigger and saw Seward fall, hit in the back, and already he in his turn was racing down the slope between the upended stones and broken walls.

Palafox rode forward among the first of his horsemen, watching Parton run down towards the spot where Maria-Dolores then Seward had fallen. He frowned, perplexed. Of course he had always hoped for something like this, that Maria-Dolores and the Jacobite would join forces to give Parton trouble. Of course – not that there had been the slightest exterior sign of his feelings – he had been unable to repress a surge of relief at the sight of his mistress running back to prove her loyalty. But something was wrong about it all. Why had Parton been running through the ruins with Maria-Dolores and Seward? What had happened to weaken his vigilance? The Englishman had come hundreds of miles without faltering and now both Maria-Dolores and Seward had escaped him within the space of a minute. Something else was going on, something that Palafox could not see and which could explain Parton's apparently wavering attention.

That something could only concern the boy. He could not be seen. Had other British agents taken him away, as the Inquisitor-General had sometimes feared would happen? It was unlikely. Palafox, as he had ridden up the slope, had seen the *guarda-costa*, one of six he had ordered out of Veracruz to patrol the coast and her course made him infer the presence of a second ship out of sight beyond the cape. Logic dictated that the second ship was British. The boy was not yet aboard, or why would Parton be there on the headland, running into the teeth of danger in order to retrieve what would be, in that case, perfectly useless prisoners? No, the boy was somewhere in hiding, doubtless with the other girl, the black-haired one and probably somewhere among the ruins, waiting to get out to the ship . . .

Parton was playing for time, that was it. He was with Maria-Dolores now, lifting her. She was leaning back against him, obviously dazed or hurt. Parton had a pistol in his hand. Palafox struggled against the desire to yell his men forward faster, to concentrate his forces on the single objective of saving his mistress. No, it was what was happening elsewhere, over the top of the headland, that really mattered. Maria-Dolores had to be considered as secondary. If the boy rejoined his treacherous father – and the bad news from Veracruz was that Torres Mendieta had disappeared from the town two days before, no one knew how or where for – then the English would have won the battle, would have held the Inquisition and Palafox himself up to ridicule, would have obtained information it was vital to Spain to keep secret.

'Modesto!' he called. 'Half the men only are to go after them. There is to be no shooting – Doña Maria must be rescued unharmed and I want the Englishman alive if possible. The rest of us will ride up there—' he gestured towards the top of the slope, '—and take a look at what's happening on the other side.'

'Very well, Excellency,' approved Modesto, giving brief orders and wheeling his horse alongside Palafox's. The distant rumble of cannon came to them on the wind and the mercenary turned his scarred face seawards. 'There's a fight on but . . . Excellency, look at that!' he exclaimed.

Palafox reined in beside him and followed his pointing finger. Beyond the ruins where Parton was retreating with Maria-Dolores, a small craft combining sail and oars was fairly shooting across the calm water towards the tip of the headland.

307

'It's a pinnace,' said Modesto. 'Looks like one of ours.'

Palafox's brows knit as he watched. The sound of a second broadside came from the vessels hidden behind the cape. The pinnace was surely too small to try to intervene in the fight. Then what . . .?

The pale eyes widened abruptly. 'Modesto!' he snapped. 'Change of orders! Send one man up to the top to report. The rest of us, at all costs, must get out to the end of the headland!'

'What the hell are they doing?' muttered Parton, backing off through the ruins with Maria-Dolores and watching Palafox. A moment before, he had been fearing for Fernando and Gabriela as half the Inquisition force had turned towards the top of the rise, but now, suddenly, the group had turned again and was riding straight towards him. Something out at sea had attracted their attention, but Parton's view was blocked by the ruins. He too had heard the cannon, but surely Palafox could not see the seafight from where he was. Whatever the reason, it was a relief. On the most optimistic reckoning, the boat might just be reaching the beach and Fernando was far from safe yet, even supposing that the sloop defeated the *guarda-costa*. Now the Spanish were staying on the side of the headland Parton wanted to see them on, the first among them dismounting at the edge of the ruins where riding was impossible. They were not firing on the escaping couple, which was encouraging because it probably meant that Maria-Dolores's act had convinced Palafox that she was still faithful to him and useful because it allowed Parton to move slowly as the Spanish approached, the better to play for time.

'Parton . . .'

The sound had been weak and Parton and Maria-Dolores rounded a corner before seeing Seward on his side in the rubble, blood welling from the wound in his back. There would be no taking him back to Jamaica, thought Parton, the more's the pity.

'I'm dying.' Seward's good hand clawed feebly towards Parton. 'My . . . my family, Parton. Please . . . would kill my mother . . .' A spasm racked him and he coughed blood. 'And . . .' He caught breath with an immense effort, the air bubbling in his throat. 'Remember . . . I didn't want . . . harm to . . . Gabriela . . .' He slumped back and the bubbling in his throat stopped.

Parton watched for a second in silence, a taste of bile in his mouth, his thoughts torn between anger and pity, as Seward's eyes glazed over. Maria-Dolores touched his arm. 'They're getting close,' she whispered.

They threaded their way more quickly now through the ruins. The Spaniards were coming on fast, fanning out into an encircling movement.

'Damn!' Parton swore as he ran, seeing in a backward glance the rider Palafox had ordered up to the top of the slope. How long would it be before the man, who was now looking over into the bay, would reach Palafox with news of what he had seen? Would the ship's boat be far enough from the shore by then?

'We can't go any further!' panted Maria-Dolores. A smooth stone wall some ten feet high blocked their way to the end of the headland, which could now only be a few hundred yards away.

'There're steps up there!' Parton pointed. They ran towards the steps and climbed them, jumping the gaps where the large stone blocks had been smashed or had crumbled away. The first dark-cloaked Inquisition soldiers were at the foot of the steps as they reached the top and found themselves at the edge of a stone-paved plaza over a hundred yards wide and almost as long. A high wall at the opposite end sealed off the tip of the headland. Parton looked anxiously out to sea.

The first news was good. The *guarda-costa*, partially dismasted and in any case disabled, was drifting with the wind towards the shore where she would shortly run aground. The sloop, further out to sea, seemed to have suffered little damage and was putting about to take a course back into the bay. Where was the boat? Parton and Maria-Dolores ran across the plaza until they saw it in the middle of the bay, well away from the shore but still far from the sloop. A figure in grey and a smaller, darker figure sat in the sternsheets. Gabriela and Fernando were in the boat and, in a matter of minutes, the boat and the sloop would meet. But, during those long minutes, Parton realized with a chill, the boat and its occupants would be terribly vulnerable to musket fire from the vantagepoint of the plaza, and Palafox would surely not hesitate before the cold-blooded murder that that would represent. It would be the Inquisitor-General's last chance to stop the boy reaching his father and hence to scotch British plans. Parton caught Maria-Dolores by the arm and turned her.

'We must stop them getting up the steps for as long as we can,' he said.

'Too late!' gasped Maria-Dolores as they ran back. The first Spaniards were at the top of the steps, three of them were over and there were more behind. Parton fired his last pistol and the man in the middle fell back with a cry. Parton hoped he would dislodge some of his fellows on the steep steps in his fall. But there was no holding back the tide and there were five or six of them now, watching Parton and Maria-Dolores with coldly calculating eyes, spreading out slowly as they came on. Parton held Maria-Dolores close to him and backed away little by little. Whatever time could be gained for the boat had to be. In the middle of the plaza, the Spaniards had fanned out into a semicircle. Before they had reached the back wall, Parton and Maria-Dolores were completely surrounded, although at a respectable distance and held at gunpoint.

'Musketeers!' Palafox came over the top of the steps and was already running towards the side of the plaza overlooking the bay. 'Take up positions along the edge and fire on that boat!'

The rider from the top of the slope had reached him before he had climbed the steps, thought Parton, and he had had time to decide on his course of action. Out in the bay, the boat seemed to be moving terribly slowly, although Parton knew that the oarsmen were most certainly pulling for their lives. The first muskets banged out and plumes of spray pocked the sea not far from the boat.

'Palafox!' he yelled, clutching Maria-Dolores in front of him. 'Order them to cease fire or I'll kill her!'

There was a moment of silence, the musketeers hesitating, as Palafox looked across towards Maria-Dolores and Parton. Parton would have given a great deal to have understood what was going on in the man's mind at that moment. The eyes were, as always, expressionless, but there was something brusque in the way Palafox shook his head which suggested emotion beneath the surface. The Inquisitor-General turned sharply.

'A hundred dollars for the man who hits the boy!' he called crisply. 'And twenty for the man who sights the pinnace!'

Parton frowned and looked out to sea. There was no sign of a pinnace, only the sloop bearing in on the breeze and the *guarda-costa* aground on the opposite shore. And the boat, coming under fire for the second time . . . Some of the musketeers, strung out along the low parapet at the edge of the plaza, had chosen precision and were driving forked iron rests into cracks between the tightly jointed flagstones, while the others had chosen speed and were firing off as many shots as they could, reloading quickly, all of them feverish at the idea of the price Palafox had set on Fernando's head.

'Palafox!' It was not going to work and Parton knew it. Soon the iron rests would be set up and the occupants of the boat would be under withering fire. '*She's going to die!*'

The feeling of failure was sickening. Palafox simply turned to a man beside him, spoke rapidly and gestured towards Parton. Did he no longer care what happened to Maria-Dolores – that didn't fit with the fact that he had not had her fired on – or was he simply calling Parton's bluff? Hadn't he guessed that Parton would never execute his threat? The subordinate was walking over now, calm and confident, while a cheer went up as one of the rowers in the boat was hit. Parton could see the grey of Gabriela's dress in the bottom of the boat. She was protecting Fernando. 'Oh my God,' he groaned. 'What can we do?'

'Let me try,' breathed Maria-Dolores, her head close to his. 'I think he wants me back. He's decided the boy's more important, that's all. Let me go free and I'll do what I can to stop them shooting.'

The man Palafox had ordered over was facing them, tanned and scarred, lean and efficient. A mercenary and no beginner, thought Parton. The man nodded abruptly and the ring of men closed in. Parton held the empty pistol to Maria-Dolores's head. The mercenary grinned and spat.

'You fired it a few minutes ago,' he said calmly. 'I saw you. There's no point in trying to fight. You've lost.'

Maria-Dolores stirred to remind Parton of her words. Out in the bay, an injured rower had gone overboard and the boat was slowing, an easier and easier target. Parton lowered the pistol, relaxing his grip on Maria-Dolores. She struggled, kicking back at his shins and as she did so, she contrived to turn her head towards his and their eyes met for a fraction of a second. Then she broke away and ran.

Parton was overwhelmed and tightly held in the instant that followed. He fought to raise his head. As the first two or three of the musketeers who had chosen to set up the iron rests finished their preparations and began to take murderous aim, Maria-Dolores stopped some yards away from Palafox, sobbing. The Inquisitor-General turned slowly to face her, an unusual hint of doubt in the habitually stony eyes. In the sudden silence, even the musketeers holding fire, Maria-Dolores stared at him, beseeching.

Palafox said: 'Maria-Dolores . . .'

Maria-Dolores ran to him.

At the last second, either some sixth sense or more probably something he read in her eyes warned Palafox of danger, because he stepped sharply aside as Maria-Dolores flung herself at him.

'*No!*' she screamed as she stumbled and went over the edge of the stone parapet behind him. On Palafox's face, the odd expression of doubt became an anguished rictus then suddenly, open-mouthed astonishment as Maria-Dolores, falling, grasped desperately at the folds of his wide black riding-cloak and he was jerked bodily back and out into empty space.

In the moment of shock which followed, Parton felt his gaolers' grip on him loosen as several of them left to join the musketeers peering over the edge. Parton shook free and ran among them, looking down.

The side of the Indian plaza was a sheer stone wall thirty to forty feet high, dropping down to rocks and sea. As soon as he saw it, Parton knew what he would see next and he didn't want to look. He forced himself. On the blood-splashed rocks lay Maria-Dolores, broken, spread-eagled, and beside her, his body twisted and his head lapped by the waves, Palafox. Parton fought against a flood of pain and grief for Maria-Dolores which threatened to double him up and close his eyes. Later, he promised. Now was not the time. The sea down there was clear and he could see the sandy bottom without being able to judge the depth. Better not to risk diving. He pushed two Spaniards aside, stepped on to the parapet and jumped into the sea beyond the rocks and the two bodies.

The fall was surprisingly short but he had the impression that something new had come into sight before he hit the water noisily, bending his knees as he went down. A small craft rowing across the bay, he thought as his feet hit the bottom and he flexed further, pushing upwards, kicking off his boots as he rose. A pinnace. The pinnace Palafox had mentioned. His head broke into the light and he snatched breath, pulling off his jacket, blinking salt water from his eyes and seeing the pinnace again, cutting through the sea towards the invisible ship's boat, the bellying sails of the sloop as she sailed in still too far to win the race. If the pinnace – and she was Spanish, he could see the men, black-haired and swarthy, on the bow oars – picked up Fernando and Gabriela now and hurried them ashore before the sloop arrived, Maria-Dolores would have died for nothing. He swam towards the pinnace. Musket balls smacked the surface of the water near him. He dived and swam underwater.

He came up several times and was forced down again by fire from above before he found himself out in the middle of the bay, feeling the tug of the current. He trod water and looked round, fearing the muskets less now. The sloop was coming in quickly. And the pinnace . . .

The pinnace was bearing down on him.

He kicked out and raised his head higher from the surface. Just before the single mast in the pinnace, unmistakable, stood Gabriela. Fernando was not in sight, but there could be no doubt that the Spaniards had captured him too. And now they were out for Parton himself.

He dived and swam underwater towards the craft. It was not going to happen as the Spanish thought, that was all. He could make out the hull and the six oars against the greenish light ahead. As he came close and his breath began to fail, he seized the first blade, toppling the rower out of the pinnace with a sudden lurch. There was a tug on the oar as another man took it and Parton pulled, kicking away, bringing the bows of the pinnace round. He felt rather than saw the hull keel over as the wind caught the sail abeam and the pinnace heeled. Lungs bursting, Parton came up for air, already planning his next move. He had created havoc on board, now he must climb up and finish it. He reached for the pinnace's side. His fingers touched rough wood and tar.

A boathook hit him a hefty blow behind the head and he lost consciousness.

When he came to, Gabriela was leaning over him, staunching the blood which was flowing from the wound behind his ear. Parton could not see clearly. He touched the wound gingerly and grimaced.

'They hit you hard, the brutes,' said Gabriela gently. 'But they thought you were going to take over the pinnace single-handed and there was no time to explain.'

Explain? wondered Parton. His eyes began to clear and he looked round, then back up at Gabriela. 'We're on the sloop,' he said.

Gabriela nodded and smiled. 'Fernando's father and his servants were manning the pinnace. It had been hidden along the coast from Veracruz, waiting for the day the message would come to tell him to move. They were off the tip of the headland when they saw we were being fired on in the boat and they sailed across to save us. Then I saw – what happened . . . and you were in the sea and I told them they had to save you too.' She hesitated. 'Maria-Dolores . . .?'

Parton shook his head. It hurt.

'I'm sorry.'

'Seward died too,' said Parton to change the subject. 'He spoke of you.'

Gabriela shrugged, but the movement was graceful. 'I don't know if I'm sorry or not. Perhaps I am, a little. Perhaps he wasn't as bad a man as all that.'

'Perhaps not.' Parton didn't really care.

'You nearly tipped us into the sea!' said a boyish voice and Parton looked round, sitting up. Fernando stood proudly holding the hand of a stocky, black-bearded man whose decisive dark eyes swept quickly over the boy's face as if to check every detail and Parton guessed that it was for the hundredth time in the last few minutes. 'So he did,' said Torres Mendieta with a short laugh.

It had all been for this, thought Parton, for this and what Torres can bring us. For Fernando to be there, tired but well and happy, leaning his head on his father's arm, far from the echoing prison-schools of the Inquisition. Father and son didn't look alike apart from the dark complexion, he thought, but it was striking the way they seemed to belong together as if they had never been separated at all. He struggled to his feet, the tension of the last few days still filling him but on the ebb, exhaustion taking its place. Maria-Dolores came to mind and he looked back sadly. The low-lying coast of New Spain had already dropped out of sight behind the sloop and only the distant mountains in which they had suffered so much could be seen.

'Señor,' said Torres Mendieta. 'After all that Fernando has told me of you, I don't know how I am ever to thank you . . .'

Parton shook his head. 'There's no need. But you can answer a question, if you will.' He steadied himself against the shiny black gun and looked at Torres. 'You knew full well right from the start that Fernando wasn't in any ordinary school or seminary, didn't you?'

The Spaniard's gaze was level. 'Señor, what I am about to say may seem unduly sentimental, but I loved Fernando's mother as, I believe, rarely a man loves a woman. She died . . . after his birth. Fernando is all I have, all that is left and they stole him away from me while I was away on the King's business. I knew that he was being held as Palafox's hostage along with sons of other prominent officials and I was determined to get him back. I was constantly under watch and I could not act alone. There was no help for me in Palafox's New Spain. I needed help from elsewhere and I found it, for which I thank you.' Torres smiled. 'But if I had told your agents all I knew, if I had admitted how impossible the mission was likely to be, do you think your superiors would have agreed to help me? Do you think my son would be here beside me now?'

Parton stared at the Spaniard for a moment, then shook his head. He grinned at Fernando, kissed Gabriela and went wearily below to sleep.

CHAPTER SIXTEEN

'Torres is a most fortunate man,' said Cameron, closing the door to his tiny room in Port Royal and ushering Parton to a seat. 'He was in the right place with the right intelligence to offer. Thanks to that, he got his son back from the Inquisition.'

Parton detailed his commanding officer's dry, lined features, and wondered yet again if the man was really human. To his knowledge, Cameron had never been married, had no children, had never been known to have a mistress or a lover. He had spoken of the exchange of information against a real, living child which Parton had carried on his back, feared for, fought for, as if he had been speaking of the price of soap. All that mattered to Cameron was that Torres was now on his way to London in a British Navy frigate and that he was to spend the next years working with the Admiralty's chartmakers. For Parton, there was still Fernando's happy, laughing face just before the frigate had sailed an hour earlier; there was his passionate farewell to Gabriela too, black-eyed, so beautiful Gabriela, on her way back to Europe, engaged by Torres to look after Fernando during the voyage. She would do what she had set out to do, she would find her father and live the life she had chosen, of that Parton was sure. But she had almost wavered, almost wanted to stay: in the end, she had said to Parton, 'If I stay, I'll be taking someone else's place and I don't think I'd be able to live with it.' And she had gone.

That someone else, Parton realized, would be an ache for a long time. He remembered the last brief exchange of glances before Maria-Dolores had gone to her death to save them all and he knew that their eyes had promised that, if there were to be a new life to share, they would take the chance and share it – she who so desperately needed it, and he . . . Didn't he need it too? He stood up and looked out of the window at the sun beating down on the Port Royal anchorage and tried to think of something else.

'And we can congratulate ourselves on having obtained the man's services,' went on Cameron imperturbably, 'not only because of his knowledge of the Spanish Pacific, but also because he's one of the dozen best chartmakers in the world. You know the Spaniards have long been fine chartmakers along with the Portuguese and now the French and the Dutch too – the least we can say is that we're lagging behind the other maritime nations and that, over the next few years, Torres will help our chartmakers make up lost ground.' He paused. 'Yes, it's a major success, Lieutenant. Palafox's death is an excellent thing too. I'm sorry to have to say, after all that, that you let me down with Seward.'

Parton stiffened but did not look round. In a few words that he would have such pleasure in pronouncing, he could give Cameron a shaking of the kind the Scot was unused to. With a little more revengefulness, he could report back to London, have Cameron hauled over the coals and demolish Seward's comfortable, important family. If they were to be unmasked as crypto-Catholics and Jacobites, their lives as wealthy and respected merchants would be over. Were such people truly dangerous? From far away in America, Parton found conflicts over true kings and religions derisory and the kind of passion Seward had apparently felt for them over-dramatic. The truth was that Seward had been a foolish and idealistic young man who had got mixed up in an affair of espionage and had believed it glorious to help his country's enemies. Now he had paid – and it was true that he had not hurt Gabriela when it had been in his power to do so. Parton couldn't summon up the hatred to make his family pay double price.

'We were under heavy fire,' he said flatly. 'I explained it to you. He was killed only yards from freedom. There was nothing I could do. It was just bad luck.'

'Bad luck of a kind I'd be grateful if you avoided in the future, Lieutenant.'

I won't forget this, Cameron, thought Parton, turning to meet his chief's steely regard. You sent me into danger with an untrustworthy man, a man you hadn't checked. As the thought came to him, Parton realized that he was keeping secrets from Cameron, that he was holding future means of attack or defence in his relationship to his commander and that he was somehow glad of it. He had come back to Jamaica to find his family problems as intensely difficult as before and not a word on his prospects, not a penny more than his meagre pay to count on.

'Thank you for reminding me, Captain,' he said softly, 'that I'm *still* a Lieutenant.'

Cameron cleared his throat and attempted a smile. 'Now, they're pleased with you in London, young man. . . . Our efforts against Law and French finances are paying off and you played your part in that . . .' He breathed down his nose and pursed his thin lips. 'But I think I should warn you, Lieutenant, not to expect a Captaincy. Never to expect a Captaincy. The particular conditions of your entry into the Service work powerfully against your nomination to the Captain's List.'

So that's it, thought Parton. I killed a man and the Navy saved me from hanging and now, years later, he's telling me Lieutenant's as high as they'll let me go.

'A ship won't move without wind in her sails,' he said. 'I'm not proud enough to refuse something other than rank. The prize money on those emeralds, for example.'

Cameron looked up sharply. 'The particular conditions of your entry into the Service also mean that you're in no position to bargain,' he said quietly. There was a brief silence. Parton was about to speak when Cameron held up his hand. 'However, dispatches tell me there's hope on the prize money,' he said with a tight smile. 'By which I mean that you're likely to receive something at least – although when, I don't know. But first let's talk about what you're to do now you're back . . .'